MORTGAGED TO DEATH
TONY SAUNDERS

APS BOOKS
Yorkshire

APS Books,
The Stables Field Lane,
Aberford,
West Yorkshire,
LS25 3AE

APS Books is a subsidiary of the APS Publications imprint

www.andrewsparke.com

©2024 Tony Saunders
All rights reserved.

Tony Saunders has asserted his right to be identified as the author of this work in accordance with the Copyright Designs and Patents Act 1988

First published worldwide by APS Books in 2024

This is a work of fiction. Names, characters, places and incidents either are products of the author's imagination or are used fictitiously. Any resemblance to actual events or locales or persons, living or dead, is entirely coincidental.

No part of this publication may be reproduced, stored in or introduced into a retrieval system, or transmitted, in any form, or by any means (electronic, mechanical, photocopying, recording or otherwise) without the written permission of the publisher except that brief selections may be quoted or copied without permission, provided that full credit is given.

A catalogue record for this book is available from the British Library

MORTGAGED TO DEATH

1

Day 1.
Tuesday 19th February.
CID Office, First Floor, Woodchester Police Station, Kent.

It was a gloomy day outside and the late winter drizzle hung in a cold, dark cloud over the town. Detective Inspector Jim Trussell sat at his desk, peering absentmindedly through the window at the Weaver Street multi-storey car park further along the High Street, just visible through the murk. His untouched coffee, long grown cold, still sat on his desk where DC Mark Green had put it an hour earlier. His computer monitor, unused, had slipped into screen saver mode.

Detective Sergeant Jackie Joynton wasn't fooled by this apparent reverie. She had a pretty good idea what was going through Trussell's mind because she had seen this every year since she joined his team. The sixth anniversary of his wife Annette's death was approaching, and to compound his unhappiness, his only daughter, Liz, had recently gone off to university. He was now totally alone at home and feeling it. But she knew that wasn't the complete story this time.

He was seriously concerned about his team.

Six months ago, it had been in great shape, until Detective Constable Lucinda Brakeford, in her late twenties, had decided to take the Sergeant's examination. She had passed first time and had now moved back into uniform elsewhere in the county. Trussell felt her loss keenly - she had been a real asset and he was sorry to see her go. She had been replaced by DC Mark Green, of similar age, transferred from the uniformed branch for his first appointment with the CID. *He was bright enough*, thought Trussell, *but lacking Cindy's experience.*

Then a couple of months ago there was another blow, when the other Detective Constable, Stan Gardner, had reached retirement age and decided that the lure of the quiet life was impossible to resist. His experience would be very difficult to replace.

And that was just the beginning of Trussell's problems.

He recalled a fateful day a month ago when he had been summoned by the boss, Detective Chief Superintendent Charlie Watkins, to discuss the situation. He was apprehensive given that there was history between them going back to Trussell's first CID appointment as a Detective

Constable at Brandford in East Kent, and now he tried to avoid the DCS as much as possible.

He had taken the lift to the hallowed eighth floor, walked along the corridor to Watkins' office and had tapped on the half-open door. He could see Watkins sitting at his desk, glasses perched on the end of his nose.

'Come in, Trussell. Sit down. I've thought about your staffing problems and I think I've got the ideal solution. I've found a ready-made replacement for DC Gardner with the experience to match: someone who will certainly strengthen your team.'

'Sir?' said Trussell, instantly suspicious, wondering how Watkins had conjured up someone out of nowhere. He thought he knew most of the people with the right experience. What was coming? It was certainly unlike Watkins to do him a favour.

'I've decided to transfer DC Sprawson from Brandford. The CID there's under new management and DCI Simpson has brought in his own team. Eddie's face doesn't fit now. A change of scenery for him will benefit all parties.'

Trussell was horrified. He remembered DC Sprawson only too well.

'Not Fast Eddie, Sir? You can't be serious. I didn't think that he was still on the force. Wasn't there some inquiry at Brandford?'

'Yes, there was, but Sprawson was exonerated.'

Whitewashed, more likely, thought Trussell to himself.

'I want you to forget about that, Trussell. As far as I'm concerned, he starts with a clean sheet here and it's up to you to see that it stays that way.'

'Didn't you say something on his behalf at the inquiry, Sir?'

'Be careful, Trussell,' warned Watkins. 'I grant you that Eddie has had his problems, but you're the right man to sort him out and get the most from his experience. He should certainly fill the gap in your team.'

Trussell had thought back to his first appointment as a Detective Constable over twenty years ago. He had been posted to Brandford police station in East Kent. The main housing estate in the area, built in the sixties, was a hotbed of criminality at all levels. It was a tough place to police and the local station was known as the Alamo by anyone unlucky enough to be posted there.

Watkins had been a Detective Sergeant there before the first of his rapid promotions. Sprawson had been quite close to Watkins at the time and had cultivated some very dubious people as informants. Some of his colleagues were unsure from time to time as to who was controlling whom. There had been rumours about his behaviour and connections, but nothing was ever proved.

Trussell had been strictly unimpressed by what was going on around him at all levels. There was more than a whiff of corruption about the place but as a new Detective Constable, he couldn't be seen to rock the boat. He was already smart enough to realise that having Brandford on his CV might just be career-threatening in the future and he'd arranged a transfer away as soon as possible.

He had a fair idea there were more problems bubbling up at Brandford now and Sprawson needed to get away. Not just because a new team had arrived. He had called in a favour from his old boss. Or maybe Watkins just wanted to extricate him from the clutches of some of his unsavoury friends before anyone outside started to dig into the past. He was probably just protecting his own back.

Now Trussell was stuck with someone he regarded as a serious accident waiting to happen. Quite how he and Jackie Joynton would control him and get the job done too, was another headache. They'd discussed it as soon as he'd left Watkins. Trussell knew that Jackie was a strong character and would provide the right sort of immediate leadership for the two Detective Constables - she didn't appear fazed by any potential problems ahead. He remembered Sprawson's first day at Woodchester only too well. The sergeant on the front desk had called to say that his new Detective Constable had arrived.

'Ask him to wait there, Alan. I'll be right down. Is the interview room free?'

Trussell walked down to the lobby by the front desk to collect his new Detective Constable.

Sprawson stood there, waiting.

Trussell had looked at him with a certain amount of loathing. He was just as he remembered him, although Sprawson had put on a few pounds since they last met and his familiar toothbrush moustache had been supplemented by designer stubble. *He must be about forty five now* thought Trussell. About five feet eight. Nothing else had changed: the greasy slicked back hair, the baggy, flashy suit, the overconfident air. His appearance had always screamed spiv whenever Trussell had seen him.

'Nice ter see you agin, Jimmy. It's been a while,' he said, holding out a hand to Trussell. The sound of that all too familiar coarse voice with the East Kent accent grated, as it always had done.

Trussell ignored the hand, and pointed to the interview room opposite.

'In there, Sprawson,' he said coldly.

Sprawson seemed stunned by his reception, but went into the interview room, his new boss following and closing the door behind them.

'You will always address me as Detective Inspector or Guv until I tell you otherwise, Sprawson. I didn't want you here and I told the DCS exactly that. He's fully aware of how I feel. I'll be watching you very carefully and the first time you step out of line, you'll be on your way out the door. Don't even think about going to the DCS. He knows the score.'

Sprawson listened, open mouthed, to this rather forthright welcome.

Trussell told him exactly what was expected of him and had left him under no illusions as to the consequences of crossing the line. Somehow, he had to make use of Sprawson's experience whilst keeping him on a tight leash. One of his biggest concerns was the other DC, Mark Green who was new, short on experience, but looking promising. Trussell didn't want him to be influenced or tainted by Sprawson.

'You'll be part of a team of four: me, DS Jackie Joynton, DC Mark Green and you. You'd better come up now and meet the other two.'

A somewhat chastened Fast Eddie had followed his new boss up to the CID office on the first floor.

It was a long room, divided into two parts by a double bank of filing cupboards, back-to-back. 'This is our part,' said Trussell, turning right into the area occupied by his team. 'DI McIndow's team live up the other end.'

There were four desks all fitted with computer screens and keyboards. In the corner stood a small table, containing a kettle, coffee percolator, a teapot and assorted cups, saucers and some well-used mugs. There was a half-full box of teabags and a coffee jar. A battered metal biscuit tin stood at the back. A laser printer was sitting on top of one of the low cabinets. A coat-stand stood by the door, with assorted coats hanging from it.

Trussell introduced Sprawson to Jackie Joynton and he stared at her. Slim, attractive, thirty, about five feet six tall, with short blonde hair and blue eyes. She would get the attention of most men, but the way Sprawson had looked at her was positively indecent.

'I'm pleased ter meet yer Jackie,' he leered, holding out a hand.

She ignored it. 'I'm sure you'd be pleased to meet my other half, Mike, as well. He's six feet three and plays rugby. You call me Sarge,' she said, staring back at him, daring a response.

He got the message and then nodded politely to Mark Green when he was introduced.

What a contrast, thought Trussell, as he looked at his two Detective Constables. Sprawson shorter, overweight, scruffy, loud; Green in his late twenties, about six feet tall, slim, dark hair, reserved, always smartly dressed in a sports jacket and neatly pressed trousers.

Mark Green indicated the empty desk opposite his own.

'That's yours. I'll show you where the tea and coffee are kept. I collect the money every week for that. You'll probably want to get your own mug like the rest of us. There are plenty of shops in the High Street.'

A rather subdued Fast Eddie thanked him and sat down at his desk. He wondered just what he would have to do to achieve some sort of acceptance from his new colleagues. He had been taken aback by the overtly hostile reaction from Trussell and the cool welcome from Joynton. Even DC Mark Green had been non-committal. This hadn't been what he had expected. He waited for the usual team briefing to see what was going on and what was expected of him. Trussell had already told him firmly that there was no point in talking to DCS Watkins.

A month on, and this sequence of events was still fresh in Trussell's mind. Sprawson's presence in the office was a reminder of a time in his own career that was best forgotten and a constant source of irritation to him. It was not conducive to a happy team. No matter how hard he tried, he still couldn't convince himself that Fast Eddie had changed in any way. The more he could get him out of the office on non-controversial stuff, to reduce the overall workload, the better Trussell liked it.

2

Day 1.
Tuesday 19th February.
CID Office, Woodchester Police Station. The same morning.

Apart from Trussell and Joynton, the office was empty and eerily quiet. The other CID team, led by DI McIndow, were out searching for a gang responsible for ram-raiding village stores and stealing cash machines.

DC Eddie Sprawson had been sent to a local branch of the national supermarket chain, Supercheap, to look into a pilfering problem that seemed to be turning into something much more serious. Stock had been disappearing from their warehouse on an increasingly regular basis. Now the management had called the police to look into it. DC Mark Green had gone with him for the experience, and Trussell was waiting for a report from them before deciding the next step.

Jackie knew that she needed to distract Jim from his dark mood. Brooding wouldn't help him. He needed to lighten up. She couldn't begin to imagine what it was like for him, going home to an empty house every night now that his daughter was at university. A lesser man might have turned to the bottle but that was not Trussell's style. She tried to break into his reverie and start a conversation. Ask him about his daughter.

'Have you heard from Liz lately, Jim?'

'Eh? Oh, yes. She phones me a couple of times a week.'

'How's she getting on at Uni?'

'She seems to have settled in OK. She's enjoying her course. She tells me that she's making friends.'

'What about you, Jim? You need to get out a bit more. Socialise. Meet people. Sometimes the job isn't enough. I know exactly what's going on with you.'

'Keep this up and you'll make a great agony aunt, Sergeant. You sound like Liz.'

Before Jackie could think of a suitable reply, the phone on her desk rang loudly. She picked it up. 'Good morning. CID office. DS Joynton speaking.'

It was the duty sergeant on the front desk downstairs. 'Morning, Jackie. It's Alan here. We've got a Missing Person being reported at the moment. Not normally your problem at this stage, but it's the Manager of the

Woodchester branch of the High Weald Building Society who's disappeared. It seems he had a dinner appointment last night and failed to come home. His wife's here at the moment and she's in a bit of a state. I think you should talk to her.'

'One of us will be down in a moment. Where is she?'

'I've put her in Interview Room 1.'

'What's her name?'

'Maureen Scoular.' He spelt it.

Jackie turned to Trussell and relayed the information to him.

'Right, Jackie, we'll both go down and talk to her.'

Just what Trussell needed - a possible new enquiry? Things had been unusually quiet these last few days. He stood up, now fully alert, shaken out of his reverie, galvanised. He picked up his mid-grey suit jacket from the back of the chair and adjusted his tie. It was an automatic yet unnecessary gesture - he was always immaculately dressed. Appearance and presentation had always been important to him.

They walked down the stairs to the front desk, nodded to the sergeant, and headed for the interview room.

A distraught woman sat on a chair by the table, a handkerchief clutched in one hand, dabbing her eyes. Jackie reckoned that she was in her thirties. She had a pale complexion, no makeup. Not unattractive. Her eyes were swollen from crying and there were tear stains on her cheeks. Her light brown shoulder-length hair was untidy - barely brushed, damp. She had obviously walked through the rain to the station without an umbrella. A brown woollen winter coat emphasised her drabness. She looked thoroughly miserable. A female uniformed officer sat with her. There was a cup of tea on the table in front of her but she was too distracted to drink it.

'Mrs Scoular?' Trussell introduced himself and Jackie. 'Please tell us what's happened.'

'My husband, Barney, had a dinner appointment last night,' she sobbed. 'Business,' he said. 'I've no idea where he was going. I work at the Building Society as well. I left work early because I had a bad headache and went home to bed. When I woke up later, I realised that he hadn't come home, so when I went into the office this morning and there was no sign of him, I came straight here. None of the others had any idea what could have happened to him. I checked his desk and his passport is missing. He's always kept it there.'

Trussell picked up on the mention of the passport. 'How many people knew that your husband kept his passport in his desk drawer in the office?'

She dabbed at her eyes again. The tears were still flowing as she tried to concentrate on the questions.

'Well, obviously I knew. Maybe Stevie did as well. I don't believe that the others would have known about it.'

'Who's Stevie?'

'Stephanie Winterden. She thinks that she's the unofficial assistant branch manager.'

'What about the dinner appointment? Was there any entry in his diary?'

'Not a thing. We have a small team and I'm sure that he would have said something to someone. But nobody knows anything,' she sobbed.

'We'd better take down a few details,' said Jackie, 'and then we'll visit the Society office. It's the branch in the High Street, isn't it?

Maureen Scoular nodded, still dabbing at her eyes.

'Barney's been with the Society since he left school, almost twenty years. He's worked his way up and they promoted him a couple of years ago when the previous manager, Mr Thompson, retired. I believe that he recommended Barney to the management. They'd worked together for quite a while. The Society is relatively small with only a dozen branches around Kent and East Sussex.'

'What about you, Mrs Scoular. How long have you been there?'

She dabbed at her eyes again before continuing. Concentrating on the questions seemed to distract her and the sobbing had subsided.

'About five years. I used to work for a major bank in the City but found the commuting too expensive and stressful, so I decided to work locally when this job came up.'

'How many people are there in the branch?'

'Let's see. Apart from Barney and myself, there's Stephanie - she's been there about ten years – I've mentioned her already. Then there's Janet McDuff. She's been there quite a long time. Scottish, as you'd expect from her name. The three of us cover the two tills during opening hours.

Then there's Susie, er, Albright. She's a trainee who covers our admin while she learns the business.'

'Is there anyone else?'

'James Howditch is our financial adviser. He spends most of his time processing new mortgage and investment applications. He also deals with people who have questions about our products. Occasionally, Barney becomes involved if there are any large or unusual applications, but he usually leaves most of the day-to-day stuff to James. The two of them have a short meeting at the close of business so that Barney is up to speed with what's happened during the day. After all, as Branch Manager, he's ultimately responsible for what goes on.' Her last statement seemed to convey a lot of pride in her husband's status.

'Can you tell me how long you've been married, Mrs Scoular?'

'Nearly two years.'

'Was there any surprise or resentment in the office?'

'No. That's a strange question?'

'I'm just trying to get a sense of the dynamics in the branch. With such a small number of people working together in a very close environment. Is it ever claustrophobic? What about disagreements?'

'No. We're all different but we still manage to work as a team' She thought for a moment, reviewing the other staff members in her mind, before continuing. 'Stephanie, or Stevie as she prefers to be known, is a total fitness freak. She's absolutely obsessed with martial arts. Always down the gym or going to her Judo club. I believe that she's very highly qualified. I think that she still has an aspiration to compete at the highest level.'

'What about the others?'

'Well, Janet is older, late forties and has a family, so for her it's just a job with the bonus of a cheaper staff mortgage. James is in his mid-thirties and has a young family. He tends to rush off home as soon as he's finished for the day. Susie is in her early twenties. She has very little in the way of responsibility at the moment so she doesn't hang around at the end of the day either.'

'Do you socialise as a team?'

'Not really. Stevie and I used to go out for a drink or meal quite often before Barney and I got together, but we don't do that anymore.'

'Well, thank you for that information, Mrs Scoular. We'll need some more details - your husband's description, physical details, what he was wearing. Oh, and a photograph of him would be very useful. A recent one if you have it.'

'I thought that you might ask that,' she said, opening the large tan handbag in front of her. 'I've got one taken on our holiday a few months ago.' She fumbled in her bag and as she took a photograph out, a small cardboard box fell onto the table. She grabbed it quickly and replaced it in her bag. Jackie Joynton noticed and scribbled something in her notebook. Mrs Scoular recovered her composure and handed the photograph to Trussell.

He looked at it. A slightly built individual in a tee shirt and shorts, probably in his late thirties, stared at the camera. Mrs Scoular, standing next to him, seemed marginally taller. The photo had been taken on a beach in a sunnier place.

'That was taken in Spain,' she said, proudly.' We spent two weeks there in July.'

'We'll need a note of your address, of course.'

'We live at The Hollows, the new estate in Frattenden, just outside town. It's supposed to be THE place to live now, especially judging by the prices of the houses. It's only right that someone in Barney's position should live there. We're at number 29, The Avenue. It's a detached house.' Her evident pride in her husband's position shone through, again.

'Thank you, Mrs Scoular. Now, if you wouldn't mind, can you give Detective Sergeant Joynton a description of your husband and what he was wearing yesterday?'

Jackie Joynton had her notebook open, pen poised as Mrs Scoular started to describe her husband.

When she had finished and answered a couple of questions to clarify something, Trussell said 'I think that we'll walk down to the Society now and talk to the staff to see if they have any more news or ideas. Your husband will probably turn up later, admitting that he overdid things last night and was too embarrassed to come home.'

'I think that's unlikely, Detective Inspector. Barney doesn't drink.'

3
Day 1.
Tuesday 19th February.
Woodchester High Street.

Trussell and Joynton left Mrs Scoular with the uniformed officer to return to their office.

'Did you notice the box that slipped out of her bag while she was searching for the photo, Jim?' asked Jackie, as they walked up the stairs. 'Did you see how quickly she picked it up? As if she didn't want us to see it.'

'Yes, but I don't know what it was.'

'Well, I do. I've seen something similar before. It took me back to my teenage years.'

'What dark secrets are you about to admit to, Sergeant?' laughed Trussell. 'I'm intrigued.'

'When I lived in London, I belonged to the local amateur dramatic society,' said Jackie. 'I quite enjoyed it. The group was quite a mixed bag. There were a couple of older members who had acted professionally over the years, and I learned quite a bit from them. You could see that they knew a lot.'

'Interesting, Jackie,' said Trussell. 'I'm sure that this is leading somewhere.'

'I remember asking one of the older ladies how they managed to burst into tears and cry so convincingly on stage. They shared the secret with me. They used something called menthol tear sticks. They dabbed them under their eyes. It was the fumes which caused their eyes to water. Practising the right facial expressions in front of a mirror would prolong the tears and a clever actor or actress could certainly give a very creditable, or in this case, convincing performance of being very upset.'

'Do you have doubts about Mrs Scoular, then?'

'I'm pretty sure that the small box that fell out of her bag contained menthol sticks. It just looked familiar. It struck a chord. I wondered whether she had one in her handkerchief to prolong the effect.'

'We'll have to find out a bit more about her,' said Trussell. 'Well spotted.'

Back in the CID Office, Trussell and Joynton quickly collected their coats, before leaving the station and setting off along the High Street.

The miserable weather had decimated the normal crowds of shoppers. No need to dodge the usual hordes, too busy texting on their phones to watch where they were going. Despite the rain, there was no let up with the traffic: there was a constant swish of tyres on the wet road and the occasional splash from one of the puddles as vehicles passed through them.

It was a ten-minute walk along the High Street past the shops to the High Weald Building Society. They arrived outside the branch, easily identified by its bright blue exterior in the Society's corporate colours.

Trussell pushed the door open and they went in. It seemed surprisingly busy. There was a queue waiting at the windows of the two tills at the back of the bank. To the left was seating for customers and a table covered in leaflets describing the Society's savings products and latest mortgage deals. The wall on that side was similarly covered in posters. In the centre, adjacent to the tills, there was a closed door, on the right three glass-fronted offices. Two were unoccupied, each containing just a small circular table and four chairs. In the third was a man in his mid-thirties, dark hair, medium build, concentrating on the computer monitor on the desk in front of him. Trussell guessed he must be James Howditch and tapped politely on the open door. The man looked up and smiled.

'Can I help you?'

'Mr Howditch? I'm Detective Inspector Trussell,' he said, showing his warrant card. 'We've just been speaking to Mrs Scoular at the station. Has there been any further news about her husband?'

'Not a word as far as I know. I think you'd better speak to Stephanie Winterden,' he said, indicating the younger of the two women behind the glass partition. 'She seems to have taken charge of things for the moment, although she isn't officially the assistant manager.'

There was a certain irony as he echoed what Mrs Schoular had said earlier.

The door at the back of the bank opened and a young woman walked into the public area, carrying a couple of files. She was of average height, slim and wearing the Society uniform - a blue blouse and skirt. Her blonde hair was tied back neatly in a ponytail and she was wearing minimal makeup. *Quite pretty*, thought Trussell. *Not much older than my own daughter.* She walked towards James Howditch, holding out the files. 'Here's the information you asked for, James.'

'Thanks, Susie. Just leave it on the desk. I'll look at it later. These two visitors are from the police, asking about Mr Scoular.'

She smiled at the two detectives, put the files down and returned to the door at the back, closing it after her.

Thanking Howditch, Trussell and Joynton joined the queue in front of Stephanie Winterden's till. The customer at the window finished transacting her business and turned to leave and Trussell replaced her at the front of the queue.

'Good morning. How can I help you?'

Trussell discreetly showed his warrant card.

'Miss Winterden? Can we talk somewhere more private?'

'Yes, of course, Detective Inspector.' She turned to her colleague. 'I've got to close for a moment, Janet,' she said quietly. 'This gentleman is from the police.' She shut the till, opened the self-locking door, stepped out of the cashiers' area and then closed the door behind her.

Trussell studied her. In her mid-thirties, tall, about five nine or ten, he thought. She was wearing the Society mid-blue uniform with a pair of blue low-wedge shoes. Dark brown hair, cut very short in an almost masculine style, pale complexion with the merest hint of make-up and brown eyes that returned his searching look without flinching or turning away. She had a toned appearance and seemed very self-confident. She offered her hand and Trussell grasped it. The handshake was dry and very firm as he introduced Jackie Joynton.

'You've obviously come to talk about Mr Scoular, Detective Inspector,' she said, opening the door of one of the glass cubicles. 'I assume that you've spoken to Maureen. We can talk here. By the way, please call me Stevie. May I offer you some tea or coffee?'

Trussell thought that he detected a very slight accent. What was it? Of course. East Kent. It reminded him of his time in Brandford and of Fast Eddie.

'No thank you,' he replied. 'We just need to talk about Barnaby Scoular.'

She showed them into the glass fronted office and closed the door after them.

'You can imagine that things are a bit difficult with Mr Scoular apparently missing,' she said. 'I've already been in contact with our Head Office. They're sending someone senior down. They also told me that they want to look at the last year's mortgage applications. There are some suggestions of a problem or irregularity. I've already mentioned it to James. He's very worried, of course.'

'So, when did you last see Mr Scoular?'

'It was when we closed the office yesterday evening. He's always the last to leave and lock up.'

Trussell studied her expression as she spoke. It gave nothing away.

'I assume you have a set of keys too, if you were able to open the office this morning?'

'Yes. That's always been the case since the last manager retired. I was surprised that Barney wasn't already here.'

'Did Mr Scoular mention a dinner appointment last night?'

'Not to me. I checked his diary this morning when Maureen arrived. She told us he hadn't come home last night. I was surprised. There wasn't any reference to any appointment.'

'Do you have any idea who he might have met, then?'

'He had said something earlier in the week about some mortgages that he had put through. There seemed to be a problem with them. He was trying to arrange a meeting with the borrowers because they couldn't come in during office hours. Maybe that's the answer.'

'How did he seem?'

'Worried, I'd say. I've known him for quite a while - since I joined ten years ago. Absolute workaholic. Seems to live for the job. He's always seemed to be - how can I put it? Unflappable? I don't know what the problem was, but it looks as though he was obviously hoping to fix it before anyone found out. Now I'm not so sure. I wonder whether the visit from Head Office is connected with it.'

She seemed quite relaxed under the circumstances. Maybe she was ambitious and saw promotion coming her way if the manager had created a problem for himself. Trussell exchanged looks with Jackie Joynton, who had been making notes. *She looks calculating to me,* he thought.

His thoughts were interrupted as the main door opened and two men walked into the branch. One was older, maybe in his fifties, greying hair, glasses, average height and build. He was wearing a beige overcoat with a dark velvet collar. The second man was much younger, slightly taller, fresh-faced, neat dark hair with a short navy-blue coat over his dark grey suit. He was carrying an executive case. The younger man was deferential and stood aside to let his colleague in first.

Stephanie Winterden noticed them as well.

'Excuse me, Detective Inspector. Those are the visitors from Head Office. Things must be serious. That's Philip McDriscoll, the Deputy Chairman. The young man is his bag carrier. I don't remember his name. I'd better go out and talk to them. Can we continue this discussion a little later, please?'

He nodded and watched her go out to welcome the visitors. They looked in Trussell's direction as they spoke and then she showed them into the other vacant office, closing the door after them.

'Well, Jackie, it seems Miss Winterden's career prospects are more important than her missing manager. I suggest that we go back to the office,' said Trussell. 'We need to take stock and look at all of the actors in this little play to see if anything's known about any of them. Anything and everything you can find out about them. Find their family details and where they live. What sort of cars they drive. Financials. The usual stuff. Then we can arrange to talk to them individually.'

'I suppose that there's always a slim chance that Barnaby Scoular may yet reappear, Jim. I think that we should check the local hospitals. It's possible he might have had an accident or suffered loss of memory or something like that. If he's under serious stress at work, it could've brought on some sort of temporary amnesia.'

'Can you contact Greeno, Jackie? Get him back to the office. We'll pass him Scoular's details and he can make a start on that. He can go to the Woodchester Hospital and talk to A & E. Find out whether they've seen Mr Scoular or anyone who resembles him. If he draws a blank there, then he'll have to start doing the rounds of the doctors' surgeries and clinics. Someone must have seen him. Eddie Sprawson can manage at the supermarket on his own at this stage.'

Trussell looked back at Stephanie Winterden, deep in conversation with the two visitors. Files had been produced and spread across the table. The three of them were looking at the contents. He saw her shake her head vigorously in answer to a question. *Creating an alibi, Stevie? Or even an opportunity?* he wondered.

4

Day 1.
Tuesday 19th February.
Woodchester Police Station.

Trussell felt a sense of unease about the situation as they walked back along the High Street to the Police Station. He glanced at the CCTV cameras along the street and wondered whether they might be able to solve the mystery of Barnaby Scoular's disappearance.

'Somehow, we'll have to find out where Mr Scoular went last night. Can you contact the control room, Jackie - see whether they have any video covering the Building Society office from, say, five thirty onwards last night?'

'I'll do it as soon as we get back. Shall I start looking at the staff members to see if anything's known while you talk to Greeno?'

'Please. I'd be surprised if there are any problems there. They seem a pretty straightforward bunch. But Stevie interests me. There may be another side to her. I think the grieving wife may be worth our attention, as well.'

'It sounds like your famous intuition again, Jim.'

'Call it what you like, Jackie. But Stevie seems like a pretty cool customer. Did you watch her body language when she was talking to the visitors? And then we have the wife's tears to consider. Were they genuine or not?"

'Stevie acts like the assistant manager when it suits her. But I think that she was stepping back at that moment. As if she was just one of the team. She's playing company politics.'

Mark Green was waiting when they arrived back in the CID office.

'What news from the supermarket, Greeno?'

'There's definitely something going on there, Guv. Stuff has been disappearing from their warehousing area and it seems a bit too regular. It's only small amounts at a time, and the sort of consumables that can be easily sold in the pub or somewhere like that. Eddie's interviewing the staff. He certainly has a fairly robust attitude to these things. Probably put the fear of God into the workers. I expect that the problem will probably go away now, at least for a while, even if we can't identify whoever's been responsible at the moment. He thinks it's organised.'

'I'll call him in a moment and then discuss the matter when he gets back. In the meantime, I've got another, urgent job for you. Jackie and I have just been to the High Weald Building Society. The manager seems to have disappeared. Apparently, he had a dinner appointment last night that no one else knew about, and he never came home afterwards.'

'What d'you want me to do, Guv?'

'Will you go to the Woodchester A & E to see if he turned up there last night. Could have been an accident or amnesia or something like that. It's unlikely to have been a drink problem because his wife tells us that he doesn't touch alcohol. But you never know. I suppose there's always a chance someone spiked his orange juice.

'OK, Guv. What do we know about him? Do we have a photo?'

'Jackie will give you his details and description. If you draw a blank there, Greeno, I'm afraid that you'll have to start doing the rounds of all the doctors' surgeries and clinics in the area. If you still can't find any trace, then contact the nearest hospitals immediately outside our area. Bit of a tough ask for you, but be meticulous. List everyone you've spoken to. We need the info as soon as possible.'

'OK, Guv.'

'Keep in touch. As soon as Eddie gets back, he can give you a hand.'

'I'll start making a list of all the surgeries and clinics before I go.'

'OK. Do that and then get Mr Scoular's details and picture from Jackie and make a start.'

Turning to Joynton, he said, 'The more I think about this case, I'm beginning to wonder whether there's something else going on. I think Mrs Scoular probably has good reason to be worried, genuinely or not, especially if there is some connection with mortgage problems at the High Weald. Can you speak to the control room about the CCTV as soon as you've briefed Greeno?'

'I'll go down there straight away.'

Trussell thought for a moment. He'd better contact Eddie at the supermarket now and let him know what was going on. He picked up his phone and scrolled down the directory until he found his number and hit the call button.

It rang three times and then he heard that familiar grating voice. 'Yes, Guv?'

'Eddie, I've pulled Greeno off the supermarket enquiry for the moment. We've got a Missing Person to deal with. It's a local Building Society manager. I've asked Greeno to start the usual hospital checks. How are you getting on at Supercheap?'

'There's definitely something going on, Guv. Frankly I'm not convinced that the management have a proper vetting system in place to check anyone who turns up for a job.'

'I see,' said Trussell. 'I suggest that you ask the manager for a list of all the employees with their names and addresses and any other info he might have. Then you can get back to the office and start running some checks on them. See if anyone is known.'

'OK, Guv. That shouldn't be a problem. The manager wants it sorted as soon as possible. Otherwise, it's going to raise a red flag with Head Office. Not good for his career path if he's ambitious.'

'Come back as soon as you've got the list of workers and info. We'll have a look to see where we go from there. I'll come down there with you next time. Have a look for myself.'

'OK, Guv. I'll organise it.'

'When that's done, Eddie, I'd like you to give Greeno a hand, checking the surgeries and clinics, if he draws a blank at A & E.'

'OK, Guv.'

Trussell finished the call and put the phone down. He was confident that Eddie could handle whatever was necessary at Supercheap for the moment.

When Mark Green had left for the hospital and Jackie had gone to check on the CCTV from the previous night, Trussell took an A4 pad from his desk and started making notes. His favourite approach at the beginning of any investigation was to start with mind maps - small box shapes on the page into which he scribbled names and those few facts he knew about those people at that point. Most of these details would eventually be posted onto the white crime board in the office.

The next step was to see if he could connect any of these information-filled shapes in any way. Some of his colleagues, in the past, had always chuckled when they had seen him reach for that A4 pad. *Jim's off again, drawing pictures'* was the usual comment. Jackie had noticed that this logical approach, together with his famous intuition, usually produced results.

He put all the names of the individuals in their own boxes with Barney Scoular in the centre and sat back to contemplate the big picture. The first thing he noticed was that he had, subconsciously, ringed round the box with Stevie's name in it several times. There was obviously something nagging at the back of his mind.

He was still studying the notes when Jackie returned.

'I've looked at the CCTV, Jim. Scoular was caught on camera leaving the Society at 17.50 last night. He walked west along the High Street but he wasn't picked up by any other camera down there. They had some technical issues with the next block of cameras at that time last night. It was fixed this morning, so that doesn't help us.'

'Where could he have gone? What's in the street along there? Restaurants? Pubs?'

'There are several eating places along there, including the Blue Dragon, that new Chinese restaurant. I hear that it's quite good. It seems fairly popular. Then there's the Castle Inn, of course. They've got a decent restaurant.'

'If Greeno and Fast Eddie draw a blank with the hospitals and surgeries, then we'd better start looking at the restaurants and pubs that serve food. We'll have to get some help from uniformed with that part, if necessary. Better speak to Alan on the front desk. See what manpower he might have available, if we need it. PCSO's as well.'

'There's one more thing. When I was reviewing the tapes, I started at 5.30, when the Building Society closes. Three or four minutes later, I saw Susie Albright leave, just as Maureen Scoular said. She doesn't hang around after work. But she only walked a short way along the High Street and then stood in a shop doorway out of the rain. I wondered what was going on. Then, two minutes later, James Howditch left the Society and walked towards her. She smiled at him, grabbed his arm and they walked off together. They looked quite comfortable in each other's company. Obviously, I couldn't say where they went because of the problems with the CCTV I mentioned earlier.'

'What about Stephanie Winterden? Surely, she was picked up by the CCTV?'

Jackie Joynton consulted her notes again. 'Janet McDuff left next just two minutes later. Stephanie Winterden left at 17.45. She walked in the opposite direction to the others. She could have been heading for the Weaver Street car park, of course. We'll need to check. They must have

CCTV. It shouldn't take too long to see if she went there. We know roughly what time she would have arrived. It would be useful to know what sort of car she drives.'

'Get Greeno to look her details up when he gets back. The car she has. Where she lives. When we have that info, get Eddie to pop round to Weaver Street and ask to look at the CCTV. He'll see what time she left and which direction she took when she exited the car park.'

'OK, Jim. As soon as they come back.'

The snippet of information about Susie and James Howditch went into Trussell's memory bank, to be added to the mind map later. Maureen Scoular's suggestion that all was sweetness and light at the Society was beginning to look less plausible. It would be interesting to talk to Janet McDuff. After all, she had been there longer than anyone, apart from Barnaby Scoular.

What secrets might she divulge? Intriguing, he thought.

5

Day 1.
Tuesday 19th February. Later that morning.
Woodchester Police Station.

Trussell decided that now was a good time to talk to the staff at the High Weald individually. He had thought about interviewing them at the branch, but on consideration, wondered whether this might inhibit them and it would be a waste of time if they would only tell him what they felt constrained to say, so he decided to invite them to the police station one at a time to see if a more informal chat would encourage them to be more forthcoming. Jackie had run their names through the PNC, but none of them had any sort of record - not so much as a parking ticket.

He rang the Society from his desk and spoke to Stevie, to tell her that he would be inviting the staff individually to attend Woodchester police station. He stressed that these would not be official interviews under caution, but just a chance to see if anyone had any further information. He told her he had decided to invite Janet McDuff first, on the basis that she had been there the longest, apart from Barnaby Scoular, and asked for her to be sent to the station.

Fifteen minutes later, there was a call from the front desk to advise him of her arrival so, Trussell asked the sergeant to show her to one of the interview rooms he had already reserved. He collected Jackie Joynton and quickly walked down the stairs to the main floor, nodded at Alan, the duty sergeant, and opened the interview room door. Janet McDuff sat at the table with a cup of tea in front of her. She had dark brown curly hair cut in a shorter style, a pale complexion and a pair of glasses with dark plastic frames. She was of average height, slightly chubby and still wearing her High Weald uniform, just visible under her coat. She looked somewhat uncomfortable. Trussell guessed that she had probably never seen the inside of a police station in her life. The spartan décor in the interview room wouldn't help.

He tried to put her at her ease. 'Good morning, Mrs McDuff. Thank you for taking the time to help us. I thought that somewhere away from the Society would be a bit more relaxed. I just want to stress that this is just an informal chat to see if you can throw any light on Mr Scoular's disappearance. Anything, however small, that could help us to piece this matter together.'

'I'm nae sure what I can tell you, Inspector. It's a verra strange situation.' Nearly twenty years in Kent had hardly blunted her Scots accent which became more marked when she was stressed. 'It's verra unlike Barney. He's always been so reliable. Works verra hard.'

'How long have you known him, Mrs McDuff?'

'These seventeen years past, ever since I started there. He was just a wee lad when I arrived. Mind you, he's always been on the short side. I always thought that he and Stevie made an unlikely pair, with her bein' so tall, and him on the small side.'

'When was this? Were they a couple?

'Yes. I think that it started soon after she joined the Society.'

'How long did it last?

'It was over before Maureen arrived. I think that old Mr Thompson, the manager, at that time, took a bit of a dim view and spoke to Barney about it. He was a wee bit old-fashioned and thought it wasnae guid for staff relations.'

'What do you know about Stevie? She's been there about ten years, I understand.'

'Yes. She worked in an office in toon somewhere. She wasnae doing anything exciting with her career so I guess she was looking for a new direction. Then there was a vacancy at the High Weald and she came in for an interview.'

Janet McDuff looked around her for a moment in a rather conspiratorial manner, as if she was worried that someone else might overhear the conversation. Then she continued. 'Winterden's nae her original name, ye ken. She changed it by deed poll. She came from Brandford and has tried to disguise it by changing her accent. Sometimes, when she's stressed, the East Kent accent comes back. I've always felt that she was a wee bit ashamed of her roots and was trying to build hersel' a new life. The martial arts thing is part of it. She has ambitions in the sport and trains verra hard. Always doon the gym. I think that might hae been one of the reasons why her relationship with Barney came to an end. Mind you, I still believe that she has some sort of power over him, although he married Maureen.'

'Do you have any idea about her previous name?'

'No, I've always known her as Winterden.'

'So how do you know about the name change?'

'Someone from her past came looking for her. I think I was the only one who heearrd the conversation. Mind you, I had tae pretend that I hadnae heearrd anything. I'm sure that she wouldnae be verra pleased if she found oot that I'd overheearrd them talkin'. She made the man leave after she'd promised to contact him later.'

Trussell made a mental note to ask Jackie to look into it discreetly.

'What do you mean?' he asked.

'Weel, Detective Inspector, I mind that Stevie isnae a person to cross. I wouldnae want to get on the wrong side o' her, with all that martial arts stuff she does. I'm sure that she can look after hersel'. She's a big strong girrrl.'

'Have you ever seen her lose her temper, then, Mrs McDuff?'

'No. She's a strong personality and she does like to give the impression she's the assistant branch manager. She's just assumed the part and nae one dares argue with her. Not even Barney.'

'What about James Howditch?'

'He looks after the mortgage applications and financial products. He's a verra clever fellow. He should be in charge.'

'Does he get involved in office politics? How does he feel about the others?'

'You'll have to ask him yersel', Detective Inspector.'

'What about Susie Albright?'

'The wee girrl's only been there about four months. She's trying to leearrn the business and she should stick to it. Not involve hersel' in other people's business. She'll destroy his marriage, d'ye ken.'

'What do you mean?' Trussell feigned ignorance to hopefully draw more information from her

'I've said enough. I dinna want to cause any problems. It's nae ma business.'

Trussell tried to move the conversation on, to cover the awkward silence.

'What about Mrs Scoular. Was she aware that her husband had been in a relationship with Stevie? I understand that the two women used to go out together for meals and drinks before the Scoulars got married.'

'Aye, that's right. Always out together on the toon. Then it stopped suddenly. Something musta happened. There was a verra definite atmosphere for a while. It seems to have blown over the noo.'

'Do have any idea what could have happened to Mr Scoular? Did he say anything about any meeting or dinner last night?'

Trussell was counting on Janet McDuff perhaps overhearing something, as she obviously knew what was going on there day to day.

'No. Not tae me. It's all a bit of a mystery.'

'What about Mrs Scoular. Does she have any family nearby to support her? I assume that there isn't a child from the marriage?'

'She hasn't any family at all. I heearrd she was abandoned as a baby and brought up in a children's home. She's had tae look out fer hersel' since she left it. I'll give her credit because she's worked hard to educate hersel.' I ken she's a clever girrl.'

'What about friends?'

'Weel, she belongs to a local amateur dramatic society in Woodchester. She's got quite a few friends there. She loves acting and usually takes one of the leading parts. She's always appearing in a new play. They put on four productions every year, I ken. It certainly shows. She can be a wee bit of a drama queen, sometimes.'

Joynton gave Trussell a knowing look which said 'I told you so'.

He locked that snippet away in his memory bank for later. Maybe he should look at Maureen Scoular in a different light. What was it that caused the rift between her and Stevie? That would need revisiting.

'Do you remember her maiden name before she married Mr Scoular?' he asked.

She thought for a moment.

'Yes, it was Atherton,' she said. 'She still uses it at the Dramatic Society. She told me that her friends called her Mo.'

'Thank you, Mrs McDuff. You've been very helpful. I won't take up any more of your time. Can I just ask you not to discuss our chat with any of your colleagues?'

She nodded in agreement and got up to leave, looking relieved. She obviously didn't want to stay in the police station a moment longer than necessary.

Trussell looked meaningfully at Jackie Joynton as they walked back up the stairs to the CID office. 'Definitely something is going on. It's not all sweetness and light, as Maureen Scoular would have us believe. Can you track down the Woodchester Dramatic Society and find a contact there so that we can find out more about Maureen Scoular?'

'OK, Jim. Soon as we've finished here.'

Let's talk to James Howditch next. He didn't seem very impressed by our friend Stevie when we first went to the branch.'

Trussell allowed Janet McDuff sufficient time to return to work and then he called Stevie again. 'Ah, Miss Winterden. It's DI Trussell. Would you ask Mr Howditch if he could spare us a few minutes and pop down to the station for a chat? Yes, now, please.'

'Are you going to tell him about the CCTV, Jim?' asked Jackie.

'Let's just see what he has to say first. Don't want to put him on the defensive. We're trying to keep this informal. No reason to believe that he's connected with Scoular's disappearance.'

Jackie's phone rang. It was Mark Green. She spoke to him and then turned to Trussell. 'That was Greeno, Jim. He's drawn a blank at Woodchester A & E. He's going to make a start on the surgeries and clinics now.'

'OK. We'll see where that goes. I think we can go down to the ground floor now. We might as well wait in the interview room for Mr Howditch. He should be here any minute.'

6

Day1.
Tuesday 19th February.
Interview Room 1 at Woodchester Police Station.

As Trussell and Joynton arrived at the main desk, Howditch appeared coming in through the main doors and they showed him into the interview room.

'Thank you for sparing us some of your time, Mr Howditch,' said Trussell. 'I'd like to stress that this is just an informal chat. I thought it would be better away from your office at the moment to avoid distracting your colleagues.'

'I understand that talking outside the office might be conducive to better understanding the branch dynamics and the people in it,' said Howditch. 'But, having said that, I'm not sure how I can help you as far as Barney is concerned.'

'Let me be the judge of that, Mr Howditch,' said Trussell. 'How long have you been there?'

'About six years now.'

'What can you tell me us about the staff and their interactions?'

'This is a bit difficult for me, Detective Inspector. It might sound a bit like sour grapes, but Stevie does take a lot of stuff over. She assumes power and considers herself the unofficial branch assistant manager. I wonder sometimes whether she might still wield a bit of influence over Barney. I think that there was something going on between them before Maureen arrived here and Barney started seeing her outside of work. By right and by qualification, I should have been promoted and given the job. Yet Barney seemed to let Stevie get away with it. Janet would certainly not have said anything. She's not interested in the politics of the place and she's definitely not ambitious. Happy just to do the job, stick to the exact hours and enjoy the perks. I happen to know that she would never have got the mortgage she has, anywhere else. Her husband is a nice guy, reliable, hardworking but not a big earner. So, she keeps her head down and says nothing.'

'What about Maureen Scoular?' asked Trussell. 'Is there anything going on there? How does she get on with Stevie?'

'When she first arrived, they became very good friends, it seems. They were always socialising outside of the office. Then something must have happened.'

'Do you have any idea what that was?'

'They appear to tolerate each other now and there's never any overt nastiness or even any perceptible atmosphere. I don't think that she resented Maureen because she became involved with Barney and then married him. I rather thought that whatever was going on between Barney and Stevie was finished long before Maureen arrived here.'

'Can you tell me anything else about her? How is she coping with her husband's disappearance? Does she have any family support?

'There isn't anybody, as far as I know. I believe that she was brought up in a children's' home. She'd been abandoned as a baby. Don't know the details. I've always considered her a fairly strong personality.'

'What about friends outside the office? Does she ever mention anyone?'

'Her life seems to revolve around her amateur dramatics. I believe that she's quite an accomplished actress who generally seems in control of herself.'

'What about her reaction to her husband's disappearance?'

'Unusually emotional for her, I'd say. But who knows how people react in those circumstances?'

'What about her relationship with her husband, as far as you could guess from life in the office?'

'Not up to me to pass any comment on that Detective Inspector. All I would say is that they hardly behaved like newlyweds from the moment they married. I thought that it was rather curious. Almost like a marriage of convenience, I'd say. But who am I to speculate about other peoples' lives?'

OK. Moving on, what can you tell me about your admin assistant?'

'Susie Albright is a trainee, so she's obviously not caught up in any undercurrents or office politics here.'

'Does she work particularly closely with any member of the team?' asked Trussell. 'I noticed that she brought you some files while we were there and there seemed to be a degree of familiarity in her tone.'

'No more than any normal office routine.'

Jackie looked at Trussell.

He nodded.

'Mr Howditch,' she began, 'we studied the CCTV on the evening that Mr Scoular disappeared, hoping that it might show us where he went after he left the office. Prior to him leaving, we saw Miss Albright leave and then you followed her out of the door a couple of minutes later. She appeared to be waiting for you further down the street and then you walked off together. Her greeting seemed to suggest more than just work colleagues. Can you explain that, please?'

Howditch maintained his composure. 'I don't see the relevance of my private life to your enquiries into Mr Scoular's disappearance. What happens outside the office is really nothing to do with you,' he said.

'It seems that Mr Scoular followed you down the High Street and we need to know what happened to him,' said Trussell. Please answer the question, Sir.'

'Well, Detective Inspector, we certainly didn't see him at any time.'

'You still haven't explained your behaviour,' Trussell persisted.

Howditch looked exasperated. 'Well, Detective Inspector, if you really need to know, we were going to the new restaurant, The Blue Dragon. We had arranged to meet my wife, Sarah, and her younger brother, Michael. It was a family occasion. Mike and Susie have been an item for a couple of years now, and as it happened, he proposed to her at the table last night. As usual, Mike managed to screw things up. When he produced the ring, it was too big, so they've got to take it back at the weekend to resize it. Otherwise, you would have seen Susie wearing it this morning when you met her, which might have avoided this unpleasantness. So, Susie will be my wife's sister-in-law at some point. There's nothing more to it than that.'

'I see...'

'The other reason why I was annoyed is that I introduced Susie to Barney. He had mentioned to me that he was looking for a trainee to add to the team. None of the others know about the family connection, and Barney wanted to keep it that way.'

'So, you're sure that there's nothing really that you can tell us about Mr Scoular's disappearance, then?'

'I'm afraid not. I'm as mystified as you are. Barney never gave me any hint that he had a problem. There are these suspect mortgages lurking in the background, but I can't offer any opinion on them. They're not anything that I've been involved in, but I'm as concerned as the management. No one seems to know about them. We have systems in place for mortgages. Everything is supposed to go across my desk, but these seem to have bypassed me.'

'Has anything like this happened in the past?'

'No. Not as far as I know.'

'Thank you for your time, then, Mr Howditch. I don't think that there's anything else. Please do not discuss this conversation with anyone. Not even Miss Albright.'

Howditch nodded. He looked thoughtful as he got up to leave.

'What do you think, Jim?' asked Jackie after Howditch had left. 'He seems fairly straightforward. Is it worth speaking to Susie Albright?'

'I think it might be. She lives in that back office, which apparently is next to Mr Scoular's. There's always a faint chance that she might have seen or heard something without realising the significance.'

Jackie picked up the phone and rang the High Weald branch. Stevie Winterden answered. 'James Howditch should be back shortly. Could you ask Susie Albright to come to the station, please?'

Stevie made disapproving noises but agreed. 'OK, I'll send her round immediately. Hopefully that will be the end of your interviews and we can get on with the business of serving our customers without any further disturbance.'

She sounded quite annoyed.

7

Day 1.
Tuesday 19th February.
Woodchester Police Station. Interview Room 1.

Trussell and Joynton stayed in the interview room to await Susie Albright's arrival and it wasn't long before the desk Sergeant was showing her into the room. Jackie Joynton gave her a welcoming smile and indicated one of the two chairs on the other side of the table. 'Please sit down,' she said.

'Ah, Miss Albright, thank you for coming here and sparing us some of your time,' said Trussell. 'We're just trying to see whether any of the staff can throw any light on Mr Scoular's disappearance. I think that I'm correct in saying that you work in the office next to Mr Scoular?'

She moistened her lips and clasped and unclasped her hands, looking around the interview room uncomfortably before she spoke.

Trussell sensed her nervousness and tried to put her at her ease. After all, she didn't seem that much older than his daughter, Liz. 'Would you like some water?' he asked, picking up a glass and reaching for the jug on the table.

She shook her head. 'No thank you. I'm not really sure how I can help you, Detective Inspector,' she began. 'I've only been there for about four months and I really don't get involved in much of the day-to-day work there. I look after the paperwork, although I don't profess to understand a lot of what comes to me for filing at the moment. But I do answer the phone sometimes if Mr Scoular can't pick it up immediately.'

Jackie gave Trussell a knowing look, and carried on making notes.

'I'm less concerned about the day-to-day stuff, Miss Albright,' said Trussell. 'I'm more interested in anything unusual you may have seen from your office at any time. What about visitors? Did Mr Scoular see many people in his office?'

'Very occasionally,' she answered. 'I tend to get in early. Although we don't officially open until nine in the morning, Mr Scoular is always first there. Around eight-thirty, I believe. I'm usually next around five minutes later. I get a lift into town from my fiancé, you know. The others always tend to arrive just before nine. I do remember Mr Scoular having a visitor already there when I arrived on one particular morning. Must have been around three weeks ago, I guess.'

'Can you describe that visitor?'

She thought for a moment.

'Well, Detective Inspector, it was about three or four weeks ago and it's not my place to take too much notice of these things.' She gazed absentmindedly at the far wall as she tried to recall that day. Trussell knew that it was a long shot, but worth asking.

'Was it a man or a woman?' asked Jackie, trying to help her.

'Definitely a man,' she said. 'He looked about fiftyish, I suppose. Shaven head. Don't they call that a number one? He was casually dressed. It's coming back to me now. I thought Mr Scoular looked a bit uncomfortable when he saw me walk past his office, as if I wasn't supposed to know about the visitor.'

'Did you see him leave?'

'That's the strange part. I went out to the front of the office to put some files on James' desk, and when I came back, the visitor had gone. I can only think that Mr Scoular must have let him out of the rear door on the other side of the staff area. That door is kept locked and isn't normally used. In fact, I don't think I've ever seen it open since I joined the Society. But Mr Scoular must have a key to it.'

'That's interesting, Miss Albright. Did you mention this little event to anyone else? To Mr Howditch, perhaps?'

'No, no one. I didn't think that it was my place to discuss anything involving the manager.'

'Did Mr Scoular say anything to you afterwards?'

'Not a word. Looking back, he seemed a bit…' she thought for a moment, choosing her words carefully, 'embarrassed, sheepish. Like a guilty conscience. As if he had been caught doing something he shouldn't have done.'

Jackie looked at her.

'You mentioned answering the phone on occasions. Were there any calls for Mr Scoular that you can remember? Anything unusual?'

'There were a couple from a man. He didn't leave his name. His voice was different.'

'Did he have a foreign accent?'

'No, it was a sort of, like an East Kent accent. It's hard to describe unless you hear it.'

She thought for a moment. 'Sounds a bit like Stevie when she's stressed.'

'Would you know that visitor again if you saw him?'

'I'm not sure. It was a brief look and it was three or four weeks ago.'

'One last question. Can you just describe the office layout behind the door at the back?'

She thought for a moment.

'When you go through the door, Barney's office is the first on the left, then the office I use is immediately behind it.' She thought for a moment and then continued. 'Opposite is what we call the staff room. That's where we make teas and coffees, or eat our lunches if we don't want to go out. There's also a staff toilet in there.'

'What about the locked rear entrance that you mentioned?'

'There's a door that leads through a short corridor to that outside door. Inside, on the right is the room used for our archives, where we keep all of our filing. I spend a certain amount of time in there as part of my job. Either filing or collecting files if they're needed.'

Trussell was trying to picture the layout as she spoke. 'What about on the left, opposite the archives?'

'There's a room of some sort there,' she continued. 'Perhaps it's some sort of storage room. I've never seen inside it. The door seems to be permanently locked, so I've no idea what it might be used for. Perhaps one of the others might know. After all, I haven't been there very long.'

'Thank you, Miss Albright. We appreciate your assistance. It's been quite useful. Every little detail helps us to build up a picture. If you think of anything later, perhaps you would give me a call,' said Trussell, handing her one of his cards.

Realising that the interview was over, a very relieved Susie Albright stood up and stepped towards the door. Jackie opened it for her and showed her the way to the main door.

When Jackie returned to the room, she looked thoughtful. 'We've heard a lot today, Jim. Is it worth getting Stevie in here to hear what she has to say?'

'I think we'll let her stew for a while. We may learn more in a day or so if she thinks that we've left her out of things. I believe that she likes to be the centre of attention. She's obviously ambitious. But the one thing nagging at me is the Brandford connection.'

'What would you like me to do first?'

'We'll have to check on her name change. It has to be posted in the London Gazette. See if you can find the entry, then that'll give her original name. I suppose that you could also try the DVLA, the Passport Office and HMRC. Someone must have some details of her previous identity.'

'Shall I start looking now, Jim? I assume that you want to keep that one away from Eddie if it involves Brandford.'

'Yes, please. Let him see as little as possible. This enquiry is complex enough already without chucking in the Brandford factor. Frankly, Jackie, it bothers me that we're being forced to work on two levels here. Watkins expects me to make the most of Eddie's experience, and goodness knows, we could certainly use it.'

'We'll just have to manage the situation the best we can, Jim.'

I know, but, I'm still nervous about letting him hear everything. It's the Brandford connection again. I don't know who he might still be in touch with over there. If any of his former contacts are involved in mortgage fraud, then I wouldn't want our progress to be shared with anyone in Brandford.'

8

Day 2.
Wednesday 20th February.
Woodchester. Bank Street.

'Now's as good a time as any to visit the management at High Weald,' said Trussell. I'm interested in those apparent mortgage problems. I want to know whether it might be connected with Scoular's disappearance. Grab your coat, Jackie. We'll wander round there right now.'

They left the police station forecourt and turned right down the High Street. Fifty yards further on, they joined a handful of shoppers waiting at the pelican crossing for the lights to change. Crossing over and turning right, they continued for another fifty yards, and then turned left into Bank Street. The four-storey High Weald head office, with its distinctive blue exterior and logo, was a short way down on the opposite side.

The automatic doors glided open as they approached, and they walked into the lobby. It was brightly decorated with some contemporary seating in the Society blue. A small table containing Society literature and a few magazines stood in a corner. Trussell walked to the reception counter.

'Can I help you?' asked the receptionist, who was wearing the same society uniform that they had seen at the branch.

'Please. I'd like to see your Deputy Chairman, Mr McDriscoll. My name is Trussell.'

'Do you have an appointment? He doesn't normally see casual visitors.'

Trussell offered his warrant card. 'I believe he'll see us.'

The girl picked up the phone and tapped in an extension number, spoke quietly and then replaced the phone. 'Mr McDriscoll's assistant is on her way down, if you wouldn't mind waiting.'

Trussell nodded.

Two minutes later, the nearby lift doors opened and a blonde woman, average height, in her thirties, smartly dressed in a medium grey business suit, walked over to them. 'Good afternoon, Detective Inspector. I'm Mary Waterhouse, Mr McDriscoll's Personal Assistant. He's in a meeting with the CEO at the moment, but he'll be available shortly.'

'That's fine.' said Trussell, as he offered her one of his business cards. 'I've no doubt that your CEO will want to be involved in our conversation.'

She led the way to the lifts and pressed the call button. The doors opened almost immediately and she stood aside to allow them to get in first. The lift took them up to the fourth floor and they followed her into the executive reception area. She indicated a couple of comfortable chairs. 'Please take a seat and I'll tell him you're here.'

She disappeared around the corner, to return two minutes later, accompanied by the man Trussell had seen at the Building Society branch speaking to Stephanie Winterden.

'Good afternoon, Detective Inspector. I'm Philip McDriscoll. How can I help you?'

'Can we talk somewhere less public, Sir?'

'Yes, of course,' he said, indicating an office behind him.

Trussell and Joynton went in, followed by McDriscoll and he closed the door behind them. He stepped behind the large antique desk and looked at them expectantly, indicating the two chairs opposite his desk. 'Please sit down. Perhaps you can tell me why you're here.'

'Yesterday morning, Maureen Scoular visited Woodchester Police Station to report her husband as missing, and then, while we were at the Building Society, making enquiries, you arrived, which ended our discussion with Miss Winterden. I understand that there may be some issues with mortgages, and I'm now wondering whether this is connected with Mr Scoular's disappearance.'

'It's possible.'

'Do you want to share the information with us?'

'I'm afraid that it could be considered commercially sensitive.'

'So is Mr Scoular's disappearance. If a crime is suspected, then we need to know.'

'Wait just a moment, Detective Inspector. I think that our CEO should be part of this discussion. I'll ask him to join us.'

He rose from behind the desk and left the room.

Trussell looked at Jackie and raised an eyebrow. 'There's more going on than he wants to tell us. We'll see what his colleague has to say.'

Two minutes later, McDriscoll returned, carrying some files, accompanied by a slim, balding man of average height, wearing dark-rimmed glasses. He was dressed very conservatively in a dark grey suit and navy blue tie. He looked rather studious and Trussell immediately thought, *Accountant.*

'This is our CEO, Douglas Hartman,' said McDriscoll.

'Perhaps you would care to enlighten us about your problems, Mr Hartman,' said Trussell. 'If a crime has been committed, then we'll need to know now.'

'It's a rather delicate matter,' began Hartman. 'If the information gets out now, it could have a very serious effect on this Society and its future. I must ask for your discretion.'

'What exactly is the problem?'

'Well,' he began, 'it has come to our attention that some mortgages were granted a while ago on properties in Brandford, through the Woodchester branch, possibly by Mr Scoular, it seems. The borrowers seem to have defaulted on the loans almost immediately. We've carried out a preliminary examination of the details of the properties on which they were granted. It now seems that they have been dramatically overvalued for mortgage purposes. As the borrower has defaulted, the only remedy open to the Society is to seek repossession. Unfortunately, the costs of this and then disposing of them on the market at their current values will leave the Society seriously out of pocket.'

'By how much?' asked Trussell.

'We are trying to quantify the losses at the moment, but our best guess is that it could be at least six figures, maybe seven.'

Trussell whistled in astonishment.

'There is a further complication which makes matters even worse. It looks as though the buyers who took out the mortgages do not exist. The names have turned out to be fictitious. This will make it very difficult to repossess and sell the properties to recover at least some of our money.'

Trussell looked at Joynton, who had been taking notes. Her face reflected his amazement.

'You can see why I described this as commercially sensitive,' said McDriscoll. 'If this gets out into the public domain before we're prepared, then it could have very serious implications for our Society and its future. We are not a large Society in our marketplace, and we're always at risk of some sort of hostile takeover from one of the major societies. As a mutual, our members have the sole voting rights over the Society's affairs, and I'm sure that they would sooner be swallowed by a major competitor than go out of business.

'Who else knows, outside of this room?' asked Trussell.

'The people in the branch are aware there's a problem, but, as far as they know, the details are not available yet,' continued Hartman. 'There is no need for anyone who hasn't been directly involved to know any more at the moment. Obviously, we're in your hands, Detective Inspector. We must depend on your discretion at this stage. I should also tell you that we don't believe that this particular deal is the only problem. We have reason to believe that there are similar cases out there.'

'How did this slip through the net? Properties have to be valued for mortgage purposes and then there must be a legal paper trail,' said Trussell. 'I won't profess to understand your business, Mr Hartman. My own experience is limited to buying my own house fifteen years ago. I still remember all the legal enquiries, the paperwork. The whole process seemed very tightly controlled and rather convoluted even then.'

'You're absolutely right. The system can only be bypassed with the connivance of professionals, usually a surveyor and solicitor. There's been criminal activity somewhere in the chain.'

'Please explain.'

'The way it works is this; buyers seek out distressed sellers and then beat the price down even further, by whatever means it takes. Then they find a surveyor to overvalue the properties. When the sales are finalised, they pay the sellers as little as they can get away with and then pocket the difference from the mortgage monies advanced to them.'

Jackie Joynton had been taking notes as usual. 'What about estate agents?' she asked. 'Someone must have been aware of what was happening?'

'We'd have to assume that they were party to the deal, or at least knew what was going on.'

'Where did the money go on completion of the sales?' asked Trussell.

'We do know that it went to a local branch of a major bank, which, of course, has international connections. We now think that it would probably have been sent electronically along a pre-arranged chain to some offshore account where it can't be traced. The money would sit there until it can be laundered and then returned by another route to this country where the perpetrators can spend it legitimately. The accomplices, the surveyor and solicitor, would have had to be paid, of course. Any estate agent involved would have been paid by the sellers of the properties, so their fees wouldn't have been part of the money that the fraudsters had taken.'

'So, that's where we start,' said Trussell. 'If you can give us the details of the transactions, we'll look into it. We mustn't lose sight of the fact that this whole thing started with Mr Scoular's disappearance.'

'The first thing I can tell you,' said Hartman, 'is that we believe the business was referred to Woodchester by our branch in Brandford. That is the area where the properties are located. Our office there is very small - just three members of staff. The sheer size of the transactions is beyond their local remit.'

Trussell groaned inwardly. Would he never be free of anything associated with Brandford? It seemed that whatever the crime, wherever it occurred, the trail inevitably led back to Brandford. The place continued to haunt him, despite his relatively short stay there at the beginning of his career.

McDriscoll continued. 'There's been a fair amount of redevelopment down there with two new estates being completed in the last couple of years. It has meant a lot of new mortgage business for us. Our local staff can handle most of that without any difficulty. But the problem we're talking about is something completely different.'

'Can you explain, please?'

'Yes, of course. Aside from the new estates I've mentioned, which were built on green field sites, the problems concern possible major redevelopment of older properties. It would mean whole streets of sometimes derelict properties being levelled to provide space for new houses. This is where the overvaluation has occurred. Someone was gambling on the appropriate planning permission being given. Then there were cases of landlords wanting to dispose of their portfolios of buy-to-let properties, but we haven't got to those yet.'

'And someone at High Weald has accepted these valuations and advanced the money on that basis?'

'Yes. Everything points to Scoular,' said McDriscoll. 'Could be the reason he's disappeared. What do you think, Detective Inspector?'

'We're keeping an open mind, Sir. We're just treating him as a missing person for the moment.'

'And now we're stuck with overvalued properties, while the borrowers and the money have disappeared,' said Hartman. The concern showed plainly on his face. 'We could be facing the end of the Society, with its long history of supporting the local community.'

'Who was the surveyor responsible for these valuations?'

McDriscoll consulted the file on the desk, open in front of him.

'His name is Edmund Royston. He's done a lot of work for the Society over the years, mostly straightforward individual valuations. I'm surprised that he got involved with something of this size. I think he's a one-man band. I would've thought that this sort of project was a bit out of his league.'

'So, who appointed him?' asked Joynton.

'That's what we've been trying to establish. It certainly looks like Mr Scoular. Could this be the reason why he's disappeared? Once the money had gone, he knew that it would only be a matter of time before there was some sort of enquiry. According to one member of the staff, he was aware of some unspecified problem, and was trying to rectify it before we found out. It obviously didn't work.'

'That wouldn't have been Miss Winterden?'

'Yes. She mentioned it the other day when we visited the branch.'

'Are you proposing to install another manager, even on a temporary basis?' asked Trussell.

'Yes, of course. Miss Winterden seems quite capable, but we are sending someone properly qualified to run it until Mr Scoular reappears, or his situation is resolved.'

'It would be quite useful, Mr Hartman, if you could supply us with details of these transactions,' said Trussell.

'I've asked Miss Winterden to make a search of the archives in their offices to see whether anything has been filed away, accidentally or deliberately. In fact, she suggested that we should look there first.'

Trussell looked thoughtful, but said nothing.

'What about the purchasers of these properties?' asked Jackie Joynton. 'Surely they would have to have been identified for the sales to go through? Wouldn't the Land Registry be involved?'

'They turned out to be fictitious, as I've already told you,' said McDriscoll. 'That could only be accomplished with the involvement of a solicitor.'

'Right,' said Trussell. Let's start with the surveyor. We'd like his details. Is he self-employed, in a partnership or a limited company? Do you have his address?'

'It appears that Royston is self-employed. No office as far as we can see. I think that he must just use his home address. I'll find it for you right now.'

'By the way, before we continue, Mr McDriscoll, I understand you're the Society Deputy Chairman, and Mr Hartman the CEO? Shouldn't the Chairman be involved in this as well?'

'The Chairman, Geoffrey Donnington, is purely a figurehead. It's a non-executive position and he takes no part in the day-to-day running of the Society. He just chairs any executive meetings. Frankly,' said McDriscoll, 'we'd rather keep him out of this at the moment. He's not known for his discretion. He tends to say too much on occasion. If he finds out, then it may well hinder your enquiries as well as do harm to the Society.' While speaking, McDriscoll had been looking through one of the files in front of him. 'Here it is. Royston lives at Number 3, Cloth Yard, Woollenden.'

'I know where that is, Jim,' said Jackie, noting it down.

'OK. Now, what about the solicitors? Do you have any names?'

'Not yet, but we're trying to find them. The relevant papers seem to have disappeared.'

'I take it that Mr Scoular didn't have any records in his office?'

'It doesn't seem so. He must have taken them with him. They've certainly gone.'

'So, as I understand it, you're just working from the small amount of information sent to Head Office?'

'Correct. The paper trail's a bit limited at the moment. We're trying to get the details from the Land Registry, but I don't think that'll help us, as the identities of the new buyers will be bogus anyway.'

'So, that complicates things for you, Mr McDriscoll, if I understand the situation correctly,' said Trussell. 'You'll be trying to repossess properties owned by fictitious people, who appear to have defaulted on their mortgages.'

'That's right. You can see the problem that we're facing now. That's why it's so important to keep this quiet for the moment.'

'As we're trying to find Mr Scoular, then it would seem logical for us to talk to Mr Royston,' said Trussell. 'We don't need to mention mortgage problems to him at this stage. If he could confirm who appointed him, then that'll be a good place to start.'

McDriscoll nodded.

Trussell stood up to leave. Joynton followed his lead, putting her notebook and pen back in her bag,

'Thank you for your time, gentlemen,' he said, opening the door. 'I'll be in touch again shortly. Please contact me immediately if there are any further developments.'

Mary Waterhouse, McDriscoll's personal assistant, stepped from behind her desk, showed them to the lift and pressed the button for them.

'Thank you, Miss Waterhouse,' said Trussell. We can find our own way out.'

'No longer a simple missing person case, then, Jim,' said Jackie as they left the building.

'Next stop Woollenden,' said Trussell. 'We'll visit Cloth Yard, see if Mr Royston is home and ask him about his valuations.'

9

Day 2.
Wednesday 20th February.
Woollenden.

They walked back to the station, and ten minutes later, they were in Trussell's dark blue Skoda, heading through the rain to Royston's address. The large village of Woollenden was on the eastern side of Woodchester, in the direction of Brandford.

'Here's a history lesson for you, Jackie,' said Trussell as they drove along the B road leading to the village. 'This area was well known in Medieval and Tudor times for the wool trade – all those Romney Marsh sheep. Then the weavers arrived from the continent and started producing broadcloth. It was a very popular and expensive product in those days. The weavers used to export quite a lot of it. That's where a lot of the early wealth came from in the area.'

Trussell had been born in Dover and had spent all his life in the county. History had been one of his favourite subjects at the local grammar school and he had kept up a lively interest in the subject ever since. In contrast, Jackie, a Londoner, wasn't too aware of the County's past. She had transferred to Kent Police from the Metropolitan Police after some personal issues and had now made a new life for herself in Woodchester. She had met her partner, Mike, on an advanced driving course and was now happily settled in a new flat within walking distance of the station.

They arrived on the outskirts of the village ten minutes later, passing the white wooden gate sign bearing its name and confirming the 30-mph speed limit. The road widened and divided as they saw the triangular village green in front of them. On the left was the village church of St Cedric, a grey, stone building with a square tower betraying its Norman origins. On the right of the green stood the village pub, The Fleece, a half-timbered building, probably dating back to Tudor times. The Green was surrounded by houses of different sizes and ages, underlining the history of the village.

Jackie looked around and then pointed to a turning on the right near the pub.

'Over there, Jim.'

Trussell followed her directions and they found themselves in a side street of very small, old half-timbered terraced houses. *Probably weavers' cottages,* he thought, *judging by the larger leaded light windows*. They found Number 3 without any difficulty. It had a rundown look about it. The black paint on the wooden window frames was peeling, the leaded windows were in serious need of urgent attention and the metal studded varnished oak front door also showed signs of neglect.

They pushed the rickety wooden gate open and walked up the very short front path. The small front garden was overgrown. There was a doorbell, but pressing it gave no clue as to whether it was actually working. Trussell waited a few seconds and then rang it again. No response, so he rapped loudly on the door with his knuckles, but still no answer. He looked at Jackie and shrugged his shoulders.

'Can I help you?' said a voice.

They turned to see an elderly woman standing behind them, an old grey coat wrapped tightly around her against the chilly drizzle. She regarded them with suspicion.

'I live next door,' she said. 'He's not at home. What do you want?'

'Do you have any idea where he is?'

'He's probably at work. One can never tell. He seems to keep very strange hours.'

'I'm sorry. I don't believe I caught your name,' said Trussell.

'I'm Maggie Dodds. Mrs. Who are you, then? Asking all these questions. Why should I tell you anything?'

'Police,' said Trussell, producing his warrant card. 'Just answer the questions, please.'

'I'm not surprised the police are calling,' she said.

He gave her a quizzical look and then continued. 'Is he married? Does anyone else live here with him? Does he have any regular visitors?'

'No, no and sometimes,' she answered crossly.

'What can you tell me about his visitors?' Trussell persisted.

'I don't know any of them because I never see them. I just hear cars and voices late at night. It's nothing to do with me. I'm not looking for trouble.'

'In that case, I'll give you two of my cards,' said Trussell. 'Please would you pass one to Mr Royston and ask him to ring me? The number's on the card. The other one is for you, in case you can think of anything that might help us.'

She accepted the cards with bad grace and just nodded. She turned her back on them and stumped off to her own house.

'There's nothing else for us here, Jackie. We may as well head back to the station.'

They returned to the Skoda and Trussell turned the car in the direction of Woodchester.

'Miserable woman, wasn't she, Jim?' said Jackie. 'I might just look her up to see if she's known. She seems to have a real attitude problem.'

'Don't bother. I think that she's a bit suspicious of Mr Royston and doesn't want to be involved. We'll just have to keep digging and hope that he does phone us. Frankly, I'm not holding my breath. If he's involved in anything dodgy, then he'll probably disappear too, when he gets the message.'

'It'll be just another missing person to add to the list, in that case.'

'We'll have to see whether McDriscoll comes up with anything new. I think that the solicitor's identity is key to all of this. He or she would be right in the middle. Track them down and we might get closer to tracing the identities of the dodgy purchasers who've taken the money, although there's always a chance that they may have just been prepared to front the deal for a pay-off. They may not even know who was actually behind the scam.'

'We can only wait for McDriscoll to contact us at this point,' said Jackie. 'By the way, Jim, I've tracked down someone at the Woodchester Dramatic Society. Actually, they're known as the Woodchester Repertory Company and the man I spoke to is Charles Preston. I contacted him and asked if we could pop round for a chat as soon as possible. I didn't give any reason. I just reassured him that neither he nor his society, were in trouble. He's the Secretary and, being retired, is available any time. I could call him now if you like. He lives in town in that rather smart apartment block, Barham House.'

'Yes, good idea. Let's see what he can tell us about his friend, Maureen.'

She picked up her phone, consulted the directory where she had already stored the number Preston had given her, and hit the call button.

It was answered after three rings.

Ah, Mr Preston,' she began, 'it's Detective Sergeant Joynton. You'll recall we spoke earlier.'

'How can I help you?'

I'd like to call round to see you, if it's convenient. Say, fifteen minutes' time? I'll be accompanied by Detective Inspector Trussell. We think you may be able to help us.'

'That's perfectly alright.'

10
Day 2.
Wednesday 20th February.
Barham House, Woodchester.

Twenty minutes later, they arrived back on the outskirts of Woodchester. They found the relatively new brick-built, four-storey apartment block quite easily and took one of the spaces reserved for visitors in the small private car park.

'I remember these flats being built about five years ago, Jackie,' said Trussell. 'They were quite expensive for the town then, so goodness knows what they're worth now.'

They approached the locked entrance door and Jackie tapped in the flat number on the security doorbell keypad and pressed the call button. A moment later, a disembodied voice answered from the speaker.

'Can I help you?'

'Mr Preston? It's Detective Sergeant Joynton.'

'Yes, of course. Please take the lift up to the third floor. I'll wait for you there.'

A buzzer sounded and an automated metallic voice told them that the door was now open. Trussell pulled the door outwards and they walked into the lobby. The lift was right in front of them.

When the doors opened at the third floor, Charles Preston was waiting for them. *He looks about seventy,* thought Trussell. His appearance was unmistakably theatrical. He was of average height, slightly overweight, with an unruly mass of white hair, curling over his collar at the back. He was immaculately dressed in a brightly striped blazer with a pale yellow shirt complete with a blue paisley patterned cravat. A pair of sharply creased chinos and a pair of suede shoes completed his outfit. He looked at Jackie.

She showed her warrant card and introduced DI Trussell.

'I can't imagine what you want of me,' he began,' but you'd better come into my apartment. It'll be more private.'

He led the way through the open door and via a small lobby into a bright, comfortably furnished living room which was dominated by a very large and expensive green velvet three-piece suite. The rest of the furniture carefully placed around the room, screamed quality. Theatrical memorabilia, signed photographs of long-forgotten actors, posters and statuettes were everywhere, suggesting a long career in the entertainment industry.

'Thank you for sparing us the time, Mr Preston,' said Jackie.' There is nothing for you to be alarmed about. We were just hoping that you might be able to help us with some information.'

'Oh dear, is it about those boys who caused a fuss last week and threw stones at the cars?'

'No, it's nothing like that. DI Trussell will be able to enlighten you,' said Jackie, reaching into her bag for her notebook and pen.

'Mr Preston, we would like to talk about the Woodchester Rep,' began Trussell. 'We should appreciate it if our conversation stays between the three of us for the moment.'

'How can I help?'

'We would like some information about one of your members,' said Jackie. 'Mrs Maureen Scoular, to be precise. I think that you may still know her as Atherton.'

'What has Mo been up to now?' asked Preston, rather breezily, an amused smile playing around the corners of his mouth.

'You make my question suggest yet another problem. Does she have any sort of history with the Rep?' asked Jackie.

'Nothing illegal,' said Preston rather hastily. The look on his face suggested some sort of inner conflict. How much should he tell them?

'Mo, that's what she prefers to be called, is a fine actress. She usually takes the star part in our productions. But she can be very demanding of her fellow actors. She's a bit of a prima donna. She always looks for perfection in her roles and expects it of the rest of the cast. If anyone fluffs their lines, she seems to take it as a personal slight. She treats them as if they're doing it deliberately just to embarrass her. She can be a bit domineering.'

'What do you think causes this, Mr Preston?' asked Jackie Joynton.

'Who can be sure? It's been suggested that her early life has left her with a bit of a chip on her shoulder. She was abandoned as a baby and brought up in a children's home, you know.'

'Yes, we are aware of that, Sir,' said Trussell. 'How long has she been a member of the Rep?'

'Ever since she moved to Woodchester. It must be about twelve years, I think. She was obviously looking to be around people after her difficult start in life.'

'She's been married for less than two years. What do you know about that? How does she get on with her husband?'

'Yes, that's a strange one,' said Preston. 'She never seemed like a newlywed from the outset. Knowing her pretty well, it seemed to me that this was just another step along the road to help her forget about her childhood.' He suddenly went red in the face and shifted in his chair. 'I've probably said more that I should have done,' he added, looking embarrassed.

'Is she prone to mood swings, angry outbursts, or anything like that?'

'She can certainly look after herself. Having met her husband once or twice, I'd think that she must be the dominant one in the marriage.'

'Interesting,' said Trussell. 'We appreciate your help and candour. By the way, did you know that Mr Scoular is missing?'

Preston looked genuinely taken aback.

'No, I hadn't heard that. What's happened?'

'That's what we are trying to discover, Sir. It appears that he went out to dinner with a person or persons unknown, and hasn't been seen since.'

'How has Mo taken it?'

'She appeared to react badly. She was in a near hysterical state when she came to the police station to report it.'

'Doesn't sound like Mo,' said Preston. 'She's usually very unemotional. In fact, she can be quite cold and self-possessed sometimes.'

Trussell and Joynton exchanged knowing looks. This case got stranger by the minute. No one was actually what they seemed to be…

'What about friends within your company?' asked Trussell. 'Is she particularly close to anyone?'

'Well, there's Alex Peterson,' said Preston. 'He normally takes the male lead in most of our productions. They've known one another for several years, ever since Alex joined the Rep. There were stories about them being somewhat close.' He chose his words carefully. 'Of course, it's not for me to comment on members' private lives outside of the group,' he added, hastily.

'Where can we contact him, if necessary?' asked Joynton.

'I'll have to look his address up and let you have it.'

Trussell nodded at Joynton to indicate that they had asked enough questions for today.

She replaced her notebook and pen in her bag and she and Trussell stood up.

'Thank you for your assistance, Sir,' said Trussell. 'We should appreciate it if this conversation remains between the three of us for the moment. If you would be good enough to find an address and telephone number for Mr Peterson and then contact DS Joynton or myself as soon as possible, that would be very helpful.'

Preston nodded and led the way to the front door to let them out.

They made their way to the lift and pressed the call button. Two minutes later, they left the building and headed for Trussell's Skoda.

'Seems like the main actors in this little drama are a mystery in themselves, Jackie,' said Trussell. 'More info for the mind map.'

'If I don't hear from Mr Preston about Alex Peterson's details by tomorrow, then I'll be on his case, Jim. It'll be interesting to see how Peterson fits into the picture. Is the Scoulars' marriage just one of convenience? There's another little triangle to add to your diagram. It's beginning to look like a geometry lesson now!'

Trussell smiled wryly at her comment. Preston's contribution had certainly added a further layer of mystery to Maureen Scoular's personality.

11

Day 3.
Thursday 21st February.
Woodchester Police Station. The CID Office.

Mark Green was alone in the office, sitting at his keyboard, updating information for the file. He had already got the details of Stephanie Winterden's car, a silver Range Rover, and had passed them on to Fast Eddie to check the CCTV at the Weaver Street car park.

Eddie Sprawson was doing the rounds of the town's restaurants and eating places to see if anyone had noticed Barnaby Scoular on Monday evening and he had also arranged to visit Weaver Street car park to ask about CCTV footage as a part of his enquiries.

Trussell and Joynton had taken the opportunity to visit Supercheap to have a quick look for themselves and speak to the management about the pilfering problems.

The phone rang on Trussell's desk. Mark Green reached across and picked it up. 'CID Office. DC Green speaking.'

A man asked to speak to DI Trussell. He sounded agitated.

'I'm sorry, but he's out of the office at the moment. Can I take a message for him? Who's calling?'

'My name is Royston. Edmund Royston. Detective Inspector Trussell called at my house in Woollenden yesterday evening and left his business card with my neighbour. He asked me to phone him.' The voice was definitely shaky.

'Are you alright, sir?' asked Green.

'Er… no, er… not really. Something's going on. I can't continue. I need to speak to him as soon as possible. I can't leave it any longer. Things have gone too far. I'm scared that something's going to happen. I knew that it would get out of control. I wish I'd never got involved. Please tell Detective Inspector Trussell that I need to talk to him about it as soon as possible. I'll give you my number.' The words just tumbled out.

Mark Green was carefully noting the conversation down as Royston spoke. 'OK, Sir. I'll see that he gets your message as soon as he returns. Where are you at the moment? I know that he was anxious to see you.'

'Just ask him to call me on the number I've just given you. Make it as soon as possible. Please. It's urgent. Sorry. I must go.' He sounded desperate. With that, he hung up.

Mark Green very carefully wrote down the conversation as he recalled it, and then tried to call Trussell on his mobile. It clicked in to his voice mail. Green left him a message, mentioning the urgency. He stressed the need for him to contact Royston as soon as possible. He'd done all that he could. He just hoped that Trussell picked it up and was able to contact Royston. The man had certainly sounded pretty desperate. He returned to his keyboard and stared at the screen, trying to concentrate on the job in hand. The last call had worried him. He felt powerless. The man was in a bit of a state.

Whilst thinking about this last conversation, he was disturbed by Trussell's phone ringing again. He reached across to the DI's desk and picked up the phone. A man's voice asked for Detective Inspector Trussell. 'I'm sorry but he's not here at the moment, Sir. This is DC Green speaking. May I leave him a message?'

He listened and made a quick note.

'Yes Sir, I have your name. Charles Preston. Yes, I've made a note of Mr Peterson's address and phone number. I'll see that the DI gets the message as soon as he returns. Yes, Sir, I will share the information with Detective Sergeant Joynton. I'll tell her you phoned. You may be sure of that. Thank you for your call.'

He put down the phone, puzzled. The DI hadn't mentioned anyone called Preston or Peterson. Where did they fit in to this jigsaw?'

12

Day 3.
Thursday 21st February. Later that morning.
Woodchester.

Trussell looked at the address and telephone number on the note handed to him by Mark Green when he arrived back in the office. Charles Preston had provided Alex Peterson's details to him, as promised. Now Trussell had to make a decision about the next step. Whether he should contact Peterson or do a little digging first. He thought he'd discuss it with Jackie as she'd spoken to Preston as well. *Wonder what she gleaned from their conversation, if anything?* He'd been a little cagey when he'd mentioned Peterson.

Trussell had another flash of intuition. He kept thinking about the number of people who'd commented on the Scoulars' marriage. Was it a marriage of convenience in some way? Was Peterson involved with Maureen Scoular? Did this mean more than just a friendship? Barnaby Scoular had had relationships with two women who were both far taller than him, and then he had married one of them. His brother had mentioned that Barnaby Scoular had been very close to his mother when they were both growing up. His mind wandered for a moment and the thought of an Oedipus complex popped into his head. Or was he reading too much into things? Yet he couldn't dismiss the thought so easily. There were a lot of factors in play here.

'Greeno, run Peterson through the PNC, will you?' he said, handing him back the details. 'See if anything's known. I'd also like to find out more about him. Does he have a car? If so, what make, model and colour? We'll need the registration details as well, of course. Contact the DVLA if necessary to get the information.'

Mark Green was slowly getting used to Trussell's apparently off the wall requests. There always turned out to be a logical reason behind them. But, why was he interested in whether this mysterious Mr Peterson had a car? What was important about the colour, if he did? Something was going on in Trussell's mind. He hadn't even met the man yet and knew nothing about him.

'When you've got those details, Greeno, get a generic picture of that type of car. The right colour, of course. The internet should help. Then I want you to take a trip to Frattenden. There's a new estate out there called The Hollows. Do you know it?'

'No. but I'll find it. What am I looking for, Guv?'

Find a road called The Avenue, and then knock on a few doors in the street in the vicinity of Number 29, but don't mention that house to anyone you speak to. Ask the residents if any of them have seen that car around the area at any time. I'm particularly interested in the evening of three nights ago - Monday 19th February.'

'The night Barnaby Scoular disappeared?'

'Correct. I want to know whether his wife really was suffering with a headache as she claimed when she left work early. She knew that her husband was going out to dinner so wouldn't be home for several hours. That might have offered an opportunity to Mr Peterson to call. Worst case it would have offered an alibi if anything has happened to Mr Scoular.'

'Do you consider her a suspect, then, Guv?'

'No one's above suspicion at the moment, Greeno. I'm interested in what Mr Preston told us about Mrs Scoular's longstanding friendship with Mr Peterson. I want to know whether there was any more to it beyond a common interest in acting with the Woodchester Rep. We can't overlook what Jackie noticed when Mrs. Scoular came to the station to report her husband missing.'

'Faking the tears, you mean?'

'Yes. It was a convincing performance. I would have believed it if Jackie hadn't spotted the box that fell out of her bag. She certainly looked like a woman seriously concerned about her husband's disappearance.'

'Right, Guv,' he said, turning to his keyboard. 'I'll get right on it now.'

Trussell unlocked his desk drawer and took out the A4 pad, adding Peterson's details to the mind map. He connected his name with Maureen Scoular and sat back, deep in thought. Would a relationship between them lead to designs on Barnaby Scoular? Trussell had had a niggling feeling for a while now that something might have happened to him. He didn't seem to have any obvious outside interests or pursuits that would require any sort of major embezzlement or need to be part of a scheme to defraud the High Weald. *Could it be blackmail?* Trussell wondered.

Greeno pulled the keyboard towards him, logged onto the PNC and started searching. He soon found Alex Peterson's details, and armed with this, connected to the DVLA. It only took a moment for details of Peterson's car to appear on the screen. He carefully noted them down and logged off the site. *What a piece of luck* he thought. The man would just have to own a yellow Caterham. At least that would make it easier when he started knocking on doors at the Hollows. It was a fairly distinctive sports car and a brightly coloured one as well.

He looked on the internet for one or two suitable pictures and then printed them off.

'Any luck, Greeno?'

'Yes, Guv. Real luck at last! The guy drives a bright yellow Caterham sports car. People would be bound to notice that if it was left in the street. Shall I get over there right away and start knocking on doors?'

'Yes please. Give me a call if you turn up anything and then add any witness information to the file when you get back.'

'You seem fairly certain that I will, Guv.'

'Right, Greeno. The more we learn about the Scoulars, things seem to point towards a marriage of convenience. The question remains, though. What was in it for Barnaby Scoular? We can guess at Mrs Scoular's motives. She wanted the security of a marriage after her unfortunate start in life, but she seems to want the continuing benefits of her previous life as well.'

'What will you do, Guv?'

'If you can get some proof that Peterson's car was seen near the Scoulars' house on the night that the husband disappeared, then we'll pull the boyfriend in and ask him about it.'

Mark Green collected his coat and keys and headed for the car park.

13

Day 3.
Thursday 21st February. Late afternoon.
The CID Office. Woodchester Police Station.

Trussell's phone rang. 'Yes, Greeno? What have you found?' He listened for a moment. 'That sounds interesting. Have you got the witness's details? Excellent. Get back here as soon as you can.'

He turned to Jackie Joynton. 'Greeno's found someone who reckons they saw Peterson's car parked around the corner from the Scoulars' house on the night that Barney disappeared. Apparently, it was there for several hours. The witness remembered it because she's seen it there on a number of occasions and wondered who owned it.'

'What's the next step, Jim?'

'I reckon we'll call on Mr Peterson and ask him what he has to say for himself, If he isn't in a talkative mood, then we'll bring him in to question him as a material witness. Perhaps that will encourage him to say something.'

'How long before Greeno gets back?'

'He said twenty minutes. As soon as we've got the details, I think that we should knock on Mr Peterson's door.'

Jackie looked at her watch.

'Mr Preston didn't give us a clue about Peterson's job, did he? I wonder what sort of hours he keeps?'

'Well, if he's not there, then the number Preston gave us is a mobile phone. We should be able to contact him if he's not at home. Obviously, it would be better to surprise him on his own doorstep.'

'How are we going to handle this one, Jim?'

'I'll ask him outright what he was doing at Scoular's house that night. I'll tell him that we're aware of his 'friendship' with Mrs Scoular and see what he has to say for himself. Get him on the back foot straight away.'

'Perhaps he can throw some light on the Scoulars' marriage.'

Trussell unlocked his drawer and pulled out the A4 pad. There were a few more details to add to his mind map.

The sound of footsteps announced Mark Green's arrival back in the office. He looked please with himself. 'I visited half a dozen houses before I struck lucky, Guv,' he said. 'A Mrs Johnson at Number 38 gave me the confirmation about Peterson's car. Her house was around the corner from Number 29. She said that she'd been a bit curious that it seemed to be there parked outside her house from time to time, but she'd never seen the driver arrive or leave.'

'Did you tell her to keep quiet about your visit?'

'Of course. She was intrigued but I told her nothing. I said that I'd be in touch if we needed anything more.'

'Well done, Greeno. Where's Peterson's address?'

Mark Green handed Trussell the details.

'Right, Jackie, grab your coat. We'll go and surprise Mr Peterson.'

They left the office and headed downstairs for Trussell's dark blue Skoda.

'Where are we going then?' asked Jackie, as he reversed out of his parking space.

'Peterson lives at 26 Archer Street in Waverley. It's on the west side of town. I know the area. Quite old. Several streets of old Victorian railway workers' cottages. A lot have been smartened up and it's becoming a bit more fashionable to live there now. Property prices are on the up. Usual story. Convert a few of the old shops to trendy wine bars and coffee shops. Now people want to live there.'

They found themselves in the middle of rush hour traffic as everyone seemed to be headed home at that time so the journey took a little longer than they expected. Jackie was unfamiliar with this particular part of Woodchester, but spotted Archer Street, a turning off the main road. Trussell was correct in his description. Rows of Victorian terrace houses, in the characteristic red brick of the period and with front doors opening directly onto the pavement.

'Typical of the time,' said Trussell. 'Two up two down. I wonder how many of them still have outside toilets out the back?'

Most of the houses seemed to be quite well kept, reinforcing Trussell's comment about the improvement in the area.

He pulled up opposite Number 26 and they both got out. There was no sign of the yellow Caterham outside the house.

'I wonder whether our man is at home?' said Trussell. He looked up and down the street. 'The houses have been smartened up,' he said, 'but there's no sense of privacy. I'll wager that everyone knows everyone else's business here.'

'If there's anything going on with Maureen Scoular,' said Jackie,' I bet Peterson hasn't brought her here.'

There was a large brass knocker on the red wooden door. Trussell banged it loudly twice but there was no response. He glanced in the front window. The curtains were open - the room was unoccupied.

They were aware of a woman standing behind them. 'Can I help you?' she asked.

Trussell showed his warrant card. 'Have you seen Mr Peterson?'

'I live next door. He's not home. He left here late last night in a bit of a hurry, judging by the sound of his engine and the way the tyres squealed.' She pointed to the rubber marks on the road outside the house.

'Does he have many visitors?' asked Jackie Joynton.

'Not really,' said the woman. 'I know that he works from home but he tends to keep himself to himself.'

'I didn't get your name,' said Jackie, 'just in case we need to talk to you again.'

'It's Jackson. Sarah Jackson. I live next door - Number 28.'

'Thank you,' said Trussell. 'We'll let you know if we have any further questions. I'll give you my card and telephone number. Perhaps you'd let us know when Mr Peterson comes home.'

They returned to the Skoda.

'I think that it might be worth contacting Mr Preston again,' said Jackie. 'I wonder whether he said anything to Peterson. He seemed rather too talkative. Bit of an old woman.'

'We'll go there now and have that conversation with him.'

Fifteen minutes later, they pulled into the private car park at Barham House.

Jackie Joynton pressed the doorbell for Preston's apartment. He answered after a short pause. 'Mr Preston, it's Detective Sergeant Joynton. Can we have a quick word with you, please?'

'Certainly,' he said and the automated voice announced that the door was open. They took the lift up to the third floor where Preston was again waiting for them by the open door of his apartment.

He beckoned them inside. 'This is a surprise,' he said. 'Did you not get my message?'

'Oh yes, Sir,' said Trussell. 'Mr Preston, did you tell Mr Peterson that we wanted to contact him?'

'Oh yes,' he said. 'We had our rehearsal last night for our latest production. Alex was there and I did mention it in passing.'

'Well, Sir, said Jackie Joynton. 'As a result of that indiscretion, it appears that Mr Peterson disappeared in something of a hurry late last night, according to our information. We shall have to waste time and resources trying to find him now, thanks to you.' Preston looked embarrassed. 'We asked you to keep our conversation just between the three of us, Mr Preston,' said Joynton.

'Do you realise that you might have laid yourself open now to a charge of obstruction, or possibly assisting an offender? asked Trussell. 'These both carry prison sentences on conviction.'

Preston's jaw dropped and the colour left his face. 'I didn't mean any harm,' he protested. 'It was just in the course of conversation.'

'How did that arise then?'

'Maureen didn't turn up for rehearsals and her understudy had to read her part. Alex said that she must be upset as her husband had disappeared, so it wasn't surprising that she wasn't there. I mentioned that you wanted to speak to him. It just sort of slipped out. It wasn't intentional.'

'Have you any idea where he could have gone?' asked Jackie Joynton. 'What about family or friends?'

'No. He's never talked about his family. Judging by his accent, I think that he must have come from somewhere up north. Yorkshire, maybe?'

'That's a big county,' said Trussell sarcastically. 'If he should contact you in any way, then please get in touch with us immediately. I am reminding you once again not to discuss this matter with anyone else. Especially Mr Peterson. Failure to comply with my instructions this time could lead to fairly serious consequences for you.'

A somewhat chastened Preston nodded in dumb agreement.

'We may as well go back now, Sergeant' said Trussell. 'This has just complicated things.'

They let themselves out of Preston's apartment, leaving a very pale, worried thespian behind them.

'I wonder whether Peterson's contacted Maureen, 'asked Jackie, as they took the lift down to the ground floor. 'I'd be surprised if he hadn't.'

'Tricky,' said Trussell. 'I don't think that's a question we can ask at the moment. We'll just have to keep an eye on the distraught wife and see what develops. In the meantime, we have his mobile number. We could try calling him.'

They climbed into the Skoda for the trip back to the office.

14

Day 4.
Friday 22nd February. Mid-morning.
Wilmhurst Green, Woodchester.

Jean Oatley, late sixties, greying now, slightly built and round-shouldered, trudged slowly along Prescott Drive carrying two bags of shopping, carefully avoiding the puddles. She was wearing a maroon woollen winter coat and a plastic rain hood of a type still popular with her generation. The weather was overcast, but at least the heavy rain had stopped now, although there was still plenty of standing water. She was headed for Number 29, where she had lived for the last thirty years since the estate was built a couple of miles outside Woodchester town centre.

Jean had been a nurse in those early days and lifting patients over the years had eventually taken its toll on her health. Her husband, Cyril, had been a chartered accountant. They had moved into their brand new four-bedroom detached house with their two young daughters and it had seemed a real adventure, a step up. They had seen neighbours come and go over the years, but she thought that the whole place these days had gradually changed for the worse. Now that they were both retired and with their two daughters married with their own families, she and Cyril no longer needed the space, and downsizing seemed a good idea.

She could see her house with its high hedges on either side of the gate. The estate agent Tillworth and Co.'s green and white For Sale board was fixed to the gatepost. It now carried an additional sticker, showing that a sale had been agreed, subject to exchange of contracts. Their prospective buyers, a young family named Taylor, seemed quite keen to progress the sale and the Building Society had sent a surveyor, Edmund Royston, round today to carry out a mortgage valuation survey.

She was surprised to see that his silver Ford Fiesta was still outside. He should have finished the survey a while ago.

Has he found something that might jeopardise the sale? she wondered. *There must be a problem. I hope not. We really don't want to stay here any longer.*

Royston had told Jean that the survey would take about forty minutes. Whoever had called her to arrange the survey had told her that there was no need for her to be there. She had taken the opportunity to do some shopping, telling him to close the self-locking door when he had finished. It was over an hour since she had left. She had had misgivings about leaving a stranger in the house, but he had insisted on total freedom of access. She had his business card and everything seemed in order. There was one thing nagging at the back of her mind. She had detected a hint of alcohol about him when he arrived, although he appeared in control of himself and seemed familiar with the properties on the estate and he'd asked all the right questions.

She pushed open the metal gate and walked up the short path to the front door, putting the shopping down on the doorstep while she fished in her bag for her house keys. Turning the key in the lock, she opened the door and picked up her bags to go inside, then promptly dropped them in astonishment, letting out an involuntary scream. The surveyor was lying face down just inside the door on the light oak wooden laminate hall floor at the bottom of the stairs. He wasn't moving and his head was twisted at an awkward angle. Some blood was running from underneath his body. Her nursing experience suggested that his neck was broken. Her eyes travelled slowly up the stairs towards the landing, where the loft hatch was still open, and his telescopic ladder lay on the carpet beneath it. It looked like a very unfortunate accident. She checked for a pulse but found none. Shocked, she reached for her mobile phone and dialled 999.

'Which service do you require?'

She thought for a moment, then, reasoning that he was beyond help, asked for the police.

The call was put through, and she gave the police brief details of what she had found, mentioning that she had not yet called an ambulance because her training had shown that the surveyor was dead. The emergency operator told her that someone would be sent immediately.

From years of dealing with the police in her time in A & E, she decided not to disturb anything and wait outside until they arrived. She stood on the pavement outside the gate, the colour draining from her face and she began to tremble as the shock began to set in, despite her years of training.

Ten minutes later, she heard the sound of a siren, and a marked car with blue flashing lights appeared.

She waved to the police car and it stopped outside the house. Two uniformed police officers got out. 'What's happened? Are you OK?' asked the first police officer, noticing her very pale complexion.

'Yes, I think so. I've just had a nasty shock. It's the surveyor. He's inside, exactly as I found him when I got home. I'm sure that he's dead. Our house is on the market, and the buyers arranged a survey today. I left the man to get on with it while I did some shopping. He told me that it would take about forty minutes. When I came back over an hour later, I was surprised to see that his car was still outside. Then I opened the front door and found him lying at the bottom of the stairs. I used to be a nurse in A & E, so I checked for a pulse. There was no sign so I called the police first. I think his neck is broken.'

One of the two police officers looked inside at the body lying on the floor. 'Must have been a very unlucky fall from up there,' she said, pointing to the loft hatch.

'I think we should call the CID as a precaution,' said her colleague. 'We'll let them look around before we move him. They can make the decision.' He called it in and got an immediate response. 'The CID and the paramedics will be here shortly. In the meantime, we'd all better stay outside, in case there's a problem.

'Any chance that I can make us some tea while we're waiting then?' she asked, more in hope than anything. 'I could really do with a cuppa.'

"Fraid not. We'll have to wait outside on the pavement. We mustn't contaminate a potential crime scene until the CID have cleared it.'

After twenty minutes of stilted conversation in the front garden between Jean and the two police officers, a dark blue Skoda Octavia pulled up and two people got out. One was a man in his early forties, slightly above average height with neatly styled dark brown hair. A smart medium grey suit showed under his open gabardine raincoat. The other was a young woman around thirty, about five feet six with short blonde hair. She was wearing a grey trouser suit, with a quilted raincoat over it.

The man greeted the police officers, showing his warrant card. 'DI Trussell, and this is DS Joynton,' he said.

'You'd better take a look inside, Guv. By the way, this is Mrs Oatley. She lives here and found the body.'

Jean quickly repeated what she'd already told the others, mentioning her previous nursing experience. 'I could see that he was already dead, so I called the police immediately.'

'Thank you. Let's have a quick look inside the door, Jackie,' he said. 'We'll need to be suited up to go inside. We'd better leave that to the CSI team.

'So, this is Mr Royston, Jackie,' said Trussell. 'I'm beginning to wonder whether this is connected in any way with his phone call. I tried to get hold of him, but he didn't pick up the call.'

'What do you think about his injuries, Mrs Oatley' asked Trussell? 'With your experience, are they consistent with a fall from up there?' pointing to the loft hatch.

Jean shrugged her shoulders.

'From that height to here, head first, possibly.'

Trussell looked at the hall: the staircase went straight up the left side. At the top there was a galleried landing to the right. The open loft hatch was at the far end. There was no direct line from the hatch to where the body had apparently landed on the wooden laminated floor by the front door.

'I saw a couple of similar incidents years ago when I was in uniform, Jackie,' he said. 'I had to deal with people who had fallen out of lofts. They were tragic accidents. Desperate situations for the families involved. I don't recall either of the victims missing everything and arriving straight at the front door. You'd expect that this one would've bounced off the landing or several stairs before he wound up here. If he'd fallen directly from the loft, then he would've been found more or less underneath the landing. ' He pointed to a spot beneath the landing. There was no obvious sign of anything there. No blood. No marks of any kind. In fact, the wooden floor looked clean - very clean - too clean… 'Given where we found him, then he must have swerved in mid-air. That's quite a feat of aerodynamics for a falling body. Isaac Newton would have had a problem explaining this one. I don't buy it. Jackie, can you call the Crime Scene Investigators and ask them to get here as soon as possible. Tell them we have an accident that now looks suspicious.'

He turned to Jean. 'Did he tell you which Building Society had sent him to carry out the survey?'

'I believe it was the High Weald in Woodchester. It was a valuation survey for our buyers, Mr and Mrs Taylor.'

'Who contacted you to arrange access to your property? Was it the High Weald or the estate agent?'

'I'm afraid I can't think. My memory is not as good as it used to be.'

'We'll need to talk to the High Weald mortgage adviser, James Howditch. Maybe he can tell us something about it.'

Trussell stepped away to make the call. He scanned through his phone directory, found the Woodchester branch number and called them. He identified himself and asked for the mortgage adviser.

'Ah, Mr Howditch. It's DI Trussell here. Did you send a surveyor named Edmund Royston round to a house in Wilmhurst Green today? Mortgage application in the name of Taylor? You didn't? That's strange. The house owner was sure that it was your Society. No, I'm afraid you can't speak to Mr Royston. He's unavailable, in a manner of speaking. In the meantime, would you mind checking with your colleagues to see if anyone else knows anything? Thank you. I'll pop round to see you later.'

'Right,' he said, turning to the two uniformed officers. 'Have you got any incident tape in the car? We'll need to seal the house off until the Crime Scene techs gets here. No one allowed inside.'

Trussell thought for a moment. 'Have you spoken to your husband, Mrs Oatley? he asked. 'I'm afraid that you won't be able to get back into your house until our investigators have finished their work and if the coroner decides that this wasn't an accident, then I'm afraid that your house will become a crime scene. Do you have somewhere to stay in the meantime?'

'Cyril has gone out for the day with a couple of friends. I haven't been able to reach him so far. We'll probably have to ask one of our daughters to put us up until we get our house back. I'd better call Jane now. She'll have to collect me. Cyril's got the car.' The awful reality had just hit Jean. The Taylors probably wouldn't want the house now. Some people could be terribly superstitious about deaths in houses. This had probably blighted the sale of their property. They would be stuck there forever now, growing old as the area continued to go downhill around them. Cyril would not be happy.

Her thoughts were interrupted by the sound of another siren as an ambulance appeared. The two paramedics rushed towards the house carrying their large equipment bags.

Trussell showed his warrant card. 'I don't think there is anything you can do for the man inside,' he said. 'Would one of you just check that he's definitely dead, please? Try not to disturb anything. We'll leave it to the police doctor to certify it. We can't move him until the CSI have had a look round.'

It only took a moment for them to corroborate Jean's diagnosis. 'Nothing we can do here, Detective Inspector. We'll leave it with you,' said one of them as they walked back to their ambulance.

Trussell said, 'Tell me, Mrs Oatley, did you lock the front door when you left to go shopping?'

'No, I didn't, Detective Inspector. Mr Royston asked me to leave it on the latch, as he would probably need something from his car.'

'So, if the door was open, it would have been possible for someone to enter the house, perhaps without Mr Royston being aware of it?'

'Yes, of course it would. But why would anyone want to do that? Do you think an opportunist thief might have entered the house while Mr Royston was here?'

'It's a possibility.'

'Our new doorbell,' Jean Oatley exclaimed suddenly. 'I'd forgotten about that for a moment. It has a video function and we pay a subscription to save the recordings. Useful when we're away. Just a minute,' she continued, hastily searching her phone. 'Here it is. I did get the usual beep to tell me that someone was at the door, but I must admit I ignored it this time. I thought that it was just the surveyor going backwards and forwards.'

Trussell looked at the phone screen. A man identified by Mrs Oatley as the surveyor, Edmund Royston went in and out of the house a couple of times as he fetched something from his car.

Then later recordings revealed a figure in some sort of dark blue anorak and what looked like blue jeans and trainers, arriving on a black framed mountain bike. The hood was pulled up and the figure was wearing some sort of mask. *A ski or a medical mask, perhaps?* It was an obvious attempt to disguise their identity. The individual was wearing a backpack or rucksack and carrying something that looked like a black plastic sack - a bin liner. The time was there. It was about fifteen minutes after Mrs Oatley had left to go shopping. The next video was about another fifteen minutes later, showing the back view of the figure leaving the house, closing the front door behind them, carrying the plastic sack which appeared to be bulkier now. The figure carefully wiped the door handle on the way out. It was not possible to identify the person in any way. The figure climbed back on the bike and nonchalantly rode off in the direction of Woodchester.

'There's one answer, Jackie,' he said. 'Something definitely going on. When Forensics have finished, I think we'll head for the High Weald. We'd better take Mrs Oatley's phone and get that video downloaded and saved. It could turn out to be important evidence.'

'Are you beginning to see some sort of connection with the Building Society, Jim? Do you think the surveyor's accident is related to the manager's disappearance?'

'It does seem a bit coincidental. We'll have to get Mr Howditch to make a thorough search. There must be a mortgage application there somewhere. Mrs Oatley was adamant that he'd been sent by the High Weald. And if so, who instructed Mr Royston?'

'What about the Estate Agent, Jim? Jackie asked. 'He's been dealing with the buyers. He must know something about their mortgage application.'

'OK. We'll start with Tillworths before we go to the High Weald. They're both in Woodchester High Street.' He turned to Mrs Oatley. 'Was Mr Royston carrying any file or papers relating to the survey?'

'I'm afraid that I don't remember,' she replied.

'Look, Jackie, someone has to stay here until the CSI have finished. We haven't any choice. We'll have to call Eddie Sprawson. See if he's finished at the supermarket for today and get him over here. I don't want to take Greeno off the missing person inquiry at the moment. Fast Eddie has enough experience to oversee a crime scene. Royston must have brought some sort of documentation or file with him. We'll ask Eddie to search for it when the CSI team have finished here. We need to follow up on this mysterious survey that no one seems to know about. It may well hold the key to Mr Royston's untimely death.'

Jackie made the call. 'Eddie will be here in fifteen minutes. I'll brief him. By the way, we'd better get someone to help Mrs Oatley. She still looks a bit shaken. We'll have to arrange for transport to her daughter's house.'

A van arrived outside the house and two men got out. 'CSI,' said Trussell. 'I'll have a quick word with them.'

The senior man walked towards them, waving to Trussell, while his assistant went to the back of the van to begin unloading their equipment. 'Hello, Jim. What have you got for us this time?'

'Morning, Maurice. Body at the bottom of the stairs that seems to have defied the usual laws of gravity.' Trussell showed them inside the door. 'Not entirely clear how he arrived here, if he fell from the landing.'

'I agree with you, Jim. It's certainly a curious place to end up.'

'I've not looked closely. It just seems odd. That's your job, but the whole of this wooden floor looks rather too clean. I think you might look very closely at the entire hall floor, and also check the stair carpet. You'll check the folding ladder up there for prints?' he added, pointing to the landing. 'Can you also check the door handles as well, particularly the outside one? We'll have to eliminate the owners and Mr Royston, of course, but it seems there was another caller while Royston was supposed to be alone in the house. Difficult to establish their identity from the doorbell video at the moment, but we'll check it separately.'

'OK, Jim. We'll look at everything and take some pictures and measurements. We'll put everything in the report as usual. With a bit of luck, you should have it in a couple of days. I'll email it to you in advance.'

'Thanks, Maurice. Jackie and I'll hang around a little longer until DC Sprawson gets here. He can take over and sort out the crime scene. He has enough experience. He'll know the drill. As soon as the doctor arrives to certify Mr Royston's death, then we can arrange to have the body removed for the post mortem. When you've finished, then we'll have to secure the house and put someone outside 24/7 until the matter's been resolved. That's going to be a difficult time for the owners, Mr and Mrs Oatley.'

15

Day 4.
Friday 22nd February.
Woodchester High Street.

Having left Fast Eddie in charge of the crime scene, Trussell and Joynton drove back to Woodchester Police Station in the Skoda, parking in its allocated space. The next stop for them was the estate agents, Tillworth and Co, located ten minutes' walk away further down the High Street.

The estate agency was unmistakable. It was painted in the same gaudy green and white colours they'd seen on the board outside the Oatleys' house. Trussell pushed the door open and they went in. The shop, containing the usual wall to wall photos of properties for sale, was empty apart from an attractive girl in her mid-twenties, sitting at a desk, typing on a keyboard. She looked up from her computer screen and smiled. 'Can I help you?'

Trussell showed his warrant card and introduced himself. 'We'd like to speak to Mr Tillworth, please.'

The girl didn't look overly surprised. Almost as if she was expecting their visit. 'I'm afraid he's out on a call at the moment. May I ask what it's in connection with?'

'When will he be back? It's very important that I speak to him.'

She opened a desk diary, consulted the page for that day and said, 'I think he may be on his way back now. He has another appointment here in fifteen minutes' time.'

'In that case, we'll wait,' said Trussell.

Five minutes later, the door opened and a man rushed in, looking harassed. Trussell immediately thought of Sprawson. The man could have been his brother. About five feet nine, overweight, thinning slicked back dark hair, florid complexion, thin moustache, a brown check jacket straining at the buttons and a pair of casual trousers that looked as though they hadn't seen an iron in recent times. A pair of worn scruffy brown shoes completed the impression of a complete lack of sartorial elegance.

'I got held up,' he said to the girl sitting at the desk, ignoring Trussell and Joynton. 'I haven't missed them, have I?'

She shook her head and indicated the two detectives. 'Arthur, these two are from the police. They were asking for you.'

He turned towards them, a look of surprise, colour starting to drain from his face. Then he regained his composure. 'I'm Arthur Tillworth. How can I help you?'

Trussell produced his warrant card. 'Detective Inspector Trussell. I believe that you are handling the sale of a property in Wilmhurst Green - 29 Prescott Avenue?'

'Correct. A nice four-bedroomed detached. Well maintained. The owners are getting on a bit and it's too big for them now. I'm afraid that it's already under offer, though.'

'I'm fully aware of that. Did you know that a surveyor was inspecting the property today?'

He thought for a moment, and then said, 'Yes. On behalf of the High Weald, I believe.'

'Who arranged it at the Society?'

'A lot of questions, er, Detective Inspector. May I ask why you're interested?' Tillworth licked his lips. He had begun to look uncomfortable with this apparently innocuous line of questioning.

'I'm not at liberty to reveal that, Sir. Please just answer the question.'

'Their mortgage advisor, I guess. His name is James Howditch. We know him quite well. He usually deals with surveyors as part of their mortgage process.'

'Not in this case, Mr Tillworth. Please try harder. Who was it? You must have spoken to the Society so that you could advise your clients, the Oatleys, that someone would be calling round today. It's a perfectly straightforward question. I only need a name.'

A bead of perspiration appeared on Tillworth's forehead. He looked at the girl. 'Did you keep a note, Sharon?' he asked. 'Can you remember who phoned?' He was obviously trying to buy himself some time. The girl just shook her head.

'It seems that we can't really help you. I'm afraid you'll have to ask the High Weald, Detective Inspector, if it is really so important. Does it really matter who instructed the man? Why don't you just ask the surveyor? I'm sure that he'll be happy to tell you. After all, it's all perfectly legal, isn't it?'

What a curious choice of words, thought Trussell. *No allegation had been made.*

He spoke to the girl again. 'Did anyone call while I was out? I left my mobile on my desk.'

'Stevie called. She said that she would catch up with you shortly. There was also a call from Brian, but he didn't leave any message.'

Tillworth looked sharply at the girl who had answered his question quite innocently. It was as if he didn't want this information to slip out.

'Well, if there's nothing else I can do for you, Detective Inspector,' he said, opening the door for Trussell and Joynton, 'then you'll have to excuse me. I have clients arriving any moment now.'

They stood on the pavement for a moment, looking back at the shop.

'He's hiding something,' said Jackie. 'His assistant mentioned Stevie. It must be the High Weald Building Society? Do you think that's yet another coincidence?'

'One to think about,' said Trussell. 'Let's head for the Building Society. I might just ask whether Miss Winterden had been trying to contact the estate agent this morning.'

It was just a short walk along the High Street to the High Weald Building Society.

16

Day 4.
Friday 22nd February.
High Weald Building Society, Woodchester High Street.

Trussell and Joynton arrived outside the Society branch, opened the door and went in. Maureen Scoular, very pale, was standing by the glass partition and gave a nod of recognition before she continued talking to the customer in front of her. They noticed that Susie Albright was there with her.

Stevie Winterden appeared from the office on the right and walked towards them, her best customer-friendly smile spreading across her face.

'Good morning, Detective Inspector. How can I help you?'

'We'd like a word with James Howditch, please.'

'Oh dear, is he in trouble?' she smiled, leading the way to his office. 'I'll see if he's free.' She pushed the glass door open, without tapping on it first. 'James, the police are here again. They want to talk to you.'

Howditch looked up from the paperwork he was reading and turned pale, picking up on their sombre faces. 'What can I do for you, Detective Inspector?'

'Thank you, Miss Winterden,' said Trussell. We'd like to speak to Mr Howditch alone, please. Would you close the door after you?'

Stevie gave them both a dirty look and walked out with as much dignity as she could muster under the circumstances.

'How can I help you?'

'It's simply this, Mr Howditch. We spoke earlier about a survey that was carried out at Number 29, Prescott Avenue in Wilmurst this morning by Edmund Royston, apparently on behalf of this Society. Did you manage to discover who instructed him?'

'It didn't sound familiar. Can you remind me of the names of the applicants? That would make it easier for me to identify the address.'

'The applicants were named Taylor.'

Howditch tapped the name into the keyboard, moved the mouse around, clicked it a couple of times and then stared at the screen.

'I'm afraid that nothing's coming up on the system at the moment. Are you sure that it was for us? I certainly know Edmund Royston. He's carried out a number of surveys on our behalf in the past…the usual valuations for mortgage purposes. All fairly run-of-the-mill stuff, nothing contentious. I think that he works for most of the other Societies and Banks in town. To tell you the truth, he's not the man he was. He's had a few problems in his life recently.'

'Would you care to elaborate?'

'Not sure what they might be, but I think he's started drinking a bit and I understand that his business has suffered somewhat. He's a one-man band, so there is no one to help him out. But he is local and it's always been our policy in the Society to support local businesses. He does a professional job on the straightforward valuation surveys at a reasonable price and he does know the property in the area very well.'

'The owner was adamant that the survey was for the High Weald.'

James Howditch looked dumbfounded.

'It's very strange. I handle the vast majority of the standard valuation surveys. The only other person here who could have been involved is the manager, Barney Scoular but obviously we can't ask him at the moment. Frankly, I'd be astonished if it was him. He does oversee all of the applications and covers for me during holidays, but he always brings me up to speed when I get back. I wouldn't have expected him to have organised a straightforward local valuation survey. It's just odd that there isn't any trace of the application on the system.'

'Would anyone else know anything?' asked Jackie. 'Is it possible to override your system?'

'I suppose anything is possible, although I'm not sure how one goes about something like that.'

'What about Stevie Winterden? Would she have seen it? Would she know how to manipulate the system?'

'Unlikely. We can ask her, but I think that if anyone knew, it would have to be the manager. After all, he's been here about twenty years, I believe. He worked closely with the previous manager.'

'Can we call Miss Winterden in here and ask her if she knows anything about this application?'

'Certainly,' he said, rising from his chair.

'Don't worry,' said Jackie Joynton. 'I'll do it.

She left the office and returned with Stevie, a moment later. The latter still looked cross.

Trussell gave her a searching look. 'Miss Winterden, we're interested in a survey carried out this morning by Edmund Royston at a house in Wilmhurst for one of this Society's mortgage applicants by the name of Taylor. Did you instruct Royston?'

She looked hard at Trussell. Was she feigning surprise, or was her response genuine? She was hard to read. 'No, of course not. That's usually your job, James,' she said, looking at Howditch.

He shook his head. 'Not one that I'd seen, Stevie.'

'Well, if neither of you sent Royston, then who did?' asked Trussell.

'Why don't you ask him, Detective Inspector?' said Stevie. 'That would save a lot of time.'

'Unfortunately, that's not possible. He met with an accident at the house.'

Trussell watched their faces for any reaction.

'That's terrible, Detective Inspector,' said James Howditch, looking shocked. 'Is he OK?'

Stevie said nothing. Her face didn't betray any emotion.

'I'm afraid not,' said Trussell, and made no further comment.

'Someone must have arranged the survey, Miss Winterden,' said Jackie Joynton. 'We can always ask the buyers, the Taylor family. They must know where they applied for a mortgage. Perhaps they can give us a name.'

'I doubt that they would know who appointed the surveyor, even if they did apply to us for a mortgage,' she replied. Something like that is usually arranged by the Society, although if James doesn't recognise the applicants' names… It's all a bit of a mystery, isn't it?'

Trussell thought there was something almost mocking in her response. He tried another tack. 'Did you phone Tillworth and Company for any reason this morning, Miss Winterden?'

'I don't think so, Detective Inspector,' she replied.

'By the way,' said Trussell, 'I notice that Miss Allbright seems to be helping with the customers at the till today.'

'Yes, that's right,' said Stevie. 'It's part of her training. Mr Scoular wanted her to learn that side of our business. Now is a good time as I'm searching the archives for any trace of these missing files. You'll remember the visit from Head Office.'

'Have you found anything yet?' asked Joynton.

'No, nothing. No trace at all. Given the urgency and importance of the search, I need to be there on my own. There's not space for Susie in the room while I'm looking. And of course, it is confidential. I've told the others I'm not to be disturbed while I'm in there. If they need me, then I've told them to call me on my phone.'

Trussell saw no future in pursuing any other lines of enquiry with Stevie at that moment, so he thanked them both for their time and indicated to Jackie that they should return to the office. 'There's something going on there, Jackie,' he said as they walked back along the High Street towards the station. 'Someone must know who appointed the surveyor. If I believe Howditch, and there's no reason not to, then this one has bypassed their system.'

'Seems strange,' agreed Joynton. 'What seems such an innocuous survey.'

By now they had reached the station and they walked up the stairs to the CID office on the first floor.

'I'll try to contact Peterson now,' said Trussell as he sat down at his desk and picked up his phone. He tapped in the number given to him by Preston. It rang several times, and just as he was about to cut it off, a voice answered.

'Mr Peterson?'

'Yes. Who's that?'

'This is Detective Inspector Trussell of Kent Police. I need to talk to you urgently. May I suggest that you leave wherever you are and return home immediately. I shall arrange to visit you there next Monday. Shall we say six pm?'

'I don't know. What's all this about?' He sounded frightened.

'I'll tell you when I see you. I should warn you that failure on your part to comply with my request will result in a warrant being issued immediately for your arrest. Have no doubt, we shall find you. Do I make myself clear?'

'Yyyes,' he stammered. 'Very well, I'll be there at six on Monday.'

'Thank you,' said Trussell, terminating the call.

17

Day 7.
Monday 25th February.
Woodchester Police Station.

The forensic report had arrived on Trussell's desk. Jackie Joynton was at the mortuary, attending the post-mortem on Edmund Royston. She had taken Mark Green with her for his first experience of this very important procedure while Eddie Sprawson was busy writing up the reports of his visit to the supermarket and his subsequent involvement in the aftermath of Royston's death.

Trussell opened the large manila envelope and pulled out the A4 sheets containing the forensic report. Some photographs fell out. As he read the contents, he felt vindicated because it confirmed that Royston had fallen straight over the landing and had hit the floor immediately below. Scrapes on the landing handrail left by the folding ladder pointed to the place where he had started his downward journey. Minute traces of blood at the impact point, a slight denting in the laminate flooring and then traces of a trail of blood to where he was found at the foot of the stairs. The report confirmed that there had been attempts to clean all traces of blood but whoever was responsible had not succeeded completely. Small splashes had also been found on the wall. The surveyor's ladder had been checked for fingerprints, but there were none, not even Royston's, and he had certainly not been wearing gloves. It had been wiped completely clean by someone. Then there was the question as to how Royston had ended up by the front door. The obvious inference was that he had crawled there after the fall, looking for help. But how did he manage to get there with an apparently broken neck? Trussell would have to wait for the results of the post-mortem to see how this medical miracle had occurred. Logic would suggest that a man with a broken neck would be unable to crawl fifteen feet towards the front door to seek help. Perhaps he was only injured in the fall. *If so, how was his neck broken?* Trussell's thoughts immediately returned to the video which had shown the figure leaving the house. It was beginning to look more like murder.

There was a further clue. Some wet footprints had been found on the stair carpet. The forensic team had included photographs and had commented that the sole pattern was from a limited-edition trainer. Probably size eight or nine. *Did they belong to whoever had interfered with Royston's ladder?* In response to Mrs Oatley's request, the surveyor had put plastic covers on top of his own brogues, so the footprints did not belong to him.

Trussell thought about the mysterious figure in the doorbell video. That was obviously key to discovering who had been in the house even if it had been impossible to identify the person leaving the house. *What was in the black sack that the figure had been carrying?* The search for fingerprints on the outside door handles had been equally fruitless. Just like the ladder, they had been wiped clean. This pointed to a very meticulous person. Then there was the missing file. *Did it contain information which might incriminate someone?* It was hard to imagine, as the survey was just a straightforward one for mortgage valuation purposes. Eddie Sprawson had told Trussell that he'd searched for it and couldn't find any trace. Could Trussell rely on him?

Trussell cast his mind back to Mrs Oatley's doorbell video and the mysterious figure in the anorak, carrying a large plastic sack. Perhaps the missing file had been removed by that individual.

The inquiry had now moved to a different level. Someone had wanted the surveyor dead. *Why?* He was carrying out an apparently non-contentious valuation survey for a reputable local building society. And yet, on enquiry, no one would admit to instructing him. Obviously, the house owner was blameless in this, but the estate agent had been rather off-hand and somewhat evasive. *What was going on? Was there a connection with the buyers' mortgage application, or was it aimed specifically at the surveyor? Was he the intended victim, for some reason? Was his death totally unconnected with the Oatleys' house?*

Trussell thought back to the phone call from Royston taken by Mark Green which he'd noted down. He had seemed very worried, according to Green. He was afraid that something was going to happen. And it had…

The post-mortem results were even more important now. He would have to wait for Jackie Joynton to get back. She knew the pathologist, so she could probably get some ideas from him before his official report was completed and circulated.

18

Day 7.
Monday 25th February.
Early afternoon.

Jackie Joynton walked into the office, accompanied by Mark Green. His first experience of a post-mortem had not gone well and he'd left his lunch in the car park drain outside afterwards. He still looked distinctly queasy and uncomfortable.

'What news?' asked Trussell.

'Interesting,' said Jackie. 'You were right about the circumstances. We're definitely looking at murder. Dr Jacobsen was certain that his neck was not broken by the fall. Someone with the right knowledge and strength broke it for him afterwards. They just twisted his head until his neck snapped. He wouldn't have been able to put up much resistance after his fall. It was surprising he managed to crawl as far as he did before it happened.'

Sprawson looked up from his report writing. He had been listening to the conversation and was showing interest.

'How would someone do that, Guv?' he asked. 'Was the pathologist absolutely certain? It sounds a bit far-fetched to me. I've never heard of anything like that happening before.'

'We go with the expert on this one, Eddie,' said Trussell. 'We have to start looking into Royston's background. Maybe he's upset someone somewhere. I don't believe that his death was in any way connected with the Oatleys' house or the Taylor mortgage application. I think that the circumstances just provided an opportunity for someone to kill him. We'll have to make Mr Royston our number one priority.'

'What about Barnaby Scoular, Guv?' asked Mark Green.

'You'll have to press on with that until we've exhausted all of the likely places. You've covered A & E and most local surgeries and clinics, haven't you?'

'Yes, Guv. Not a sniff anywhere. We've got just got a couple of surgeries left. I believe Eddie is going to check with the two hospitals just outside our area, and then we're done. There's no trace of Scoular anywhere.'

'Then I'm afraid that we've done all we can for the moment. Mr Royston has just become our number one priority now. That won't be much comfort to Mrs Scoular, though. We'll have to think about the usual media appeal.' Turning to Jackie, he asked when Dr Jacobsen's report would be available.

'A couple of days, he said.'

'OK. Let's start with Royston's background. Jackie, can you contact James Howditch at the High Weald to see what information he can give us. We'll need to speak to the estate agent, Arthur Tillworth, again. He should be able to fill in some background info about our man. Royston seemed to be fairly well known locally.'

He turned to Sprawson. 'Eddie, when you've checked those last two hospitals, I'd like you to make a list of all the estate agents in and around Woodchester. You'd better include the other Building Societies who have branches in town. I can think of two. Check with the banks as well. Speak to anyone who might have used the services of a surveyor. It'll be a good opportunity for you to get to know our patch a bit better. We need to find out who knows anything about Royston. I want everything they can tell us. Information, gossip, rumours, connections - anything at all. I want a complete picture of the man's life. Leave Tillworth off the list – we'll deal with him. Remember, I want everything documented.'

'Righto, Guv. I'll finish these two reports later. I'll get straight out to the two hospitals and eliminate them from the Scoular search list then I'll start on the estate agents as soon as I get back.' He got up from his desk, picked up his phone, grabbed his coat from the rack by the door, and rushed away.

Mark Green looked at Trussell. Questioning. 'What about me, Guv? What d'you want me to do?'

'Right, Greeno,' said Trussell, looking at the still slightly pale Detective Constable, 'first of all, I want you to make yourself a strong cup of tea.'

'OK, Guv.'

'When you feel a bit better, I want you to see Tillworth. You'll need to be on your guard. We thought that he was a bit evasive when Jackie and I spoke to him about the survey. He'll probably try to fob you off with some spurious meeting as an excuse to get rid of you. Be persistent. If he's difficult or uncooperative, tell him that I'll invite him to come to the station to talk to us. Make it official. He'll get the message. We need to build a complete picture of Royston.'

'OK Guv. I'll go round there as soon as I've finished my tea.'

DC Mark Green left his desk and returned a couple of minutes later, mug in hand and sat down.

'If Tillworth isn't there, Greeno,' continued Trussell, 'then speak to the girl who runs the shop and answers the phone. I believe he called her Sharon. She was quite nice looking. Probably about your age, so you can use all your charm to see what she can tell you. We thought that she knew more than she showed when Jackie and I spoke to her. She might be a bit more forthcoming with you if the boss isn't there. But be professional and behave yourself,' he added, smiling.

'OK, Guv,' said Mark Green, hurriedly draining the mug. He stood up, straightened his tie, picked up his raincoat and headed for the door and the stairs to the ground floor. He could not have known that carrying out the DI's simple instruction was about to change his life.

'Keen, isn't he?' said Jackie, smiling. 'You don't think that your description of Tillworth's assistant, Sharon, had anything to do with it, do you?'

Trussell grinned. 'I've deliberately sent Greeno to see Tillworth because I just think that he's more likely to relate to the girl. Eddie would probably terrify her. He has a rather single-minded approach to questioning people and it surely won't work with either Tillworth or his young lady. I'm actually hoping that Tillworth himself won't be there. But we'll see.'

'If Tillworth's there, Jim?'

'Then it'll give Greeno a chance to show us what he's made of,' said Trussell, smiling again.

19

Day 7.
Monday 25th February.
Woodchester.

As Mark Green stepped out of the main door, he immediately turned his collar up. There was an icy drizzle in the air as he headed down the High Street past the shops towards the estate agency. There was hardly anyone about. The weather was still keeping most people inside.

He arrived outside the gaudy green and white painted shop, pausing briefly to look in the window at the various properties on offer. Only a few carried *sold* or *under offer* stickers across the pictures. That didn't seem to fit with the current state of the market around Woodchester as he understood it. Tillworths was obviously not very successful at the moment.

He pushed the door open and went in. It wasn't much warmer inside. No sign of a heater. The place was full of photographs of properties for sale on the inside of the window and on the walls. The lack of *sold* or *under offer* signs confirmed what he had seen outside.

A girl sitting at a desk on the right looked up from her keyboard, in anticipation of a customer. She had shoulder-length, light brown hair and was wearing a brightly-coloured, boldly striped, heavy jumper. Just a touch of make-up. A hint of lipstick. The DI had been right, she was nice looking. In fact, Mark Green thought her very attractive. Her name, Sharon Webster, was engraved on a brass plate at the front of her desk.

'Can I help you?' she asked, giving him a winning smile. 'What are you looking for? A flat, perhaps? We have a nice new development nearing completion just outside of town. Within easy reach of the centre. On the main bus route, if you don't want to use your car.'

Flustered, he felt in his pocket for his warrant card. That was embarrassing. He should have had it ready to hand. He found it. 'I'm Detective Constable Green. I'm looking for Mr Tillworth'

He offered his warrant card and before he could retrieve it, she grasped his wrist to look at the card more closely.

'You realise that assaulting a police officer is an arrestable offence?' he said, trying to keep a straight face and maintain some sense of gravitas.

'I'm sorry, Detective Constable Mark Green,' she said, smiling, with the accent on his first name. 'I was just checking your identity. I needed to be sure.' Smiling, she continued, 'Are you going to arrest me now?' as she held out her two hands, palms down, for the imaginary handcuffs.

He felt somewhat embarrassed by her very direct and flirty response. His developing observational skills kicked in. *Slender pale hands. Well-manicured nails with a very light polish. Not wearing any rings or any other jewellery on either hand. Just a watch with a gold band on her left wrist.*

'I'm making a note of your name for future reference, Sharon Webster, in case you persist in obstructing our enquiries,' he said, trying not to smile. 'Now, is Mr Tillworth here, please?'

'I'm sorry, but he's out on an appointment. I'm afraid that he won't be back for a couple of hours, so you'll have to question me instead. I'm his secretary, personal assistant, salesperson, and filing clerk and I make the tea. Meaning, there's only me here most of the time. Would you like a cup?'

He shook his head.

'Why don't you pull up that other chair, then? It'll be more comfortable than standing. What is it you want to know?'

He did as he was told and sat down. He took out his notebook and a pen from his pocket. 'My boss, the DI, was here a couple of days ago asking about a survey on a property in Wilmhurst, carried out by Edmund Royston. It was one of your properties; Mr Tillworth seemed unable to recall who had instructed the surveyor on behalf of the High Weald. Do you know?'

'It wasn't me, so it could only have been him, Detective Constable Mark Green. He probably discussed it with Stevie Winterden on one of her visits to the shop. We would have suggested to the Taylors that they spoke to the High Weald about a mortgage.'

'You've heard about Mr Royston's unfortunate accident? Did you know him?"

Her expression changed and a look of sadness replaced her natural smile for a moment. 'Yes. He used to do a lot of work for us but he hasn't done so much lately.'

'Did you notice anything different about him recently?'

'Yes. I think he'd begun to drink a bit. He seemed to be worried about something.'

'Any idea what the problem was?'

'No, but I heard Arthur shouting at him one day last week in the office.'

'Any idea what it was about?'

'I didn't hear all of it because the office door was closed. Arthur can be a bit loud sometimes. He told Edmund that he'd better keep his mouth shut if he knew what was good for him. He said that there was too much at stake. This was not the time to get cold feet.'

Mark Green noted that down.

She continued. 'When the door opened and Edmund came out, he looked very pale and shaken. He just walked out of the shop without a word. He normally passed the time of day with me. He always had a laugh and a joke. He was such a nice friendly man.'

She pointed to the closed door at the back of the shop. 'That's Arthur's office. He keeps the door locked all the time unless he's here. He's obviously got something to hide these days. I'm never allowed in there. The only people who go in there are Arthur and some particular visitors who turn up from time to time. Some of them are distinctly odd. To tell you the truth, Detective Constable Mark Green, I'm getting a bit fed up with it and I'm a bit worried about what might be going on. I don't want to be involved if there is anything dodgy happening. In fact, I'm thinking about giving in my notice. There's not enough day-to-day stuff to keep me occupied. I don't believe that Arthur is concentrating on our vendors and our actual business here. Frankly, I'm surprised that most of them haven't taken their houses to one of the other agents in town.'

'Who are the visitors? Are they the same people? How many? Male or female?'

'There are one or two regulars. There's a man named Brian. I think that he comes from Brandford. They've got some sort of business deal going on there. Then there's a rather shifty character that comes in, maybe once a fortnight, and usually delivers a couple of packages. I don't know his name. I've no idea what's in them. Arthur never shows me and there's never anything to go in our recycling bin.'

'Tell me about Brian. Do you know his other name?'

'No. Never been mentioned.'

'Can you describe him?'

'About five-ten. East Kent accent. Roughly spoken. Heavily-built. Number one haircut. Clean-shaven. I hope that doesn't sound too judgemental. Fiftyish, I'd say. He's always casually dressed, usually in a tee shirt, black leather jacket and jeans. Intimidating. Not the sort of man you'd want to cross.'

'Anyone else we should know about?'

'I've already mentioned Stevie Winterden from the High Weald Building Society. She comes here from time to time. Not surprising, as we recommend all potential buyers to them for mortgage advice. I guess that she wants to make sure that they're first on the list when we talk to prospective buyers.'

'Interesting,' said Mark Green. 'Have you ever seen the High Weald manager, Barnaby Scoular, here?' He produced the photograph of Scoular he had been using whilst touring the hospitals and clinics. 'Here he is. Look familiar?'

'Yes, I'm sure I've seen him here recently. Yes. I did. He came here in the last couple of weeks or so. He went into Arthur's office. The door was closed after he went in. I couldn't hear what was being discussed in there, but when he left, he didn't look very happy.'

'Can you recall anyone else who might have visited Mr Tillworth?'

She thought for a moment. 'Yes, of course. There is another man. I can't be sure of his name. Unusual one. I think that it was Marcus or something like that. Man in his forties, I guess. He's always smartly dressed. He never says much when he comes in. Just goes straight into Arthur's office. I think that they also meet outside of the office. Socially, but I think that there might also be a business connection. He comes here from time to time carrying an executive case as if he has papers. He usually seems to be carrying a small package when he leaves. Looks rather like one of those parcels that the shifty-looking chap brings in.'

'Thank you, Miss Webster, that's been very helpful,' he said. 'I'll give you one of my cards in case anything else occurs to you. I wouldn't leave it lying around, though, if I were you. You can call me on the mobile number anytime.'

'Anytime? Do you mean that?'

'Yes. Anytime. And please be careful. From what you've told me, I can understand your concerns. There's just one more thing. I'd better take a note of your address, just in case you do decide to leave this job and move on. We may need to contact you. It looks as though you could have valuable information.'

She picked up her multi-coloured leather handbag from the floor, opened it and took out a bulky matching purse. It contained a selection of bank cards, store cards and other items. She found her driving licence and offered it to him.

'My address is there. I still live with my parents at the moment. No chance of a mortgage on what Arthur pays me.'

Mark Green carefully copied the details into his notebook and handed the licence back. She put it back in her purse, together with his card. He replaced the notebook and pen in his pocket.

'Thank you, Miss Webster.'

'Sharon,' she said, smiling again.

Mark Green stood up, replaced the chair where he'd found it.

'Take care,' he said, opening the door. She smiled at him again.

He stepped out into the rain to return to the station.

Sharon Webster dominated his thoughts. *The DI was right. She is very attractive. I bet that she has a whole queue of admirers. No chance. I'm surprised that she still lives at home though. Put her out of your mind, Greeno. Concentrate on the enquiry. We have a murder to solve.*

He'd have a lot to tell the DI and realised that it would be best to share the information about the Brandford connection when Fast Eddie was out of the office.

He'd only walked about a hundred yards when his phone warbled, indicating an incoming message. Must be the DI chasing him. He took it out of his pocket and glanced at it. He didn't recognise the number. He opened the message. It said simply, *'I'll let you know if I hear anything else. I thought that you might need my number.'* It was signed. *Sharon.*

Damn, he thought. *I don't need complications. Remember what the DI said about professionalism.* He was torn.

By now, he had reached the police station and walked up to the first floor.

'How did you get on, Greeno?' asked Trussell, not even giving him time to hang his raincoat on the rack. 'I hope that Tillworth wasn't a problem.'

'No Guv, he was out. I had a chat with his young lady.'

'I bet you did, Greeno,' laughed Jackie Joynton.

Mark Green coloured slightly, but tried to ignore the inuendo.

'And…?' asked Trussell.

He consulted his notebook and repeated everything that Sharon Webster had told him. 'Frankly, Guv, I'm a bit concerned for her safety. She's worried about some of the things happening there and is talking about leaving before she gets caught up in any of the problems. By the way, I got her details in case she moves on.'

'I'm sure you did, Greeno,' chuckled Jackie. 'Phone number too, I'll bet!'

'Leave him alone, Sergeant,' laughed Trussell. 'There's a lot of helpful stuff there that Tillworth certainly wouldn't have mentioned to us. I doubt that the young lady would even have shared that information with you or me. Good job, Greeno. Well done.' He continued, 'You'd better keep an eye on that estate agency, Greeno. Be discreet, but check with the girl there when you get a chance. Preferably when Tillworth's out. It sounds as if there's a lot going on there.'

'OK, Guv.' He could certainly live with the boss's instruction to keep in touch with Miss Webster.

'Some of that is beginning to tie in with what we were told at the High Weald Head Office,' said Trussell. 'We'll need some more information from them, so we'd better arrange to see them tomorrow. Jackie, can you give the Deputy Chairman a call and arrange a mutually convenient time, please?'

'OK, Jim,' she said, picking up the phone.

'I've got another idea that might save some time and help us move this on,' said Trussell. 'When we see McDriscoll, I'll ask for a look at the personnel files for Stephanie Winterden and both Maureen and Barnaby Scoular. You can make a search while I keep McDriscoll and Hartmann occupied discussing their main problem. We'll need Stevie's date of birth, so that we can track her down. The General Registry Office can provide us with a copy of her birth certificate once we have her birth name. That might prove revealing, with her apparent Brandford connection. I still think that she's a fairly important piece of our jigsaw puzzle. It will be useful to see what information the Society has about the Scoulars as well.'

20

Day 7.
Monday 25th February pm.
Waverley.

Trussell had arranged to meet Alex Peterson that evening at his home in Waverley. He set out for Number 26 Archer Road with Jackie to arrive at the agreed time of six pm. They pulled up outside the small red brick terraced house behind a yellow Caterham and got out of the Skoda.

'Seems your phone call paid off, then, Jim,' said Jackie, pointing to the Caterham.

Trussell nodded as he seized the large knocker on the door and gave it a heavy double blow. Maybe it was his frustration with Peterson finally surfacing. There was no immediate response.

He was about to repeat it when the door opened and a man stood there, looking at them. He was about six-feet-tall, fair-haired and slim build. Probably in his late thirties. Maybe forty. 'Can I help you?' he asked, as if his visitors were unexpected.

'Mr Peterson?' asked Trussell.

'Yes. You must be DI Trussell?'

Trussell nodded as he showed his warrant card and introduced Jackie.

Peterson looked concerned. 'What can I do for you?'

'Can we come in, Sir? It would be better to talk inside.'

Peterson seemed reluctant at first, but stood aside and beckoned them into the narrow hallway. He indicated the first door on the right. 'We can talk in there,' he said.

The door opened into a small, dimly lit front living room. Dull décor matching the age of the property. A small Victorian fireplace against the party wall. A large dark leather settee and matching armchair dominated the room, barely leaving space for a small coffee table in the middle and a wide-screen television in one of the two small alcoves either side of the fireplace.

Peterson followed them in. 'Now, what can I do for you?'

Jackie Joynton produced her note book and pen from her bag.

'Perhaps you can start by explaining why you left in such a hurry on the night of Wednesday the Twentieth of February?'

'I'd been told that the police were looking for me and I panicked. I couldn't think why. I've done nothing.'

'Let us be the judges of that. First of all, can you tell us where you were in the evening of Monday the Eighteenth?' asked Trussell.

'Certainly. I was here working on a project for my business, as I am now.' He indicated an open laptop on the coffee table and some papers scattered around it.

'Really, Sir? That can be verified. We'd just need to look at your laptop. That would confirm it or otherwise. Do you want to reconsider that statement?'

'I don't see the relevance.'

'How can you account for the fact that a yellow Caterham, identified as yours, was seen by witnesses, parked in The Avenue at Frattenden that evening? In fact it's been seen there on a number of occasions.'

Peterson looked embarrassed and swallowed hard. He began to flounder. 'I don't know what you're talking about.'

'I put it to you that you were visiting Maureen Scoular at her home. Do you want to tell us about your relationship with her?' persisted Trussell. 'This wasn't an isolated visit, was it? I'm sure that you're aware that her husband, Barnaby Scoular is missing.'

'If you know anything,' said Jackie,' this is your chance to tell us. Unless, of course you'd rather accompany us to the station and discuss it there.' She was playing the bad cop in this conversation.

Peterson sat down on the settee. He had turned pale. He was clasping and unclasping his hands, looking about him, as if for inspiration.

'You may as well tell us everything,' said Trussell. 'We're aware of your longstanding friendship with Maureen Scoular prior to her marriage to Barnaby Scoular. The marriage doesn't appear to have interrupted your relationship.'

'What's happened to Barnaby Scoular?' asked Jackie Joynton. 'He hasn't been seen since the night he disappeared. You'd better tell us what you know.'

'I know nothing about that,' he said, now looking rather shaken. 'Nor does Maureen.'

'How can we be sure of that?' asked Trussell. 'Could be a very convenient way of establishing an alibi, if you admit that you were together that evening.'

Peterson didn't reply. He just looked down at the carpet, distracted.

Trussell and Joynton stared at him. Keeping the pressure on. They were encouraging him to say more. 'What can you tell us about the Scoulars' marriage? It seems a little unconventional.'

Peterson thought for a moment, took a deep breath and then answered them. 'I first met Maureen Atherton, about seven years ago, after I joined the Woodchester Rep. She was already a member. I was in a marriage that was going nowhere at the time, and Maureen and I became close. My wife refused to give me a divorce and then, by the time she had changed her mind, Maureen had married Barney Scoular.'

'That didn't seem to deter you, Sir, did it?' said Jackie Joynton.

'Maureen had a difficult upbringing and she craved security which I couldn't offer her at the time. Barney could, but on different terms. He needed a mother figure in his life, so it suited both of them. There was no love in the arrangement.'

'Did he know about you?' asked Trussell.

'I don't think so. He was totally committed to his position as Branch Manager. Absolute workaholic. I think that he had some difficulties there recently. Maureen said that he seemed preoccupied in recent months, but didn't want to discuss whatever the problem was.'

'So, Maureen Scoular had no idea what was going on, then?'

'No. But frankly, we weren't bothered. Their lives seemed to exist in separate compartments. It made it easier for us. The irony is that after my divorce came through, I could have offered Maureen the security she wanted, as we were already committed to one another.'

'We could be talking about motives here, Sir,' said Jackie Joynton. 'Mr Scoular has disappeared and we're trying to work out who might profit from that.'

'Not Maureen and I, if that's what you mean. Nothing has or would change for us.'

Trussell thought for a moment. 'We've not finished with you yet. We shall want to speak to you again. Do not communicate with anyone at the Woodchester Rep until I tell you otherwise, unless you want to find yourself in one of our cells. Do you understand?'

The man nodded dumbly, still looking shaken.

'That includes Maureen Scoular as well. I think that's all we need at the moment. I must ask you not to leave Waverley in case we want to talk to you again.'

Jackie Joynton finished writing in her notebook and replaced it in her bag as she followed Trussell out of the house. 'What do you think, Jim?' she asked as they got back into his Skoda.

'Frankly, Jackie, I don't think that he knows anything about Scoular's disappearance. He's not a very good liar. By implication, I don't think that Maureen Scoular is involved either. I think that they just share a guilty secret about their relationship and I suspect that they don't know it's not as secret as they think. I'm not letting him off the hook, though, until I'm absolutely sure he's in the clear.'

'Where next then, Jim?'

'We'll go back to the office and see whether Greeno and Fast Eddie have turned up anything new.'

21

Day 8.
Tuesday 26th February.
CID Office, Woodchester Police Station.

Jackie Joynton's phone rang. She picked it up. It was the desk sergeant.

'I've got a gentleman here who just walked in, Jackie. He claims to be Barnaby Scoular's brother. To be honest, he doesn't look anything like our missing person. Will you talk to him?'

'Of course, Alan. I'll come down right away.'

She relayed the news to Trussell who was studying his A4 pad containing the mind maps. It was becoming more convoluted as time went on. The office whiteboard reflected this information to a lesser degree. That dealt in facts, whereas Trussell's was more concerned with ideas and speculation. It was a system that had served him very well in the past.

'We'll both see him, Jackie,' said Trussell, putting the pad back in his drawer and carefully locking it.

They walked down the single flight of stairs into the main entrance. The sergeant indicated the first interview room. 'I've put him in there.'

They opened the door and the visitor stood up. Trussell introduced himself and Joynton, whilst he studied the man. He certainly bore no resemblance to the missing man's photo or description. He was about six feet tall, which was certainly at odds with Barnaby Scoular's apparent height from the photograph provided by his wife.

'I saw the news of Barney's disappearance on the television news and felt that I had to come and talk to you,' he said.

'Hadn't you spoken to Mrs Scoular, then?'

'No. We hardly ever speak. Barney has always done his own thing. We're rarely in contact these days.'

'Is there any other immediate family, then?' asked Trussell. 'Other siblings?'

'No, just my parents and myself. It may seem unlikely to you, but Barney and I are non-identical twins.'

Trussell indicated a chair and invited him to sit down. Joynton, as always, had her notebook and pen to hand.

'Can we start with your full name and address, Mr Scoular, just for the record, please?' she asked.

'Robert James Scoular,' he said. 'I live near Maidstone.'

'Do you have any form of ID, Mr Scoular? A driving licence, perhaps?'

'Certainly,' he said, reaching into his jacket pocket and producing a wallet. He extracted his licence and put it down on the table.

Jackie Joynton picked it up, looked at the photograph on it and at Scoular and quickly made a note of his address.

'Do you have a phone number where we can reach you, if necessary?' she asked. He gave a number which she duly recorded.

'I know it must seem improbable that Barney and I are twins, because we are both so different in every way - appearance, attitudes, thinking. I'm the eldest by about twenty minutes. Our mother had a difficult time with his birth. There were complications. I've often wondered whether that accounts for us being so different.'

'Interesting,' said Trussell. 'What can you tell me about your brother?'

'There seems to be a certain amount of speculation in the press linking Barney's disappearance with some mortgage problems,' said Scoular. 'I don't believe that fraud is Barney's style. He's always been scrupulously honest. I do know that he was incredibly proud of the fact that he had become the branch manager. After all, he started there more or less straight from school with no real qualifications. The previous manager hired him and obviously saw something in him.'

'We have an open mind at the moment, Sir,' said Trussell. 'We're just interested in finding him. What else can you tell us about him?'

'Well, we were completely different from the beginning. Being much smaller, he got more attention from our mother. He wasn't really academic or sport-minded. He just seemed to drift through his teenage years. Kept himself to himself. Definitely a bit secretive. A bit of a loner.'

'Where were you both brought up?'

'Just outside Woodchester. Our parents still live in the same house, although they're retired now. They're very worried about Barney, naturally.'

'What about friends? Girl friends? Did he have any?"

'I don't remember anyone specific in those days. Despite our relationship, we moved in different circles from a very early age. He was bullied a bit because of his size, and sometimes I did have words with the people concerned. That put a stop to it, but we still weren't close. Unusual for twins, I guess.'

'What about his wife? Did you attend the wedding? What can you tell us about her? Is there a problem with her? Have there been any family disagreements?'

'No. The wedding all seemed a bit sudden. It surprised us all. Took place in a Registry Office. Obviously, I've met Maureen. Likes to act in her spare time, but I think that it's part of her persona. You're never quite sure who you're meeting when you're with her. I don't know what Barney sees in her. She's taller than him. Rather like that other woman at the Building Society, Stephanie. Barney had a relationship with her for a while but the manager was a bit old-fashioned and didn't approve. She was much taller than him as well. Perhaps he likes being dominated. It's a throwback to his childhood. Maybe he still needs a maternal figure in his life.'

'Do you believe that it really was the manager who finished his relationship with Stephanie Winterden? Do you know anything about her?'

'I met her in those early days. She's changed quite a bit over time. She's into martial arts now and I don't think that would interest Barney in the least. Anything rough isn't his style. Curiously, she changed her hairstyle as well. She had it cut really short, almost in a masculine style. She said that it was better for her martial arts training, but somehow, I doubt it. There's always been something odd about her. I couldn't quite work out what it was. Perhaps that contributed to the parting of the ways.'

'Do you think that she had any influence over Mr Scoular?'

'It's possible. Barney did say that she wanted to be the Branch assistant manager when he was promoted.'

Joynton thought about the conversation with James Howditch on the morning after Barnaby Scoular disappeared. All sorts of questions chased each other around her head. *What hold did Stevie have over the manager? Was it connected with their past relationship or was it something more sinister? Did she know about the mortgage problems and had she been using it as a weapon to achieve her own ambitions?*

The list of suspects was growing and yet she and Trussell were still unable to establish what was going on. *Had Scoular realised the game was up as the dodgy mortgages had come to light?* This theory was certainly reinforced by the fact that his passport was missing. And yet, there was no proof that he had left the country. *Is he in hiding somewhere, waiting for an opportunity to disappear abroad?* That would need some assistance. *Is Stevie implicated? Or maybe even his wife?* Jackie Joynton had noticed the box of menthol tear sticks which might discredit her as the distraught wife. *Was she involved in the mortgage plot?* The alternative theory was that something might have happened to him, and the absence of the passport was designed to put them off the trail. All these thoughts went through her mind as she looked at Scoular's brother.

'Thank you for coming to see us, Mr Scoular,' said Trussell, handing him one of his cards. 'If anything else should come to mind or you hear from your brother, then please let us know.'

Scoular nodded.

Jackie Joynton stood up, ready to show him out of the station. When she returned, she looked quizzically at Trussell. 'What do you think of Mr Scoular, then, Jim,' she asked. 'He seems to have added another dimension to the case.'

'He's certainly shed a bit more light on our missing manager,' he said. 'What is it that attracted the two women? More to him than meets the eye.'

Joynton nodded and then reminded Trussell that they had an appointment that afternoon at the High Weald Head Office with the CEO and the Deputy Chairman. 'I wonder if they've got any more info on the dodgy mortgages yet, Jim? Surely they must have tracked down some of the other parties involved?'

They walked back up to their office on the first floor, where they found Sprawson looking at the white board. 'There seems to be quite a few gaps here, Guv,' he volunteered. 'Where d'you reckon this is all going? There doesn't seem to be any sign of Scoular. We've covered all the possibilities. Checked all the Hospitals, Doctors' surgeries, and Clinics. There's absolutely no trace of him leaving the country, either. Perhaps he's lying low, waiting for the heat to die down before he scarpers with the money.'

'I don't think that it works quite like that, Eddie,' said Trussell. The money would probably have been transferred electronically through a series of accounts and then sent out of the country. This is a white-collar fraud, not some sort of old-fashioned blagging. It's a bit more subtle than the sort of crime you've grown up with at Brandford. It's a different world now.'

'How's that, Guv?'

'You know that bank robberies are relatively unusual these days, Eddie. Computer crimes seem to be the way forward nowadays for the criminal fraternity. Emptying peoples' bank accounts electronically is so much easier than walking into a bank with a sawn-off shotgun. No need for any getaway car. Less dangerous, too.'

'What about the restaurants around town, Eddie?' asked Jackie Joynton, changing the subject. 'If he was supposed to be having dinner the night he disappeared, then someone must have seen him. Yet no one's come forward. We'll need to recheck those. How are you getting on with the estate agents, by the way? Have you found anything about Mr Royston?'

He consulted his notebook. 'I've been getting the same response just about everywhere I've been, Sarge. He appears to have worked fairly widely for the local banks and building societies for simple valuations over the years. Most people seemed reluctant to say anything really bad about him. He seemed to be liked by the majority of the people I spoke to, but I got the general impression that he wasn't quite up to it anymore. He seemed preoccupied, lately, although, if he was worried about something, he certainly wasn't sharing it. One or two people mentioned an apparent drinking problem, but they chose their words carefully.'

'Did you pick up anything about Scoular's disappearance at any of the other building societies and banks?'

'A couple of people asked me in a fairly low-key way what was going on, Guv,' said Sprawson. 'I got the impression that there's a fair amount of speculation at the moment, but they didn't want to discuss it with the police.'

'What about the CCTV at Weaver Street? Did you see Stephanie Winterden leave the car park?'

'No, Sarge, the CCTV couldn't help.'

'Thanks, Eddie. Well done. Can you get it all written up while it's still fresh in your mind?'

22

Day 8.
Tuesday 26th February.
Woodchester.

Trussell and Joynton left the office to walk round to the High Weald head office in Bank Street. It was still quite cold but at least the rain had stopped. The High Street was busier now as they threaded their way through the shoppers rushing in all directions. There was definitely more traffic about now and the constant background noise made conversation difficult.

They arrived at the building in Bank Street that was now becoming familiar to them. The automatic doors glided open to let them through. Trussell went to the reception desk and asked the girl behind the counter for Mr McDriscoll's personal assistant, showing his warrant card.

She picked up the phone, quietly mentioned that the police had arrived and then asked them to take the lift up to the fourth floor.

When the doors opened, Mary Waterhouse was waiting for them. 'Please come this way,' she said, holding the lobby door open for them.

They walked to McDriscoll's office where he was waiting for them along with Douglas Hartman, the CEO. A third man was also there. He was of medium height, dark hair and complexion, fortyish and soberly dressed in a dark grey suit. There was a serious look about him.

McDriscoll made the introductions. 'Detective Inspector, this is Jack Adams, our head of security. He's been looking at our mortgage problems.'

Trussell nodded and introduced Jackie Joynton.

McDriscoll continued. 'Can you update these officers, please, Jack?'

'So, Mr Adams, what have you discovered so far?' asked Trussell.

'Well, Detective Inspector, I understand that the CEO and Deputy Chairman have already told you about the illegal mortgages. We have been trying to piece the story together here from the limited information available to us. We just don't have the complete paper trail. A search of the branch has yielded nothing further so far. The death of Edmund Royston, the surveyor apparently implicated in this, was unfortunate, to say the least. It isn't at all helpful to our efforts to unravel the problem.

As soon as we have the names of the other parties implicated in this matter, then, we shall share them with you, of course.'

'What about any solicitor involved in this business?'

'We haven't been able to find the individuals involved so far. A call to the Land Registry hasn't produced anything useful. They've promised to look into it and get back to us. But I expect that they're snowed under at the moment with normal business. There's a lot going on in the property market at this time. Mortgage applications are off the scale.'

'I believe that at least some of this business may have come from Brandford. What about your local people? Are they aware of your concerns?'

'We have arranged to call the three staff members from our Brandford Branch to Head Office to discuss the matter. The branch will be officially closed that day for staff training as far as the public are concerned.'

'How much have you told them so far?'

'They know nothing at all about the mortgage problems. They think that they're being called in to talk about the future of the branch – after all, it's our smallest one and its viability is suspect, now that the major new developments there have all been finished and the houses sold. Not much personal investment business in the area at the moment. There's not a lot of spare money about over there. However, the CEO and Deputy Chairman are in a better position to clarify these matters for you.'

'Have you discussed the matter with the police at Brandford yet?' asked Trussell.

'No. Should we?'

'I'd rather you didn't. As the matter started with Barnaby Scoular's disappearance being reported to us, then I think that we should control things here in Woodchester to avoid duplication of effort and any delays. If any local help is needed, then we'll arrange it.'

'As you wish, Detective Inspector.'

'Right,' said Trussell, 'moving on, Mr McDriscoll, I've a couple of requests to make.'

'They are...?'

'First of all, we'd like to look at the personnel files for Stephanie Winterden and both Maureen and Barnaby Scoular, if that's possible.'

'Staff files are confidential,' said McDriscoll. 'We might create a problem for ourselves if they're shared with anyone outside of the authorised inhouse group. The Data Protection legislation is a nightmare.'

'Well, Mr McDriscoll, I'm sure that you'll appreciate that I have a good reason for asking. I had hoped that we could all work together on this. If you're unable or unwilling to co-operate, then I'll simply get a judge to issue a court order. It may take a day or two, but it will happen and inevitably arouse public interest, which could reflect badly on the Society.'

He looked embarrassed. And indecisive. 'What's the second thing?'

'Do you have contact details for Mr Thompson, the previous branch manager? I assume that he's on your pension scheme.'

It was Hartman who got up, left the room to speak to Mary Waterhouse and then returned to his seat. 'That's organised, Detective Inspector,' he said. 'You'll have the files and Edward Thompson's details in ten minutes. Will you need to take the files away? We'll need a receipt, of course.'

'Thank you, Mr Hartman. If Detective Sergeant Joynton can borrow an office, she can skim through them. She knows what we're looking for. That should suffice. If we need to take them away, then of course, we'll give you the proper receipt for them.'

Adams opened the file in front of him. 'This selection of mortgages covers the potential redevelopment of Harbour Street and The Parade in Brandford,' he said. 'Rows of very old terraced houses built for the port workers in Victorian times. They aren't really fit for purpose in today's market. It came as no surprise that someone had been buying them up with a view to knocking them down. No problems with that. Normally, they would hope to get planning permission and then sell the houses on to another developer at a profit. After all, it's a prime location for today's apartment market as it overlooks the gentrified port area and the new marina. Unfortunately, the valuations put on them by Mr Royston seem to have been rather exaggerated. It seems that there was no need for the perpetrators to worry about the possibility of future profits. They got those from the Society immediately with the mortgage money lent to them. It's obvious now that they had no intention of pursuing the project. The aim was just to scam us, pocket the profits and disappear.'

McDriscoll looked very concerned. 'You see what this sort of information would do to the Society if it gets into the public domain before we're ready to release it?'

Mary Waterhouse tapped on the glass door at that moment. She was holding some light brown files. Hartman beckoned her to come in. 'I've got Mr Thompson's details, Mr Hartman,' she said. 'He lost his wife last year and he's now living with his daughter, a Mrs. Jenkinson. The address and phone number are in the file.'

'Thank you, Mary,' he said, as he took the files and handed them to Trussell, who in turn passed them to Joynton.

'So, could Detective Sergeant Joynton borrow an office and desk for a few minutes, please?'

'Certainly,' said Hartman. 'Have we got a spare room, Mary?'

She nodded. 'This way, Detective Sergeant,' she replied, leading the way to a room on the other side of the floor.

Trussell knew that he could leave the information gathering with Jackie Joynton. She needed to see what the files revealed about the three individuals, particularly when they first joined the Society. She should also find Stephanie Winterden's date of birth in her file and it would be interesting to see whether there were any other clues to her background. He was also still intrigued by Maureen Scoular and her past. *Was there anything in the comments made by Barnaby Scoular's brother about his choice of women?*

Trussell continued. 'As you've had no luck in tracking down the solicitors who were involved in these transactions,' he said; 'we'll have to chase the Land Registry ourselves. The case has grown beyond the disappearance of your Branch Manager. We now have a murder connected with your problems. There would have to be substantial incentives for any solicitor to get involved, because discovery would inevitably lead to criminal charges and the firm probably being struck off.'

'We'll be happy to share what information we have, Detective Inspector,' replied Adams.

McDriscoll was looking very uncomfortable. He could only think of the potential consequences for the Society and the damage to his own reputation. He was positively wringing his hands as he felt that control of the situation was slowly ebbing away from him.

Adams pulled some papers from the file in front of him. He turned to Hartman. 'If we can have these copied, Mr Hartman, perhaps they may prove useful to the Detective Inspector,' he said.

'Ask Mary to arrange for copies to be made now and put in a file for these police officers to take away with them,' said Hartman. 'We have to work together on this - we have a common interest.'

Adams left the office to speak to Mary Waterhouse to arrange for the copying of the file. As he returned, he was followed back into the room by Jackie Joynton, carrying the three personnel files.

'I think we have all we need for the moment, Mr Hartman, thank you,' she said, handing them back. 'Please arrange for the files to remain available to us in case any further information is required. It's important that our involvement with them remains confidential. Please do not discuss this even with your HR department.'

Hartman nodded. 'Of course, Detective Sergeant. Just let us know if you need anything further.'

'Copying the other documents should take about fifteen minutes,' said Adams. 'Can we offer you some tea or coffee while we're waiting for them?'

Trussell politely declined the offer and told them that he and DS Joynton would be quite happy to just wait for the copies. 'Obviously, the identity of the solicitor involved in this matter is of paramount importance now. Please let me know the moment you get that information.'

'Before you leave, Detective Inspector,' said Hartman, 'there's someone I think that you should meet. It may help you with your investigation.' He opened the door again and called across to Mary Waterhouse at her desk. 'Mary, would you ask John to spare us a minute please?'

She nodded in response, left her desk and walked around the corner. A moment later she returned, accompanied by a man in his forties, hastily pulling on his grey pinstriped suit jacket as he walked. He had dark brown thinning hair and was of average height and medium build. He did not seem fazed by this sudden summons. He came into the office where Hartman introduced him to the two detectives.

'This is John Hansworth. He was manager of our largest branch until he was promoted recently to a senior role here in our head office,' said Hartman 'We've asked John to take over the management of the Woodchester branch until such time as we have some sort of clarity about Barnaby Scoular. He has the necessary experience to get a grip of whatever is going on there at the moment and as an outsider, he won't be concerned about existing relationships in the branch.'

They shook hands.

'That will certainly make our lives easier,' said Trussell. 'We've spoken to all of the staff there on an informal basis at the police station, with the exception of Miss Winterden.'

'Has she been uncooperative?' asked Hartman.

'No, not in the least. In view of her apparent assumed responsibilities, we thought it best to leave her until such time as her absence from the branch would be less disruptive,' said Trussell.

Hartman nodded, as if in approval. Hansworth just looked thoughtful. He guessed correctly that Trussell was just telling them only what was necessary.

Now wasn't a good time to reveal details of her change of name. He wanted to discover the reason for it first. Having Hansworth at the branch would make his life so much easier in that respect. From his initial look at the man, Trussell thought instinctively that he could work with him. 'What about the future management of the branch if Scoular is unable to resume his role for any reason?' he asked.

'That's a tricky one,' said Hartman. 'On paper, James Howditch would be a logical choice, as he is suitably qualified. On the other hand, should we cause potential problems with the rest of the staff by bringing someone in from outside the branch? We might run the risk of Howditch resigning, which would be a loss to the Society.'

'We have to try to find Barnaby Scoular first,' said Trussell. 'Then we have to track down whoever was responsible for the death of Edmund Royston and follow the trail on the mortgage fraud. The two are obviously linked.'

'We plan to put John in place tomorrow,' said Hartman. 'We have already told Miss Winterden that she must post a notice that the branch will be closed tomorrow morning from 9.00 to 9.30 am for staff training. That's when we shall introduce John and tell the staff what's happening.'

'When would you like to speak to Miss Winterden, then, Detective Inspector?' asked Hansworth.

'I'll let you know when the appropriate time comes,' said Trussell.

Hansworth was not fooled by this. He looked knowingly at Trussell, but said nothing. He had already guessed that there were good reasons for the delay in speaking to her.

Mary Waterhouse tapped on the door and Hartman nodded. She came in, carrying the file of copied documents relating to the Brandford mortgages. Hartman took them and handed them to Trussell.

'Now you know as much as we do, Detective Inspector,' he said.

'We won't take up any more of your time, gentlemen,' said Trussell. 'Thank you for your assistance.' He indicated to Jackie that it was time to get back to the station. That would give him a chance to see what she had found in the personnel files.

23

Day 8.
Tuesday 26th February.
Woodchester.

As they walked out of the building through the automatic doors, Trussell looked enquiringly at Joynton.

'Well. What did the personnel files tell you, Jackie?'

'I've written everything down, but as you'd expect, Jim, Stephanie Winterden's file confirmed her place and date of birth and exactly when she joined the Society. Born and bred in Brandford. It also gave her current address. A rather smart one. It's an apartment in one of the new developments just outside town. Breckenridge Tower in Whitford, it's called. Do you know it? A bit above her pay grade, I would've thought.'

'That's interesting. I wonder how she affords it? It might be worth looking into that. A call to the Land Registry might be useful. It'll tell us who owns it, and whether there's a mortgage on it. That is, unless she shares it with someone, of course. I just wonder whether it's connected in any way with her relationship with Barnaby Scoular. A lot's being made of her apparent assumption of the assistant manager's job. Does she still have some sort of hold over Mr Scoular? I wonder how much he's told his wife about his previous relationship with Stevie?'

'Some sort of blackmail, you mean, Jim?'

'The thought had crossed my mind. Was there anything else of note?'

'Her previous job was in the offices of a local engineering company here in Woodchester. She started there straight from school and worked in their accounts department.'

'What about education?'

'Surprise, surprise! She attended Brandford High School and seems to have done reasonably well, if her list of GCSEs is correct. She left at sixteen. Lists her hobbies and interests as martial arts and keep fit.'

'What about references when she applied to join the Society? I can't imagine they'd take anyone without looking into them?'

'All supplied and checked by the Society at the time, Jim. I've made a note of the source, although it's ten years down the road. The individual may not be around now.'

Another thought occurred to Trussell. 'Did she nominate anyone as next of kin? Banks and Building Societies would need that sort of information for pension funds and the life insurance that usually come with them.'

'Yes, she did. I've got the details written down. Someone in Brandford. A man.'

'No mention of her mother, then?'

'Apparently not.'

'OK. What about Mr and Mrs Scoular?'

'Mr Scoular joined the Society straight from school in a very junior capacity. He attended the old Woodchester Comprehensive. He must have been in the A-Stream, because he came away with a very commendable bunch of GCSEs. No wonder they took him on. I read through his old annual appraisals and he appears to have performed quite well since joining the High Weald. His annual appraisals all seemed to be very satisfactory in terms of his work performances. There's no mention of his private life or the manager telling him to stop seeing Miss Winterden. They didn't seem to have too many reservations about him stepping up to take the manager's position when the previous incumbent retired. In fact, Mr Scoular got quite a glowing recommendation for promotion.'

'I presume that he lists Maureen Scoular as his next of kin?'

'Yes. He changed his expression of wish, as they call it, when he got married. Previously anything would have gone to his parents. I've noted their details as well. The address is the same as that given by his brother.'

'Lastly, what about Maureen?'

'Everything tallies with what we've learnt about her. We know where she was born and when and her early life in a home was documented as well. Her marriage is noted, of course.'

'What about her insurance and pension details? I assume Barnaby Scoular is the beneficiary?'

'Correct. But here's the interesting part. Before her marriage, she had nominated one Alexander Peterson! She changed it just over two years ago.'

'What about Thompson's contact details?'

'I've got those. Why do you need them, Jim? He's been retired for quite a while. He won't have been aware of today's mortgage problems, surely?'

'I'm more interested in what he might be able to tell us about Scoular's relationship with Stevie Winterden and why it stopped. I'll call him shortly to arrange a meeting.'

Trussell's intuition again, thought Jackie.

By now, they had reached the police station entrance.

'In view of the Brandford connections, Jackie,' said Trussell, as they walked up the stairs to CID Office, 'I think that this information should stay locked away as part of the mind maps collection. I'm still uneasy about Fast Eddie and who he might still know and contact back in Brandford.'

Trussell sat at his desk, and, taking Thompson's details, picked up the phone. He tapped in the number and when the call was answered, asked to speak to Mr Edward Thompson.

'I'm sorry, he's not here at the moment,' said a woman's voice. 'I'm afraid he's on holiday. Who's calling? Can I take a message for him?'

'Am I speaking to his daughter, Mrs Jenkinson?' asked Trussell.

'Yes. Who is that?'

'My name is Trussell,' he began. 'I don't want to alarm you. I'm a Detective Inspector with Kent Police.'

There was a gasp at the other end of the line. 'What's wrong? Why do you need to speak to my father?'

'There's nothing for you or your father to be concerned about. I just need to ask him a couple of questions about his time at the High Weald in Woodchester. He may have some information which might be helpful to us with our current enquiries.'

'Is it anything to do with the manager's disappearance? Dad read about it in the papers. He was shocked by the whole thing.'

'When will he be available?'

'Unfortunately, he's just left on a long cruise. He'll be away for four weeks. He's due home on the Fourteenth of March. We lost my mother last year and the family thought that it would be good idea for dad to get away. We finally persuaded him to do something. Meet more people. See new places.'

Trussell was disappointed but didn't let it show.

'Thank you, Mrs Jenkinson. I'll make a diary note to contact your father on the Fifteenth, if that's convenient. I would reiterate that there's absolutely no reason for your family to be concerned. It may just be that Mr Thompson has some information that could assist us. Thanks again. Bye.'

He hung up.

'Seems that we'll have to wait for that one, Jackie,' he said, as he made the entry in his diary.

24

Day 9.
Wednesday 27th February.
Woodchester.

It had now been over a week since Barnaby Scoular disappeared. The search had drawn a complete blank. Nobody had seen or heard anything of him. They had trawled the restaurants and eating places in Woodchester, but no one remembered seeing him. His photograph had been widely circulated and shown on local television, but to no avail. His wife, Maureen, had confirmed that her husband had always kept his passport locked in his desk drawer in the office. Now it was missing. With the looming question of the fraudulent mortgage advances, everything pointed to his disappearance being planned.

Questions were already being asked in the Press. Had he been involved in illegal activities? Speculation was rife and it made for a very uncomfortable time at the High Weald Building Society. Phillip McDriscoll had been rather circumspect in his press releases. Some reporters had found him evasive. Now, some of the bigger building societies were beginning to look at the High Weald in a predatory way. The vultures were circling.

Trussell had used his overworked team resources to organise checks on airport, ferry and dock records, but the searches had not revealed any trace of Scoular. Now, his wife was preparing to make a public appeal for information. A press conference had been set up by the police and Trussell would need to be there. A local hall had been booked. A long table was in position at the front with four chairs behind it. The microphones were ready. The hall was full. The tension was palpable.

A television camera and crew from BBC Southeast were there to cover the event. Their regular reporter was just speaking to the camera when Maureen Scoular walked in, flanked by Trussell and Joynton, and accompanied by an officer from the Police Public Relations team. She was wearing a plain brown dress and had tried to tidy her hair and apply some makeup, but this could not change the impression of a deeply unhappy woman. She dabbed continually at her eyes with a tissue. The four sat down at the table and the room went quiet. There was an air of expectation.

The Public Relations officer opened the proceedings and introduced everyone and then Trussell spoke. 'As you are all aware now, the manager of the local branch of the High Weald Building Society here in Woodchester, Barnaby Scoular, has gone missing. He went out to keep a dinner engagement here in the town on the evening of Monday Eighteenth of February and has not been seen since. His wife, Mrs Maureen Scoular, would now like to make a public appeal for information.'

He nodded at her. She had done her best to be strong, but the strain was evident in her face, and, particularly, in her eyes. There were dark circles under them, which seemed to bear testimony to her many sleepless nights since her husband had vanished.

She cleared her throat and began nervously. 'My husband, Barney, has just disappeared,' she said, dabbing at her eyes with a handkerchief. 'I miss him terribly and I want him back. If he can hear this, please, Barney, get in touch and let me know that you're OK. If there is anyone with any information, then please contact the police and share it with them. Someone must have seen him or know where he is. I beg whoever was with him on the evening he disappeared to get in touch. Someone must know something.' With that, her brave front seemed to collapse and she was reduced to tears, sobbing loudly. Jackie Joynton put a reassuring arm around her shoulders, while Trussell, trying to divert attention away, picked up the theme again.

'There have been rumours circulating, particularly in the Press, about certain issues at the High Weald Building Society which have been linked to Mr Scoular's disappearance. I can state that, at this time, there has been nothing to link Mr Scoular positively with this, and the police are treating him solely as a missing person at this time. It is too early for us to draw any conclusions about these matters. In the meantime, our efforts to find him are continuing. I would repeat Mrs Scoular's request for any information. The police hotline number is on the wall behind me and if anyone knows anything, then I would urge them to get in touch as soon as possible.'

The Police PR man now stepped in. 'We aren't taking any questions today. We're asking for information, not giving it out,' he said, in response to one persistent reporter. 'When we've something definite to share there'll be another press conference.'

With that, the meeting was closed and the four stood up and left the table. When Maureen Scoular had gone home, Trussell felt that he had to ask Jackie the one question that had been bothering him. 'Did you see her use any menthol tear sticks, Jackie?'

'No, Jim, I didn't, but she could have concealed them in the handkerchief she was using to dab her eyes.'

25

Day 10.
Thursday 28th February.
The CID Office. Woodchester Police Station.

'Yesssss!' exclaimed Jackie Joynton. She punched the air as she stared at her computer screen. Her voice was a mixture of excitement and relief. 'I've found it at last.'

Trussell looked askance at this unusual outburst by his Detective Sergeant.

'It's Stephanie Winterden's change of name by Deed Poll. It was eleven years ago, a few months before she joined the Building Society.'

'Come on, share it with me,' said Trussell. 'What was her previous name? What was so bad about it that she needed to change it?'

'It was Jessica Ann Flimwell.'

'An unusual name, but not disastrous' said Trussell. 'I wonder what she found so objectionable about it, that she needed to change it as an adult. Perhaps there were family problems. Connections she wanted to forget. There could be all sorts of reasons. So, our next move is to get hold of her original birth certificate. Maybe that will provide a clue. The General Register Office should be able to help us. You'll find them online, Jackie. Get onto them and ask for a copy. Tell them it's urgent.'

Joynton returned to her screen and brought up the GRO site, scribbled down a few details and reached for the phone. She tapped in the number and then listened for a moment. She made notes on a pad in front of her, hung up and went back to her keyboard. She moved the mouse around, clicked it a couple of times, and scrolled the screen downwards. 'Damn,' she said. 'You wouldn't believe it. There are three girls born in the first quarter of that year with the same name. How do I find the right one?'

Trussell thought for a moment. 'Stevie has an East Kent accent. We look for a Brandford connection. You know her date of birth. You'll just have to order all three birth certificates and hope that the right one is among them. You can't get the info over the phone. You'll just have to stress the urgency to the GRO.'

Five minutes later, Jackie closed the website and sat back in her chair, heaving a sigh of relief. 'That's done, then,' she said. 'I've ordered all three. Not cheap, but they'll be here within a few days.'

'I suppose you'll expect me to approve your expenses this month, then, Sergeant?' said Trussell, straight-faced, as he watched Jackie slip her credit card back into her bag.

'If you want to solve the murder and the other crimes, Guv, then definitely,' was the response. 'Otherwise, the information is all mine until I'm reimbursed!'

'Remember that withholding evidence is an arrestable offence, Sergeant' said Trussell. 'Not to mention misconduct in public office.'

Joynton poked her tongue out at him.

'Insubordination as well,' laughed Trussell.

She ignored him.

'Moving on,' said Trussell, 'Hansworth has been in place down the road at the High Weald as the temporary manager for a couple of days now Jackie. I think it's time that we talked to Stevie Winterden.'

Joynton agreed. 'She's certainly had time to wonder why we haven't called her in yet, Jim.'

'We've let her stew for long enough, now. Let's see what she has to say about life in general in the branch and Mr Scoular's disappearance in particular.'

Trussell picked up the phone and called the Society's number. 'Mr Hansworth, please,' he said when the phone was answered. 'Sounded like Susie Albright,' he told Jackie. 'I wonder how the new temporary regime is going down in the High Street branch.'

He heard Hansworth pick up the phone. 'Good morning, Mr Hansworth, it's DI Trussell speaking. You'll recall that when we met, I mentioned that we would still like to talk to Miss Winterden at some stage. We'd just like an off-the-record chat, the same as the others. I wonder whether you can spare her this morning?'

'Yes, of course, Detective Inspector. Shall we say, half an hour's time?'

'Thank you, Mr Hansworth. Please stress to Miss Winterden that this is purely voluntary. It's just an informal chat about Mr Scoular's disappearance. Just ask her to call at the main desk and we'll meet her there.' He replaced the phone.

Jackie Joynton looked at him. 'How do you want to play it, Jim?' she asked. 'Will you ask her outright about her change of name? What she knows about the identity of her father?'

'No. We'll let her do the talking. We'll just offer her a question to start with. See where the conversation takes us. Can you call the front desk and reserve one of the interview rooms, please?'

'Of course,' she said, reaching for the phone. 'I just wonder if she'll be prepared to talk about her Brandford connections, or whether we'll have to lead the witness on that one. Jim?'

'Right, Greeno, we'll leave you to hold the fort while Jackie and I talk to Miss Winterden. Call me if anything dramatic happens while we're downstairs with her.'

Mark Green nodded and returned to his keyboard. He needed to update the file while Fast Eddie was back at Supercheap continuing his enquiries into the thefts from their warehouse, armed with the information about some of the employees. His research into the backgrounds of the employees there had been illuminating. There were some with form and the management had not picked it up. There was a serious conversation to be held with the manager about apparent slackness in their vetting of potential employees.

26

Day 10.
Thursday 28th February.
Woodchester Police Station

Trussell and Joynton awaited Stephanie Winterden's arrival in the interview room. They had only been there a couple of minutes when the desk sergeant tapped on the door and showed her in. She was her usual composed self; exactly the same as the first time they'd seen her on the day after Barnaby Scoular had disappeared. Her eyes gave nothing away.

'Please sit down, Miss Winterden,' said Trussell, indicating the chair on the other side of the table. 'Thank you for sparing the time to help us. I would stress that this is just an informal opportunity to see whether you can throw any further light on Mr Scoular's disappearance.'

'I'm not sure that I can assist you, Detective Inspector,' she said in that flat, emotionless voice. 'Barney didn't tell me about his apparent dinner arrangements.'

'Let's talk about the High Weald's relationship with Tillworth and Co,' said Trussell. 'I understand that your branch transacted quite a bit of mortgage business through them.'

'That's right, although we do get a lot of referrals from most of the other estate agents in town.'

'How well do you know Arthur Tillworth?'

'Only from the mortgage business he brought to us from their purchasers. No better than any of the other local estate agents.'

'I understand that you visited the estate agency fairly frequently?'

'No more than some of the other estate agents in town who sent clients to us for mortgage advice.'

'Wouldn't that have been James Howditch's responsibility, rather than yours? Doesn't he deal with most mortgages, apart from those occasions when the manager becomes involved?'

'He was certainly responsible for vetting and granting most mortgage applications. But I do the PR bit. Mr. Scoular thought that it was important to have a regular presence with the local agents to ensure that we remained their first port of call for any new business.' Her eyes gazed steadily at him as she spoke, unflinching, not blinking. Her voice was quietly authoritative. She was someone totally in control of herself. She exuded self-confidence.

Trussell needed a way to catch her off balance. She seemed as unflappable as she had described Barnaby Scoular to be. 'How are things at the branch now, Miss Winterden. Has life settled back to normal?'

'What passes for normal, I guess. It's not the same without Barney there.'

'Has the arrival of Mr Hansworth changed the dynamics? What is your role now?'

'It's the same as ever. I still hold the set of keys to the office and share the till duties with Maureen and Janet.'

Trussell looked at Jackie.

'Tell me, Miss Winterden,' she began, 'what caused the breakdown of your relationship with Mr Scoular. Did the previous manager demand that you stop seeing one another?'

'I don't think that's any of your business,' Stevie replied sharply.

'And what caused a rift between yourself and Maureen Scoular? I understand that you were quite good friends when she first arrived at the branch.'

'I'm sorry. I don't see the relevance of any of this to Mr Scoular's disappearance,' she retorted.

'Let us be the judge of that, Miss Winterden,' said Trussell. 'We have our reasons for asking.'

The mask slipped for a moment. 'It's personal,' she snapped.

'Was it over Barnaby Scoular? When did Maureen Scoular start dating him? Was this the reason why you fell out?'

'No. We just had different views on life in general. As we were opposites, there didn't seem any future in any sort of close friendship. As far as I'm concerned, she's just another work colleague. My time with Barney was just an interlude, a diversion. It wasn't serious, as far as I was concerned. He was a sad person. He didn't want a girlfriend. He needed a second mother with benefits. Something to do with his upbringing, I guess. Anyway, I got bored with it.'

'You used him to gain more influence in the branch?'

'Your words, not mine.'

'So how did you end the relationship?'

'It was quite simple. The right word in the manager's ear and he did the necessary. Mr Thompson was old-fashioned and told Barney that it wasn't good for staff relations in the office. I had to pretend to Barney that I was hurt by the manager's involvement as well, but had to accept it. That seemed to satisfy him – he didn't suspect a thing, so we carried on our normal professional relationship after that.'

Trussell tried another tack. 'Perhaps you'd care to tell us why you changed your name eleven years ago? What was there about the name Jessica Ann Flimwell that you didn't like?'

This almost caught her off guard but she quickly regained her composure. 'It's nothing to do with you. It was all perfectly legal. I got tired of the old one.'

'Do you know the identity of your father? If not, perhaps we can help you. It's amazing what DNA can tell us these days.'

She looked annoyed. 'If you must know, my mother was abandoned by the man who made her pregnant, when she was sixteen.'

'Do you know his identity?'

'Yes, my mother told me later. That helped with my choice of name when I changed it. I wanted something which was the complete opposite, to erase him from my identity and my life. His name was Sommer or something like that. It sounded German to me. That's why I chose the name Winterden. I saw it in a book somewhere and thought that it would be ideal. I just liked the name Stephanie and took that for my new identity. I wanted to make something of myself and this was the best way to erase the past.'

Trussell looked at Joynton and raised an eyebrow. *Is she holding out on us? Sommer is Summer in English. Could the actual name have been Summerton?* It was one that he knew only too well from his days at Brandford and her mother had come from the town. If it was the man he was thinking of, then that would involve Fast Eddie. As far as Trussell could remember, Jack Summerton had been Sprawson's informant in those early days.

'Did you have any contact with your father while you were growing up?'

'No. He just deserted my mother when he heard that she was pregnant.'

'Your mother married, though. How did you get on with your stepfather?'

'I had a series of *stepfathers* or *uncles* when I was growing up until Colin Tompkins appeared, although he didn't stick around for too long after the wedding.'

'Were there any other children?'

'I'd rather not discuss my mother's life. It was hard enough growing up in her households.'

'What is your mother doing now? Are you in contact with her?'

'Not often. We are completely different. We have nothing in common now. As I've already told you, I didn't have a happy life growing up. My mother was quite selfish. There seemed to be a succession of men in her life. She works in a factory unit in Brandford. I'm not sure exactly what she does. All I know is that she's screwed up her life and I want no part of it now. I'm concentrating on my own life and my martial arts and fitness. It takes up most of my spare time. I'm determined to make something of myself.'

'As you seem to visit Tillworth on a fairly regular basis, what can you tell us about his Brandford connections? I understand that there was a significant amount of mortgage business coming from that area.'

'Nothing. I was not involved in those applications. It's rather unusual that they've bypassed James as well. Barney did mention that there were some issues with mortgages that he was trying to address, but never shared the details with me.'

'So, you can't throw any light on Mr Scoular's disappearance, then? You didn't see him after you left the office on that last day?'

'No,' she said rather sharply.

'We noticed from the CCTV that evening that you walked in the opposite direction to everyone else when you left. Where were you going?'

'To the Weaver Street car park to collect my car, as usual.'

'Where did you go that evening?'

'Let's see... it was a Monday. I would have been going to the gym.'

'Would anyone have seen you there?'

'Quite possibly. The gym is always busy after working hours. It's difficult to remember that particular evening. There was nothing unusual about it. After all, Barney hadn't gone missing at that moment. It was a couple of weeks ago. I'm a regular there. I go there several times a week.'

'Tell me, Miss Winterden, do you own a bicycle?' asked Trussell. 'Quite useful for maintaining fitness, I would have thought. Especially as that's so important to you.'

I wonder where Jim is going with this? thought Jackie.

'I don't have any room for a bike in my flat,' said Stevie. 'I can get that sort of workout on the exercise bikes at the gym. I've already told you that I go there several times a week. Besides, cycling is getting more dangerous on the roads these days. There always seem to be accidents involving cyclists.'

'I see,' said Trussell. 'Is there anything else you can add that might assist us in our search for Mr Scoular? He didn't offer any hints?'

'None at all. I'm afraid there's nothing more I can tell you.'

'Thank you, Miss Winterden. We won't take up any more of your valuable time. I'm sure that you're needed back at the branch. We appreciate your time and assistance,' said Trussell, rising from his chair to indicate that the interview was over.

Stevie stood up from her chair, nodded and opened the door to leave. 'You know where to find me if you need anything else,' she added as a parting shot as she walked out of the interview room.

'A very self-confident lady,' said Jackie.

'I wonder,' said Trussell, thinking back to that first day when he had started on his mind map.

27

Day 11.
Friday 1st March. 9.00 am.
Woodchester Police Station.

Jackie Joynton sat down at her desk and looked at the buff coloured official foolscap envelope addressed to her, lying there awaiting her arrival. Puzzled, she turned it over in her hands and then saw the General Record Office return address printed on the back. The birth certificates had arrived at last.

She took a paper knife out of her drawer, carefully slit the back of the envelope and took out the three certificates. The first had the correct name, Jessica Ann Flimwell, but the date of birth was wrong and the place of birth was questionable – Wolverhampton. The second carried the same name, but again, a different date of birth and the place of registration was Newcastle.

That left the third certificate as the only possibility.

She unfolded it, conscious of the moment, holding her breath, scarcely able to take in the details. Yes, the date of birth matched that of Stephanie Winterden. The place of birth was given as Brandford General Hospital. She looked along the columns... no father's name was mentioned. The mother's name was given as Shirley Ann Flimwell, occupation, waitress. Address of mother, 24, Tyler Lane. Brandford. This would give them something to work with. They would need to track down Shirley Ann Flimwell to see if she could shed any light on her daughter's need to change her name. *What's happened to the mother in the intervening thirty odd years? When had she married?* Their next job would be to find the answers to those questions.

She showed the certificate to Trussell. 'I reckon this must be the right one, Jim. It all fits.'

He looked at it closely and agreed that the next job was to try to trace the mother. He immediate concern was that there was yet another connection with Brandford. 'The usual rules apply, Jackie,' he said. 'This has to stay on the mind maps pad at the moment. We have to keep this information away from Fast Eddie.'

'I agree,' she replied. 'What's the next step?'

'I'm afraid that you'll have to go back to the GRO website to see if you can find any trace of Shirley's marriage to Mr Tompkins. It might be helpful if we could find him to see whether he can add to the story. Start searching after the date that the baby was born, although the marriage must have taken place quite a bit later. I'm afraid there's nothing in our budget to hire a professional genealogist, Jackie. Who knows, you might even get a taste for this sort of research! Build your own family tree.'

'You'll be lucky,' she said, making a face at Trussell, which suggested that she was not about to take up a new hobby.

'I reckon that Brandford is a pretty safe bet for any marriage location, as we know Stevie came from the area. We need to track down the mother. It may give us some sort of confirmation as to why Stevie decided to change her name. If we find her, we have to hope Shirley will be prepared to confirm the father's identity.'

28

Day 14.
Monday 4th March.
CID Office, Woodchester Police Station.

'Uniformed on the phone,' said Jackie, holding the receiver as she spoke to Trussell. 'They've just been called to a suspicious death. Looks like a suicide, but they want a separate opinion.'

'Where is it?'

'Somerville Avenue in Brackenden. Neighbours called it in. When the postman called about nine o'clock this morning, he heard a car engine running in the garage behind a closed door. He mentioned it to the neighbours who took a look and then dialled 999 straight away. When uniformed arrived, they couldn't get any answer from the house and decided to force the garage door. They could hear the engine still running and found a hose pipe pumping exhaust fumes into the car. They could see someone inside and managed to get the car door open and turn the engine off. The paramedics were called but it was too late. The man was dead.'

'Have they identified the individual?'

'Magnus Culverton, the homeowner. He's a local solicitor. He's the sole partner in Fotherby and Company in Woodchester.'

'Are there any relatives?'

'No. Apparently he lives alone. He was divorced a long time ago.'

'Tell uniformed not to disturb the scene any further. Say we'll be there in fifteen minutes. We'll probably have to call in CSI. We seem to be having a run of these 'accidents' at the moment.'

**

Trussell and Joynton arrived in Somerville Avenue and had no problem finding the house. There were two marked police cars outside and an ambulance. A crowd had begun to gather on the pavement opposite.

Somerville Avenue was one of the more exclusive roads in the area, tree-lined with large detached houses, built mainly in the 1920's on substantial plots, each set back from the road with a large front garden. Culverton's house was screened from the road by trees and bushes. No one would have noticed anything if the postman hadn't called with a couple of letters.

As they walked up the neatly paved drive, they were approached by a uniformed constable. Trussell showed his warrant card and identified them both.

'It's this way, Sir,' said the officer, pointing in the direction of the garage, with its red-painted wooden doors wide open. He lifted the police incident tape so that Trussell and Joynton could duck underneath. One of the doors bore signs of forced entry and the smell of exhaust fumes still hung heavily in the air. They could see the car inside through the blue smoky haze, with the driver's door open. A man wearing a dark grey suit was slumped in the front seat, eyes staring. Almost as if he had suffered a shock. The two paramedics from the ambulance were standing outside the garage, chatting to another police officer. They looked in Trussell's direction.

'No doubt about him being dead, then?' asked Trussell.

They both shook their heads.

'Thanks,' said Trussell. 'No point in you hanging around any longer. We'll wait for the police doctor and forensics and then we'll arrange for the body to be moved. There'll have to be a post-mortem, of course.'

'I wonder who will benefit from this?' asked Jackie. 'Houses on this road don't come cheap.'

'His firm, Fotherby and Co will have to be told as soon as possible. I wonder whether he left a will? Maybe they have it on file, if he wrote one,' said Trussell. 'We'll make that our first priority as soon as we can.'

Another car pulled onto the drive. A middle-aged man with grey receding hair and dark-framed glasses, wearing a navy blue suit, got out and walked towards them, carrying a small bag.

'It's the doc,' said Jackie. They greeted him and indicated the body in the car. He put on a pair of blue plastic gloves to carry out a quick examination. He looked puzzled for a moment and then lifted the head and looked again.

'Well, DI Trussell, I can confirm that he is dead and I'll write out the certificate,' he said. 'But there's something strange going on here. I'll be interested to hear what the pathologist has to say after the post-mortem.'

'What do you mean?'

'Well, he was in a car filled with exhaust fumes which would point to suicide. But I'm not convinced.'

'Why? What makes you unsure?'

'I think that he was dead before the fumes reached him. Did you notice his facial expression? He looked surprised. I've examined his eyes and his skin hasn't taken on the cherry-red colour usually seen in these cases. It's grey. There's no sign of retinal haemorrhage which you'd expect to see with carbon monoxide poisoning. A post-mortem should show if he had any sign of it in his lungs.'

'If that's the case, then, Doctor, what do you think killed him?'

'That's anyone's guess at this point. I think that'll be your problem. Hopefully the pathologist will have some ideas about exactly what happened.'

Trussell asked Jackie to call the Crime Scene Investigation team. She took out her phone, consulted the directory and tapped in the number.

'They'll be here in half an hour, Jim.'

'It might be worth using the time while we're waiting to talk to the neighbours, Jackie. You start with the people who spoke to the postman, and I'll talk to the people on the other side.'

29

Day 14.
Monday 4th March.
Brackenden. The same afternoon.

The CSI team arrived within the promised half hour, and Trussell greeted the team leader.

'Afternoon, Maurice. We've got a death that looks for all the world like a suicide, but the doc isn't happy. He reckons the man was dead before he went into the car and the engine was started. We'll hang around for a while. Let me know if you notice anything interesting, will you?'

He watched the team collect their equipment and suit up before going into the garage to examine the body and the car and to take photographs. Then Trussell noticed that they were concentrating on the garage floor. More photographs.

Then the team leader called Trussell. 'Get yourselves some coveralls, Jim. There's something you need to see.'

'What have you found, Maurice?'

'Come and look.'

Trussell and Joynton grabbed spare coveralls and plastic shoes and then, suited up, they walked through the garage to where the CSI team had gathered by the side door.

'Unfortunately, there's been a fair amount of movement and crime scene contamination around the car and the garage doors by the people who attended first,' said Maurice. 'Not unreasonable, as they thought that it was a suspected suicide and perhaps still a chance of saving the poor chap. They couldn't have known that it would become a crime scene. Fortunately, most of the activity was confined to those immediate areas.'

He pointed at the dusty floor of the garage and to some long scrape marks that started outside the garage and tracked through the side doorway almost to the driver's side of the car. 'They start at the side door of the house and there are similar marks in the kitchen,' said Maurice. 'They match the backs of the deceased's shoes. They're badly scraped. The concrete floor is quite abrasive in that respect. My guess is that he was killed in the kitchen or somewhere else in the house and dragged out here to the car. As the main garage doors were closed, no one outside would have seen it. I think someone probably put their hands under his arms to lift him and dragged him backwards out here.'

'Anything else in the kitchen?' asked Trussell.

'No. Nothing. Complete lack of fingerprints on the door handles. No signs of anything. Everything's been wiped clean. Even the car ignition key is clear apart from a smudged print from one of the police officers who turned the ignition off. You've got a meticulous suspect here, Jim.'

'Another one? Just like Mr Royston,' said Jackie Joynton.

'Not even a sign of a struggle?' asked Trussell. 'Culverton must have let the killer into the house if there's no sign of forced entry.'

'We're checking for that now.'

'Do you think that there's a possibility that Culverton knew his killer, then?' asked Joynton.

'That's a possibility that we can't ignore.' Trussell looked thoughtful. 'We'll wait until the team have finished their checks. Then we'll have to start looking ourselves for anything that might tie him in with our other enquiries. It looks more than coincidental. We're looking for a solicitor who might be part of a mortgage fraud, and suddenly one turns up dead.'

'Something else just occurred to me, Jim,' said Jackie. 'When Greeno spoke to the girl at Tillworth's, she mentioned that there was a regular visitor to the shop. She described the man as in his mid-forties, smartly dressed and having a name something like Marcus. I wonder if it was Magnus Culverton. The name's pretty close.'

'You could be right. We'll have to get a picture of him and show her. It would be better if we could find one taken recently rather than something the CSI have taken today. Don't want to upset the poor girl with a picture of a dead man. She's had enough trauma already. It looks increasingly like Mr Tillworth has a lot of explaining to do.'

'We'll look around the house and see what we can find. I suppose there's always a chance that Fotherby and Co might have a photo in their offices. We'll have to ask.'

Their work completed, the CSI team collected their equipment together and left, promising Trussell a report within two days. The usual discreet black private ambulance with dark side windows collected the body and took it away to the mortuary where it would await a post-mortem by a Home Office registered pathologist. The house and garage had already been taped off and secured as a crime scene and a couple of PCSOs had been summoned to guard it. They stood there, arms folded, impassive, as a curious crowd looked on. The sound of their voices carried across the road. Speculation was rife.

Trussell and Joynton had already spoken to the neighbours but their conversations had yielded little worthwhile information. Magnus Culverton seemed to be a quiet professional man who kept himself to himself. Most people couldn't recall him having any regular visitors, and he didn't seem to have any close relations. However, one elderly neighbour living almost opposite remembered seeing someone on a mountain bike call there quite early that morning. She thought that it was just some sort of delivery. Maybe a newspaper. Her memory was hazy but she thought that the rider was wearing a dark blue jacket or anorak with the hood up and jeans. She hadn't been sure that she could describe the individual though. Just a tall figure on a bike.

Trussell and Joynton returned to the Skoda and set off back to Woodchester. Trussell was still thinking about the figure on the mountain bike. *Could it be the same person seen leaving the Oatleys' house after Edmund Royston was killed?*

'The doctor seemed to think that Culverton's death was suspicious, then,' Joynton said. 'D'you think that we might have stumbled on the solicitor implicated in the mortgage fraud?'

'It's beginning to look that way.'

'It does seem a bit coincidental that another body's turned up. The deeper we get into this, the more likely it seemed that a solicitor would turn up dead. After all, there's been no sign of the Building Society manager who seems to have advanced the mortgage money and the surveyor who agreed the valuations has met an apparent accident. Someone's one step ahead of us each time.'

'I still think that Tillworth is the key to all of this, but we can't just pull him in on suspicion without any proof. Any lawyer would have him out of the door in a flash and we'd probably have a lawsuit on our hands.'

'So, what's the next step, then, Jim?'

'I think a visit to Fotherby and Co. First of all, we have to break the news to them about Culverton's death, and that will no doubt, produce a reaction that might be helpful. We shall see.'

Fifteen minutes later, they pulled into Trussell's allocated parking space at Woodchester Police Station.

30

Day 14.
Monday 4th March.
Woodchester.

'We'll walk straight down to the solicitor's office now,' said Trussell, 'so that we can tell them about Culverton's unfortunate demise. We shan't mention the manner of his death, of course. If anyone asks, we'll just tell them that we have to wait for the results of the post-mortem,'

They soon found the address in the older part of town, tucked away in a small cobbled square down a narrow lane off the High Street. The trees in each corner obviously attracted birds, because they could hear them calling to one another. The silence after the noisy High Street was almost eerie. It was like entering a time warp: a haven of peace away from the hustle and bustle of the traffic in the High Street. The buildings were probably Victorian and didn't look as though they had had much attention since that time. It was very evocative. Trussell, with his interest in history, could visualise Victorian gentlemen in their frock coats and tall hats, gold-headed canes in hand, walking to their places of business.

'Number two. There it is,' said Jackie. A small brass plaque on the wall, tarnished with age, was etched with the name - Fotherby and Co. - although it was barely legible. Old green paint was peeling from the door and window frames. The building showed years of neglect.

Trussell pressed the doorbell and was surprised to hear it actually work.

The door was opened by a middle-aged woman, shabbily dressed in a long faded grey skirt with a well-worn red cardigan. Her grey hair was piled up in a bun on the top of her head. Her appearance added to the Victorian impression. 'Can I help you? Do you have an appointment?'

Trussell introduced himself and showed his warrant card.

'I'm afraid that Mr Culverton, the managing partner, isn't here at the moment,' said the woman.

'I'd like to speak to whoever's in charge in his absence,' said Trussell, offering her one of his cards.

'You'd better come in, officer. I'll see if Mr James, the Chief Clerk, is available.' She indicated a small dimly lit room on the left and asked them to wait. It contained four rickety wooden chairs arranged around a small circular table holding a few magazines of indeterminate vintage. The drab decor matched the furniture. A couple of faded prints hung on the wall.

A musty smell pervaded the place. It didn't even appear to have been cleaned recently. There was a layer of dust on the table.

'A bit Dickensian, to say the least,' said Jackie. 'I wonder when the cleaner was last here. I certainly didn't expect to find a Health and Safety issue at a solicitor's office.'

The door opened and an elderly man with thinning white hair and a slight stoop walked in. He was wearing an old grey, pin-striped suit with a maroon tie that had seen better days and his white shirt had a slightly frayed collar. He peered at them through a pair of glasses with very thick lenses as he looked at Trussell's card in his left hand.

'Good afternoon, Detective Inspector. My name is Godfrey James. How may I help you?' he asked in a very soft voice, full of old world civility. It suited him.

'Mr James, I have to tell you that Mr Magnus Culverton was found dead at his home today. I'm making enquiries into the matter and need to know something about him.'

Mr James was thunderstruck. 'What happened? Was it a heart attack or something? I know that he has been under a great deal of stress recently.'

'Do you know what might have been the reason for that stress?'

'It's no secret that the business is not doing well. It was in decline when old Mr Fotherby was the managing partner. We had hoped that Mr Culverton might have been able to change things when he took over, but that doesn't seem to have happened. The firm is a very old one and unfortunately the clients who have been with us for many years have been slowly dying off. After we've dealt with their estates, then that's the end of the relationship. We don't seem to be able to attract many new clients apart from a substantial amount of conveyancing that Mr Culverton has brought in. He seems to have a good working relationship with Tillworth and Co. in the High Street.'

Trussell looked across at Jackie at the mention of Tillworth's name and she raised an eyebrow. She had been busy taking notes and had picked up on it. Someone else with links to Tillworth was dead.

'On the subject of wills, Mr James, do you know whether Mr Culverton has left one? I understand that he was divorced a long time ago. Are there any living relatives? Is there anyone we should contact?' asked Trussell.

'Mr Culverton had no close relatives,' said Mr James. 'He was divorced some years ago and I understand that there were no children. His will is held here in our vault.'

'So, what can you tell me about his will?' asked Trussell. 'What will happen to his estate? I presume that he owned the house in Brackenden?'

'Yes, he did. But I happen to know that there was a substantial mortgage outstanding on it. Through the High Weald Building Society, I believe.'

'Even so, there must be significant amount of equity in the house. The road must be one of the most expensive in the area. Who benefits from all of this? Who's his executor?'

'Between you and I, and I don't want to speak out of turn, Detective Inspector, I doubt whether there will be much left after all the expenses are settled. Mr Culverton did have a penchant for the finer things in life. And, unless he had some other outside source of income, he certainly wasn't able to balance the books on what we make here as a company. I only know this because he asked me to witness his will.'

'When was the will signed?'

'Two weeks ago.'

'It was as recently as that? How interesting,' said Trussell. 'I wonder whether Mr Culverton had some sort of premonition. How old was he?'

Godfrey James thought for a moment. 'He must have been about forty five.'

'So, who are the beneficiaries?'

'There are a couple of distant cousins. They live up north somewhere. From memory, I believe that one of them is the executor. They will have to be told about Mr Culverton's demise. How did he die? Was it a heart attack or something like that?'

'I'm afraid I can't comment on that, Sir. We'll have to wait for the post-mortem. You mentioned his interest in the finer things in life. Would you care to elaborate?'

'Forgive me. I was being ironic. I hate to speak ill of the dead, Detective Inspector but I believe that he might have had a taste for the high life and certain illegal substances. I think that people refer to them as recreational drugs these days. I can't imagine why, when you consider the harm they cause.' Godfrey James had chosen his words with considerable care.

'Where do you think that they came from?' asked Trussell. 'Can you tell me anything about his life outside of this firm? What about friends or acquaintances?'

'I believe that he did spend a certain amount of time with Arthur Tillworth, the estate agent. I know that we have received a substantial amount of conveyancing business from them in the last year or so, but I think that they used to socialise as well. He may be able to tell you more.'

Trussell looked at Jackie. She raised an eyebrow. That name kept cropping up. And yet, Tillworth and Culverton seemed such unlikely bedfellows.

'There was also a woman who phoned him sometimes. She never left a name so I can't enlighten you on that one, I'm afraid.'

'A client, or was it personal?'

'I have no idea. You could talk to our secretary, Mary. She usually answers the phone here. She may know.'

'I won't bother you any more today, Mr James. You have my card. Should anything else occur to you, please give me a call. In the meantime, could I ask you to contact the executor and ask him to phone me as soon as possible on the number I've just given you? Unfortunately, Mr Culverton's death is now part of a major enquiry into other matters, so speed is of the essence.'

'Yes, of course, Detective Inspector. My first duty is to call the Law Society and acquaint them with Mr Culverton's death. I've never come across this situation before, when the sole managing partner has died suddenly, leaving a rudderless ship, in a manner of speaking. They'll know what to do. There is client money to be safeguarded, of course, and I'll certainly not have the authority to run the firm. I'm worried for our small number of staff, as well. They'll expect to be paid as usual. It's going to a very worrying time.' He was wringing his hands as he spoke.

Trussell felt rather sorry for him. The situation had become very stressful for someone who appeared to be well beyond retirement age. 'I understand, Mr James. But I must also ask you to give equal priority to my request. I need to speak to Mr Culverton's executor.'

'Of course I will, Detective Inspector. If that's all for this moment, allow me to show you out. There's a lot to be done now.'

'Thank you for your time, Mr James. I'll be in touch. We shall need to look through the conveyancing files you mentioned.'

He closed the door behind them. Jackie made a face at Trussell. 'It's like a time warp in there, Jim. Welcome back to the real world.'

31

Day 14.
Monday 4th March.
CID Office, Woodchester Police Station.

Trussell turned to speak to Joynton as they retraced their steps to the police station. There was no chance of their conversation being overheard as they walked along the High Street.

'There's another connection with Tillworth. I think we should go back to talk to Mr James tomorrow to go through the property transactions that he mentioned. I'm sure he'll cooperate. He has nothing to lose now with the demise of the managing partner. He strikes me as a man of old-world morality and values. I'm ready to lay money that their conveyancing business involved mortgages with the High Weald.'

'Isn't it amazing? Just a couple of weeks ago, things were so quiet, and now I wonder whether we have enough resources.'

'Charlie Watkins certainly won't sanction any overtime or extra people from outside.'

'Business as usual, Jim. We'll manage. We always do.'

'You're right. I know that John McIndow and his team are busy as well, so we can't expect any help there. They can hardly keep up with the thefts of cash machines from village stores. It's becoming a bit too frequent. Mac is short of resources as well. He's just lost Smithy to the Met. I'm not sure when he'll get a replacement.'

'What next, then, Jim?'

'I'm beginning to think that we might also progress matters by visiting the High Weald again to talk to Hartman and McDriscoll. They'll cooperate now that we seem to have a common objective. At least Hartman will. I think McDriscoll is out of his depth.'

'In view of the possible Brandford connection, how much do you want Eddie to see, Jim? Should we let him carry on with the Supercheap problems as well as assisting us with Scoular's disappearance? He could start checking the local eating places to see whether Scoular was seen in any of them on the night that he disappeared. After all, Scoular was supposed to have had a dinner appointment. Someone must have seen him, surely? I'll get him to document every enquiry he makes. We'll just tell him that we don't want to go over the same ground twice.'

'Yes. Good idea, Jackie. Let him run with that one while we concentrate on the High Weald's other problems. It's best that you direct Eddie's effort as his DS, rather than me. It's important that he's made to feel part of the team without hindering our efforts.'

'We can't stop him seeing progress on the white board in the office, Jim. Eddie's not stupid. After all, he'll be adding to it with whatever he turns up.'

It worried Trussell that he had to be secretive about the case when he needed all of his resources. But he still had nagging doubts about Eddie Sprawson and his Brandford connections, especially in view of the mysterious frequent caller, Brian, at the estate agents.

'The only thing we can do is confine the sensitive stuff to the mind maps on my pad. I don't believe that Eddie knows about that. Better tell Greeno not to mention it. I'll keep the pad locked in my drawer when I'm not adding to it.'

He had drawn Barnaby Scoular at the centre, and then connecting lines to boxes containing the names of Stephanie Winterden and Maureen Scoular. Thinking about their apparent previous friendship, he now drew a line connecting the two women. Sitting back and studying his work, he realised that he had created a triangle from the three names. A thunderbolt moment. *Am I looking at the classic eternal triangle?* But he had to include Alex Peterson in the mix as well.

His instinct had told him to keep it away from Sprawson's eyes, in view of the apparent Brandford connection. Fast Eddie had spent so much time there that he might know the answers already, but Trussell couldn't afford to allow him to be involved. He was inwardly cursing Watkins for putting him in this difficult position. With that thought in mind, he replaced the pad in the drawer and turned the key, Stephanie Winterden exercising his mind.

'Jackie, can you go to the control room and look at the CCTV covering the High Weald branch entrance? I'm interested in the timing of staff members' arrivals this morning.'

'OK, Jim. What time do you want me to search from?' She wondered where this one was going. *Trussell's intuition kicking in again.* There was always a reason for sudden off-the-wall requests like this one. *Have to wait and see what happens.*

'Susie Albright told us that she used to arrive about five minutes after the manager, around 8.35. Start looking a bit earlier. What time did Miss

Winterden arrive today? I wonder whether she still opens the branch before Hansworth arrives? It's worth checking.'

'OK, Jim, I'll go there now.'

Half an hour later, Jackie Joynton returned to the office. She was looking puzzled. 'That was interesting,' she said. 'I looked at the CCTV video covering the High Weald branch starting at nine o'clock and worked backwards. Janet McDuff arrived at five to nine, James Howditch a couple of minutes earlier, at the same time as John Hansworth. Susie Albright arrived as usual at eight thirty-five, the door being opened from inside by Stevie Winterden. Made me wonder exactly when Stevie had arrived. So, I started running the video back… and back. You wouldn't believe it, Jim. She arrived at the branch and unlocked it at six thirty this morning.'

Trussell was surprised. 'Wonder what devotion to duty persuaded her to turn up so early for work?' he mused. 'Might be worth asking her to explain.'

32

Day 15.
Tuesday 5th March.
CID Office, Woodchester Police Station.

When Trussell arrived at his desk that morning, there was a large manila envelope waiting for him. He recognised the address on the back. 'Looks like the post mortem report on Magnus Culverton has arrived, Jackie,' he said.

'We'll see whether the doctor was right, then,' she replied. 'He seemed fairly sure that the cause of death wasn't related to the exhaust fumes.'

Fast Eddie looked up from his computer screen.

'It all seemed pretty conclusive to me, Guv. I saw it. The guy was sitting in a car full of exhaust fumes with the pipe stuck through the back window and the engine had been running. Looked like a classic case of suicide to me.'

Jackie Joynton caught his eye. She discreetly shook her head. She was indicating it was best not to pursue the subject with Sprawson.

'Well, let's see what the pathologist has to say.'

He opened the envelope and took out the typewritten sheets of the report. There were several photographs with the papers. He would read it later in detail, but he skipped right to the end to the conclusions section and the report confirmed that death had occurred before the exhaust fumes had reached the body - there was very little trace of carbon monoxide in the lungs. The pathologist had attributed death to asphyxia and deprivation of blood to the brain. From damage around the victim's neck and throat, he had deduced that some sort of choke hold had been applied to Culverton, resulting in death within about twenty seconds. This had occurred outside the vehicle, and the body had been placed in the driver's seat shortly afterwards, before connecting the hose and starting the engine. It was obviously premeditated and skilfully executed. Trussell glanced at the photographs that accompanied the report, just to refresh his memory.

Sprawson persisted. 'Well, Guv, what did the doc say?'

Trussell told him. He read out the concluding paragraph, as much for the benefit of Jackie Joynton and Mark Green.

'Well, it looks as though we have another murder enquiry on our hands, then,' said Jackie Joynton. 'Where do we start with this one?

'Obviously with Tillworth,' said Trussell. 'There seemed to be contact between them.'

He watched Eddie Sprawson out of the corner of his eye. He had made no further comment but Trussell noticed that he had discreetly scribbled something on a piece of paper and put it straight in his pocket. *What is he up to?*

33

Day 16.
Wednesday 6th March.
CID Office, Woodchester Police Station.

Mark Green sat at his desk, working his way through the list of surgeries and clinics he and Eddie Sprawson had visited. He wanted to be sure that that they hadn't missed anything before he passed it all over to Trussell.

No one had seen or heard of Barney Scoular. He seemed to have disappeared off the face of the earth. Even Maureen Scoular's tearful press conference hadn't yielded any fresh information. Trussell had already voiced his opinion to his team that he had begun to fear the worst. Had Scoular disappeared with part of the profits from the scam, or had he been silenced by the people behind it?

Mark Green's thoughts were disturbed by his phone warbling. It was another incoming message. He picked the phone up and looked at the screen. The message was from Sharon Webster at Tillworth and Co. It said simply 'Can you meet me? Something serious has happened. I'm scared. Do you know The Coffee Shop in the High Street? I'll be outside at one o'clock. Please come.' It was just signed Sharon.

He looked at his watch. 12.45. He walked over to Trussell's desk and showed him the screen. 'Should I meet her, Guv? It's the girl at the estate agents. I told you that I was concerned for her safety. I've kept in touch with her as you suggested but there haven't been any further developments.'

Trussell read the message and simply said, 'Yes. See what she has to say, but keep it professional, Greeno.'

He typed in his reply. 'Leaving now. See you there,' and walked over to collect his coat.

Trussell looked at Joynton, who had heard the short conversation. 'It looks as though we got lucky Tillworth was out when Greeno went round there,' he said, thoughtfully. 'I wonder what she wants?'

Mark Green walked briskly along the High Street, impervious to the cold wind, and arrived outside The Coffee Shop ten minutes later. He stood there, looking up and down until he caught sight of Sharon Webster walking quickly along the road. She was wearing a navy blue, quilted coat and the multi-coloured leather handbag swung from her shoulder as she rushed along the pavement. She was rather taller than he remembered.

About five feet seven, he thought. She had a worried expression as she hurried towards The Coffee Shop, frequently looking over her shoulder, but her look changed when she caught sight of Mark Green. Her face lit up with a big smile as she rushed up to him. She whispered, 'Look pleased to see me, I'm being followed,' as she reached up and put her hands on his shoulders before planting a kiss on his cheek.

Although taken aback, he maintained his composure, opened the door, and motioned her to go in. 'That was unexpected, Sharon,' he said.

She blushed. 'I had to make it look as though we were friends on a pre-arranged date. 'It's that thug. He's following me. I didn't want him to think that I was alone.' Concerned, she looked over her shoulder again. The worried look had returned.

'Let me just sort out some coffee and cakes,' he said. 'Then you can tell me what's going on. Go and find a quiet table in a corner, if possible, where we won't be overheard.' A couple of minutes later, he carried a tray over to the table where she was sitting, and sat down opposite her. 'Now tell me what's happened. Who's following you?'

'It's been uncomfortable for me since the beginning of last week,' she said. 'I told Arthur Tillworth that I was going to look for another job because I didn't have enough to do. Being there most of the day on my own didn't help, either. The shop just wasn't busy enough. I was trying to give him enough time to find a replacement.'

'How did he take it?'

'Very badly. He didn't want to discuss it. He just stormed off. He went into his office and slammed the door behind him. That was bad enough, but it got worse.'

'So, who's following you?'

It started a couple of days after I'd spoken to Arthur. The man from Brandford, Brian, came in, only this time he wasn't alone. There was a younger man with him. He was wearing a black leather jacket and jeans and carrying a motorcycle helmet. They called him Jason. Frankly he looked a thug. Number one haircut, tattoos everywhere. He was full of himself. I wondered whether he might be Brian's son. There was a definite family likeness.'

'What happened?'

'As Brian went into Arthur's office, he told Jason to *look after me.* I wondered what was coming.'

'So, what did Jason do?'

'He came over to me, dropped his helmet on my desk and sat on the edge. Started trying to chat me up. When I told him to let me get on with my work, he turned very threatening and talked about me needing to watch my step. He told me that people were taking notice of me. Since then, I've seen him whenever I've been walking around town. He always seems to be there, wherever I go. That's the reason why I had to put on a show when I met you. I wanted him to think that I wasn't alone.'

'That's my hopes dashed then,' said Mark Green, grinning now.

'It wasn't hard for me to do that,' she admitted, blushing again. Then a look of panic crossed her face. 'He's just come in and he's looking over here.'

'Don't worry, Sharon. Nothing's going to happen. He won't try anything with me here and a shopful of people. He's just trying to put the pressure on you.' He turned around and located the man, standing just inside the door. He was exactly as Sharon had described him. He stared hard at him and half rose from his seat. The man returned his look for a brief moment, averted his gaze, glanced around the coffee shop and left.

'He's gone. How much time do you get for lunch?'

'About an hour,' she replied. 'I was thinking about going to the job agency down the High Street today, but that man frightened me and made me reluctant to go anywhere.'

'Well, I think that you should go there right now,' he said. 'I'll come with you and wait while you talk to the people in there.'

He received a grateful smile in response. 'Are you sure you don't mind? What about your work?'

'Not a problem. I showed your message to the DI and he told me to come here straight away. He's aware of your situation. I can take as much time as you need.'

Finishing their coffees, they stood up from the table and made for the door. As they went outside, Sharon looked around nervously.

'Don't worry. He's disappeared for the moment. Let's find the agency.'

She grabbed his arm as they walked down the High Street. She felt safer with him. 'That's the place,' she said, pointing to a shop with *Woodchester Staff Recruitment* in bold black lettering on the window.

Mark Green opened the door for her. 'Just go and tell them that you want another job. Convince them that you're the best candidate who's walked through the door today,' he said. 'Don't worry about Jason. I'll wait by the door. He won't be bothering you. Just concentrate on what you have to do.'

He received a grateful smile in return.

He stood just inside the door, carefully watching the street. No sign of Jason. Sharon had spoken to a woman sitting behind one of the desks and had now taken a seat opposite her. He was so absorbed in looking up and down the High Street that he scarcely noticed that time had flown by until Sharon suddenly appeared next to him and spoke to him.

'We can go now,' she said. 'Will you walk back to Tillworth's with me?'

'Of course I will. How did you get on? I was too busy watching the street.'

'They seemed to like me and my qualifications and experience,' she said. 'The woman I spoke to told me that she has at least four jobs that would suit me, so she's going to arrange interviews with them. They're all offering quite a bit more money so it could be good news all round.'

'What sort of jobs? With other estate agents?'

'Yes. They're all so busy at the moment that they need extra staff.'

'Are the jobs all here in town?'

'Three are. The other one is closer to where I live. I'll just have to see what happens.'

'The most important thing is to get you away from your friend Arthur and his circle of undesirables. You will let me know what happens, won't you?'

'Yes, of course. Perhaps we can meet again for coffee if it's convenient.'

'Anytime you like. Just don't let Jason intimidate you. Tell Tillworth that you won't stand for it. Give me a call if there are any more problems or threats. If that Neanderthal's stalking you around town, then we can soon put a stop to it. There are laws against that sort of thing now.'

By now, they had reached the estate agent's shop, and catching sight of Tillworth inside, staring at her through the window, Sharon gave him another peck on the cheek, and whispered, 'Thank you.'

'Was that for show as well?' he asked.

She smiled and vanished inside. He turned away to walk back to the station, somewhat confused.

34

Day 16.
Wednesday 6th March.
CID Office, Woodchester Police Station. Early afternoon.

Mark Green returned to the office still slightly bemused by the turn of events at lunchtime. He gave Trussell a quick account of what Sharon Webster had told him and mentioned seeing the individual who had threatened her.

'Make a note of everything, Greeno, so we can add it to the file.'

He sat down at his desk, pulled the keyboard towards him and started typing. He had realised that Sharon Webster was genuinely frightened by what had happened and he felt concerned for her safety. If things were really going on at Tillworth, then she had every reason to worry.

'I think that we could contact Mr James at Fotherby and Co, now, Jackie,' said Trussell. 'We've got to start somewhere with that conveyancing business that he mentioned.'

'I'll ring him now so we can arrange to see him this afternoon.' She picked up the phone and rang the number. When the call was answered, she said, 'Ah, Mr James, it's Detective Sergeant Joynton here. We met yesterday… That's right. Detective Inspector Trussell and I would like to come round shortly to talk about that conveyancing business that you mentioned during our visit. Say, in about an hour?…You'll have everything available? …Thank you. That would be most helpful.'

'All arranged, Jim,' she told Trussell.

'I'd better add Fotherby and Mr James to the mind map.' He unlocked the drawer in front of him and took out the A4 pad which now carried a lot more information than the whiteboard even before he added Fotherby to it.

'What d'you think about Fotherbys then, Jackie?'

'Dickensian is the first word that comes to mind. I think that this is probably the most exciting thing that's happened there in living memory.'

'I agree. I feel sorry for Mr James. He'll have a huge sense of duty towards their remaining clients and the small staff there. He'll certainly feel the need to see things through. My worry is that whoever the Law Society sends in might be a bit too modern thinking for him.'

Three quarters of an hour later, they left the office to walk to Fotherby and Co. They left the High Street and walked down the narrow side street towards the run-down Victorian terrace in its small quiet square.

The door was answered fairly quickly by the same woman who'd greeted them on their first visit. She was still wearing the long grey skirt and the shabby red cardigan from the previous day. 'You're here to meet Mr James. I believe. Detective Inspector,' she said. He'll see you in our conference room.' She led the way down a gloomy corridor with faded dark wallpaper, lit by a single dim bulb on a pendant fitting, and showed them into a room at the back of the building. There had been no pretence of cleaning the room. Dust lay everywhere.

'I hope we're not putting our health at risk here,' said Jackie, grinning as she looked around the room.

Trussell made a face. 'I wonder what the temporary solicitor thinks about what he found here, before he even looks at the way the firm's been run?'

'I think we're about to find out,' she said quietly, as the door opened.

Godfrey James walked in, followed by a serious-looking individual of about forty. Medium height and build, thinning dark brown hair, in a smart dark-grey suit, neatly pressed white shirt and flawless tie. A contrast with James' dated attire. He frowned, peered suspiciously at Trussell through dark-framed glasses as James made the introductions.

'This is Jeremy Twistley, the solicitor sent by the Law Society to help us through our present difficulties, Detective Inspector.'

'What is it you want know, Officer?' asked Twistley, rather pompously. 'Frankly, this place is a shambles and it needs to be sorted out as soon as possible. I haven't really got time to chat.'

'I rather hope that you will cooperate with us, Sir,' said Trussell. 'The information we need from Fotherby and Co. forms part of a murder enquiry now, as well as a possible fraud.'

'Yes, yes. Well, what do you want? Get on with it.'

Trussell contrived to ignore Twistley's patronising tone. 'I believe that Mr James is already aware of the subject of our enquiries. We're concerned with conveyancing business brought in by Mr Culverton.'

Twistley looked at Godfrey James, somewhat disdainfully. 'Have you got the information ready?' he asked.

'What little I could find, Mr Twistley,' said James. 'I just don't understand it. The files seem to be missing. I can't believe that Mr Culverton would have taken them away from the office. Why would he do that?'

'Don't be naïve, man. If he was engaged in anything illegal, he'd hardly be likely to leave the evidence behind, would he?' As Trussell listened to this exchange, he couldn't help feeling sorry for Godfrey James.

'We searched his office thoroughly,' said James. We had to force the lock on his drawer. Mr Twistley authorised it. But there was nothing of any value or interest in it, except for a few personal items. His filing cabinet was empty, save for these few pieces of paper. They seemed to have fallen out and were underneath the empty hanging files. I think that one of them had come loose.'

'Perhaps Mr James could show us what he's found, then, Mr Twistley,' Trussell said, evenly. 'I'm sure that you're interested in justice being served and seeing this matter brought to the correct conclusion.'

'Yes, alright, get on with it, then, James. I'll leave you with him, Officer. I've got too much to do, sorting this place out. Unbelievable,' he muttered, half to himself, as he walked out of the room.

Godfrey James looked embarrassed. 'I'm really sorry, Detective Inspector. I really don't think that he wants to be here. I'll show you both what little I've found. If you'll take a seat, I'll bring the paperwork in here.' He returned two minutes later, clutching a small bundle of papers. 'This is all I could find. It shows that we had some conveyancing business referred to us by Tillworth and Co in the High Street. It seems to concern a number of properties in Brandford. It's extraordinary. I didn't realise that Tillworth had an office there as well.'

He put the papers down on the rather dusty table and looked apologetic. 'I'm sorry about the state of the table. We never use this room these days and Mr Culverton wasn't very keen on paying out money for cleaning. Our small team certainly doesn't have time to even think about it, but it's not their job anyway. As people left, Mr Culverton didn't bother to replace them. We're a very small office indeed, now.'

Trussell and Joynton glanced at those few pieces of paper. They showed details of some properties that were to be redeveloped. There were copies of surveys carried out by Edmund Royston, which confirmed his complicity in the affair. There was nothing to tell them where the instructions had originated. Nor were there any names for the purchasers or any reference to mortgages. Culverton had obviously taken that information away with him. Trussell made a mental note to search his house in Somerville Avenue just in case there were any papers or other items still there. It was already secured with PCSOs in attendance. They had left Fast Eddie in charge of the crime scene, but he hadn't mentioned finding any paperwork. That began to ring alarm bells in Trussell's head, but he made no comment.

'I think that we'd better take these with us, Mr James,' said Joynton. 'As you say, there's not a lot there, but these papers are just a few more pieces of a very large jigsaw.' She produced an evidence bag and put the papers inside before sealing it.

'What about accounts?' asked Trussell. 'Was there any record of money being paid in or out?'

'No. I've spoken to Mary, who has had to take over responsibility for just about everything these days. She couldn't find anything relevant in the accounts at all. No record of any cheques being paid in or out. It leads me to the rather unsavoury conclusion that Mr Culverton must have been dealing in large sums of money in cash. Not really the way to do things, you know. Old Mr Fotherby would never have allowed anything like that. Standards seem to be so different these days.' He looked genuinely pained by this apparent departure from his accepted norms.

'When we spoke yesterday, Mr James, you mentioned callers. You told us that the secretary, Mary, would have taken any phone calls in Mr Culverton's absence. Is it possible to have a quick word with her, please?'

'Of course. If you'll excuse me for a minute, I'll fetch her and you can ask her yourself.' He left the room and returned a minute later with the middle-aged woman who had answered the door earlier. 'I believe that you have already met Mary,' he said. 'Please ask her whatever you wish.'

Trussell looked at her. 'I understand that you might have answered the phone in Mr Culverton's absence. We'd like to know who phoned him.'

She looked at them nervously.

'It's perfectly alright for you to tell these officers, Mary,' said Godfrey James. 'You don't need to worry about confidences.'

'Well, Sir,' she began, clearing her throat nervously and fidgeting with a sleeve of her cardigan. 'Mr Culverton did receive calls fairly frequently. Some were from Arthur Tillworth, the estate agent. There was also a lady who called. She was always very precise and, erm, economical with her words. Direct. That's the word. She had a very serious tone to her voice.'

'Did she leave her name?'

'She didn't give one to me, but I do recall Mr Culverton addressing her once by name, but I'm afraid that I can't remember what it was.'

She looked at Godfrey James, as if for reassurance, before she continued. He nodded and she said, 'I'd say that Mr Culverton sometimes looked uncomfortable after he'd spoken to her.'

'Was there anyone else?'

'There was a man who didn't give his name. He had a rather gruff voice and some sort of accent. I must say that Mr Culverton looked rather worried after they had spoken.'

'What about any visitors?'

'There were none that I can recall who were connected with this business. We did receive occasional visits from our longstanding clients, and as the only managing partner, Mr Culverton certainly met them.'

'You can give us details if we need them?'

'Of course, Detective Inspector,' said James.

Trussell nodded to Joynton, who picked up the papers. 'Thank you for your time, Mr James,' he said. 'We appreciate your assistance at what must be an incredibly difficult time for you. We won't take up any more of your time. You have my card. Perhaps you would be kind enough to phone me if anything else occurs to you.'

James nodded. 'Allow me to show you out,' he said, and led the way back down the gloomy corridor to the front door. He opened it and stood aside for them to leave.

As the door closed behind them, Joynton heaved an exaggerated sigh of relief. 'Welcome back to the twenty first century, Jim,' she said. 'That solicitor, Twistley, is a nasty piece of work. The way he treated Godfrey James was nothing short of scandalous.'

Trussell shrugged his shoulders. 'I didn't enjoy the spectacle either, Jackie,' he said, 'but he's been lumbered with a job which he realises he doesn't want, and it shows. We can't change things. We just need to get these papers back to the office and add them to the file.'

35

Day 21.
Monday 11th March.
CID Office, Woodchester Police Station.

Mark Green's phone rang. He picked it up and looked at it. The caller was Sharon Webster. Rather self-consciously, he looked around him, but nobody was paying any attention.

'Hello,' said that familiar voice. She still sounded worried. 'I need to talk to you urgently. I've got some news.'

'Hello Miss Webster. What's going on? I hope you haven't had more problems with Tillworth and his friends.'

'Well, I've got two things to tell you. First of all, I've been offered all four jobs through the agency and I've accepted the one with Thompson Granby in the High Street.'

'That's great news. Well done. Not too far from here, either. What's the second thing?'

'I've just given in my notice to Arthur.'

'How did he take it?'

'Very badly. Threw another tantrum and slammed the door. I heard him on his phone. I've told you how loud he can be sometimes. I couldn't hear exactly what he was saying, but I believe he was telling someone about me. Frankly, that rather scared me.'

Green could hear the concern in her voice. He looked at his watch. It was almost lunchtime.

'Do you want to meet me at The Coffee Shop? We can talk about it if you're really worried.'

'Are you're sure? Say, ten minutes time?'

'I'll be there,' he promised.

He relayed the conversation to Trussell, who was engrossed in his mind map, trying to make sense of the various actors in this particular drama and the latest developments.

'You'd better see her, Greeno. Find out what's going on. Be careful.'

He nodded as he stood up, grabbed his coat and headed for the stairs. Ten minutes later, he was outside The Coffee Shop waiting as Sharon Webster hurried along the High Street, looking around her nervously.

'Hello, Mark. Let's go inside,' she said quickly, looking over her shoulder again. 'I'm scared that Arthur might send that thug Jason after me now.'

Mark Green tried to reassure her, but she was obviously very worried. He ordered two cappuccinos and cake while she found a quiet table at the back of the shop. It was only about half full at that moment.

'I can't wait to get out of there,' she said. 'I know that working my notice is going to be very uncomfortable.'

'You mentioned that Tillworth was talking on the phone after you'd spoken to him. Did you hear anything he said?'

'His voice was a bit muffled, but I'm sure that he was talking about me. I thought that he said something about someone knowing too much and that they'd have to do something about it. What can it mean, Mark? It frightens me now. He knows some very dodgy people who call round to see him. Who can tell what they're capable of doing? Do you think I'll be safe at my new job? I'm so looking forward to starting there. They seem such nice, friendly people. It's at the other end of the High Street, but he'll know where I am. Worse still, he knows where I live, of course.'

She was managing to keep her composure, but the strain was evident in her face. She was fidgeting with the coffee mug while she was speaking, holding it with both hands and twisting it nervously one way and then the other on the table. She kept looking in the direction of the door. Her usual smile was missing.

'Look, Sharon, I'll share this with the DI and let's see what he thinks about it. I'll let you know when I've spoken to him. Try not to worry. Just make sure that you keep in touch with me regularly so that I know what's going on. I'm pleased about the job. That's a real step forward.'

She tried to smile at his attempts to reassure her. 'When you first came to Tillworth's shop, you said that I could call you any time. Is that still true?'

'Yes, of course. Would you like me to walk back to the shop with you when we leave here? Just so that he can see that you have some support?'

She nodded.

They left the coffee shop and began walking down the High Street towards Tillworth's when she grabbed his arm again. *For show or because she really needs the comfort?* he wondered. As they arrived outside they saw Tillworth through the window. He was glaring at Sharon.

'You see what I mean?' she whispered. It's going to be a very difficult month for me.'

'Just keep in touch. Let me know if there are any problems at all.'

She smiled at him, opened the door and went inside. He hovered outside, watching Tillworth carefully through the window and letting him know it.

Sharon took off her coat and sat down at her desk and Tillworth disappeared in the direction of his office. She raised a thumb to indicate that she was OK, and the detective left to return to the station. He needed to share the information with Trussell. Tillworth's veiled threats could complicate matters even further.

36

Day 21.
Monday 11th March 2.00 pm.
CID Office, Woodchester Police Station.

Mark Green returned to the office to tell Trussell about his lunchtime chat with Sharon Webster. He stressed her concerns about Tillworth.

'I know that this won't be difficult for you, Greeno, so I want you to keep in contact with Sharon Webster. See if anything else develops at the estate agency. I don't think that there's any doubt that Tillworth is up to his neck in the whole thing, but we can't move until we have something definite. Just note down what she told you and keep me posted. Make sure that you keep all your dealings with her on a professional level, though. She's an important witness and we wouldn't want to compromise any future legal proceedings.'

'OK, Guv.' He sat down at his desk and switched on his computer. He pulled the keyboard towards him and began to type, making a record of their lunchtime conversation. He was only distracted by his mobile ringing on the desk next to him. He glanced at the screen to see who was interrupting his train of thought. It was Sharon Webster again so he picked it up. 'Yes, Sharon? What's happening?' He listened carefully to her for a minute and told her to come to the station immediately. 'I'll see you at the main desk. If you get there before me, ask the desk sergeant for me and tell him that you've come to give a statement.'

Trussell looked askance at the conversation he couldn't help overhearing. *What the hell's going on now?*

'That was Sharon Webster again, Guv. She sounded quite upset. There's been an interesting development. She gave her notice in this morning, and when she went back after lunch, Tillworth threw his toys out of the pram, told her to clear her desk and sod off. My words, not hers. You get the picture. He told her he'd pay her what was due in lieu of notice, but didn't want her on the premises a moment longer. He obviously thinks that she's seen and heard too much. Damage limitation from his point of view, I guess. She's very worried that something might happen to her. I reckon that she's genuinely frightened for her life now so I told her to come straight round here.'

'Good call, Greeno. Talk to her in one of the interview rooms. Take a note of everything she says. It could turn out to be a useful development. Do your best to reassure her that we're taking all this very seriously.'

Mark Green lifted his jacket from the back of his chair, put it on and picked up a notepad from his desk. He left the CID office and walked quickly down the stairs to the main desk to find a very pale Sharon Webster waiting for him. He smiled to try to put her at ease and indicated the open door of the interview room, but the strain showed on her face. Her usual smile was missing.

'Thank you for coming, Miss Webster. We can talk in here,' he said with a straight face, strictly for the benefit of the desk sergeant, who was watching with a slightly bemused look. 'Would you like some tea or coffee?'

She shook her head as she walked into the room. He indicated the nearest chair, which had its back to the door, while he took the chair opposite her. He had left the door slightly ajar. 'Now tell me exactly what happened today, from the moment that you gave Tillworth your notice,' he said, with his pen poised over the pad.

Before she could reply, Mark Green heard a familiar voice outside at the front desk. There was no mistaking that coarse voice with the East Kent accent. He saw a look of recognition flit across Sharon's face.

'I've heard that voice before,' she whispered. 'It was someone who came in to see Arthur recently. I was in the staff room at the back, making tea for Arthur and myself, so I never saw who it was.'

Mark Green looked through the gap left by the door which was slightly ajar. Fast Eddie Sprawson was talking to Alan, the duty sergeant on the desk.

'Do you remember any of the conversation?' asked Mark Green, putting a finger to his lips, indicating that she should keep her voice down.

'Not really,' she whispered. I wasn't listening deliberately. It was just that voice. It's very distinctive and carries. The man did mention something about speaking to Jack. Said it was important. Jack might not be very happy about something. I don't know anyone of that name. Certainly, hasn't been to the shop while I've been there.'

Alan must have said something because Sprawson looked across at the interview room and saw Mark Green through the narrow gap left by the partly open door. He walked across and peered at him. Sharon Webster was sitting behind the door, beyond his line of sight. 'Who've you got in there, Greeno?

Mark Green shook his head. 'Not now, DC Sprawson. I'm taking a witness statement. It's another matter. I'll catch up with you shortly. I think the DI's waiting to hear about your enquiries at the other estate agents.'

'OK,' said Sprawson. 'See you back in the office,' and he turned to walk towards the stairs to the first floor.

Mark Green immediately picked up his phone and tapped in Trussell's number.

'What is it, Greeno?'

'Please can you come down to the interview room right now, Guv? Something really important has just come up. Don't mention this conversation to anyone else or say where you're going, particularly to Eddie. You'll understand why when you get here.'

Sharon looked apprehensive. 'What's up?'

'This is getting more complicated by the minute. Wait for the DI and you'll understand.'

Two minutes later, Trussell walked into the room. Mark Green hastily shut the door behind him.

'Good afternoon, Miss Webster. What's with all this cloak and dagger stuff, Greeno?'

'I was just making a few notes when we heard a voice outside at the desk. Miss Webster recognised that voice immediately. It was Eddie. Tell the DI what you just told me, please, Miss Webster.'

She repeated the conversation.

'Do you remember when this happened?' asked Trussell. 'Exactly when did the man visit Tillworth?'

'In the last couple of weeks,' she replied.

Turning to Mark Green, Trussell said, decisively, 'I want a full, signed witness statement from Miss Webster now, please, Greeno. You'll find some forms in the drawer in front of you.'

Sharon Webster looked alarmed.

'Don't worry, Miss Webster,' said Trussell. 'We just need a record of what you've just told us. I'm really sorry that you've become involved in this matter now and what you've just shared with us could be very important. However, I must ask you not to discuss the matter with anyone outside of this room. Not even your family or friends.'

She nodded, rather confused by this turn of events, even more worried now.

'What will you do when you leave here, Miss Webster?' asked Trussell, concerned about her nervous state.

'I suppose I'll get the bus home to Hammerton. There's no point in hanging around the town as I don't start my new job for a month,' she replied. 'I just hope that Jason or one of his friends isn't waiting for me somewhere. I'm really frightened now after today's events. There's just no telling what they might do. Arthur Tillworth was really angry with me.'

Trussell thought for a moment. 'In view of Miss Webster's importance as a witness now, we can't allow her to put herself at risk by travelling home on the bus alone today, DC Green. Will you drive her back to Hammerton when you've finished the paperwork? It's a straightforward matter of witness protection.'

'OK, Guv.'

'I'll leave you to it then,' he said as he stood up. 'Thank you again for your help, Miss Webster.'

Fifteen minutes later, statement completed and signed, Mark Green smiled as he said 'I'd better carry out the DI's instructions now, Miss Webster. Are you ready to leave?' She nodded, so he opened the door for her and then led the way to the car park outside. 'My car's the white Hyundai over there,' he said, pointing at it. 'I should get you home in about fifteen minutes.'

'No need to hurry on my account,' she smiled, more relaxed now.

Safely belted up, he started the engine and reversed the car out of his space, heading for the car park exit. 'There's one thing I ought to clarify, Sharon. I must keep our conversations on a formal basis from now on. Those are DI Trussell's instructions. We're involved in a major enquiry and you're now an important witness. Familiarity could compromise our case if any defence lawyer caught a sniff of anything else. Please address me as DC Green or Officer if we're seen together in public, until the case is concluded. We can't have it any other way.'

She swallowed hard, thought for a moment and then asked, 'And when the case is over, DC Green?'

'We'll deal with that when the time comes,' he said, slightly embarrassed. 'You need to get out with your friends. Be around people. It might help to take your mind off these problems. I'm sure you've got a good circle of friends?'

'Well, not really,' she said. 'Not any more. I've lost touch with most of them. All of my oldest friends are married now. Some of them even have children.'

'What about you? You must have a boyfriend?'

'No. Not at the moment. I guess that I just haven't met the right man. At least not until now.'

'We'll talk about this again when the case is over,' he said, colouring slightly. 'What about your home? Do you have any siblings?'

'No. There's just my parents and me. Oh, and a dog called Fred. My dad sometimes calls him Heinz. His idea of a joke, I suppose.'

'That sounds like a German breed. What is he? A Dachshund or a Schnauzer or something?'

'No, he's a mongrel…a real mixture. Heinz, as in fifty-seven varieties.'

Mark Green laughed at the joke. It seemed to ease the tension, although he could see that she was still preoccupied. The journey passed all too quickly and they soon arrived in Hammerton and she pointed to the next turning on the right off the main road.

'That's where I live. Graham Road. Our house is on the right. The semi with the antique coloured-glass panels in the front door.'

Green followed the line of neatly kept Edwardian semi- detached houses until he reached Number 36 and pulled up outside. 'Do keep in touch,' he said,' particularly when you start your new job. Call me anytime. I have to keep an eye on you. Those are the DI's orders. After all, you're an important witness,' he said, rather self-consciously, searching for the right words.

'Do you want to come in?' she asked hopefully. 'Can I offer you a cup of tea or coffee? I suppose that you've got to get back, though,' she added, somewhat wistfully.'

'No, I mustn't stop. Things are moving very quickly in this case. No telling what's happened in the last twenty minutes. Just keep in touch. Let me know what's happening.'

Sharon opened the door and stepped out, smiling as she closed the car door. He waited until she had reached the house, opened the front door and waved. The he turned the car round and set off back to Woodchester.

37

Day 22.
Tuesday 12th March. 10.00 am.
CID Office, Woodchester Police Station.

Mark Green's mobile rang where he had left it on his desk as he updated the file after the previous day's events. It was Sharon Webster calling again. 'How are you today, Miss Webster?' was his first question. The enforced formality difficult for him.

'I'm much better, thank you, Detective Constable Mark Green.' She certainly sounded more cheerful than when he had left her outside her home the previous afternoon. He felt relieved.

The circumstances of her abrupt departure from Tillworth had left her rather shaken, but now she had had time to think, she had investigated her precise job status using the internet. She had found several solicitors' websites which had stated that payment in lieu of notice, without any contractual conditions attached, meant she was free to start her new job whenever she wanted. 'I've spoken to Thompson Granby and explained exactly what happened to me. They've told me that I can join them as soon as I like. I've agreed to start next Monday. I'm really looking forward to it.'

'That's great news,' he said. 'Just make sure that you keep in touch with me and let me know what's going on. The DI has told me to stay in contact with you,' he added, somewhat lamely.

'Of course,' she said. 'I've got to pop into town today to complete some paperwork for Thompson Granby before I start there. Perhaps I could meet you at lunch time, like before. We can make sure that I've told you everything about my time at Tillworth. I'll try very hard to think about it. Make sure that I haven't forgotten anything.'

'That sounds a good idea. While everything's still fresh in your mind. Anything extra you can recall would be very helpful. Where would you like to meet?'

'Are you sure you're free today? We could meet at The Coffee Shop, the same as before. One o'clock?'

'OK,' he said. 'That's fine. I'll be there.'

He cleared the phone and attracted Trussell's attention and told him about the conversation.

'By all means meet her, Greeno, but remember that she's a potential witness. We don't want to prejudice any future legal action.'

'OK, Guv. I'll be very careful.'

Trussell wasn't fooled. He could see the direction in which things were heading, but there was no doubt that the information produced from the various interviews with Sharon Webster had been very valuable in moving the case forward. He knew that she might not have shared as much information with him or Jackie. He was also aware that her safety was still of paramount importance even if there had been no further sightings of the man known as Jason since the day that he came into The Coffee Shop when Mark Green and Sharon Webster had met for lunch.

Jackie Joynton had been listening with a certain amount of amusement, but decided that it was best to leave well alone this time.

'Don't forget to make a note on the file when you get back, Greeno,' was Trussell's parting shot.

**

On his return to the office, Mark Green sat at his desk and pulled his keyboard towards him to update the file.

'Well, Greeno, did you learn anything new?' asked Jackie. 'Or was it just her excuse to see you?' She was grinning as she spoke, intent on embarrassing him.

'It was interesting, Sarge. She remembered something which had been lurking in the back of her mind for a while, but she'd overlooked it with all the other stuff going on.'

'Come on, Greeno, share it with us,' said Trussell.

'Well, Guv. It might be something or nothing at all. Sharon, er, Miss Webster, said that every time that Stevie Winterden visited the shop, she thought that Arthur Tillworth was rather deferential or respectful. She thought it rather strange, as Stevie was supposedly there on some sort of PR exercise to drum up business for the High Weald. She wanted to make sure that her Society had first pick of any new mortgage business. She should have been the one politely deferring to him as she was trying to attract new business, not the other way around. It was almost as if she had some sort of hold over him. Miss Webster thought that Tillworth was almost frightened of her.'

'Interesting,' said Trussell. 'He didn't strike me as the politest person I've met. Add it to the file, Greeno.'

'I doubt that Miss Webster will have any further information for us now, Guv. She starts her new job at Thompson Granby on Monday.'

'No doubt you'll stay in touch, though, Greeno,' said Jackie Joynton, grinning mischievously. 'There may be more information that she's holding back to keep you interested. Drip feeding all these snippets to make sure that you stay in touch.' She was determined to extract the maximum embarrassment out of this ongoing saga.

38

Day 23.
Wednesday 13th March.
CID Office, Woodchester Police Station.

Trussell consulted his diary.

'Time to try to talk to Mr Thompson, the former High Weald manager,' he said. 'He should be back from his cruise now. Hope his daughter hasn't worried him too much about this.'

He picked up the phone and tapped in the number. It rang several times before it was picked up. 'Hello, Mrs Jenkinson? It's DI Trussell at Kent Police in Woodchester. We spoke some time ago. Is your father back now?...Good…Would it be convenient to call round and have a quick chat with him?...Of course you can be there…Not a problem. Shall we say this afternoon at two o'clock?...Thank you.'

'That's fixed, Jackie. We'll need an hour to get there. He lives somewhere near Dover. I suggest we leave at one. I know the village quite well. I grew up in the area.'

They left Woodchester in Trussell's Skoda and headed for the motorway. It was busy as usual with trucks heading for the Dover Ferryport or the Eurotunnel at Cheriton. Trussell turned off the motorway onto the A20 in the direction of Dover. After passing through the road tunnel, he turned off towards the village, almost a suburb of Dover these days. The streets were reminiscent of Waverley. – parallel roads of well-kept Victorian red-brick, terraced houses. They found the address easily enough and were lucky to find a space for the car outside the house.

A knock on the front door produced an instant response.

'I saw you arrive,' said the woman who answered the door. 'I'm Angela Jenkinson. I assume that you're Detective Inspector Trussell?'

He nodded, offered his warrant card as confirmation and introduced Jackie.

'Please come in. My father is waiting for you in the living room.' She opened the first door inside the narrow hallway. It gave access to a small room with a Victorian fireplace and shelves on either side containing a variety of books. A small television sat on a unit in one alcove.

An older man in his late sixties stood up as they entered the room. Casually dressed in an old comfortable cardigan and neatly pressed dark trousers. He had an impressive tan, testament to his recent extended cruise. 'Please sit down,' he said, indicating a large sofa, as he resumed his seat in the corner armchair. His daughter took another chair. 'How can I help you? I've been retired a couple of years now so I'm rather out of touch with the High Weald. Dreadful business about Barney. Is there any further news?'

'I'm afraid not, Sir,' said Trussell. 'We'd like to talk to you specifically about the way the staff interacted while you were still in charge. We gather that Barnaby Scoular was involved with Stephanie Winterden before he married Maureen Atherton. Do you know why he stopped seeing Miss Winterden?'

'Yes. I recall that quite well. I think that Stephanie became bored with Barney and looked for a way to let him down gently. She came to me and asked If I would speak to him discreetly. Tell him that it wasn't quite the thing to carry on with another staff member in such a small team.'

'How did you feel about their relationship, personally?'

'It really didn't matter to me as long as it didn't cause any problems in the branch with the others. I certainly wouldn't have said anything if Stephanie hadn't mentioned it.'

'How did Mr Scoular take it when you asked him to stop seeing Miss Winterden?'

'Surprised. He didn't think it was my business. I calmed him down by telling him that I was recommending that the management promote him to take over as Branch Manager when I retired. He was very competent and totally devoted to the business.'

'What about Miss Winterden?'

'Very thorough and ambitious. A bit pushy, to be frank.'

'Do you think that she would be able to wield any influence over him?'

'It's quite likely. She must have learned quite a bit about him while they were together. I think that she was also jealous of James Howditch. Although he joined us after her, he was obviously highly qualified and very clever.'

'What about Maureen Atherton?' asked Trussell. 'I understand that she and Miss Winterden became quite friendly when she first joined the Society, but that friendship cooled after a while. Do you know why?'

'I can't be sure, and I have to be very careful about what I say, but I think that around this time, Miss Winterden began openly showing an interest in women as well as men. She changed her image…shorter masculine hairstyle, for example.'

'You think that this might have influenced Maureen Atherton's view of her, then?'

'I suspect so, but nothing was ever said, at least to me. They seemed to tolerate each other after that. There were no problems.'

'Was everyone surprised when Maureen Atherton married Barnaby Scoular?'

'I suppose so. It did happen rather quickly. I guess that they were each looking for a different sort of security, and it seemed to work for them.'

I think that we've learned as much as we can today, thought Trussell. 'Thank you for your time, Mr Thompson,' he said, standing up. 'We really appreciate it. I hope that we won't have to trouble you again.'

Jackie Joynton followed Trussell's cue, putting het notebook and pen back in her bag.

Mrs Jenkinson opened the door and showed them out.

They returned to Trussell's Skoda for the trip back to Woodchester.

'Well worth the journey, Jackie,' said Trussell. 'Back to the station now. That's more information for the mind maps.'

39

Day 24.
Thursday 14th March.
CID Office, Woodchester Police Station.

No real progress had been made in identifying the mysterious figure seen leaving the Oatleys' house after Edmund Royston's death. More effort was needed and Trussell decided to broaden the investigation. 'Jackie, can you take Mrs Oatley's doorbell video and download a couple of reasonable pictures of the mysterious cyclist? The clearest you can get.'

'OK, Jim. What next?'

'I think we must cast the net a bit wider to try to identify the individual on the bike. When you've got the pictures, I suggest that we contact the media. BBC Southeast have their studio in Tunbridge Wells, so it might be helpful to ask them to include an item in their regular local news slot.'

'You want me to do that?'

'Please. Can you also contact the local newspaper group and ask them to run an article on it with the photograph? The usual statement. *The police are anxious to speak to the individual in the picture in connection with two murders. If anyone recognises that person then they should contact the police on the usual number.* Let's see if that generates any response.'

A quick look on the internet and Jackie had the BBC number. She rang it and asked to speak to the news editor. Having explained what was required, she arranged to meet him that afternoon with the details. The next call was to the Kentish Express group to arrange for them to run an article in the paper, but more importantly, in their online edition, to reach a wider audience. The same details.

'Right, that's fixed, Jim,' she said. 'I'm seeing the BBC at three o'clock.'

The two Detective Constables, working at their desks, had heard this exchange. 'Better watch out, Guv,' said Sprawson in his irritating grating voice. 'Once the TV people meet the lovely Sarge, they'll be poaching her to appear on the telly. You might lose her.'

Mark Green very sensibly kept quiet.

'How are you getting on with the Supercheap problem, Eddie?' asked Trussell. 'Now you've had a chance to check on the complete list of employees. Have you got any obvious candidates yet for the thefts there?'

'There are a couple of people with form who might fit the picture, Guv. I haven't shared it with the manager yet, I thought that it might be better to look into them a bit more before we move. There's always a slight chance that that they might not be involved. I'll share the list and details with you as soon as it's complete.'

'OK, Eddie, Soon as you can, please.'

'Greeno, I assume that there's been nothing further from your star witness?'

'No, Guv. But I'll check again to make sure that we have everything,' he said, reaching for the phone.

40

Day 26.
Friday 16th March. 9.00 am.
CID Office, Woodchester Police Station.

'How did you get on at the news studio yesterday, Jackie?' asked Trussell.

'It was a new experience, that's for sure,' she replied. 'They were very helpful. The appeal went out several times yesterday and they're going to repeat it today. The two murders certainly received a fair amount of on-air exposure. I just hope that it was worthwhile and we get some sort of response. Someone must recognise the figure on the bike.'

'Fingers crossed, we just need to wait for the calls to start rolling in,' said Trussell. 'Uniformed are manning the telephone line downstairs and will get details of any calls to us straight away.'

'I expect it'll be a case of filtering them,' said Greeno. 'We'll get the usual hoax calls and anonymous calls from people trying to settle grudges by giving us names.'

'When the results start coming in, I dare say that we'll have a number of people to talk to,' said Trussell. 'We'll share them out. Just remember to be meticulous when you start interviewing people.'

An hour later the messages started coming in from the team manning the phone line. They had done their best to filter out obvious hoax calls, but everything else would need to be followed up. 'We'll concentrate on this for the moment as it's key to the two murder enquiries,' said Trussell. 'We've done as much as we can at the moment as far as Barnaby Scoular is concerned.'

Jackie Joynton was collating the messages as they came in to divide them between the team members in a workable way. 'Here's an interesting one, Jim,' she said. 'It's a message from a Mr Braithwaite, the secretary of the Woodchester Country Club and Spa. He thinks that the photo resembles one of his members - Frederick Charles Durnford. He apparently regularly cycles there where he uses the gym. Braithwaite knows him well, so this is not just a casual sighting.'

'Interesting, Jackie. Would you like to follow that one up immediately?'

'Certainly. It sounds quite positive, compared with some of what's coming in.'

Mark Green picked up the pile of messages handed to him. Shall I start on this lot, Guv? Most of them are fairly local. I might be able to eliminate them quickly.'

'Do that, Greeno. Keep in touch and let me know how you get on.'

Eddie Sprawson, too, picked up the pile allocated to him.

'I'll look into these now, Guv,' he said.

'OK, Eddie. Keep in touch.'

That left Trussell alone in the office, so he took the opportunity to unlock his drawer and retrieve the pad with the mind-maps. He had a couple of items to add to it, so he looked at it again, trying to make sense of all these pieces of the jigsaw. *I must be missing something,* he thought.

41

Day 26.
Friday 16th March. 11.30 am.
CID Office, Woodchester Police Station.

Trussell was still studying the mind-maps at his desk when his phone rang. It was Jackie Joynton.

'Jim, I'm with Mr Braithwaite. I think that you should come down here straight away. There's something you should see.'

'OK. I'll leave now. See you in about twenty minutes.'

He grabbed his coat and car keys and headed for the car park. Within two minutes, he was in the Skoda, heading southeast out of town to the Country Club. He had been there over the years on a number of occasions to attend functions and fundraising dinners. It brought back memories as he had usually been there with his wife, Annette, but he had to try to put that association out of his mind and concentrate. He knew that Jackie must have had a good reason to ask him to meet her at the Club.

Twenty minutes later, he arrived at the imposing wrought iron gates and brick pillars which marked the entrance to the grounds of the Country Club, and took the long narrow road which bisected the golf course, up to the main building. He parked in the main visitor area and walked to the reception. Jackie Joynton was waiting for him, in company with a smartly dressed man in his fifties, in a dark grey suit, average height and build, thinning hair and metal-framed glasses.

She made the introductions. 'Jim, this is Mr Braithwaite, the Club Secretary,' she said. ' He believes that the figure on the mountain bike is one of his members.'

'It certainly looks like Freddie,' said Braithwaite. He usually wears a blue anorak and jeans in this weather when he cycles up here to use the gym. A number of members have commented on the likeness. It was on the news yesterday.'

'So, when does this gentleman use the facilities here, then, Mr Braithwaite? Is it on a regular basis or just occasionally?'

'Freddie's a very active member. He's always here. Never seems to be working yet he's not short of money. He seems to prefer cycling here although I'm sure that he must have a car.'

'Before you ask, Jim, said Jackie,' I've already got his details from the Club records. But the reason I've asked you to come up here is to look at the security camera footage. Mr Braithwaite has shown me recent footage of the CCTV outside and you can see the gentleman arriving on his bike.'

'I take it he's not here at the moment?'

'No, but he could turn up at any time.'

Braithwaite showed them into his office. There was a security screen on one wall divided into half a dozen smaller pictures. Using a remote, he rewound the video on one of them.

'Watch this, Detective Inspector,' he said.

A figure on a dark mountain bike cycled up the road towards the building, and as he approached it, slowed down and swung his right leg over the frame and coasted to a stop with his weight on the left pedal. He dismounted and wheeled his bike to the rack, where he parked it and added a security chain. As he walked towards the camera, it certainly looked like the figure captured on the Oatleys' doorbell video. The rider was the right height, the clothing seemed identical and the bike looked the same. *Too much of a coincidence?*

'I think that we should talk to Mr Durnford and ask him to explain his movements on the dates in question, don't you, Jackie?' said Trussell. 'One more thing, Mr Braithwaite. Could I look through your register of members, please?'

'Of course. Detective Inspector,' said Braithwaite. If you'd care to look at this screen, I'll put the list up for you.' He indicated the computer monitor on his desk, and moved the mouse around, clicking it several times in the process. 'There it is. Just scroll down. The members are all listed alphabetically. It's bang up to date.'

Jackie Joynton looked quizzically at Trussell, but said nothing. *What is he up to now?*

'Thank you, said Trussell, settling into the chair at the desk. 'This shouldn't take a moment.' He scrolled rapidly down the list, pausing occasionally to check something, before continuing to the last page. Satisfied, he stood up from the chair.

'Thank you, Mr Braithwaite. That was most enlightening,' he said.

'What's next, Jim?' asked Jackie Joynton. 'Shall we go back to the station and contact Mr Durnford? We can invite him to attend voluntarily at this stage,' she said.

'I agree,' said Trussell. 'Thanks again, Mr Braithwaite. This could prove to be very helpful. Can I ask you not to share this conversation with anyone, particularly your member, Mr Durnford?'

'Of course, Detective Inspector. I'm happy to do anything I can to help you. Do you want me to let you know if Freddie turns up today?'

'Please,' said Trussell, indicating to Jackie Joynton that it was time to go.

42

Day 26.
Friday 16th March. 2.00 pm.
CID Office, Woodchester Police Station.

'Right, let's call on Mr Durnford and see what he has to say for himself, Jackie,' said Trussell.

She had been surprised that Trussell hadn't wanted to dash straight round to the man's home to interview him as soon as they had seen the CCTV footage at the Country Club the previous day. His lack of urgency suggested to her that he wasn't completely convinced that Durnford was the man they were seeking.

'I get the feeling that you don't really think that he's involved in the two murders,' she said.

'We'll see,' said Trussell, enigmatically, as they headed down the stairs towards the car park.

Once in Trussell's Skoda, they left for the address given to them, a rather exclusive development forming part of the village of Rillenden.

Twenty minutes later, they were looking for the name of the street given to them by Braithwaite. The detached houses were relatively new, rather large and certainly well-finished and cared for. The open lawns, well-manicured, bore testament to the quality of the neighbourhood. Where there were cars on drives, they were all expensive models.

'Over there, Jim,' said Jackie, pointing to one particular house. 'Looks expensive. Not bad for a man who apparently doesn't work.'

Trussell parked and the two detectives walked up the drive past an expensive SUV to the front door. They were being watched by a security camera outside. Trussell rang the doorbell.

There was a delay before the door was opened – they had obviously been checked by the occupant. A man stood there, average height, lean athletic build, short, neatly styled hair. He was wearing a tee shirt and blue jeans and had a toned appearance. Probably in his early forties.

'Mr Durnford? ' asked Trussell, showing his warrant card. 'We'd like to talk to you.'

'What about?' said the man.

'We'd like to ask you a couple of questions. Can you tell us where you were on the morning of Friday the Twenty-Second of February?'

'Frankly, no,' he replied. 'One day is very much the same as any other to me now. I tend to be a bit spontaneous in my daily life. Whatever I feel like doing when I get up.'

'What about employment? What do you do?'

'Nothing whatsoever. Private means. I've got a couple of businesses that jog along quite nicely without too much intervention from me. More like investments.'

Trussell nodded at Joynton and she produced the photograph taken from the Oatleys' doorbell video.

'Do you own a dark-coloured mountain bike? And a dark blue anorak? asked Trussell. 'Is this a picture of you?'

Durnford studied it. 'The answer is I do have a bike like that and a similar anorak, but that is certainly not me. Where was this taken?'

'In Wilmhurst Green.'

'Never been there. Wouldn't even know how to find it. Let me show you my anorak and you can see that it's different to the one in the picture. Similar, it's true but different in detail.'

'What about Brackenden? Were you there on Monday Fourth March?'

'Definitely not. I'm absolutely certain of that. I wasn't even in the country that day. I was attending a friend's wedding in Spain that weekend and didn't get back until the Tuesday. I'll be happy to show you my passport to confirm that.'

'If we can just see the anorak and bike, Sir.'

'Yes, of course. Please come in. I've nothing to hide. I'm not sure how else I can assist you.'

They followed him into the very large hall with an impressive staircase up each side meeting a large, first-floor gallery. He opened an understairs cupboard on the left, rummaged around for a moment and then produced a dark blue anorak, which he offered to them for inspection. They studied it as he held it up on its hangar, and compared it with the photograph. The pocket design and stitching were obviously different.

'Are you satisfied? he asked. 'Would you care to see my bike now? It's in the garage.'

'Yes please, Sir.'

They followed him out of the front door to the large double garage adjoining the house. He pressed a remote and the door opened. He led the way inside. A black framed mountain bike was leaning against the wall. He offered it for inspection. Again it was obvious to the two detectives that this was a much more expensive model than the one in the photo. There was no sign of any other bike in the garage.

'You own just the one, Sir'

'Yes. I only use it for getting to the gym. I like to cycle to the Country Club most days. I know that they have plenty of exercise bikes in the gym, but I prefer to do that part of my programme in the open air.'

'Then I think that we have seen as much as we need, Sir. Thank you for your time,' said Trussell, offering one of his cards.

'Might I ask why you're asking these questions?' asked Durnford.

'Certainly,' said Trussell. ' You must have missed the item on BBC local news yesterday. You resemble the person in the picture we've shown you. We need to talk to that person.'

'I'm afraid I missed that. Don't watch too much television these days. Sorry that I can't help you.'

Trussell nodded and he and Joynton returned to the Skoda for the trip back to Woodchester. As they drove off, Joynton said to Trussell, 'You knew that it wouldn't be him, didn't you Jim? That's why you weren't in any hurry to follow the lead.'

Trussell smiled. 'We just had to eliminate him from our enquiries. He's been used, although he doesn't know it. You'd be surprised who belongs to that Country Club.'

'Who has used him, Jim?'

We'll see. By the way, I'm keeping this on the mind-maps for now.'

43

Day 28.
Monday 18th March
CID Office, Woodchester Police Station.

Mark Green and Eddie Sprawson had finished checking those people whose names had come from the help line. None of them fitted the description, or had been seen in similar clothing to the figure in the photograph. Few of them actually owned a bike and no-one possessed a black mountain bike.

'I think that we've exhausted the lists, Guv,' said Mark Green. ' I don't know where we go next.'

'Just have to wait to see if any other calls come in, I suppose,' said Trussell. 'There's still a chance that someone knows the person.'

Jackie Joynton looked sideways at Trussell. She was sure that something was going on, but he was saying nothing. Maybe he was still concerned about Fast Eddie's previous connections with Brandford.

'What d'you want us to do now, Guv?' asked Mark Green.

'We must work on the Supercheap problem,' said Trussell. 'There's nothing we can do about Mr Scoular at the moment. That leaves the two murders. The figure on the bike is key but we seem to have hit a wall on that one.'

'Shall I go down to Supercheap again, Guv?' asked Sprawson.

'Good idea, Eddie. Just make sure that you have details of all the employees who were there while the pilfering was going on. Check to see if any left before we became involved.'

'OK, Guv,' he said, standing up and heading for the door.

'What about me, Guv?' asked Mark Green.

Trussell looked at his watch. 'It's getting close to lunchtime. Why don't you contact your star witness to see if she's OK. She was starting her new job today, wasn't she?' See if she's thought of anything else which might help us now that she's put her problems behind her.'

Mark Green didn't need to be told a second time. He immediately sent a text to Sharon Webster. A reply pinged back almost immediately.

'She wants me to meet her at the Coffee Shop, Guv,' he said.

'By all means,' said Trussell,' but keep it official.'

'I knew it,' said Joynton, smiling. 'She's still drip-feeding him information.'

Mark Green grabbed his raincoat and headed for the door.

**

An hour later, he was back.

'Well, what news, Greeno,' asked Jackie Joynton.

'She seems to have settled in to her new job OK,' he said. 'She did have one real concern, though.'

'What was that?'

'She thought that she saw Jason on a motorcycle at the weekend. He and a passenger were touring the roads around Hammerton. She didn't think that he noticed her, but she was certain that it was him. I told her to keep in touch and let me know if she saw him again in the area.'

'You'd better tell the DI when he comes back.

44

Day 29.
Tuesday 19th March. 10.00 am.
CID Office, Woodchester Police Station.

The phone rang on Jackie Joynton's desk. She listened to the caller and made rapid notes on a pad in front of her. She replaced the phone and then turned to Trussell.

'Fire and Rescue on the phone,' she said. 'They've just attended a suspicious fire in Hammerton. They reckon that it looks like arson, and pretty serious at that.'

'We're rather busy at the moment with the fallout from the Building Society's problems. Can't John McIndow's team deal with it?'

'I think you'll want to add this one to our list,' was her response. 'It's 36, Graham Road.'

The colour drained from Mark Green's face.

Trussell looked blank for a moment, and then the penny dropped.

'Oh my God, that's Sharon Webster's address, Guv,' said Mark Green. 'Tillworth's former assistant. She was worried about some of the things going on there. I told you that she'd begun to fear for her own safety.'

'So, what's happened?' asked Trussell.

Jackie looked at the note she had scribbled during the short telephone call.

'Someone poured an accelerant through the letterbox last night and then threw a firebomb at the door. It was an old wooden door with a couple of glass panels. It didn't stand a chance.'

'What about the people inside?'

'Fortunately, they have a dog and he woke them all up. They managed to get downstairs and out of the back door. They were taken to hospital suffering from smoke inhalation. The neighbours called Fire and Rescue.'

Trussell thought for a moment.

'Right, Greeno, as you know the girl. I want you to get down to the hospital now and check on the family's condition. See if they're able to talk and whether they heard anything. I assume that they were taken to the Woodchester?'

Jackie nodded.

Mark Green hastily grabbed his coat, checked that he had his car keys, and rushed out of the door.

'Jackie, can you get on to uniformed? Speak to Alan. See what manpower he has available. I want house-to-house enquiries. Get them to knock on neighbours' doors. Someone must have heard something. Did Fire and Rescue mention roughly when the fire started?'

'Yes. Around one a.m.'

45

Day 29.
Tuesday 19th March.
The Woodchester Hospital.

Twenty minutes later, a very worried Mark Green was at The Woodchester Hospital, and rushing into the building. All sorts of thoughts were racing round inside his head. He headed straight for the A & E reception desk, warrant card in hand.

A secretary behind the counter looked up. 'Can I help you?'

'I'm DC Mark Green, I understand that some casualties were brought in here in the early hours after a fire in Hammerton? I need to check on their condition and possibly speak to them if they're fit enough. It's a family by the name of Webster.' A name he wasn't going to forget in a hurry.

The woman consulted her screen, tapped the keyboard and clicked the mouse.

'Ah yes. The two ladies have been taken to Maidstone Ward and the gentleman to Canterbury Ward. They're all on the first floor. Take the stairs in the main reception,' she added helpfully, pointing to the sign behind him.

Nodding his thanks, he walked rapidly in the direction indicated and then rushed up the stairs.

He found the two wards without any problem. They were on either side at the top of the stairs. He convinced himself that he should talk to mother and daughter first and went up to the nurses' station. One of them was seated behind the counter, looking through a file. He showed his warrant card and explained the reason for his visit. 'How are the ladies? Are either of them able to speak with me?' he asked.

'Yes,' she said. 'They're feeling a little better. The doctors have checked them. Luckily there wasn't any lasting damage done. They should make a full recovery fairly quickly. They seemed to have got out of the house in time. I'll show you the way.'

He followed her into a side ward and saw Sharon Webster, propped up in the bed, eyes closed. She had an oxygen mask covering her face and looked very pale. Occasionally, she was racked by a nasty cough, the legacy of the cocktail of smoke that she had inhaled.

'Ten minutes only,' said the nurse, pulling out a chair for him.

He sat down and looked at her.

Her eyelids flickered, and then opened wide in surprise. 'Mark Green,' she muttered hoarsely from under the mask. 'Why are you here? What's going on?'

'That's what I'm here to find out, Sharon. How are you? Can you talk? I've been allowed ten minutes. Then I have to speak to your parents.'

'How are they? The nurses won't tell me anything.' she wheezed.

'I'll find out and come back here afterwards, if they'll let me,' he promised. 'Now, what can you tell me about last night?'

Her eyes closed for a moment and a pained look crossed her face.

'Not a lot, really, Mark,' she said in a very hoarse voice. 'I remember the dog barking. Smoke everywhere. Dad was shouting at me. He was trying to get us out. I just had time to grab my dressing gown and phone. We managed to get down the stairs before the fire took hold. We went through the kitchen and out the back door into the garden. What about our house? How did it happen?'

'That's what we're trying to piece together, Sharon,' he said.

She stretched out a hand towards him and touched his arm. 'I'm so glad you came. What's going on? How did the fire start?'

'That's what I was hoping that you might be able to tell us. Now, Sharon, I have to know. Have there been any odd phone calls, strangers seen around the area, any threats, even?'

'Surely you don't think that the fire was started deliberately?'

'I'm afraid that all the signs point to it. That's why I'm here. But I'm glad that the DI sent me. I was really worried when we heard about the fire and realised it was your address. We were only told an hour ago.'

'Threats from whom?' she wheezed.

'That's what we're trying to work out.'

'I can't think of anyone that I've upset - apart from Arthur Tillworth.'

'Remind me what happened when you told him that you were leaving?'

'He was very angry and really shouted at me. Told me to get out right away. I thought that it was just because he knew that he would have to pay someone more to replace me.' She was racked by another coughing fit, and then she continued, hoarsely. 'Surely you don't think there was any more to it than that?'

'We certainty can't rule it out. After all, you saw all the comings and goings at the estate agents, especially his meetings behind the closed office door. You saw who went in there. You've even told me that you heard some of the shouting that went on. I'm sure Tillworth thought that you knew more than you should. All the time you were working for him, he had an element of control. Once you left, he lost that. Don't forget Jason, who caused you so much worry for a while until you left Tillworth. You haven't seen him since you started your new job, have you?'

'No. Not once. You don't think that he was responsible?'

'It's possible, but it might be connected. I'm keeping an open mind. Please don't mention this conversation to anyone else. I'll be back when I've spoken to your parents.'

'I'd like that,' she said, coughing again.

He got up, carefully moved the chair and went in search of a nurse. *I might as well speak to Sharon's mother while I'm in the women's ward,* he thought.

He asked the nurse about Sharon's condition.

'She should be able to go home in a couple of days,' she reassured him.

He enquired about Mrs Webster and followed the nurse to another side room.

'Same again,' she said. 'Ten minutes only.'

He looked at the woman propped up in the bed. He could see the family likeness. Ruth Webster had the same light brown hair as her daughter although it was lightly sprinkled with grey. Her face was very pale. She was probably about fifty but difficult to tell. Slim like her daughter. She had plastic oxygen tubes clipped under her nose and seemed more alert as she looked at him. Her glance was questioning.

Mark Green showed his warrant card and introduced himself.

'Oh, so you're the young detective Sharon's always telling me about,' she said in a very hoarse voice. 'I've been so worried about her and my husband. Nobody will tell me anything. I expect the nurses are all too busy.' This short speech started a coughing fit. She looked at him apologetically.

'Please take your time, Mrs Webster. I've just seen Sharon. She seems to be comfortable, despite what you've all been through. She's still on oxygen, but she was able to speak to me. I promised that I'd go back and tell her how you and your husband were getting on.'

'Thank you. That's very kind. She's always telling me how nice you are.'

Mark Green coloured slightly. He recovered his composure and asked the same sort of questions he'd asked her daughter and received very similar answers. Her reply was punctuated by a couple of coughing fits. The first she'd known was when her husband had woken them all up. She hadn't even heard the dog frantically barking. Not seen any strangers. She was certainly unaware of any threats.

He listened patiently, and then said, 'Thank you, Mrs Webster. I won't trouble you anymore. I need to have a word with your husband now to see if he has any information. Can I give him any message from you?'

'Thank you, Officer. Tell him that I'm OK and just say that I'm thinking about him.'

Off he went again, in search of a nurse to take him to Mr Webster.

The nurse led him to another side room. John Webster was lying propped up in the bed, oxygen tubes under his nose. He was awake. He had a pale but open friendly face and thinning dark hair.

Mark Green introduced himself. He told him that he had already seen his wife and daughter and that they were comfortable, despite their ordeal. They were both still on oxygen but able to speak to him. They sent their best wishes.

'Thank you,' he said.

'The reason I'm here,' said Mark Green,' is that the Fire and Rescue have told us that the fire was started deliberately. Did you hear anyone outside before the fire started? Can you guess who might be responsible? Do you have any problems, as a family, with anyone who might have taken this sort of action? '

He looked astonished.

'Whaat?'

'All the signs point to arson,' said Mark Green. 'Do you have any idea who might have done it?'

'The answer is no. I can't think of anyone who might do something like this to us. We seem to get along just fine with all of our neighbours. They're a friendly lot. We often socialise with them.' He paused, shaken by a coughing fit. Then he took a breath and continued. 'Did I hear anything? Yes - it might be relevant. I heard a motorbike leaving. It was very noisy.'

'Was this after the fire started?'

'Yes. I heard a crash downstairs and then the smoke… Fred, our dog, was going crazy - he was in the kitchen at the back of the house. We rescued him on our way out to the garden.'

Mark Green realised that there was nothing else to be learned from this visit. He stood up, pushing the chair back against the wall. 'Thank you. Mr Webster. I won't trouble you anymore today. I may have to talk to you again. I hope that you feel better very soon.'

His next stop was to see Sharon again having promised to return after he had spoken to her parents. At least, that was his excuse. He crossed the landing and returned to the women's ward. The nurse looked up, questioningly.

'I just need another quick word with Miss Webster, if that's OK, and then I'll be on my way back to town.'

'Ten minutes, then?'

He went back to her room. She was awake and looked up expectantly.

'I'm back, just like I promised. I've seen your parents. They're OK and comfortable. They send their love.'

'Thank you.'

'I've got to get back to the office. Can I drop by again? You might remember something useful,' he added hopefully.

She wasn't taken in by his excuse.

'Of course. I'll try very hard to see if I can remember anything important. I'll see you again soon, then?'

He smiled, nodded and left the room. *Must remember some flowers next time,* he thought. He rushed down the stairs and out of the main entrance and headed for the car park. He was haunted by the memory of Sharon and her parents, lying in their beds, pale, coughing. He must do his bit to catch whoever was responsible for the fire.

46

Day 29.
Tuesday 19th March.
CID Office, Woodchester Police Station.

Twenty minutes later, Mark Green arrived back at the police station and quickly ran up the stairs to the CID office.

Trussell and Joynton looked up when he walked through the door. Eddie Sprawson was still out checking with the local estate agents for any information about Edmund Royston.

'Well?'

He gave them a quick account of what he had seen and been told.

'Mr Webster was the only one who could tell me anything, Guv. He thought that he heard a motorbike leaving immediately after a loud bang. Must have been the petrol bomb hitting the door,' he said. 'He seems like a nice chap - the sort of man who gets on with anyone. Not an enemy in the world. It was the same with his wife. I can only think that it was aimed at Sharon.'

'Can you explain that, Greeno?'

'You already know why she left her job at Tillworth and Co. I told you about that lunchtime meeting I had with her when she called me unexpectedly. She was frightened that she had seen and heard too much. Then that thug Jason started following her around Woodchester. He was trying to intimidate her. You remember when she came into the station that she mentioned Tillworth was pretty upset when she quit. He told her to leave immediately, threw a wobbly and slammed his office door. She was sure that there was something going on other than the estate agency business.'

'What are you suggesting, Greeno?'

I don't think that Tillworth personally chucked the fire bomb, but I bet he knows who did. I seem to remember Sharon told me that the young thug, Jason, who stalked her for a while, was carrying a motorcycle helmet when he first turned up at the estate agent's shop. It may just be coincidental. I think that we should talk to Tillworth, Guv. I'd like to do it.'

'He's already on the to-do list, Greeno,' said Jackie. 'Leave him to us. I wouldn't want your actions to be influenced by personal considerations.

You're too emotionally invested in this one. We can read between the lines. We saw your reaction when you recognised the address.'

'I've told the Webster family that I'll go back again in a day or so in case they think of anything else.'

'OK. You do that and leave Tillworth to us,' said Trussell. 'But keep everything professional, Greeno.'

'We'll need to track down some of those other people that Sharon mentioned, Guv. That character, Brian, from Brandford and the young thug, Jason, that he brought with him. I wonder whether Eddie knows him.'

'We'll keep that one off the agenda for the moment. I want Eddie occupied with other things. Where are we with that supermarket problem?'

'It's still ongoing, Guv. Eddie's checked the employees and some of them have got form. I think he's looking at them first.'

'I'll get him to update me on that,' said Trussell. 'We need to decide what steps need to be taken. I'll go down to the supermarket with Eddie to see the management there. Hopefully, that should show them that we're taking it very seriously.'

Mark Green went to make himself a cup of tea. He knew that it was purely psychological, but talking to the Webster family and hearing them all coughing and wheezing had left him feeling rather dry and thirsty.

Trussell turned to Jackie and spoke very quietly so that Mark Green wouldn't hear the conversation. He didn't want to put him in an even more difficult position.

'The supermarket problems and trying to find any information about Mr Royston should keep Eddie occupied and out of our way for the moment. I don't particularly like this secrecy, but we can't compromise the main inquiry now. It was enough that he was involved with the Crime Scene Investigators after that solicitor's death.'

'Maybe we should talk to Tillworth as soon as possible, Jim.'

'Grab your coat, Jackie. We'll go there right now.'

47

Day 29.
Tuesday 19th March.
Woodchester High Street.

Ten minutes later, Trussell and Joynton arrived outside Tillworth's estate agency in the High Street.

They were not alone. A group of about half a dozen people were standing in front of the door, busy talking angrily. Voices were raised. Trussell pushed through the group, waving his warrant card and saw a sign inside the door which said simply *Closed due to staff shortage*. There was no other information. No telephone number to contact.

The most vocal member of the crowd, a rather angry man in his forties, turned to Trussell, as the latest arrival. 'What am I supposed to do? My purchase has just completed,' he shouted. 'We've paid the money over and I'm supposed to collect the keys to the new house from Tillworth. How can I do that if there's no one here? I can't even get back into my own house.'

Others joined in with a whole host of complaints. It was becoming a very noisy, angry crowd.

'I've arranged a viewing today but I can't get the keys.'

'I'm here by appointment for Tillworth to put my house on the market.'

'Tillworth told me to come down to discuss some offers on my property. I just want to know what's going on.'

Jackie Joynton put her hand up for silence as she waved her warrant card. 'We're here to talk to Mr Tillworth about certain matters,' she said. 'If everyone would calm down, I'll take down your details and we can contact you when we've managed to find Mr Tillworth.'

'Does that mean that there's been some sort of fraud?' asked the first man. 'I've paid money over and can't get into my new house.'

'I can't be certain. Sir,' said Joynton. 'Your money should have been transferred between the two sets of solicitors and wouldn't have been passed through Tillworth's hands. It's just a matter of getting hold of the keys. If we can't find him at this moment, and if you're now the legal owner of the property, then perhaps you should consider getting hold of a local locksmith to open the door and send Tillworth the bill. I can't tell you to do that, officially, of course. You should phone your solicitor and seek his advice.'

The man seemed satisfied with this suggestion, thanked her, pulled out his phone and went to find a quiet corner to make his call.

Joynton lined up the other people and took their details. When the last one had walked away, she looked at Trussell, questioning.

'I think that you handled that rather well, Sergeant,' he said, with a twinkle in his eye. 'More satisfied customers. Now, what are we going to do about friend Tillworth? We can't wait for extra hands. We'll have to deal with the matter ourselves. I think that we might start by asking whether anyone in the neighbouring businesses can offer any information. You start on the east side of the High Street and I'll do the same on the west side. We need to know when he was last seen. Ask if anyone noticed anything unusual, prior to the assembly of unhappy punters that we've just seen, of course. Did he just disappear quietly, or was there any fuss? We'll reconvene outside here in. say, half an hour? That should give us enough time to cover the immediate businesses. We should also include those shops on the opposite side, too.'

Trussell headed for the curtain and blind shop next door. He identified himself to the woman behind the counter and asked whether she had seen Arthur Tillworth that day, or even better, noticed him leave the premises.

'I'm afraid that I don't normally have time to keep an eye on the other businesses around here, Detective Inspector,' she said. 'However, as it happens, I did see him leave earlier today. It seemed odd. A car pulled up outside his shop and two men got out. They both went inside. Ten minutes later, they came out with Arthur Tillworth. He looked uncomfortable and was limping. One of them was holding him by an arm and helped him into the car. He looked rather unhappy about it. Then the other one came out carrying a pile of what looked like files. That's what made me think that it was a police raid, carrying the evidence away with them. The second man shut the shop door, locked it and then he got into the car and they drove off.

'I don't suppose that you can remember the men who were with him? Can you describe them?'

'Oh yes, I've seen one of them go in and out of the shop a number of times.'

'Can you describe him?'

'Late forties, fifty, maybe? I'd say about five ten, heavily built with a shaven head. He always wears a black leather jacket and jeans.'

'Can you describe the second man?'

'I hadn't seen him before. He was about the same height as the other one. Slimmer build and dressed casually in a denim jacket and jeans. He looked Afro Caribbean.'

'Thank you. Is there anything else you can tell us?'

'I must say that Arthur hasn't been the happiest of people this last couple of weeks when I've spoken to him, but even so, he looked rather worried. That's why I thought he was being arrested.'

'Do you recall what time this happened?'

She thought for a moment. 'Must have been around ten or quarter past.'

'Do you recall anything about the car? Make? Model? Colour?'

'I'm afraid not. I don't pay too much attention to cars. I think that it was silver or grey.'

'Thank you, Miss..?'

'Jane Brownlow. Mrs. I own this business with my husband.'

'You've been very helpful. I'll give you my card. Should you see Mr Tillworth come back, then please give me a call straight away. There's no need to mention this conversation to him, of course.'

Trussell walked out of the shop and phoned Jackie. 'Any luck so far?'

'Not yet, Jim.'

'Well, it looks as though I've struck gold, Jackie, so you can stop for the moment. Head back to the office and I'll see you there.'

Ten minutes later, they were back at their desks. Trussell shared the information given to him by Mrs. Brownlow.

'Sounds like our friend, Brian,' said Jackie. We'll need to talk to him sooner or later. All roads lead to Brandford.'

'I wonder whether Tillworth went off with Brian, if it was him, of his own free will, or whether he was persuaded to go?' mused Trussell. 'Was he doing a runner or had he been summoned by whoever's masterminding this whole thing?'

Joynton shrugged her shoulders. 'We won't know until we find him, if we can' she said. 'All our suspects keep winding up dead before we can speak to them. From what you've just told me, I'm not holding my breath as far as Tillworth's future's concerned either.'

48

Day 30.
Wednesday 20th March.
CID Office, Woodchester Police Station.

Sprawson's phone rang. He looked at it, thought for a moment, then turned away from the others and spoke quietly into it. Ending the call, he thought for a moment and then looked at Trussell. That grating voice again. 'Guv, is it possible that I can have a couple of hours off? Compassionate? That was my cousin on the phone. My aunt's taken a turn for the worst. She's very ill. We've been expecting it for a while. I've gotta be there. We're very close - she helped to bring me up.'

'Of course, Eddie. Where do you have to go?'

'Brandford, Guv.'

'Off you go, then. Hope that you have some better news when you get there.'

He got up from his desk, picked up his coat from the rack and rushed out of the office.

Trussell looked at Joynton. 'That looked a bit contrived,' said Trussell and Joynton nodded in agreement. 'There's something going on, Jackie. Leave what you're doing. I want him followed. It's a poor state of affairs when you have to question the actions of your colleagues, but in Fast Eddie's case, we have to make an exception. See if the pool has an unmarked car available. Take the camera with you. I'll see you downstairs.'

'Are you coming with me, then, Jim?'

'No. I've got an idea. Just organise the car and wait outside.'

Jackie grabbed her jacket and bag, took the camera from the cupboard behind her and rushed out to find a car.

Trussell wandered up to the other end of the office, occupied by the second CID team, led by DI John McIndow. He looked up as Trussell appeared by his desk.

'What brings you down here, Jim? Slumming?' he asked, smiling.

'Not exactly, Mac. I need a favour.'

Trussell looked around the office which was empty apart from McIndow and a new face at a desk in the corner. A girl in her late twenties with short dark hair She was wearing a plain blue jumper and a knee-length dark-coloured skirt.

'Who's the new team member, Mac?'

'Detective Constable Julia Brompton,' he said. 'She joined us today from uniformed as a replacement for Smithy. You remember that he transferred to the Met.'

'Is she busy yet? Or just finding her feet?'

'Why?' asked McIndow. He was suspicious and wondered what was coming.

'I need a new face for a rush job. She would be ideal. Is there any chance that I can borrow her? It'll only be for two or three hours at the most. That's if she's prepared to volunteer. Her lack of CID experience won't be a problem.'

'What's it about?'

'It's a surveillance job with my DS, Jackie Joynton. All legal and above board, Mac, but the fewer people who know about it, the better it will be. If I don't tell you, then it won't cause you any problems.'

'OK, Jim. It's up to Julia, if she's prepared to volunteer. Do you want to ask her?'

'Thanks, Mac. Just make the introductions and if she's happy to help us, I'll take her away and brief her.'

McIndow called his new team member over.

'Julia, this is DI Trussell. He runs that team up the other end. He needs some help for a couple of hours with something. He'd like to borrow you for a job. He won't even share it with me. He assures me that it's all entirely legal. It's up to you.'

She looked at Trussell. She was unsure. She studied him keenly for a moment. His open, honest face convinced her. She thought about the benefits of networking within the office. After all, she was only looking through old stuff at the moment and finding her feet. It would give her a chance to become involved. She made her decision. 'OK, Guv. I'm happy to help, if you think that I can do something useful.'

Trussell smiled his thanks.

'I owe you one, Mac. Grab your coat, DC Brompton, and come with me.'

49

Day 30.
Wednesday 20th March.
Woodchester/Brandford.

Trussell and Brompton walked quickly out of the office and down the stairs to the main entrance.

A dark blue BMW X5 was waiting outside with the engine running.

'You'll be working with my DS, Jackie Joynton,' Trussell told her. 'It's a rather delicate surveillance operation. She'll brief you. And don't worry about her. She qualified on an advanced driving course before she joined the CID.'

'No problem for me, Guv. I spent two years on motorway patrols before I came here.'

Trussell felt infinitely happier when he heard that. He opened the passenger door for her, but leaned in first to tell Jackie.

'This is DC Julia Brompton, Jackie. She joined John McIndow's team today, so your target probably hasn't seen her before. Have you got the details of his car? I want to know where he goes and who he meets. I'm assuming that it will be Brandford. After all, that's where all his contacts are. Take as many pictures as you need.' Then he turned to Julia Brompton. 'This trip and what happens, what you see or do, must remain between the three of us. Do not share it with anyone - not even John McIndow. I doubt whether he will even mention it when you get back, unless I do. The reasons for this will become clear this afternoon. Do I have your word on that?'

'Yes, Guv.'

She climbed in and closed the door and the car pulled away, leaving Trussell to his thoughts. *If Fast Eddie is up to something, then they should be able to spot it.*

Trussell was still worried about Sprawson's former life in Brandford and his contacts there. He wasn't completely convinced that Fast Eddie had put everything behind him when DCS Watkins had arranged his transfer to Woodchester. There were still some nagging doubts at the back of Trussell's mind. They included Watkins' involvement in the whole thing. He still wondered whether the DCS's motives in transferring Fast Eddie might have had an element of self-preservation about it. Trussell had seen enough during the short time that he served at Brandford police station to be concerned.

In the car, Jackie briefed Julia Brompton about their quarry for the afternoon as they headed east towards the motorway and Brandford. Details of his car - make, colour, registration - were all shared with her.

'I'll need to put my foot down to catch up with him,' said Jackie. 'This is the only route to Brandford. I don't think that he'll be breaking any speed limits today. He won't want to draw attention to himself. I'm sure that flashing his warrant card would be enough to convince one of the patrols if someone pulled him over, but my guess is that he won't want to be noticed. I've a fair idea where he might be heading, and I'm absolutely certain that he won't want to be stopped.

They drove down the slip road and filtered onto the motorway. Traffic was surprisingly light for the time of day. The road appeared slightly damp, but it was drying out. Jackie eased the BMW into the middle lane to overtake a couple of trucks, and she stayed in that lane as she continued to accelerate. 50 - 60 - 70 - 80 - 90.... They had to find Fast Eddie's car before he left the motorway.

'Damn! Here come a couple of our friends from uniformed,' she said, as a marked police car appeared in her rear mirror, rapidly catching them, blue lights flashing, headlamps blazing, siren blaring. She waited for them to overtake, but they didn't and the siren screamed at them.

Jackie looked for their own blue lights but Julia found them first and switched them on to identify themselves. The marked car was not dissuaded. This could get tricky. If they stopped, then they'd lose their quarry.

'I'll call it in and they can get rid of our friends,' said Julia, reaching for the radio. Their car's registration was on the dashboard. She'd done this before. As Jackie concentrated on the road ahead, Julia flashed their blue lights again. Then, suddenly the car behind turned off their lights and slowed down. The message had got through.

They both searched the road ahead, looking for Fast Eddie's distinctive blue Mondeo. At last, Jackie spotted it and eased back her speed to move into the nearside lane. She kept a respectable distance between the two vehicles - far enough away not to be seen but close enough, should he suddenly leave the motorway. Sure enough, he took the next exit towards Brandford and headed for the town centre. Jackie hung back and when he turned into a side road, she stopped to see where he went. The area was rather run down, industrialised with repair garages, a tyre centre and a couple of small factories. Fast Eddie pulled into the parking area in front of a small manufacturing unit and parked his car. He got out and walked towards a door on the front.

'Quickly, give me the camera,' said Jackie. She had just enough time to focus the long lens and take a couple of pictures before he opened a door and disappeared inside.

'So that's where his old auntie lives, then,' she muttered.

'I've been here before,' said Julia. 'It's a plastics factory. I was part of a raid here a couple of years ago. There were women working at the premises so they sent another woman and me to oversee any arrests.'

'What was that all about?' asked Jackie.

'That business was a front for drugs and some of the women were illegals. The Border Force was involved as well. The legitimate business was owned by Jack Summerton, although a clever brief managed to get him off on the pretext that he had no idea that his business was being used by others.'

'It's a name I've heard,' said Jackie. 'Tell me more. What do you know about him?'

'Jack Summerton is the Mr Big round here. Nothing happens without his permission. He grew up on the Brandford estate which is a real hotbed of crime. He started life as a snout for someone in the local nick, and, somehow, he worked his way to the top and now effectively controls the area. There've been rumours about his connections with some of the local senior police officers. No one's been able to pin anything on him up till now.'

'It's time to level with you, Julia. DI Trussell swore you to secrecy about this afternoon's little excursion. The man we are following is DC Eddie Sprawson, one of our team. He was transferred to us a couple of months ago from Brandford, on the orders of the DCS, Charlie Watkins, who, coincidentally, also served there. It's no secret that Jim Trussell didn't want him, but Watkins didn't give him the option. Eddie has had his problems in the past and Jim is convinced that this particular leopard's very unlikely to change his spots. He thinks that Eddie still has connections and contacts here. We believe that the case we're currently working on has links to Brandford, so we don't want it compromised by someone like Eddie. He asked for some compassionate time off today to visit his dying aunt, but Jim saw through that, which is why we're here.

And as you only joined today and haven't met him, he wouldn't recognise you.'

'So, what do you think he's doing here today that was so urgent?'

'He might be reporting progress on our enquiries. On the other hand, knowing what he does about our current investigation, he might just be trying to cut himself a bigger slice of the deal, in exchange for even more regular intelligence on our case.'

'So, what's going on?'

'It began with a missing person, the Manager of a local Building Society. Once we started looking into that, our enquiries led to a mortgage fraud. It looks as though there are some very big numbers flying around and there's been some collateral damage as well. A couple of people connected with our inquiry have turned up dead and that may not be the end of it. Another important witness has disappeared and the home of another has been firebombed.'

Joynton was interrupted by a commotion in the street.

The door to the building opened and Eddie Sprawson backed out of it onto the pavement. A tall, gaunt and very angry man, probably in his early fifties, followed him out of the building, jabbing his chest with his forefinger and waving the other fist at him. He shouted something and Sprawson retreated in the direction of his car, still followed by the man, shouting and gesticulating.

'Quick. The camera,' said Julia. 'That's Jack Summerton doing all the shouting. He doesn't look well. Seems as though he's lost quite a bit of weight.'

'So that's the man himself,' said Jackie, picking up the camera and pointing it at Summerton.

The rapid click of the shutter of the camera confirmed that a number of pictures had been taken.

Meanwhile, Sprawson had reached the safety of his car and was preparing to leave in a hurry. He hadn't spotted the dark blue BMW further up the street with the two detectives inside.

'We'll hang around and see what happens next,' said Jackie. 'I'll phone DI Trussell and let him know. He can see the pictures later.' She called Trussell, listened to his response and then hung up. 'As I thought, he wants us to stick around to see what Eddie's up to.'

Sprawson backed his car off the parking area, still followed by a very angry Summerton, banging on the side window. Sprawson pulled away and drove off, leaving Summerton still standing there gesticulating. Then, apparently overcome by this exertion, the man sat down heavily on a pile of pallets outside the unit. He seemed out of breath and looked exhausted by his efforts.

He was joined by a stocky man wearing a black leather jacket and jeans, who leaned over Summerton, putting a hand on his shoulder, seemingly concerned about him. Jackie remembered Mark Green's visit to Tillworth's estate agency and immediately thought of Brian. The regular visitor to the estate agency. He matched Sharon Webster's description exactly. This put a whole new spin on things.

The two men exchanged a few words and Summerton pointed at Sprawson's departing car.

The two detectives watched as Brian, if it was him, climbed into a silver Mercedes parked in front of the building. The camera was busy again, recording this new evidence.

'I wonder where he's off to?' she asked. 'Nowhere that's good for Eddie, I'm sure. We'd better follow them to keep an eye on things.'

She eased the BMW quietly away from the kerb and moved along the road, keeping a discreet distance.

'How well do you know this area?' she asked Julia. 'I wonder where they're going.'

'Not well, but this is the seedier part of town, if you can believe it,' she replied. 'Most of the dodgy bars and clubs are down this way. As close to a local red-light district as you can get in Brandford, I suppose.'

'Definitely Eddie's old stamping ground, then. He's probably got connections round here. I wonder if he's trying to sell information to the highest bidder.'

'If Jack isn't buying, then he's not doing very well,' said Julia. 'I doubt that he'll get much interest anywhere else, especially with that other character trailing behind him.'

'Sounds like Eddie's status as a police officer may not be enough to protect him,' said Jackie.

'We'd better tell Jim Trussell. We may have to get some support down here if Eddie's putting himself at risk, although I doubt that we can look to Brandford for it. This is going to get tricky.'

They watched Sprawson's Mondeo turn into a small side street and park. The Mercedes pulled in further back. Sprawson got out and walked towards one of the garishly lit bars in the road. He exchanged a couple of words with the man by the door, showing his warrant card, and then went in. The man who might be Brian followed at a distance. He didn't get into the bar as a rather larger muscular bouncer stepped forward and put a hand on his chest to stop him. The camera was clicking away, recording all of this.

'I do believe that we're witnessing the beginning of a turf war here,' said Julia. 'No one would've dared bar any of Summerton's people before.' 'Perhaps your man thinks that he can curry favour with the new power in the district – Eastern Europeans. Showing his own value and weakening Summerton's position at the same time.'

Jackie reached for her phone to call Trussell. 'What's the name of this street, Julia? She asked.

'Crick Lane. The bar's called The Green Parrot.' was the reply.

Jackie called this information in to Trussell.

'We think that Eddie has just burnt his boats with Summerton, his long-standing contact,' she told him. 'We think he may be trying to broker himself a deal with the new kids on the block. They're Eastern Europeans, apparently. He must feel that Summerton's getting weaker and losing his influence. He certainly didn't look well. That might just be a dangerous mistake, though.'

She listened to Trussell's response and hung up.

'Jim wants us to wait a bit longer. See when Eddie leaves the club and how Brian reacts. Hey, look, he's on his phone. I bet he's talking to Summerton. Note the time in case we have to look at phone records at some time in the future.'

Julia glanced at her watch and then scribbled time and location down on a notepad.

Jackie Joynton continued. 'I wonder whether he's calling up reinforcements. I can't believe that he would start a war here and now. They tend to be a bit more subtle these days.'

They sat there in the BMW for about half an hour, watching. Nothing happened. There were just people going in and out of the club, after being checked by the bouncer.

'One of the fun parts of surveillance,' said Jackie. 'It's all waiting and no action. I just hope that Eddie hasn't found a back way out and that we've missed him. Mind you, he'll need a car to get back to Woodchester.'

As she spoke, Fast Eddie emerged from the club, exchanged a couple of words with the bouncer, shook his hand and walked towards his car. Brian started moving towards him, but the bouncer put his hand inside his jacket, suggesting that he was carrying a gun, and shook his head, indicating that he shouldn't go any closer. Eddie got back in his car, heaving a sigh of relief, and headed for Woodchester.

Jackie tapped Jim's number and handed her phone to Julia, as she pulled away to follow Eddie.

'Tell Jim what we've seen and that I believe that we're heading back to Woodchester now.'

As she was relaying this message to Trussell, Jackie noticed that Brian had returned to the Mercedes and was moving off in pursuit of Eddie.

'I've got a horrible feeling that this isn't going to end well,' said Jackie, as they followed the two cars at a reasonable distance. Do you know how to activate the dashcam on this car?'

Julia looked around the dashboard on her side.

'Here it is. I can switch it on anytime you need it.'

'I think that we might need some evidence,' said Jackie. 'I've got a bad feeling about the whole thing. That man, if he is Brian, has probably got some instructions from Summerton. I've got a suspicion that Eddie's luck is about to run out. I just hope I'm wrong.'

They followed the two cars up the slip road and onto the motorway. As they accelerated away, they noticed that the Mercedes was keeping its distance from Eddie's Ford. They hung back, safe in the knowledge that they had enough under the bonnet to outpace both the other cars.

The speeds increased. It now seemed that Eddie had noticed the other car, and was trying to get away. Then as they approached a straight and level stretch of the road, the Mercedes began to creep closer to Eddie's car.

'Switch the dashcam on, Julia,' said Jackie. 'Look how the Mercedes is positioning itself. I think Eddie's about to have an accident, courtesy of Mr Summerton. He's going to pay the price for double-crossing him.'

'Call Jim, and tell him what's going on. Give him the Mercedes registration number.'

As they watched, horrified, the Mercedes crept closer to the Ford, moved left onto the hard shoulder and then, in a decisive move, it swung to the right, striking the nearside rear wing of Eddie's car. The back of his car swung wildly to the right and then the vehicle flipped over towards the hard shoulder. It rolled several times, bounced, before hitting the top of the Armco barrier on the left and flying over it, hitting a tree and bursting into flames.

The Mercedes snaked from side to side as the driver fought to control it, recovered and streaked off, heading for the next exit and a probable return to Brandford.

'Call it in, Julia. They can organise Fire and Rescue,' said Jackie, as they passed the burning remains of Eddie's car. 'We can't help Eddie so there's no point in us stopping. We'll follow the Mercedes back to Brandford. See what Jim says. I need a decision as the exit's coming up pretty quickly.'

'There was nothing we could do, Guv,' Julia told Trussell. 'It all happened too quickly. Do you want us to follow the Mercedes? He's leaving the motorway and looks like he's heading back to Brandford.'

She listened to Trussell for a moment, and then told Jackie to follow the other car.

The Mercedes took the same road back towards the town centre, and then turned right at the next set of lights, signposted towards the Elton Industrial Estate. A couple of hundred yards further on, it braked and turned left through the gates of a large scrap yard.

Jackie stopped the BMW just outside and they watched Brian get out, speak to one of the employees and then head for the small office building, pulling out his phone as he walked. A man of Afro-Caribbean appearance, dressed in a denim jacket and jeans, came out of the office and greeted him. They shook hands and exchanged a few words before Brian spoke on his phone. Jackie was recording this evidence with the camera as events unfolded.

'Looks like he's reporting back to Summerton, Julia,' said Jackie. 'Can you note the time?'

As they watched, the second man signalled to someone and then a large grab on a crane moved down towards, the Mercedes, closed on it, breaking the windows as it gripped the top of the car. It was hoisted upwards, swung round and dropped into a hydraulic ram. The top closed slowly, crushing the top of the car, and then the ram started moving. The screech of tortured metal grew louder as the car was completely crushed. The remains were removed from the crusher as a metal block which was lifted out, swung around and deposited with a pile of similar items. Jackie had recorded all of this with the camera from the moment the man drove into the yard.

'Well, that's the evidence of the car destroyed,' said Jackie. 'It's time we left now. We need to get back with the pictures. This has moved to a whole new level. DI Trussell needs to see the evidence. Remember that this whole event was confidential. Not a word to anyone - not even DI McIndow, although John's a decent guy. He won't ask you any questions. He trusts Jim Trussell.'

50

Day 30.
Wednesday 20th March.
CID Office, Woodchester Police Station.

As soon as he had heard the news of Eddie Sprawson's accident, Trussell knew that he had one of the most difficult conversations of his career ahead of him. He needed to tell DCS Watkins and it would have to be face to face. He couldn't put it off. He picked up the phone, tapped in Watkins' number and heard Watkins' familiar voice on the other end of the line. 'It's Trussell here, Sir. Can I have a word? It's extremely urgent.'

'If you must, Trussell, but make it quick. I've got to see the ACC in fifteen minutes.'

'I'll come up immediately, Sir.'

Trussell took the lift to the hallowed eighth floor, wondering exactly how he was going to start the conversation. Tact was needed. He tapped on the half-open door.

'Come in, Trussell. I suppose that you've come to complain about Sprawson and tell me that you can't put up with him any longer. He's too much of a maverick for you.'

What a stroke of luck thought Trussell. He had wondered how he was going to broach the subject.

'It's certainly about DC Sprawson, Sir, but not what you think. I regret to have to inform you that he was killed in an accident on the motorway this afternoon.'

Watkins' jaw dropped. He was stunned.

'How did it happen?'

'As I understand it, he was forced off the road by another vehicle. His car rolled and hit a tree. It caught fire. It all happened very quickly. He didn't stand a chance.'

'Was it accidental or deliberate?' asked Watkins. 'I'm aware that Eddie wasn't particularly known for his silky driving skills or courtesy behind the wheel. Not a case of road rage, surely? What are we doing to trace the other driver?'

'We know exactly who was responsible and the whole sequence has been captured on video.'

'You'd better tell me everything you know, and quickly. Trussell. The death of a police officer on duty is something that will deeply concern the ACC. I'll have to tell him when I see him shortly. There may have to be a press conference or at least some public announcement.'

'Well, Sir, I don't think that you are going to like what I'm about to say, but these are the facts.'

He then recounted everything that had happened; from the moment that Fast Eddie had received the call on his mobile and had asked for a couple of hours' compassionate time off.

'Unfortunately for him, I didn't believe him, Sir. I guessed, correctly, that something else was going on so I arranged for DS Joynton to follow him in an unmarked car from the pool. She was accompanied by DI McIndow's new DC, as Eddie wouldn't have recognised her. They took a camera and had the dashcam on the vehicle.' He repeated what Jackie had told him on the phone about Eddie's movements and whom he'd seen as part of a complete breakdown of the sequence of events.

'It seems that Eddie had a falling out with Jack Summerton. It looked as though he was trying to sell him out to the new boys in town, an Eastern European gang. Summerton's man followed him and reported back. He was obviously given instructions to deal with Eddie.'

Trussell watched Watkins' face for any reaction. There was none. *I wouldn't want to play poker with him,* he thought.

After the initial shock, Watkins seemed to have mastered his emotions. 'So, are you telling me that everything has been recorded on video?'

'Yes Sir. They even watched the vehicle being crushed at one of Summerton's scrap metal yards, immediately following the event. The car was put into the crusher and emerged shortly afterwards as a block of scrap. They photographed everything. We have the identity of the driver confirmed by the photos. We can even show him as the man seen talking to Summerton after Eddie left that building in Brandford.'

'What steps have you taken to arrest him?'

'None as yet, Sir. It only happened an hour ago. I've been waiting for DS Joynton to get back with the evidence. I want to see the pictures and the video before I move on this. We've reason to believe that the man's involved in the Building Society case we're handling and we're still investigating his connection with it. It's quite possible now that Summerton may be connected with the mortgage fraud that we're looking into at the moment. We already have two other deaths that we have to deal with. Not to mention a suspicious fire involving the house belonging to the family of one of our key witnesses.'

'What was Eddie's part in this?'

'Although we tried to occupy him with other matters, I couldn't keep him out of it completely. He was aware of the case and the fact that it seemed to lead back to Brandford. I haven't any proof yet, but I strongly suspect that Eddie was feeding information back to Jack Summerton. I'm sure that you remember the name from your time at Brandford.'

Watkins nodded.

'He was Eddie's first informant during the short time that I spent there myself. Now it seems that he's the local Mr Big, controlling most of the organised crime. I'm sure that you know that, anyway, Sir. It could be that Eddie became greedy today and that Summerton had had enough. Just conjecture on my part. I'll never be able to prove that now, of course.'

'I think that you'd better haul this man in immediately, Trussell. Once you've got him here, then you can start questioning him about the other matters.'

Trussell nodded in agreement and then thought about practicalities.

'This is probably not a good time to mention it, Sir, but we're fairly stretched at the moment. Eddie was investigating organised theft at the Supercheap Supermarket just outside town, as well as looking for Mr Scoular. Things have been disappearing from their warehouse. I've been down there myself with him, but we obviously still have to deal with the problems at the Building Society and the two suspicious deaths. These must take priority at the moment. That's before anything else comes our way. I know that John McIndow has more than enough to handle at the moment so we can't ask him for any further help. He was able to loan us DC Brompton for the surveillance today as she'd only arrived this morning, but that was a one-off.'

'Well as luck would have it, Trussell, there's another new DC transferring to us from uniformed next week. You can have him. His name's Beach. I'll arrange for him to be re-deployed here instead of sending him to Dover.'

'Thank you, Sir. If that's all for now, I'd better go back downstairs. There's a lot to do now after today's events.'

With that, Trussell left Watkins' office to return to his depleted team. The discussion had been easier than he could have hoped. He privately wondered about the ramifications about Sprawson's death. *What does this mean to Watkins? Will he sleep more easily now that he no longer needs to be concerned about Sprawson?* No one knew what had happened at Brandford that required him to transfer Sprawson to Woodchester. Was there any direct link to Summerton? Trussell was obviously concerned about any further leakage of information about the Building Society case. *Any connection with Barnaby Scoular's disappearance?* All these questions were flying round inside his head as he took the lift back to the first floor.

He went back to the CID office and looked for John McIndow first. He felt that it was only right to share some information with him before Jackie Joynton and Julia Brompton returned to Woodchester. After all, the news about Eddie Sprawson's accident would soon get out. The press had probably already got hold of the information about the crash. The fact that a police officer was involved would only deepen their interest.

McIndow was sitting at his desk, studying the monitor screen in front of him. He looked up as Trussell appeared.

'Alright, Jim, what have you done with my new team member?' he asked, smiling.

'They're on their way back, Mac. But I need to talk to you about this afternoon's trip before you hear about it from anyone else.'

McIndow picked up on Trussell's sombre look. 'Has something happened?'

'Yes, I'm afraid so.'

Trussell recounted what he knew, omitting nothing and McIndow whistled.

'How did Watkins take it, Jim? After all, Eddie was his man. He brought him over from Brandford and inflicted him on you.'

'He didn't bat an eyelid, Mac. I don't know what I was expecting in the way of reaction. But he told me that he would speak to the ACC immediately. He also instructed me to pull the man responsible for the accident straight away. I'll wait for Jackie to get back and hear what she has to say before I jump in that particular direction.'

'Good luck with that'.

'Thanks, Mac. The cynic in me would say if Charlie knows, then the word might get back to Brandford pretty quickly. There's always a chance that he might talk to someone at the Alamo before I can get over there to pick up the man responsible. I know there's been a clear-out in Brandford, but the problem is that we still don't know who we can trust there at the moment. I can't ask for any local assistance in case the word gets back to the very people I want to question.'

McIndow nodded. 'I'll make sure that Julia keeps quiet about it until she's needed officially,' he said. 'Just keep me posted in case I can do anything else to help you.'

Trussell thanked him for his discretion and headed back to his own part of the office to await Jackie's return and the chance to debrief her and Julia Brompton. He would want to look at the video and the pictures taken by Jackie with the camera. He would also encourage them to write down everything while it was still reasonably clear in their minds. The statements would be needed for any enquiries, including a possible inquest, and most likely for Crown Court if Brian was arrested and brought to trial.

51

Day 30.
Wednesday 20th March.
CID Office, Woodchester Police Station.

Jackie Joynton walked back into the office, accompanied by DC Julia Brompton. She was carrying the camera and the memory card from the dashcam.

Trussell looked at them both, concerned.

'Are you two OK after this afternoon?'

'Yes. We're fine, Jim. It wasn't pleasant, but I think that we're making some real progress on the whole enquiry now. By the way, Julia has some interesting info that you ought to hear.'

Trussell looked at her, quizzically.

'Well, Guv,' she began, 'what we saw this afternoon in Brandford confirms your suspicions about DC Sprawson. We watched him have an argument with Jack Summerton before he left the factory. All recorded. I'd been there on a drugs raid a couple of years ago so I recognised Summerton. It went to court and he got off on a technicality. It probably convinced him to be a bit more careful in future. Having said that, Guv, I thought that he looked a sick man today. Don't know what the problem is.'

'It might be worth digging the records of the trial out,' said Trussell. 'I wouldn't be surprised if the solicitor involved wasn't a certain Marcus Culverton, given his dependence on recreational drugs, and Summerton's dealings in that trade.'

'Your intuition again, Jim?'

'Culverton probably knew where the money went, too,' said Jackie. 'That was just another reason to silence him. The High Weald should know who the cheques were made out to.'

'We'll need to approach Brandford Borough Council Planning Department,' said Trussell. 'They should tell us who applied for the planning permission for all the supposed redevelopment of the waterfront there. That's just one more avenue for us to investigate. You and I should do it. There's no extra help at the moment and Greeno already has too much to do.'

'Not to mention fighting off the attentions of his star witness, Jim?' she laughed. Julia Brompton looked puzzled. Jackie glanced at her, smiled, and said, 'Don't even ask, Julia!'

Trussell thanked Julia Brompton for her assistance. He mentioned that he had told DI McIndow about the afternoon's events but asked her not to discuss the matter any further. He also told her to expect to be interviewed as a witness as there would be questions to be answered at some stage.

She wasn't exactly smiling as she returned to her new desk.

52

Day 35.
Monday 25th March.
CID Office, Woodchester Police Station.

The phone rang on Trussell's desk. He picked it up and found himself addressing DCS Watkins. 'Come up, Trussell. I've got your new DC here.'

'I'm on my way, Sir.'

'That was Watkins, Jackie. He's got our new team member up there. His name is Beach. I've got to go up and collect him. I hope Charlie hasn't frightened him too much.'

'We could certainly do with some help now, Jim. Another pair of legs for the door-to-door enquiries would be very useful. Uniformed can't help us with any more manpower, and we still haven't found those responsible for the Webster family house fire.'

'By the way, Greeno,' said Jackie, turning to him, 'how're the Websters getting along?'

'They're out of hospital now and in some temporary accommodation that the Insurance Company has sorted out for them. They found them a place fairly close by. They're still suffering a bit health-wise but getting better all the time.'

'I guessed that you'd keep in touch, Greeno,' she said.

'Just following the DI's orders,' he said, looking a bit embarrassed.

'Anyway, Greeno, Congratulations are in order.'

'What for, Sarge?'

'Why, your promotion, of course. You've just moved up the pecking order to number three now that DC Beach is joining us. He'll be junior to you!'

Trussell smiled to himself as he heard the banter. It showed him that the three of them had a good working relationship and there was a real team spirit. He only hoped that the new man would fit in as well. Life had been difficult with Sprawson and there had always been a bit of an atmosphere since he joined. Trussell's initial concern about him had been justified. He was not callous, but he knew that this would be one less worry. As far as he knew, Sprawson didn't have any close family, so there wouldn't be any difficult conversations or the need to 'say the right thing,' which he knew would be dishonest. He had his values and would stick by them.

He left the office, took the lift up to the eighth floor and headed for Watkins' office. The door was open, and he saw a very nervous-looking young DC sitting in the chair opposite the DCS. He looked as if he was fresh out of school. He was wearing a tan leather jacket over an open-necked polo shirt, and jeans; casual but smart. His sandy-coloured hair fitted his name. What a contrast with the more formally dressed Mark Green, who tended to favour sports jackets, pressed casual trousers and tie.

Hope he's up to it, thought Trussell. *We don't have room for any passengers, particularly at the moment.*

Watkins made the introductions and told Trussell to put Beach to work immediately. The new man followed his new boss to the lift but when the doors opened, Trussell stood aside to let Beach go in first.

'Right, DC Beach. Tell me about yourself,' said Trussell, as he touched the button for the first floor. 'Where you've come from and what sort of experience you've managed to amass in your career to date. And, why did you apply to join the CID?'

'Well, Guv,' he began nervously, 'I've done two years around Canterbury and then I applied to join the CID. They were sending me to Dover and the DCS called me in to tell me I was coming here instead. I'd had a couple of jobs which involved the CID and thought that was what I really wanted to do."

'How old are you, Beach?'

'Twenty-one, Guv.'

'First name?'

'Tim, Guv.'

'OK,' said Trussell as the lift stopped at the first floor, 'come and meet the rest of the team. There are only two others, so you're on a very steep learning curve. There'll be very little time to find your feet.'

He led Beach into their section of the office and introduced him to Joynton and Green. Jackie spotted his sandy hair, smiled, held out a hand and said, 'Welcome, DC Beach. I think I'm going to call you Sandcastle from now on!'

'You'll have to get used to DS Joynton's sense of humour, DC Beach,' said Mark Green.

Beach, taken aback, accepted it with as much good grace as he could muster.

They'd already cleared Eddie Sprawson's desk of what few items he'd left in it. They hadn't found anything of any real personal nature, which had softened the blow somewhat, so everything was ready for its new occupant.

'Right, Jackie. Let's have a ten-minute team chat about everything that's going on here and where we are, to bring DC Beach up to speed. We can prioritise things today and then we can put Sandcastle to work.'

The nickname had already stuck.

Trussell quickly outlined progress on the cases and stressed how they all appeared to be linked.

'Right. Here's what we'll do today. Greeno, get that list of the Webster family's neighbours, and check to see how many we still have to talk to. Take Sandcastle with you and knock on those doors. It's crucial that we know whether anyone heard or saw anything on the night of the fire. Keep notes of everyone you see and any information you get.'

'OK, Guv. Where can I contact you if necessary?'

'Call me on my mobile. Jackie and I are taking a trip to Brandford to see if we can track down the mysterious Brian, if that really is his name. Luckily Jackie has seen him, so we're not just reliant on photos. If we can find, him, we'll bring him in. We'll keep an eye out for his unlovely assistant, too. He can join the party as well. What was his name, Greeno?'

'They called him Jason, Guv. I know that Sharon -Miss Webster - hasn't seen any sign of him since she left her job with Tillworth, but he's still a concern. I know that there's no evidence at the moment, but I still believe that he was behind the fire.'

Trussell and Joynton exchanged smiles at Greeno's apparent slip of the tongue.

'That's precisely why we're going, Greeno. We don't have any emotional involvement in this case other than the need to bring the perpetrators to book.'

Tim Beach seemed baffled by this exchange.

'Don't worry. Sandcastle, Greeno will explain,' laughed Jackie.

Mark Green checked through the files on his desk and found the one containing the lists of neighbours around Graham Road, Hammerton and clipped it on a board.

'Let's deal with this character, Brian, first, Jackie,' said Trussell. 'I just hope that Fast Eddie didn't tip anyone off before he fell out with them. Before we go, can you print off several copies of the pictures of our mystery man? We can use them if we run into Summerton. See what reaction we get. It might also be worth giving one to Greeno. He can show it to Sharon Webster from the Estate Agents at some point. She'll be able to tell us whether it was the same man who visited Tillworth. Oh, and by the way, we should show the picture to Susie Albright at the High Weald. I wonder whether Brian was the man she saw talking to Scoular that morning?'

A couple of minutes with the camera, computer and the office printer, and Jackie had some recognisable prints of the man they wanted to contact.

'Come long, DC Beach, let's get started,' said Mark Green, picking up his jacket from the back of his chair and checking that he had his car keys.

As they left the office, Trussell asked Jackie what she thought about their new DC.

'He seems keen enough, Jim. We'll just have to hope that he can handle the pressure. Now, thinking about Brandford, are you going to contact the Alamo first to let them know that we're on their manor? If we don't tell them, there'll be hell to pay if they find out.'

'Sad state of affairs, Jackie, but I don't know who can be trusted there. I don't want someone tipping off Summerton, to give this character, Brian, the chance to do a runner. Strictly between us two, I still have concerns about Charlie. I don't know who's still at the Alamo from his time there. There's a new man in charge, a Superintendent Ross, apparently, but who knows whether all the bad apples have been moved out.'

'Surely, you're not thinking about going to the ACC, Jim? That'd be a seriously dangerous career move.'

'Not at the moment. Let's see how things play out. If we don't tell Brandford, and they know what we're up to, then we know there's a leak.'

53

Day 35.
Monday 25th March.
Graham Road, Hammerton.

Clutching the clipboard containing the lists of addresses still to be seen, Mark Green led his new colleague down the stairs and out of the main door towards the car park. He walked towards his two-year old white Hyundai, clicking the remote to release the central locking.

'In you get, Sandcastle,' he said. 'It's only about fifteen minutes to Hammerton this time of day. I reckon that we've got about twenty doors to knock on. Let's just hope that they're all at home.'

'What did the Sarge mean when she said that you would explain everything, Greeno?'

'Well, it's a long story. Sharon Webster was working for one of the local estate agents and there was definitely something dodgy going on there. The DI sent me round to question her boss, but he was out, so I had to speak to Sharon instead. She gave me some valuable information about things going on there but she was very concerned for her own safety and wanted away from that job. She's contacted me several times and the DI knows about it. The Sarge thinks it's a bit of a hoot and keeps ribbing me about it because she thinks that there's something going on between Sharon and me. Well, there isn't. At least, not at the moment.'

'What's she like?'

'Nice girl. Very attractive. She's about my age. She still lives with her parents. Don't think that she'd need much encouragement from the way she speaks to me, but we've got a lot going on at the moment. No time to think about her. I'm keeping a check on the family while we try to find out who firebombed their house. DI's orders.'

Mark Green fastened his seat belt while he was speaking, twisted the ignition key and then when the engine fired up, reversed out of his parking space.

'Do you have any idea who might have done it, Greeno?'

'I'm pretty sure that the estate agent, Arthur Tillworth is mixed up in it. Everything seems to point to Brandford and the organised crime there.'

'What makes you so certain?'

'Not just me. The DI and the DS are looking into that. DC Sprawson came from Brandford and there were hints that he still had connections there. You heard about his unfortunate accident, I expect?'

'Yes. It's being talked about everywhere. It was definitely discussed in Canterbury. It seems Brandford has a bit of a reputation.'

'Certainly has. No one says too much, but I understand that the DI spent a short time there when he was a new DC. From what I can gather, he was a bit concerned about some of the things going on there. There were all sorts of stories about corruption at senior level. The DI didn't want any part of it and didn't stay there that long. He soon got a transfer away.'

'What sort of guy is he?'

'He's very straight and open, but no pushover. Integrity's important to him. He sticks to the rules. No corner-cutting, whatever the reason. He expects his team to operate the same way. You'll like him. He's very supportive of all of us. The Sarge told me that he lost his wife about six years ago and he's become a bit withdrawn. It doesn't seem to hold him back, though, when it comes to dealing with any cases. He's always highly focussed and very intuitive. That makes him a first-rate detective. He's in his mid-forties and the Sarge reckons that he should have easily made DCI by now, perhaps even Detective Superintendent, but I guess that his ambition stalled a bit with his personal problems. The Sarge is very good. She's always trying to get him down the pub with the rest, but he just doesn't seem to show much interest in socialising these days. It's a real shame.'

'So, what are the DI and Sarge doing today?'

'They've gone to Brandford, hoping to track down and arrest the bloke responsible for Sprawson's accident. Just between us, I can tell you that the whole thing was picked up on the unmarked car's dashcam. The Sarge got a pile of photos as well. The target's also under suspicion of being connected with the mortgage fraud. Frankly, I wouldn't be surprised if he was behind the deaths of the surveyor and the solicitor. Either him or his psychopathic sidekick.'

They had reached Hammerton now, and Greeno headed for Number 36 Graham Road. The police tapes were still in place around the Edwardian semi-detached house and a PCSO stood outside to deter any curious visitors. The brick porch had saved the house next door, but it still looked a mess with the remains of the charred front door, and its two missing glass panels, hanging open. Green showed his ID to the PCSO and asked whether he'd heard anything about the events of the previous days.

'Not a whisper,' was the reply.

Green consulted the list on his clipboard, and pointed at a house about fifty yards away on the same side of the street.

'Number 2. We'll start there, Sandcastle.' They headed for the house and walked up the path to the front door. 'Have your ID ready,' he said to his colleague, as he rang the doorbell.

The door was answered by a middle-aged man, wearing overalls who looked at them warily.

Green identified himself and mentioned the fire at Number 36. 'We're just following up on the events of the Twenty-Fifth,' he said. We're hoping that we might learn something now that people in the street have had a chance to think about it or even discuss it with their neighbours. Did you hear anything or notice anything suspicious that night?'

'Well,' he said. 'I did see a couple of lads riding round here during the day on a pretty expensive motorcycle. It was a BMW S1000RR with a red tank, fairing and front mudguard.'

'Interesting,' said Greeno. 'What makes you so sure? That's a pretty good description'

'Cos I'm an enthusiast and I've got one myself. Expensive. Beautiful bike. 998cc four-cylinder motor. 200 brake horsepower. They didn't strike me as the sort of people I'd normally associate with a piece of kit like that.'

'Interesting,' said Greeno. 'Did you notice anything about the riders?'

'Yes. The rider was wearing an Arai helmet. Red, white and blue. It's used by a lot of the professional road racers. Top of the range. Goes with the bike image, but not the rider, if you see what I mean. Neither the rider nor the passenger was wearing full leathers. Just leather jackets and jeans. They didn't seem to go with the bike or the helmet. I'm sure that they weren't from around here. They just seemed to be riding round the streets looking at the houses.'

'What time was this?'

'Late afternoon. Say about four.'

'Did you hear anything later that night? Say around one a.m.?'

'Yes, I did. I had to get up to let the dog out into the back garden. Something must have spooked him. He barked until I got up. Then I heard a crash or bang or something. It was a strange noise. That was followed by the sound of a bike being ridden away very quickly. Those BMWs have a distinct sound if you thrash them in a lower gear. I'd be prepared to say it was the same bike I saw earlier in the afternoon. As I said just now, I've got one and I'm used to the sound.'

'Thank you, Mr...'

'Browning.'

'Thank you, Mr Browning. That could be quite helpful.'

'You're welcome. I'm happy to help. Do you have any news about the Websters? They're nice people. John is the sort who would help anyone. I can't imagine why anyone would want to do this to them.'

'That's exactly what we are trying to find out, Sir. Thank you for your help. I'll give you a card with my phone number on it in case anything else occurs to you.'

Tim Beach had listened intently while Mark Green spoke to Mr Browning and noted all this down on his clipboard.

'Right, Sandcastle,' said Greeno, as he ticked Number 2 off the list. Let's try next door.'

They walked up the path and rang the doorbell. No response. Mark Green rapped on the door with his knuckle but there was still no answer.

'We'll have to revisit this one,' he said as they moved on to Number 6. It was the same again. No reply.

'I've done this door-to-door stuff several times when I was at Canterbury,' said Tim Beach. 'It's not the most rewarding part of policing.'

Mark Green glanced at the clipboard with its list and notes, looked along the street, paused for thought and suddenly had a lightbulb moment. 'Can you carry on with this for a couple of minutes, Sandcastle?' he asked, handing him the clipboard. 'I've got an idea. May not help, but worth a try. Work from the list. If you get any positive info, write it down against the house on the list. Don't forget the names. I shouldn't be more than ten minutes. I'll catch up with you.'

With that, he retraced his steps to the corner where they had spoken to Mr Browning, and turned left at the junction into Westbury Road. He knew exactly where he was going. He walked along the road until he reached Number 51, a small terraced house.

He walked up the path and rang the doorbell. A dog barked and then he heard the sound of footsteps with a woman's voice calling out, 'I'll get it.'

The door opened and a rather surprised Ruth Webster looked at him.

'Detective Constable Green. This is a nice surprise. Come in.'

'Thank you, Mrs Webster. How are you all?'

He was interrupted by the arrival of a large ginger dog of unknown parentage. It walked up to him, inspected him suspiciously and sniffed the hand that he held out. Satisfied, the dog allowed him to pat its head, licked the hand, turned around and walked back, somewhat disdainfully, the way he'd come.

'So that's Fred,' said Mark Green. 'He's the super hero – the dog that saved you all.'

'We owe him a lot,' she said. 'He seems to like you. What brings you here today?'

'This is an official call. I need to speak to Sharon, urgently, if it's possible?'

'Of course. I'm sure that she'll be pleased to see you.'

'I just need to ask her a couple of questions. I can't stop. My colleague is knocking on doors at the moment and he won't be very pleased if I leave it all to him.'

'I understand,' she said, opening the door to the living room. 'She's in here, resting. Sharon, you have a visitor.'

He walked in and saw a still pale Sharon Webster, sitting quietly on the sofa. She was wearing a pink dressing gown with matching slippers, and was obviously not yet fully recovered from her ordeal. When she saw Mark Green, her hands immediately flew to her head, as she tried to pat her hair into some sort of order and the book she'd been reading fell off her lap.

'Hullo, Sharon. How are you? I'm sorry to bother you today but this is official.'

'Oh dear, it's Detective Constable Green,' she smiled. 'You haven't finally come to arrest me, have you?'

He looked embarrassed as he recalled their first encounter. 'No. Sharon, but I want you to think about that conversation. You told me about Jason when he first came into your office and sat on your desk. You said that he was carrying a motorcycle helmet that he put down on the desk. Do you remember anything about it?'

She closed her eyes, as if trying to visualise the helmet. She was concentrating hard.

'Yes, I do remember it. It was so brightly coloured. It was red, white and blue. There was a design on it. Numbers? In blue, I think. It had a tinted visor. The full-face design made me think of the Storm Troopers in Star Wars. I wish he'd been wearing it with that visor down so that I didn't have to look at that ugly face with all those tattoos.'

She shuddered at the memory.

'That's brilliant,' he said, noting the details down. 'Thank you. It's just what I needed to know. Do you think you'd recognise the helmet if you saw it again?'

'Absolutely.'

'Just one other question,' he said, producing the copied photo of the driver responsible for Fast Eddie's accident.

'Do you recognise this man?'

She looked at it. 'Yes, that's Brian, the man who used to visit Arthur Tillworth regularly at the shop.'

'Thank you, Sharon. That's been very helpful. I have to go now.'

'Can't you stay a while?' she asked, hopefully.

'Not now. I must go. I'll call round later, if that's OK.'

She nodded.

With that, he left the room and opened the front door.

'Is everything alright?' asked Mrs Webster.

'Yes. Thank you. Sharon has just given me with some very useful information. I'll call round later when I've finished for the day, if that's OK.'

She nodded and smiled to herself as she closed the door behind him.

Mark Green hurried back along Westbury Road and turned right into Graham Road, looking for Tim Beach. He spotted him further up the road, leaving the front garden of one of the houses.

'How're you getting on, Sandcastle?'

'It's just an exercise in futility, Greeno. I feel that I'm just going through the motions,' he said. 'People are either not in or else they heard or saw nothing. I've covered the list. There are five houses where there was no reply. I've noted everything down, names and all. Is life in the CID always this exciting?'

'90% legwork and 10% excitement, Sandcastle. It won't always be as interesting as today! We'll head back to the station now and write this up. You'll soon find out that the DI likes us to be meticulous. He says that it's a good habit to get into.'

'So, where did you sneak off to then, Greeno?'

'As it happened, I went to see Sharon Webster, our star witness. The family are living just round the corner in temporary accommodation.'

'I might have known. You're skiving off and leaving me to do the legwork, while you visit your girlfriend.'

'It's not what you think. Something Mr Browning said struck a chord. I rushed round to ask Sharon a couple of questions and I think it's paid off.'

'What's that then?'

'Remember Mr Browning's description of the fancy crash helmet?'

'Yes. What's the relevance?'

'I'd remembered Sharon telling me that one of the thugs from Brandford had been carrying one when he went into the estate agent's shop. He parked it on her desk. Well, Sharon has just described it. It matches Mr Browning's description perfectly. She's certain she'd recognise it if she saw it again.'

Sandcastle looked impressed.

'That sounds like a result then, Greeno.'

'The DI thought that that guy might have had something to do with the arson attack on their house. This looks like an important clue. So, today's visit to Hammerton hasn't been completely wasted.'

'That's a relief,' said Sandcastle, with a certain amount of irony.

'I also showed her the photo of the guy who caused Eddie's accident. She confirmed that it was the same man who came into the estate agent's shop regularly.'

'Definitely worthwhile, then, Greeno.'

By now, they had reached the car, so they climbed in and set off back to the station.

'We'll update the file before the DI gets back,' said Greeno. 'We can add the information to the whiteboard in the office, too. That makes Jason a suspect now as far as the firebombing's concerned.'

Tim Beach looked thoughtful. 'You've told me about the DI, Greeno. What about the Sarge? She's quite a looker.'

'You can forget that, Sandcastle. Her partner, Mike, is a six-foot-three rugby player and they live just around the corner from the station. He's in the job as well, in Traffic division. Nice guy. Anyway, the Sarge is good at what she does. Works well with the DI. She's very supportive of him. Seems to be able to read his moods and cheer him up. She has a degree in computer sciences and I understand that her ambition is to join the Fraud Squad. It's no secret that the DI wants to keep her and hopes that he can change her mind.'

54

Day 35.
Monday 25th March.
Brandford.

Trussell and Joynton walked down the stairs and out of the station towards the parking area. They had arranged for two uniformed officers to accompany them in a van and they were already waiting in the car park.

'We'll take my car, Jackie,' said Trussell. 'You can direct me to the building where you saw Jack Summerton and his man, Brian, just before he chased Fast Eddie.'

They climbed into Trussell's Skoda and he left the car park, followed by the van, turning east along the High Street in the direction of the motorway and the journey to Brandford. Once on the motorway, Jackie was looking intently at the opposite carriageway.

'There it is, Jim,' she exclaimed,' pointing to a burnt area on the other side. A fire engine was still on the hard shoulder, with the crew examining the wreckage. 'That's where Eddie had his accident.'

Despite his views and distrust of Eddie Sprawson, Trussell wasn't totally devoid of feelings. 'An awful way for Eddie to die, Jackie. Are you OK with it, having seen it happen right in front of you? What about DC Brompton?'

'Yes. It was probably easier for her because she spent two years on the motorways so she's no stranger to accidents. She accepted it. It wasn't pleasant, but we have to get on with life.'

'OK. Let's see if can find this character, Brian, if that really is his name. You'll recognise him of course? We do have Sharon Webster's description as well.'

'I'll certainly know him, Jim. What do you plan to do?'

'Go to Summerton's building to see whether he's around.'

'Did you know Summerton from your short time at Brandford? I understood that he was Fast Eddie's first informant.'

'I might have met him once, but it was twenty years ago. I doubt that he'll remember me. We've all changed, anyway.'

Jackie pointed out the next exit to Brandford, and then directed Trussell to the small factory unit on the industrial estate where she and Julia had seen Eddie have his falling out with Jack Summerton. On the way, they passed the scrap yard where the Mercedes had been crushed.

'That's where the car finished up, Jim. We'll just have to rely on photographic evidence. There were certainly plenty of those crushed metal cubes lying around the yard.'

'Turn left here, Jim,' said Jackie. 'That's where Eddie parked. There's the door where I saw Summerton chase Eddie out.'

Trussell pulled in and parked the Skoda. As agreed, the marked van was parked out of sight of the unit. They got out and led by Trussell, headed for the door. It was a factory-style metal fire door and it appeared to be locked.

'Let's try that reception door,' said Jackie, pointing to a frosted-glazed door ten feet away.

Trussell led the way, warrant card in hand, opening the door into a small reception area. The décor was very tired and dirty. There was a counter with a glazed partition above it. A crudely handwritten sign invited callers to ring the bell for service. Trussell pressed it and waited to see whether there was any reaction from the door on the other side of the counter.

Nothing happened. He pressed it again, more insistently this time.

'Alright. I'm comin.' A loud voice from somewhere inside the bowels of the unit. He thought that the voice was female, but couldn't be sure.

The door opened and an angry-looking woman appeared. She was probably about fifty, he thought and above average height. She was dressed in some sort of baggy stained and faded blue overall. Her dark brown hair was tied back rather untidily and her face told its own story. Lived in. She was taken aback by the police presence.

'Whaddya want?' she shouted.

'I want to speak to whoever's in charge here,' said Trussell.

'Why might that be? We don't encourage visitors. Who are ya?'

'Police,' said Trussell, showing his warrant card.

'You can talk to me,' she said. I'm the manager. Now waddya want? I ain't got all day ter waste talkin' ter you.'

'OK,' said Trussell. 'I'd like to speak to Brian.'

'He ain't 'ere at the moment.'

'When will he be back, then?'

'No idea. Can I give 'im a message?'

'In that case, I'd like to speak to Jack Summerton, please. This is his business, isn't it?'

'I dunno what you're talking about.'

'OK,' said Trussell, reaching for his phone. 'I'll arrange for a warrant to be sent over right away so that I can search the place. Who knows what we'll turn up here. I'm sure that you'll find it more convenient to cooperate now. My team can be very thorough. I might even get the Border Force down here to check your employees. Big fines now for business owners if any foreign workers haven't all got the right paperwork and shared it with you. I can arrange to close you down, just like that.' He emphasised his words with a snap of his fingers. 'Just think about it, but don't take too long. Now then, where's Brian? And what's his other name?'

He started tapping a number into his phone.

'Alright. Alright. 'Old on a moment. Brian ain't here. I dunno where he is at the moment. I ain't responsible fer 'im. 'E usually gets 'ere about four o'clock every day.'

'And his second name?'

'Kirby.'

Does he have a son called Jason?'

'Na, Jason ain't 'is son, although 'e looks like 'e could be. E's a nasty little toe rag wiv a short fuse. I reckon e's a psycho. I wouldn't wanna upset 'im.'

It didn't sound terribly convincing, thought Trussell

He persisted.

'So, is he here at the moment?'

'Nah. 'E's probably out with Brian, puttin' the frighteners on some poor sod. Brian don't like to get 'is own 'ands dirty these days. Finks 'e's management.'

'What about Summerton? Is he here?

 I dunno anyone of that name.'

Trussell watched the colour drain out of her face at the mention of Summerton's name. She was badly frightened. He glanced at his watch. About ten minutes to four. He looked at the woman again.

'I think we'll wait then,' he said. 'Perhaps you'd be good enough to wait with us. Don't want you tipping them off. By the way, what was Jason's other name?'

'I fink it's Tubbitt. Funny name, innit?'

'I also want your name. If anything goes wrong, then I'll need to include you in what we're doing.'

'It's Shirley. Shirley Tompkins. I don't wanna be involved.'

Trussell and Joynton exchanged knowing looks. Now was not the moment to complicate matters. Better to concentrate on Brian Kirby.

'It seems it's a bit late for that, Shirley,' said Trussell. 'Do yourself a favour and cooperate. Stay exactly where you are.'

Trussell walked towards the outer door and beckoned Jackie.

'Are you up for this?' he asked quietly. 'If these guys turn up and resist, we could have a problem. I'm reluctant to call the Alamo for reinforcements. You just don't know who they'll send and whose side they'll be on.'

'We'll manage, Jim. The four of us should be enough to cope with them. If Jason really is as crazy as our new friend Shirley suggests, then we could have a problem but pepper spray should take care of him,' she said, reaching discreetly into her handbag.

The two detectives and the two constables stood just inside the door, just out of sight from the street. Trussell looked at Shirley Tompkins and put a finger to his lips. 'Just look as though you're doing something, and don't look at us. Don't say a word when anyone comes in.'

The clock on the wall ticked agonisingly slowly towards four o'clock and then past it.

Ten past four.

'Perhaps he's not coming back here today,' whispered Jackie. 'You don't think that he's been tipped off?'

Trussell shrugged his shoulders. 'Who can tell? Particularly as you-know-who upstairs told me to get on with this particular arrest.'

A shadow fell across the frosted glass of the door.

Trussell looked across at Jackie and nodded.

The door opened and a man came in. Jackie nodded at Trussell in recognition and pulled the pepper spray out of her bag to be ready. Trussell held a pair of handcuffs ready behind his back.

'Brian Kirby?' asked Trussell and the man turned to face him.

'Who wants to know?' said the man.

'Detective Inspector Trussell, Kent Police,' he said, showing his warrant card. 'Brian Kirby, I'm arresting you on suspicion of causing the death by dangerous driving of Edward Sprawson on or about Twenty-First of March.' He completed the caution and one of the two uniformed officers quickly secured Kirby's wrists with handcuffs before the astonished man could resist. 'You will now be taken to Woodchester Police station to be questioned about this and a number of other matters. Other charges may well follow.'

Kirby scowled at them. 'I ain't saying nothin' without a brief.'

'That's your right,' said Trussell. 'That can be arranged at the station.'

As they prepared to take him out of the building, Trussell turned and looked in Shirley's direction.

'Not a word to anyone. Remember what I said earlier.'

He knew that his words were probably wasted, and that she would probably speak to Jack Summerton as soon as they left.

The two uniformed officers gripped Kirby by his arms and led him in the direction of the van. The back door was opened and he was unceremoniously pushed into the secure part and the door slammed behind him.

'Follow us back to Woodchester,' Trussell told them before he and Jackie returned to the Skoda. 'I want to make sure that Mr Kirby is booked into a nice comfortable cell as soon as possible.'

55

Day 35.
Monday 25th March.
Woodchester Police Station.

Trussell and Joynton arrived at the station followed by the police van. The two uniformed officers removed Kirby from the back of the van and took him down to the custody suite with the two detectives following.

He was searched and Trussell told the custody sergeant that he had been arrested on suspicion of causing the death of Eddie Sprawson by dangerous driving. 'That will do for now,' said Trussell, 'but there'll be other charges to follow.'

Kirby simply scowled at Trussell and repeated his request for a lawyer.'

'Anyone in particular, Mr Kirby?'

'Yeah. I want Willoughby Frankenberg. He's in Brandford. You'll find 'im on the internet.'

'OK, we'll try to arrange that for you.

After he had been searched and the other formalities had been completed, two uniformed officers took him to the cells. They removed the handcuffs, took his shoes and belt and pushed him into a vacant cell. The heavy door slammed behind him.

Trussell and Joynton walked back upstairs to CID, Trussell looking thoughtful. 'D'you know, I'm wondering whether we might just have found Stevie's mother,' he said.

'Shirley Tompkins. Of course,' said Joynton. 'I didn't even think about it and make the connection. I was too concerned about Mr Kirby at the time. You don't think that it's just a coincidence, the fact that she has the right name and is living in Brandford?'

I don't think so. She looks the right age, as well. She's tall. Maybe that's where Stevie gets her height.'

'What about her husband, Mr Tompkins? I wonder where he is these days?'

'Who knows,' said Trussell. 'She's not much of a catch now, is she?' It'll mean another trip to Brandford. She'll have some questions to answer.'

'I wonder whether she'll be prepared to reveal the identity of Stevie's father. Or should I say, Jessica's father?'

'That's what we'll need to find out. She certainly seemed genuinely frightened when I mentioned Jack Summerton's name.'

'It's as if he had some sort of hold over her,' said Jackie.

Anyway, she'll keep for now,' said Trussell. 'She won't know that we suspect her of being Stevie's mother.'

'I remember that Sharon Webster commented on the likeness between our guest downstairs, Mr Kirby, and the young thug, Jason, who threatened her at Tillworth's shop,' said Jackie. 'This whole case is beginning to look like some sort of extended family business.'

'The lab will be on overtime processing all the DNA samples when we bring the rest of these people in,' smiled Trussell.

56

Day 35.
Monday 25th March.
Hammerton.

Mark Green left the office and headed for the car park. He climbed into his car and set off for Hammerton. He had told Mrs Webster that he would call round again after he'd finished for the day. He needed to have a conversation with her and John Webster before he spoke to Sharon. It was going to be a bit tricky.

He pulled up outside Number 51, got out of the car and walked up the short path of the terraced house to the door. When he rang the bell a dog barked somewhere inside. Fred was obviously around.

Ruth Webster answered the door. She smiled at him. 'Come in Detective Constable Green,' she said. 'We've been expecting you.'

'Thank you, Mrs Webster. I'd like to speak to you and your husband before I talk to Sharon, if that's OK.'

'Of course,' she said, looking surprised. 'Come through to the kitchen. Sharon's in the living room but I believe she's asleep.'

Mark Green followed her down the narrow hallway past the stairs to the back of the house, and into the modest kitchen-diner. John Webster was sitting at the small table, reading a newspaper. He had a cup of tea in front of him. He looked very much as Mark Green remembered him from their brief conversation in the hospital. He too was still somewhat pale.

'We have a visitor, John,' she said. 'Detective Constable Green would like to speak to us.'

John Webster put down his paper. 'Hello again. Please sit down,' he said, indicating a chair opposite him. 'What can we do for you?'

'Tea, Detective Constable?' asked Ruth Webster.

'Thank you, Mrs Webster. Milk, no sugar, please.'

Mark Green collected his thoughts as he sat down at the table. Mrs Webster put a cup and saucer in front of him and filled it from the teapot.

'Can you help yourself to milk?' she asked, handing him a small jug.

'First of all, how are you getting on?' he asked, as he poured the milk into his cup. 'Any idea when you'll all be able to return to work?'

'Another week and we should be OK,' said John Webster. 'Wish I could say the same for the house. The Insurance Company are dragging their feet a bit. No indication as to when the work will start. I doubt that we'll be back in our own house much before Christmas.'

'Have you shared your current address with any of your neighbours?'

'Of course. We keep in touch with them. They've all been brilliant in helping us. Why do you ask?'

'I don't want to worry you, but we have a fair idea who was responsible and we haven't been able to track them down yet. I wouldn't want them to come here looking for you. Can I suggest that you speak to your neighbours and ask them not to talk about where you're living at the moment? It's not widely known that you are just around the corner. I know that from my house-to-house enquiries.'

'Who's behind it, then? I can't believe that we've upset anyone round here.'

'You're absolutely correct. I should appreciate it if you would keep this information to yourselves for the moment. Unfortunately, Sharon was the target. It seems that she inadvertently overheard a bit too much at her last job and someone decided to do something about it. Not her fault. It seems that she found herself working for someone who was involved in some extra-curricular business.' John Webster looked shocked at this revelation. 'This is the main reason why DI Trussell has asked me to keep in touch with you. Sharon is a very important witness.'

Ruth Webster looked disappointed. 'I thought that you were interested in Sharon after you met her at Tillworth's agency,' she said. 'You've been taking her to lunch and you've even brought her home from Woodchester in your car. She's told us all about it and talks about you all the time. What are we to think?'

'This is the second part of what I wanted to talk to you about,' said Mark Green. 'Sharon is a very attractive girl and, it's true, we have spent a fair amount of time together.'

'She's been let down quite badly in the past by a couple of boyfriends and I wouldn't want to see her hurt again. She's too trusting,' said Ruth Webster. 'Perhaps it would be better that you don't contact her anymore. She'll get over it. She has done before.'

'You've misunderstood me, Mrs Webster. It's the official part of all this that's causing me a problem too. Sharon is a very important witness in our investigation. The DI has told me to be professional at all times to avoid prejudicing any future prosecutions. I've told Sharon that. When the legal side is done, then I won't be constrained by those rules.'

'What do you mean?'

'If I didn't have this problem, then I would have asked her out as soon as I met her. I think that we've got along rather well together under the circumstances. Where I need your help is to persuade Sharon to accept the situation as it is for the moment and treat our current relationship as a purely professional one until the process is finished.'

'And then?'

'We'll see where we go when those barriers have been removed. She's been through so much already through no fault of her own, and it's certainly not my intention to add to those problems. I'll tell you honestly that it's been very difficult for me, trying to keep this relationship at arms-length. I really enjoy her company when we meet. I think that we have a lot in common.'

'So, what do you want us to say to her?'

'First of all, ask her to take great care still when she's out and about. The people concerned know her and she still represents a threat to them. We are looking for them and doing our best to catch them. Secondly, tell her to maintain that same professional distance between the two of us when we meet. The situation won't last for ever, and then I can hopefully make it up to her.'

'Why don't you tell her yourself?'

'I will, but I just need you to help her understand the situation. I did promise her that I would pop in after I had finished, so I'm keeping my word. I would like to talk to her.'

'No need to wait,' said a familiar voice from the doorway. 'I'm awake now.'

'Why don't you take your tea into the living room, Detective Constable Green?' said Ruth Webster, smiling now.

Mark Green followed Sharon into the other room, carrying his cup and saucer. She indicated the armchair next to the settee.

'I heard the end of that conversation, Mark' she said. 'What happens next?'

'We catch the people responsible and bring them to justice and then you and I can start again. I've told your parents that I've been uncomfortable with our enforced relationship. If I'd just been a casual customer at the estate agents when you offered me that new flat, then things would be different. It's bad enough that some of my colleagues think that something is going on between us and the DI keeps reminding me to keep a professional distance. I can't afford to let anyone believe anything different at this stage of our enquiries. I hope that you understand that.'

'OK, Detective Constable Green. I'll do my best. Formality it is. But you'd better look out when all this is over,' she said, smiling. 'I still have your phone number.'

Mark Green tried to steer matters in a different direction, hoping that this conversation had resolved the situation, at least for the moment.

'What can you tell me about your time with Tillworth? When did you start working for him? When did you first notice that things weren't right there? Before you answer, you don't mind if I take a few notes in case you mention something that might assist us?'

'Of course not. Let's think. I started working there about five years ago. It wasn't Tillworth in those days. The business was owned by a Mr Trott, The agency was all a bit old-fashioned and traditional, but I enjoyed it. He was well respected and knew the local property market really well. The business was very successful in those days, but then he wanted to sell up and retire about three years ago. That's when Arthur Tillworth appeared and bought him out. It was supposed to be his business, but I always had the feeling that there was other money behind it. Anyway, he took over and changed the agency name. In fact, everything seemed to change. I began to think that our normal day-to-day business wasn't as important anymore.'

'When did you first suspect that things weren't quite right?'

She thought for a moment. 'I guess it must have been about eighteen months ago. Arthur seemed to become less interested in the business. That's when we started getting visits from Brian and the odd character, the one who brought the parcels in.'

'What about Stevie Winterden? When did she start visiting regularly? Did you see her when the previous owner ran the business?'

'No. She's only been dropping in since the business changed hands.'

'And did she always meet Tillworth in his office behind a closed door?'

'Oh yes.'

So much for Stevie's claims that she was merely visiting local agents for PR purposes, thought Mark Green. He made a note of that. Trussell would need to know. 'Do you remember when you started getting regular visits from Edmund Royston?'

'He'd always done work for the local Building Societies and would visit us from time to time to deal with valuation surveys for mortgages, even when Mr Trott owned the agency. We've seen more of him over the last year, I'd say. That didn't fit with the sales activity in the agency. Made me wonder where the work was coming from because he was taking on more valuation surveys than we had properties on offer. I didn't really think too much about it at the time, but now I'm beginning to realise that it just didn't add up.' A look of horror crossed her face as the penny finally dropped. 'You don't think that the estate agency was really just a front for something else, do you?'

Mark Green nodded. 'It's beginning to look that way.' He continued. 'What about the solicitor, Magnus Culverton?'

'I never knew his actual name. I always thought it was Marcus. Now I realise that he was the smartly dressed man who turned up from time to time. Always went into Tillworth's office and the door was shut. I never heard what was said there, but he never looked overly happy when he left.'

'Did he ever bring anything with him, such as papers or files?'

'Yes. He did bring a pile of files into the shop. It was the last time I saw him - a couple of days before he died. He must have left them with Arthur. I remember him speaking to Arthur as he left. Something like, *It's all here. It's up to you what happens to this lot now*. That was the last time I saw him.'

Her face lost its customary smile as she recalled that, yet again, she had seen two people just before they had met untimely deaths. It caused her to think about her own situation. The police were looking for some very dangerous and ruthless people and she was only too aware that she was still very much at risk.

Mark Green noticed the change and immediately picked up on it. 'We'll catch these people, Sharon. Don't worry about that. We're pretty sure that we know who they are and it's only a matter of time before we find them. We've made one arrest already but I can't talk about it. It just means that you have to be a bit careful in the meantime. I suggest that you stay indoors for the next week until you all go back to work.'

'What about Arthur Tillworth. He's my major worry. He knows too much about me. Where I live. Where I work.' Her usual smile faded again.

'What I can tell you is that he's disappeared.'

'What do you mean?'

'Apparently, he was visited by a couple of people and taken away by them in a car.'

She gasped and her hand went to her mouth 'Do you think something's happened to him?'

'We can't rule that out. Anything's possible in this case, the way things are developing. We are actively looking for him at the moment.'

'Will I have to give evidence if there's a trial?' She looked very worried again.

'I can't answer that at the moment, Sharon. That will be down to the CPS. They make the decisions. I have to say that it's a possibility. But don't worry about that at the moment. If it happens, there'll be plenty of support for you. I'll make sure of that.'

She still looked concerned, unconvinced.

'Is there anything else you can think of?' he asked. 'You mentioned someone called Jack when you recognised that voice you heard in the station. Have you thought any more about that?'

'No, it's still a bit of a mystery. I don't remember anyone of that name visiting the shop. Arthur's regular visitors were really quite a small number – Brian, the smartly dressed man, the shifty character with the parcels, and of course, Stevie from the High Weald. Luckily Jason only came into the shop just once that I can remember, although I did see him around town when he seemed to be following me. We've already spoken about that.'

'You never saw his friend, Jimmy, I suppose?'

'No. Never.'

'They've been seen riding around Hammerton recently on a bright red BMW motorcycle. You've already remembered Jason's brightly-coloured crash helmet. They both usually wear black leather jackets and jeans. If you do see them, make sure that they don't see you. They now know that we're looking for them, so hopefully they won't be round here again. But please do take care – don't let them see you.'

'Are you still concerned with witness protection, then, Detective Constable Green?' she asked, smiling.

'I have my instructions from the Detective Inspector, Miss Webster,' he replied, with a straight face. He closed his notebook, put it in his pocket and stood up. 'I'd better be going now, Miss Webster,' he said with enforced formality. 'If anything else should occur to you, then please contact me.'

'Certainly, Detective Constable Mark Green,' she said, keeping a straight face. 'I hope that your witness protection programme will include another visit soon.'

He coloured slightly, nodded and left the room.

Ruth Webster appeared as he opened the front door. 'Is everything alright, Detective Constable?'

'Yes, of course. Thank you for the tea, Mrs Webster. I think that Sharon understands and accepts the present situation. I'll call again soon.' With that, he hurried off to the safety of the car parked outside.

57

Day 36.
Tuesday 26th March.
CID Office, Woodchester Police Station.

DC Mark Green's mobile phone rang where it lay on the desk in front of him. It interrupted his train of thought as he was struggling to record everything that had happened as he typed it into a usable report for DI Trussell. He glanced at the screen, but didn't recognise the number. 'This is DC Green speaking. How can I help you?'

There was an unfamiliar voice on the other end of the line. 'Detective Constable Green? It's Mike Browning here. Number 2 Graham Road in Hammerton. You came to see me yesterday about the attack on the Websters' house?'

'Oh yes, of course, Mr Browning. What can I do for you?'

'It's more, how I can help you, DC Green,' continued Browning. 'We spoke about the two lads on the rather expensive motorcycle who had been riding round the streets during the afternoon before the fire occurred.'

'So, what can you add?' asked Mark Green. 'Do you have any further information?'

'Oh yes. They've been back, still touring the streets, looking at houses. I spoke to the guy riding the bike.'

Mark Green sat back in his chair, astonished.

'How did that happen?'

'I was just wheeling my own bike out of the garage an hour ago when they saw me and stopped. I told you that I have a similar BMW. It's exactly the same model and colour. The guy just wanted to chat. He seems mad about bikes.'

'So, you got a good look at him, then? Can you describe him?'

'I can do better than that. I have his picture, plus a picture of the bike with its registration plate. I had to be a bit careful, I can tell you. He just wanted to talk about his bike. I just couldn't stop him. He's not the sharpest tool in the box! Mind you, I wouldn't want to get on the wrong side of him. He looks capable of anything.'

Mark Green couldn't believe what he had just heard. Was this the break they needed?

'Are you at home now, Mr Browning?'

'Yes. I will be for the rest of the day.'

'Good. I'll be there in about fifteen minutes,' said Mark Green. 'Don't talk to anyone else about this, please.'

He looked at Trussell. 'I think that we may have something concrete on the Graham Road fire, Guv. That was one of the neighbours we spoke to on the door-to-door. He's seen that motorcycle again. I'm going straight round to see him now.'

Trussell nodded. 'Keep me in the loop with what's going on, Greeno.'

Mark Green nodded as he stood up, grabbed his jacket and car keys, and rushed for the stairs. Within two minutes, he was in the Hyundai, heading for Hammerton. A quarter of an hour later, he pulled up outside Number 2, Graham Road and Browning answered the door immediately.

'Thanks for the call. What do you have to show me?'

Browning produced his phone and scrolled through the images.

Mark Green looked in disbelief at the first picture. It showed Browning with another man, posing in front of the two BMWs. It was undoubtedly Jason. He had seen him on the day that he had followed Sharon Webster to the coffee shop. He had come in, looked around, seen her with Mark Green and left but Green had got a good look at him that day, so he was absolutely certain in his identification. He couldn't believe his luck.

'He got his mate to take the pictures,' said Browning. 'He called him Jimmy. The guy just wanted some photos of us together with the two bikes. He used both my phone and his. The bike is obviously his favourite toy! We spent about fifteen minutes just talking about the bikes.'

Browning then moved on to a second photo. This showed the two bikes together and then a third picture, taken from behind, clearly showed the registration plate of the other bike.

Mark Green thought for moment.

'You have my number, Mr Browning. Do you have WhatsApp on your phone? Can you send those three pictures to me, please?'

'Certainly. They're on their way,' he said as he tapped his phone screen.

Green's phone warbled. The message and pictures had landed. He nodded his thanks. 'What about the other man with him? Can you describe him?'

'Twentyish, I guess. He was wearing a black leather blouson style jacket and dark blue jeans. He kept his helmet on although the visor was open while we were talking, so I can't tell you too much about him. The two of them were similar height. From the way they spoke, they weren't from around here.'

'Did they give any indication why they were in the area?'

'They looked in the direction of Number 36 and made some comment about the terrible fire that had occurred there. They asked what had happened to the people living in the house.'

Mark Green shuddered. The thoughts of those two still looking for the Webster family was too horrible to think about. 'What did you tell them?'

'That I had no idea at all. I said they had had to leave the area as the house was so badly damaged. I didn't know where they'd gone.'

Mark Green heaved a sigh of relief. 'Should they come back and ask again, don't tell them anything.'

'That won't be difficult. I've no idea where the Websters have gone.'

'Mr Browning, I shall need you to come to Woodchester Police Station to make a statement, please. This is important evidence and we must get it documented as soon as possible. Perhaps you could call me later to arrange a suitable time.'

'Of course.'

Slipping his phone containing those valuable images back into his pocket, Mark Green thanked Browning and returned to his car. The next job when he got back to the office, after updating Trussell on this breakthrough, was to look at the PNC and obtain Jason's home address. Following that up should hopefully enable them to find the identity of the passenger with him on his bike.

58

Day 36.
Tuesday 26th March.
CID Office, Woodchester Police Station.

'About time we spoke to Mr Kirby, Jackie,' said Trussell. 'Can you find out whether his brief has arrived?'

She picked up the phone and spoke to the sergeant on the front desk. Turning to Trussell, she said, 'Someone has just arrived, Jim. We'd better go down there now.'

They walked down the stairs to the ground floor and the sergeant behind the desk indicated a man standing in the lobby, briefcase in hand. He was about average height, fiftyish with thinning dark brown hair showing traces of grey. He was wearing a woollen-check sports jacket and tan chinos that looked as though he'd slept in them. Not the duty solicitor, obviously. *Must have been paid for and sent by Summerton*, thought Trussell. And in a hurry, too. What a contrast to Trussell, immaculately dressed as usual in one of his mid-grey suits and red tie.

Trussell took the bull by the horns. He indicated the ID card on a tape around his neck.

'I'm DI Trussell and this is DS Joynton. I assume you're here to represent Mr Kirby.'

'Correct, Detective Inspector. 'My name is Willoughby Frankenberg,' he said, offering a card. 'I would like some time with my client before you start the interview process. I haven't had an opportunity to take his instructions.'

'Of course, you are entitled to have time with your client, but I suggest that you may prefer to hear what we have to say first. That may well influence your client's thoughts and whatever he needs to say to you, and, naturally, what advice you feel that you're able to give him.' said Trussell with forced politeness. He nodded to Jackie.

She turned to the Sergeant behind the desk.

Can you contact the Custody suite and ask them to bring Mr Kirby up, please. We'll use Interview Room 1.'

The sergeant picked up the desk phone and organised it.

Trussell led the way, tapping his ID card on the electronic pad and pushed the security door open, holding it for Frankenberg to follow him.

The security door closed behind them automatically. He opened the first marked door on the left and stood aside for the solicitor to enter it first, pointing to the chairs on the other side of the table. The usual recorder sat on the table, and Jackie took the chair next to it, producing a fresh disc as she sat down, placing it on the table in preparation for the interview.

A tap on the door, and two uniformed officers entered with a very surly Brian Kirby between them. He looked dishevelled, and had obviously not slept very well in the cell downstairs.

Trussell indicated the chair opposite, next to Frankenberg. 'Take a seat, Mr Kirby. This is your solicitor, Mr Frankenberg. We'll give you five minutes to get acquainted before we begin the interview. I've told him that he may have whatever time he needs alone with you to take your instructions once he understands why you're here. In the meantime, I'll remind you that you are still under caution. If you don't understand the implication of that, then I'm sure he'll explain it to you.'

He looked at the solicitor as he stood up. 'Five minutes, then, Mr Frankenberg?'

Trussell and Joynton followed the two uniformed officers out of the room. 'How's our guest behaved himself downstairs?'

'Not a happy bunny, Guv,' said one of them. 'He hasn't stopped complaining since he got here. They're fed up with him downstairs. He acts as though he owns the place.'

'How d'you want to handle it, Jim?' asked Jackie.

'We'll just tell him and his brief that we have everything on video and in pictures as far as the charge relating to Eddie is concerned. Convince him that he's already so far up shit creek that he might just as well tell us everything else we need to know, particularly what's happened to Mr Tillworth. I still think that he's central to the whole matter.'

He glanced at his watch. 'Well, Frankenberg has had his five minutes. Let's get on with it.' He tapped on the door and opened it. 'Times up, gentlemen,' he said. 'We need to get on.

He and Jackie Joynton sat down and she put the fresh disc in the recorder.

'Is there anything your client wishes to say to us before we begin?'

Frankenberg shook his head.

'We'd like to hear your evidence to back up this very serious charge, Detective Inspector. I've already told my client about the consequences of such a charge, should it be substantiated.'

Trussell nodded to Jackie to switch the recorder on.

'This is a record of an interview at Woodchester Police Station on Tuesday Twenty-Sixth of March at 10.30 am. Perhaps we can begin by identifying ourselves, then,' she said, looking in the direction of Kirby and his solicitor.

'Detective Inspector Trussell, Kent Police.'

'Detective Sergeant Joynton, Kent Police.'

'Willoughby Frankenberg, solicitor, representing the accused.'

They all looked at Kirby. Frankenberg nodded.

'Brian Rossiter Kirby.'

'Would the accused state his address for the record?' asked Joynton.

'Flat 29, Rochester Buildings, Burnden Road, Brandford.'

'I am now going to invite Mr Kirby to give us his version of events on the Twentieth of March this year which led to the death of Detective Constable Edward Sprawson on the M2 motorway at approximately 16.30 hours BST.'

'My client denies all knowledge of the event.' said Frankenberg. 'He was never there. He believes that he has been falsely accused.'

'I suggest that he reconsiders that statement, Mr Frankenberg,' said Trussell. 'We have eyewitnesses, together with video and photographic evidence of his direct involvement in this tragic event. At the moment, he has been charged with causing death by dangerous driving, which is serious enough. However, it is possible that the charge may be changed to murder. No doubt you have already informed your client of the likely outcome if he should be found guilty by the courts. If the charge is upgraded, it could result in a whole life sentence, as a police officer was involved. Meaning, he'll most probably die in prison.'

The colour drained out of Kirby's face when he heard Trussell's words. He looked at his solicitor in disbelief. Frankenberg just nodded.

'So, what's your point, Detective Inspector if you really have the evidence you say?'

'There are a number of other matters of which we believe your client has knowledge, and I want him to give us some answers.'

'Being what?'

Trussell looked at Joynton.

'What can you tell us about the whereabouts of Arthur Tillworth?'

'I don't know what you mean,' responded Kirby.

'He was seen leaving his estate agency premises on the morning of Wednesday the Twentieth of March between 9.30 and 10.30 am in the company of two men, who locked the premises before they took him away in a silver or grey car. This was seen by a witness at the time and the information was passed to us the same morning. You fit the description of one of those men. The witness stated that you had been seen visiting those premises on a number of occasions prior to that day. We can also produce other witnesses who will testify that you were a regular visitor.'

Frankenberg looked at his client and shook his head.

'No comment,' said Kirby.

'We are already investigating two murders in connection with another matter,' said Trussell. 'If Mr Tillworth should turn up as the third victim, then we shall be looking in your direction, as possibly one of the last people to see him alive.'

'You're not pinning those murders on me,' shouted Kirby. 'You're not going to stitch me up. I had nothing to do with them.'

'So, who was responsible for those two deaths then?' asked Joynton. 'It seems as if you might know.'

'No comment,' was the reply.

'Now let's turn to another event. Let's talk about the arson attack on a house in Hammerton. Where is Jason Tubbitt?' asked Trussell.

'I've never heard of him,' was the response.

'Tubbitt accompanied you to Tillworth's agency on at least one occasion. Again, there are witnesses.'

'You mean that bitch who worked for Tillworth,' shouted Kirby, losing his cool. 'She's the one who's grassed me up.'

Frankenberg touched his client's arm and shook his head.

'I think that we might break for five minutes, Detective Inspector, so that I can speak to my client, clarify matters for him and take his instructions.'

'Certainly, Sir. Just five minutes. Then we'll resume. I have a number of other matters to put to him.'

He nodded to Jackie Joynton,

'Interview suspended at 11.00 am,' she said, switching the recorder off.

Trussell and Joynton stood up and headed for the door, indicating to the uniformed officer that he should follow them.

'I'm just popping upstairs to make a call,' said Trussell. 'Can you keep an eye on things? I shouldn't be more than ten minutes.'

Leaving their colleague to stand outside the interview room, Joynton went across to talk to the desk sergeant.

Ten minutes later, Trussell reappeared and pointed to the door.

'Frankenberg's had more than enough time,' he said, 'but the rules have changed now. I've just spoken to the CPS. Let's chat to our friend Brian.'

Trussell tapped on the door as he opened it.

Frankenberg looked up. 'I've spoken to my client...' he began, but Trussell cut him short.

'All bets are off, gentlemen. I've just spoken to the CPS and laid out the facts for them.'

'And?'

'Their instructions are that Brian Kirby should be charged today with the murder of Detective Constable Edward Sprawson.'

Kirby turned red in the face and with clenched fists, he started to rise from his chair.

Frankenberg put a restraining hand on his arm. 'No, Mr Kirby. Don't make things even worse.'

'Before we go down to the custody suite to complete the formalities, I should warn you that other charges will follow. He will be kept here overnight and then put in front of the magistrates tomorrow to be remanded in custody until such time as a trial date is fixed.'

'What about bail?' asked Frankenberg.

'I would suggest that you don't waste your own or the court's time with that. The Prosecution will oppose any such application.' He turned to Jackie Joynton. 'Can you take Mr Kirby and his solicitor downstairs now and complete the formalities, please?' Then he addressed Frankenberg. 'Perhaps you will impress on your client that it is in his interests to comply now and get this process completed as smoothly as possible. In the event of him being unwilling, I can get enough help here to ensure that it happens. I'm sure that we all understand one another,' he said, looking meaningfully at Kirby.

'He won't give you any trouble, Detective Inspector,' said Frankenberg, rising from his chair and indicating to Kirby that he should follow the uniformed officer and Jackie Joynton.

Trussell returned upstairs to the CID office to make further notes for the file.

Fifteen minutes later, Jackie Joynton returned. She looked at Trussell, questioning.

'Why the change of heart on the charges for Kirby, Jim?'

'I realised that he was not prepared offer us anything more, so I spoke to the CPS. They shared my concern that a magistrate might be swayed by the eloquent Mr Frankenberg and offer Kirby bail if we went with the Dangerous Driving charge. He knows too much and might cause further damage if he's allowed to remain free. So murder it is.'

59

Day 36.
Tuesday 26th March. Pm.
The CID Office. Woodchester Police Station.

Mark Green returned to the office to share the information with Trussell about Jason, the mysterious motorcyclist. He still couldn't believe his luck. Not only had Jason reappeared in Hammerton, but he had spoken to Mike Browning and his passion for his bike had allowed him to make the fatal mistake of being photographed. One picture really is worth a thousand words, thought Green, and he had three!

His first job was to search on the PNC for the bike's registration number and get an address. Then they could track Jason down and hopefully pick him up.

'I've found it, Guv. Here it is…. Details of the bike tally with what Mr Browning told us. Registered keeper is Jason Tubbitt. Address Flat 3, Trencham Buildings, Hartley Street, Brandford. It gives the postcode. Confirms that he's insured, but I bet it doesn't include third party liability coverage for arson, though.'

'Very funny, Greeno. We'd better pick him up for questioning before he does any further damage. Is anything known about him? Any previous?'

'As it happens, Guv, yes. He does have form. A couple of violent incidents. Beat some guy up outside a pub for no good reason and was involved in a domestic. Got let off with a suspended sentence for the pub case and the complainant dropped the other charge. Looks like it might have been a friend or relative. Name of Tompkins.'

Trussell listened with amazement.

'That can't be just coincidence, surely? We seem to be encountering the same people over and over again here, Jackie,' he said. Then he thought again. 'Was Jason acting alone with the pub beating? Greeno, 'Or was anyone else involved?'

Mark Green consulted his screen again.

'Yes, Guv, right again. His co-defendant was a James Sharrell, aged 20. His details are here. He's also from Brandford. There's a surprise! He had no previous form so he was also given a suspended sentence. Wonder if he was the man on the back of the bike when Mr Browning saw them? He said that he referred to the other man as Jimmy.'

'Get a picture of him and show it to Browning, Greeno, said Trussell. 'Do it as soon as you can, please?'

He watched as Mark Green picked up his phone and tapped in a number.

'Mr Browning? It's DC Green again. Will you still be at home this afternoon?...Good. I'd like to pop round again. You recall that we discussed your visitors; I'd like to show you a photograph to see if you recognise the person concerned. Say, in about half an hour, then?...Thank you very much.'

Green finished the call and told Trussell that it was organised. He downloaded the picture from the PNC records and left the office immediately for Hammerton.

Trussell now faced a real dilemma.

How much should he share with DCS Watkins? He still had nagging doubts about the Brandford connection. Should he contact the new DCI there and share it with him? He might well need backup now, with his own limited resources, but it was a question of who he could trust and he certainly didn't want to let the enquiry go out of his own control. It was his decision alone, but he thought he'd like Jackie's input. She was always a good sounding board on these occasions. *Maybe I'll wait until Greeno gets back with confirmation or otherwise about the second man*, he thought.

60

Day 37.
Wednesday 27th March.
CID Office, Woodchester Police Station.

Peace and quiet reigned... yet it was deceptive... there was a lot going on...

Trussell was staring at the pad containing his mind map, trying to make sense of the latest information. Jackie Joynton was online, still looking for the details of Stevie Winterden's mother's marriage.

Mark Green had gone back to the Supercheap supermarket to try to progress matters as Sprawson was no longer around to deal with it. He had the list of employees and details of past convictions which had not been picked up by the management. They were certainly in for a rude surprise. There were people who would have to be interviewed again. Whatever came out of those discussions might well lead to more than one arrest. Screening of all future employees was going to be a major priority for them.

Tim Beach had been sent to Hammerton to contact the last few neighbours about the fire that had damaged the Websters' house.

Trussell just had to maximise his resources, which meant more of the load was falling on Jackie Joynton's shoulders. She didn't complain and just seemed prepared to get on with things, but Trussell was still concerned that this might encourage her to seek a transfer to the Fraud Squad, which was still very much her ambition.

The calm was shattered by the sound of rapid footsteps on the stairs outside the CID office and DC Beach burst into the office. He looked rather flushed. Was it because he had been hurrying or was it just a combination of his natural complexion, tinged with a bit of excitement?

'What's the hurry, Sandcastle?' asked Jackie. 'How did the door-to-door enquiries go in Hammerton?'

'I've seen all the remaining houses on the list, Sarge,' was his breathless response. 'I drew a blank with all but one. Number 43. I spoke to the owner, a Mr Sharples. He'd been away for the last six weeks with his wife. They own a holiday property in the Pyrenees in Spain.'

'Slow down, Sandcastle. So, are you saying that he was unaware of events at Number 36?'

'On the contrary, Sarge. He had some really useful information.'

'How come?'

His house, Number 43, is almost opposite the Websters' place. But here's the good bit. He has one of those doorbells that pick up any nearby motion as well as anyone at his door. He showed me the video from the night of the fire.'

'Could you see anything useful?'

'Oh yes, Sarge,' said Sandcastle, his voice rising with excitement. 'There were two guys on a motorcycle who pulled up outside Number 36. One got off the back of the bike and walked up to the door. He was carrying what looked like two bottles, one large with what seemed to be a rag stuffed in the top and the other was a small one. He did something to the letterbox with the small bottle, stood back and then there was a spark or something. There was a flame on the top of the large bottle. He walked back up the path, and when he reached the gate, he turned and chucked the large bottle at the door. It shattered and burst into flames. Then he climbed onto the back of the bike and they left in a hurry.'

'Why didn't your man, what was his name? get in touch with us straight away? He must have realised that a major crime had been committed?'

'Mr Sharples. He reckoned that he didn't see it until this morning because he got back late last night. He said that the Wi-Fi at his place in the mountains is rubbish, so he didn't know about anything that had happened in Graham Road. He didn't even notice the damage to the house opposite because it was dark when they got back last night.'

'Didn't any of his neighbours contact him?'

'No. He had only moved to the house a couple of weeks before he went away, so no one has any contact details for him yet. He hardly knows any of his neighbours at the moment.'

Trussell had listened to this important new information with amazement. He had been concerned about his two DC's lacking experience, and yet they'd both picked up some very important information on their own initiative. This certainly gave him hope for the future of the team.

'So, have you warned this gentleman that he's holding some fairly significant evidence, then, Sandcastle?' he asked. 'We'll need to get a hold of this video as soon as possible.'

'I told him to hang on to it and I'd be back as soon as I'd spoken to you, Guv,' he said. 'I've got his details, including a phone number.'

'Well done, Sandcastle. Good effort,' said Trussell. 'We'll need to find Jason and his friend and get them off the streets as soon as possible. We have to assume that the man who threw the petrol bomb was his mate Sharrell, as they seem to be in the habit of getting into trouble together. They still pose a significant threat to the Websters all the time they're on the loose, so it's important that we pick them up as soon as possible.'

'Mike tells me that his unit has been asked to look out for the bike,' said Jackie Joynton 'It might be worth Greeno checking with his friend, Mr Browning, to see if they've been back. Although I guess we'd have known if he'd seen them again.'

'Write it up, Sandcastle, while the details are fresh in your mind,' said Trussell.

Tim Beach sat down at his desk, produced his notebook and pulled his computer keyboard towards him. He was still flushed with his success and felt that he'd really started to contribute to the team's efforts now.

Trussell was pleased to see that Jackie had already impressed on Sandcastle the need to make detailed notes. It was essential to have a complete file available to the CPS if the matter came to court.

'We'll need to get hold of Mr Sharples' phone, Jackie, and download the video showing the attack. Can you help Sandcastle organise that, please? I doubt that he knows the drill yet.'

She nodded, almost automatically, her eyes still fixed on the screen in front of her.

'I'll sort it in just a moment, Jim. I believe that I've found the marriage details at last. There can't have been too many women named Shirley Flimwell getting married in Brandford around this time. It's a fairly unusual name. The spouse's name was Tompkins. I've got the date. I'll send for a copy of the certificate right now, and then I'll help Sandcastle with the video. I'll leave you in charge, Jim, while we go over to Hammerton to sort it,' she laughed.

'Shirley Tompkins? The name of the woman at the factory counter at Brandford when they had arrested Brian Kirby. 'It's got to be more than coincidence, Jackie.'

61

Day 37.
Wednesday 27th March.
CID Office, Woodchester Police Station.

The phone on Jackie Joynton's desk rang loudly, interrupting everyone's thoughts. She picked it up, answered and then listened to the caller. Her face was a picture ... shock, surprise...

'OK, thanks for that,' she said as she replaced the phone and then turned to Trussell.

'What's going on Jackie?' he asked.

'I think that we've just solved another piece of the puzzle, Jim,' she said. 'But not in the way we'd have liked.'

'Well...?'

'That was my other half, Mike,' she said. 'He was passing on a message from the motorway patrols. Apparently, a certain red motorcycle with two people on board was chased on the motorway heading for Brandford this afternoon.'

'And?'

'The patrol tried to stop them but they just shot off. That BMW's a very fast bike. The car couldn't catch them. Mike said that it looked as though the rider was a bit too careless in overtaking a line of cars and collided with a large truck which had pulled into that lane. Unfortunately, at the speed they were travelling, neither the rider or passenger survived the impact. They were identified at the scene as Tubbitt and Sharrell.'

'We seem fated never to lay hands on any of these people, Jackie,' he said. As fast as we identify any persons of interest, they come to an unfortunate end.'

Mark Green listened to this revelation with great interest.

'At least they won't be around to trouble Sharon Webster and her parents any more now,' he said. 'She was genuinely afraid of Tubbitt and what he might do to her. That will lift a weight from her shoulders. If we can only find Tillworth, then her problems will be over. It's been very unpleasant for her after what she had to put up with at the estate agency, through no fault of her own. Can I share this news with the family yet, Guv?'

'I don't see why not, Greeno. Give them a call and arrange to go round there. It'll be a burden lifted for all of them.'

'OK, Guv.

'Don't discuss it on the phone at all. Better to tell them face to face. Just let them think that our enquiries are continuing. Choose your words carefully. By the way, it seems as though you're off the hook now as well,' he added, smiling. 'There's no need to keep everything official any longer.'

Mark Green immediately reached for his phone.

'What about their next of kin, Jim?' asked Jackie. 'Someone will need to be told. Do we do it, or leave it to Traffic?'

'As far as Tubbitt is concerned, we have his father, Brian Kirby, downstairs in the cells. Shirley Tompkins, if she is his mother, wasn't terribly complimentary about him when we visited the factory in Brandford to arrest Kirby. Don't know whether her reaction was genuine, or just trying to put us off. Not sure about Sharrell, either. He must have some relatives who'll need to be informed. Better leave them to uniform.'

'The net seems to be closing on Summerton, now, Jim,' said Jackie. He's running out of friends. What we don't know is whether Tillworth was recalled by Summerton to keep him out of our hands, or whether Summerton just wanted him silenced like the others. It means fewer people to pay off over the mortgage fraud.'

'The big question now, Jackie,' said Trussell, 'is whether I contact DCI Simpson at the Alamo to tell him that we want to lift his Number one target in Brandford. I don't want to get into any sort of turf war with him over Summerton, when the aim is just to take the man off the street. We have enough to go on with to charge him with conspiracy over Sprawson's death, and that will give us the chance to look at his potential involvement in the mortgage fraud.'

'That's a tough call, Jim. Simpson will obviously want a big win for himself and his team to show the locals, as the new boys, that they mean business in Brandford. Maybe we can let Simpson haul him in on the conspiracy charge and we arrange to transfer him to Woodchester to assist our enquiries into the High Weald's problem.'

'Interesting thought. The one thing I can't do is to go to Charlie Watkins upstairs to get his input, He'll want to pull rank and do it all himself, if only to send a message to any of the remaining wrong'uns there.'

'I'd sleep on it, Jim, and decide in the morning. You can always call Simpson then. Unless there are still some leaks within the Alamo, a traffic accident today on the Motorway is unlikely to generate much interest in Simpson's team.'

'Good call, Jackie'

Mark Green had put down his phone and was trying to attract Trussell's attention. 'I've spoken to Sharon Webster, Guv. I told her that I'll call round later to update them. She thinks that it's still part of the witness protection programme, as she calls my visits.'

'You better watch out, Greeno,' said Jackie. 'If she's no longer at risk, and probably won't be needed as a witness any more, she'll be after you! No more using the DI's professionalism order now as an excuse. You're in trouble, Greeno. You've nowhere to hide now! It serves you right for giving her your mobile number!' She grinned at him, determined to embarrass him even further.

Trussell smiled. It was one less thing to worry about. He knew that Mark Green had struggled with that conflict of interest with Sharon Webster. At least he wouldn't need to remind him constantly about the need to stay detached.

Trussell turned to Jackie Joynton.

Can you find out a bit more about Tubbitt and Sharrell? We'll need to know when the post-mortem will take place. We'll want Tubbitt's DNA. You'd better flag that up now.'

'OK, Jim,' she said, picking up the phone.

62

Day 37.
Wednesday 27th March. 5.30 pm.
The CID Office. Woodchester Police Station.

Mark Green checked his desk, collected his coat and left the office to visit the Webster family at Hammerton, as promised in his earlier phone call.

He turned a number of scenarios over in his mind. He was really relieved that Sharon and her parents were safe now and wondered where the news would lead. He wouldn't have the opportunity to visit them in any official capacity in the future, as Trussell had told him that the need to distance himself from the witnesses was no longer necessary, following the deaths of Tubbitt and Sharrell on the motorway. *Dare I say what I really think?*

He walked out of the main door to the car park where he climbed into the white Hyundai, reversed out of his space and set off for Hammerton. *What sort of reception am I going to get?*

He made his decision. He would speak to Sharon first and see where the conversation went. She would obviously be relieved to learn that she and her family were now out of danger, although Arthur Tillworth had not yet been found. The DI had voiced his opinion that Tillworth no longer presented a threat, and indeed, thought that he was actually in danger himself since he had disappeared.

The fifteen-minute journey to Hammerton seemed to pass all too quickly with so many different thoughts whirling around in his head. Suddenly, he had arrived and turned into Westbury Road, pulling up outside Number 51. He was still in a state of inner turmoil.

He got out, locked the car and walked up the short path to the front door. As he rang the bell, the sound brought an answering bark from inside. Fred was at home.

Ruth Webster opened the door. 'Hallo, Detective Constable Green,' she said, smiling at him. 'Sharon told us that you would be calling and that you had some further news for us. Please come in.'

'Good evening, Mrs Webster,' he began, somewhat nervously. 'It's nice to see you. Hope that you are all feeling better now. I think that I should talk to Sharon first, if that's OK with you.'

'Yes, of course. She's in the living room, she said, opening the door. 'Sharon, Detective Constable Green is here to see you. Please go in. We'll talk to you shortly, then?'

He nodded as he walked into the living room and Ruth Webster closed the door behind him

**

'He's been in there a long time speaking to Sharon,' said Ruth Webster to her husband. 'It's over an hour and a half since he arrived. I hope that everything's alright. We don't need any further bad news. I don't want her upset any more than before. She's been through so much already.'

'It does seem to be taking a while but I'm sure that everything's OK,' said her husband. 'In fairness, Detective Constable Green seems to have done his best throughout the whole process. I can't imagine that he would deliberately upset her. He strikes me as too straightforward and far too considerate for that. Why don't you just put the kettle on. We'll have a cuppa while we wait to find out what's going on.'

She had just switched the electric kettle on when the living room door opened. Sharon and Mark Green emerged and walked into the kitchen. They both looked rather serious.

'Is everything OK?' asked Ruth Webster, even more concerned now.

Sharon looked at Mark Green and nodded imperceptibly.

He cleared his throat rather nervously and spoke.

'I've brought Sharon up to date with the latest developments in the case,' he began, 'and now I'd like to share some information with both of you.'

The Websters looked apprehensive.

'Go on,' said John Webster. 'What's happened?'

'First of all,' began Mark Green, 'we now believe that you are all no longer at risk. The people responsible for the fire at your house have been identified and I can tell you that they are no longer a danger to anyone now. They were killed in a road accident earlier today on the motorway on their motorcycle whilst trying to evade arrest.'

The Websters looked at one another, at the same time shocked but relieved. 'It's a weight lifted, obviously,' said John Webster, 'but I wouldn't have wanted the problem to have been solved quite that way. No one deserved that.'

Mark Green continued. 'Other arrests have been made and our enquiries are continuing. Sharon's previous employer, Arthur Tillworth, has disappeared under suspicious circumstances and we're still looking for him but we no longer consider him a threat to any of you.'

'That's really good news,' said Ruth Webster. 'It seems to have taken quite a long time for you to share this information with Sharon, doesn't it? We were beginning to wonder whether everything was alright. We were quite worried.'

'We've had a lot to talk through,' said Mark Green. 'This is probably my last official visit to this house, so I have to tell you that I intend to take Sharon into protective custody at this point.'

'Whaaat?' said John Webster, horrified. 'You're arresting our daughter? Whatever for?'

Ruth Webster just stood there, mouth open, stunned. She looked at Sharon, who still had that serious, concerned look on her face.

'No, Mr and Mrs Webster, I didn't say that I was arresting her. I mentioned protective custody. I want to protect her from now on.' He glanced at Sharon.

She looked at her parents, a smile beginning to form around the corners of her mouth. 'It didn't take Mark long to update me on the criminal part of things,' she said, grabbing his arm. 'We've spent most of the time discussing much more important matters.'

'Such as?' asked Ruth Webster, still looking worried.

'Well Mum, Mark and I have had a long chat and we've come to a most important decision,' she said, her usual smile returning. 'What Mark means about protecting me is that now all the legal barriers to our futures have been removed, we have both agreed that we want to be together, so he has proposed to me and I have accepted him. It seems that we have both been feeling the same since we first met when he came to Tillworth's. I know it all seems very quick, and unusual, but in view of all the difficulties we've been through, it's drawn us even closer together and we see no point in putting things off any longer. You already know how I feel about him. We've talked about it several times.'

'I know that I should have spoken to you both to ask for your permission,' he said, 'but I'm sure that you'd agree that the circumstances are rather unusual. I hope that you will give us your blessing.'

Before the Websters could answer, Fred walked into the kitchen, came up to Mark Green, sniffed his offered hand, licked it and wagged his tail furiously.

'If it's OK with Fred,' said John Webster, laughing, 'then how can we possibly object?'

'I realise that you don't know too much about me at the moment,' Mark continued. 'Our family is a small one, just like yours. My parents still live in the same house just outside Maidstone where I grew up. I have one older sister, Julia, who's married.'

'How long have you been in the police?' asked Ruth Webster.

'After I left school at eighteen, I thought about a career in the police and eventually joined the force at Maidstone. I have over seven years' service now.'

'Do you still live with your parents?' asked Ruth Webster.

'Not any more. When I transferred to the CID at Woodchester about eight months ago, I felt that it was time to move out and decided that I wanted my own place. The chance came up to buy a flat on that new estate on the south side of town so I took it. It's a nice bright place, very modern, with a balcony that faces south and looks out over open fields. I'm sure that Sharon will love being there. It will certainly be fine until we need more space in the future.'

'It seems that you are well organised then…Mark,' said Ruth Webster. Using his first name seemed strange.

'I think so. I told my parents about Sharon after our first meeting at Tillworth,' he said. 'I was instantly attracted to her. I told them that, but I could only hope that things would turn out OK, with everything that has happened in the meantime. I'm taking Sharon to meet them at the weekend. That is, after we've been shopping to choose an engagement ring.'

'Well, this has been a day of surprises,' said John Webster. 'You really worried me for a moment back then, with your talk of protective custody.'

'I'm sorry about that… We talked about it as a way of telling you. As I said, this is my last official visit to this house, so I'll be a guest in future. I hope that's OK.'

'I feel that we should be celebrating,' said John Webster, 'but we're fresh out of champagne thanks to our enforced move. At least we have some good news at last. We'll have to organise something.' Turning to his wife, he said, 'Well in the meantime, we'll have that cuppa!'

63

Day 38.
Thursday 28th March.
CID Office, Woodchester Police Station.

Jackie Joynton looked up as Mark Green walked into the office. Trussell and Tim Beach watched from their desks. 'Well, Greeno, how did you get on last night with your visit to your star witness and her family?' she asked. She smiled as she spoke, bent on teasing him just a little more. There wasn't likely to be much more mileage in that particular joke now that the Tubbitt and Sharrell were no longer a threat.

'Obviously the family were really relieved to hear that they were no longer at risk, Sarge.'

Jackie tried again. 'I warned you yesterday that Miss Webster is likely to be after you now that the DI's instructions have been cancelled,' she gloated.

Greeno looked a bit embarrassed. 'That's unlikely to happen now, Sarge,' he said.

Jackie Joynton looked disappointed. 'Why?'

'Because I've resolved the situation. Permanently.'

'Come on, Greeno, just tell us what's going on,' said Trussell. 'Put us all out of our misery. I don't have to remind you that we have two ongoing murder enquiries, as well as two missing persons and a major fraud. Not forgetting a theft problem at Supercheap. We need to get on and make some progress.'

'Well, if it's really so important to you all, I'll tell you what happened last night when I visited the family,' he said. 'Sharon and I had a long chat about the future and now we're engaged. That's it. I've resolved the situation,' he said defiantly to the DS.

Jackie Joynton was stunned into silence. Not the answer she'd expected.

'You should try it, Sarge,' added Mark Green, with a slight dig at Jackie Joynton's own domestic arrangements.

'No fighting in the playground, children,' laughed Trussell, intent on defusing any situation before it developed, but Jackie accepted the jibe with good grace. 'Congratulations, Greeno,' she said.

'Drinks all round then,' said Tim Beach, more in hope than anything.

The others ignored him.

'Just one more thing, Guv,' said Mark Green. 'I really have to thank you for sending me round to Tillworth that first time, otherwise I would never have met Sharon. Now, perhaps we can get on with the business at hand.'

'I guess that congratulations are in order then, Greeno,' he said. 'And you're absolutely correct. We must make some progress.' Having thought about the events of the previous day, Trussell had taken Jackie Joynton's advice and slept on the matter. It was time to be decisive. 'Right, back to business. I've come to a decision, Jackie,' he said. 'I'm going to call DCI Simpson at Brandford. If I continue pursuing things in his manor, then sooner or later the brown stuff will hit the fan. Better to get him onside now.'

'I think you're right. At least you can justify Kirby's arrest in Brandford. After all, Charlie Watkins ordered you to haul him in.'

Trussell reached for the phone and tapped the 0 button. The switchboard answered immediately. 'Can you connect me with Brandford, please? I want to speak to DCI Simpson.'

'Call you back,' was the response.

Two minutes later, his phone rang. 'DCI Simpson,' said a deep voice on the other end of the line.

'Good morning,' said Trussell. 'This is DI Trussell at Woodchester. Can you spare me a few minutes, Sir?'

'Oh, so you're the man who walked onto our manor and lifted one of our local citizens without so much as a please or thank you,' laughed Simpson.

'Yes. Sorry about that. It was on the direct order of DCS Watkins so I had little option. I'm afraid.'

'So, what can I do for you, Trussell?' boomed the voice.

'Well, Sir, it's all a bit delicate. I need to speak to you face to face. I don't want to visit the station at Brandford at present, and I'd rather we met outside of this office. I don't want Watkins to know about it at the moment. I'd like to talk to you somewhere between the two places. It'll be to our mutual advantage. You'll understand why when we meet.'

There was a silence at the other end of the line for a moment and then Simpson spoke again.

'I'm intrigued, Trussell. Do you know The Jolly Farmer at Bridgington? It's on the main road this side of Hammerton. They've got some quiet tables tucked away there and they do a decent pint too. That's probably the best place round here in terms of discretion.'

'Sounds ideal, Sir. When can we meet? The sooner the better, from my point of view.'

'Today, if you like. Say, one o'clock, if that suits you. I'll bring my DI, Phil Jennings as well.'

'Perfect. I'll bring my DS, Jackie Joynton.'

'Look forward to it, Trussell.'

'Thank you, Sir,' said Trussell, and put the phone down. He turned to Jackie. 'Right, Sergeant. It's lunch with the big boys today. Best behaviour!'

'Fine if you're paying, Jim.'

Trussell glanced at his watch. 'What do you reckon, Jackie? Thirty minutes to get to Bridgington? We'll leave in about half an hour.'

'Might be an idea to take some of our photos with us to see if Simpson and his DI know any of them, I'm particularly interested in the Afro-Caribbean guy who was seen with Brian when Arthur Tillworth disappeared. We ought to show those pictures to the woman from the curtain shop and get her to sign a witness statement. I think I'll pop round there when we get back. Ask her to come to the station.'

64

Day 38.
Thursday 28th March. Noon.
Bridgington.

Thirty minutes later, they left the Woodchester Police Station car park in Trussell's Skoda.

'How are you going to play this, Jim?' asked Jackie.

'I don't want to get drawn into long conversations and bargaining,' said Trussell. 'I'll just tell Simpson that I think that we've found a way to get Summerton off the street for quite a long time.'

'He shouldn't have a problem with that.'

'I can't imagine that he'll want to argue about it. I'll leave it up to him as to how we go about it. He can decide whether or not he wants to take the credit as the new man in charge. After all, it's his manor. I'm only concerned that we're able to question Summerton about everything that has happened in and around Woodchester. This will be a real opportunity to get some answers.'

Jackie Joynton was already well aware of Trussell's willingness to step back from the limelight and allow others to take the credit. Even so, she thought that he should be upfront on this particular arrest.

They found the pub without any difficulty, parked up and went inside.

They were greeted by the smell of food and of beer as they pushed the door open. They looked around the gloomy interior, and as their eyes became accustomed to the low lighting, spotted two men sitting at a table in the far corner. They looked up and one beckoned them over. He stood up as they approached the table. A tall man in his late forties with fair hair.

'Trussell?' he asked, extending his hand. 'I'm Ken Simpson and this is Phil Jennings,' indicating a shorter man with dark hair and sharp features.

Looks like a ferret, thought Jackie Joynton to herself. *I bet he does the dirty work in the team.*

'Jim Trussell' he said and introduced Jackie Joynton.

Simpson indicated the two empty chairs for them to sit down. 'Drinks?' he asked, beckoning the waitress over. Formalities out of the way, the talk turned to business. 'What can I do for you, Trussell?' Simpson asked. 'You called me.'

Trussell gave the two Brandford officers a brief summary of the case so far, starting with Barnaby Scoular's disappearance and moving on to the mortgage fraud, the two murders and Eddie Sprawson's unfortunate death, followed by the events leading up to Brian Kirby's arrest. He also mentioned Arthur Tillworth's disappearance.

'I think that we have enough now to bring Jack Summerton in for questioning,' said Trussell. 'I reckon that we can charge him with conspiracy over Sprawson's death for starters. We have photographic evidence and Kirby's phone log which proves that he spoke to Summerton at the crucial moments.'

Simpson and Jennings exchanged significant glances. 'This is really what we've been looking for, Boss',' said Jennings. 'What an opportunity.'

'I really want to talk to him about Scoular's disappearance, the deaths of the surveyor and the solicitor and the mortgage problems, of course. We're not in a position to hang that one on him yet, but we believe that he was behind the whole thing. Diversifying from his drugs and other businesses. The list seems endless. I daresay that the Fraud Squad will want him over the mortgages eventually. More their scene than ours. That one's down the road a bit, though.'

'That's quite a shopping list, Trussell,' said Simpson. 'What do you want us to do?'

'The question's a bit political,' replied Trussell. 'It's our enquiry with everything happening in and out of Woodchester, but there's a big Brandford connection. As Summerton's your local big fish, and you might want to make a statement as the new men on the block. Perhaps you should pick him up and hand him over to us. That's why I wanted to talk to you away from our respective stations. It's your call.'

Simpson looked thoughtful. 'What do you think, Phil?' he asked his colleague.

'Taking Summerton off the street is our number one priority, Boss,' he said. 'No matter who picks him up, it will make a statement as far as the locals are concerned. If DI Trussell has enough evidence to pull him in from Woodchester, then I'd let him do it. We can be there with him. It should send the right sort of message to the locals that we've got a long reach and there's nowhere for these people to hide.'

'I still think that the estate agent, Tillworth, is central to this whole matter,' said Trussell. We have evidence that Eddie Sprawson knew him and that they both had connections to Summerton. I thought that

Summerton was the mastermind behind the whole thing, but then I began to have doubts. I'd like to know where Tillworth fitted into the whole scheme. He seems to have orchestrated things and I always assumed that it was on Summerton's instructions. Now I've got concerns. Maybe we've been looking in the wrong direction.'

'What d'you mean, Trussell?' asked Simpson.

'A witness told us that he had been seen leaving his shop in the company of two men, one of who was identified as Brian Kirby,' said Trussell. We believe that the other man appears to work for Summerton in his scrapyard on the Elton estate. He's of Afro-Caribbean appearance.'

'That sounds like Denim Des, as he's known from his usual clothes,' said Jennings.' He's a nasty piece of work and doubles as one of Summerton's enforcers.'

'We have a picture,' said Trussell, nodding to Jackie Joynton. She opened the file she had been carrying and produced the photo taken at the scrap yard when Kirby had dropped the Mercedes off after Sprawson's *accident*. She offered it to Simpson and Jennings.

'That's Denim Des alright,' said Jennings. 'His name is Desmond Bronning. He looks after Summerton's drug business as well as using the scrapyard as a front for other activities. Useful places, scrapyards. Illegal trade in scrap metals as well as destruction of evidence to order, like your case.'

'We also have to show his picture to another witness to confirm that he was one of the two people seen leaving the estate agency with Arthur Tillworth. We're still unsure whether Tillworth was leaving voluntarily, or whether he'd been summoned.'

'Let me have a look,' said Simpson. He scanned the picture and pointed to a scruffy individual standing behind Brunning.

'Do we know this chap, Phil? He asked.

'That's Bobby Critchlow,' said Jennings. 'We believe that he acts as a drugs courier for Bronning,'

Trussell turned to Joynton. 'We'd better get Greeno to show this picture to his star witness to see if she recognises him. Could be the dodgy character that turned up at Tillworth's shop from time to time with the parcels. We have good reason to believe that he was delivering drugs regularly to Tillworth. Some of them might well have finished up with Marcus Culverton.'

'What do we know about Tillworth, Phil?' asked Simpson.

Jennings looked thoughtful.

'I understand that he works for Summerton, managing his property empire, private and commercial rentals. All legit.'

'No wonder Tillworth was rarely in his shop,' said Trussell.' The witness seemed to think that he was neglecting his everyday business. Perhaps he got greedy, which is why he was taken away.'

'The Estate Agency was probably an outlet for money laundering.'

Trussell thought for a moment. He turned to Jackie. 'D'you remember the address of Stevie's apartment in Woodchester?'

She thought for a moment, and then opened her bag to retrieve her notebook. She flicked through the pages until she found the information.

'Yes. It was called Breckenridge Apartments in Whitford. Rather glitzy. We were trying to trace the owners. It all seemed a bit opaque. We said at the time that it seemed rather pricey for someone working in the Building Society. Then there was her car. Expensive SUV. Leased. Even so, more outgoings. Her gym and club memberships. Smart clothes. They all add up.'

Simpson and Jennings exchanged glances. 'One for the Fraud Squad at some stage?'

'Does that address ring any bells? asked Trussell.

'We'll have to look into it. Can you sort it, Phil?' asked Simpson. 'Let DI Trussell know if it's part of Summerton's property portfolio.'

'It would all be a bit too coincidental if Stevie is living in a smart apartment owned ultimately by Summerton, said Trussell. 'Especially as she suggested that her father's name might have been Sommer. More and more seem to be pointing in Summerton's direction.'

'Well, Trussell,' asked Simpson, 'exactly how do you want to proceed?'

'I'd like to call on Mr Summerton tomorrow, if that fits with your arrangements. I think that we have enough now to pull him in. We'll need uniformed back up. I was reluctant to contact the Alamo because I'm still not sure what's going on there.'

'If you're referring to past problems,' said Simpson, 'let me put your mind at rest. The new Superintendent, David Ross, has done a really good job in sorting out the uniformed side. There've been a lot of changes. Turnover of staff. People opting for early retirement to avoid trouble. My team is completely new. No history there. So, you don't need to be concerned about leaks.'

Trussell looked relieved. The previous problems at Brandford had weighed heavily on him. 'I also think that we should collect our two friends, uh…Bronning and Critchlow, from the scrap yard.'

'Charges?' asked Simpson.

'Take your pick…supplying Class A drugs, conspiracy to destroy evidence, kidnap and Actual Bodily Harm….'

'That should suffice,' said Jennings. 'Just let us know the timing, and I'll organise the back up.' He handed Trussell his card. 'Call me on that number tomorrow when you're ready. We'll set it up.'

'Now let's look at the menu,' said Simpson, picking up the card in front of him. "Are you buying?"

65

Day 39.
Friday 29th March. 9.00 am.
Woodchester/Brandford.

Trussell phoned Jennings at Brandford to co-ordinate the arrest of Jack Summerton. They agreed to meet at 2.00 pm outside the factory unit at Brandford where Brian Kirby had been arrested. Trussell knew that Summerton used those premises as an office on a day-to-day basis so he had already obtained a search warrant the previous afternoon after they had returned from Bridgington, to enable them to look around.

Simpson and Jennings agreed to meet them around the corner from the unit and half a dozen uniformed officers would arrive in three cars and a van as the CID entered the premises. It had been agreed that Trussell would lead the operation and that Summerton would be taken to Woodchester.

'Right, Jackie, are you ready to leave?' Trussell asked.

'What about us, Guv?' asked Mark Green. 'Don't you want Sandcastle and me to join you?'

'Not this time, Greeno. Just push on with the other matters. I need you here to keep an eye on things. You can contact me if anything important crops up. We'll have enough local support for this afternoon as it's a joint operation with Brandford.'

When they arrived at Brandford, the others were already waiting. They got out of their car and walked towards them. Simpson was carrying a radio in his left hand. He spoke into it briefly and three marked police cars appeared from around the corner and stopped right outside.

A brief exchange of greetings as they walked to the front of the unit and Simpson pointed at the door. 'After you, Trussell.'

He led the way through the frosted glass door, followed by Jackie Joynton with Simpson and Jennings right behind them. He pressed the bell on the counter several times and heard Shirley Tompkins' familiar rough voice behind the door.

'Alright, alright, I'm comin'.' She opened the door and walked to the counter. She was wearing the same worn and stained blue overalls as before. The intervening time had not improved her looks. She recognised

Trussell and Joynton immediately and the colour drained from her face. 'Whaddya want this time? Yer caused enuff trouble last time.'

'Hullo, Shirley. Customer-friendly as usual. I'm surprised you remembered me. I've come to see Jack Summerton.'

'Told yer before. I dunno anyone of that name.'

Trussell lifted the counter flap, pushed past her, heading for the door that she'd just come through.'

'Oi, whaddya fink yer doing?' she shouted. 'Yer can't go in there.'

Trussell just waved the search warrant. 'This says I can go anywhere, Shirley. Hang onto her,' he said to one of the uniformed officers behind him. Don't let her talk to anyone or try to leave.'

He pushed the door open. He was greeted by a smell of hot plastic from the moulding machines that were working in the factory. *The sort of smell that might mask other things,* he thought.

Through the door, Trussell saw a staircase, which he assumed led to the offices on the first floor. He rushed up the stairs. Joynton, Simpson and Jennings right behind him, followed by four of the uniformed officers.

There was a door at the top which opened out into a corridor with a number of doors.

Trussell looked at the others. 'Take your choice,' he said. 'We'll check them all.' He opened the door nearest to him. There were two women sitting at desks with computer monitors in front of them, busy typing on their keyboards. 'Police. Stay where you are,' he ordered them, waving the search warrant. 'Where's Jack Summerton?'

They just looked at each other, too frightened to answer this man who had suddenly burst into their office without any warning.

'Come on, come on. I don't have all day. Where is he?'

One pointed wordlessly to the door opposite.

Trussell took two strides across the narrow corridor and pushed the door open. He was greeted by the sight of Jack Summerton, sitting behind a large desk, looking through a pile of files. Trussell immediately thought of the few documents left behind in his office by Magnus Culverton. The same sort of file. But it was the change in Summerton since they last met that really caught Trussell's attention. It was his gaunt appearance. He had lost a lot of weight and had a greyish tinge to his pinched face.

Summerton looked up at this sudden intrusion. Annoyed. 'What the hell... who d'you think you are?' he gasped. Then a look of recognition passed over his face. 'My goodness,' said Summerton, sarcastically. 'If it ain't young Jimmy Trussell. What are you doing here, boy? Bit out of your depth, aren't you?' That East Kent voice again.

'It's DI Trussell to you, Summerton,' said Trussell. 'I think that you're the one out of his depth now. I've popped round to talk to you and arrange a change of scenery for you. Long overdue, I'd say.'

'What d'you mean?'

'Jack Summerton, I am arresting you for conspiracy to cause the death of Detective Constable Edward Sprawson on or about the Twenty-First of March.' He proceeded to caution him and signalled to one of the uniformed officers to handcuff him. 'You will now be taken to Woodchester Police Station to be questioned on this and other matters. I should also mention that we have a warrant to search these premises.'

'Oh yes, and what do you hope to find?' asked Summerton.

'Who knows?' Whatever we do find certainly won't help you,' retorted Trussell.

'I'm not saying anything. I'll want a brief.'

'Of course,' said Trussell. 'That's your right.' He addressed the remaining uniformed officers. 'Right, I want this place turned over. Check every room before we start on the factory downstairs.'

'What are we looking for, Guv?'

'Paper records of any sort, files. Check his offices first. I want everything collected. We'll box it up to take it away. Look for any evidence of drugs, of course. Particularly downstairs in the factory. Anyone you find in any of the rooms must stay there until we've got their details and they've been interviewed. Nobody is to leave. Understood?'

They nodded

Jackie Joynton appeared in the doorway. 'There's someone you need to see, Guv.' Trussell followed her to a room at the other end, where a uniformed officer was standing, outside the open door, watching. They pushed past him. 'The door was locked, but luckily the key was in the lock outside,' said Jackie.

Inside was a figure, sitting on a chair. Trussell recognised him immediately despite the state of his face. He had obviously been beaten up quite badly. He was bloody and bruised. It was Arthur Tillworth. He looked in Trussell's direction.

'Who did this?' asked Trussell. Tillworth declined to answer. He thought for a moment. 'I'm prepared to trade information,' he said, quietly, through damaged lips. 'I can guess what you want to know.'

'OK. What's happened to Barnaby Scoular?'

'That I don't know,' he said. 'I've had nothing to do with him.'

'Not entirely true,' said Trussell. 'We know that he came to your shop on at least one occasion. Where is he?'

'I really don't know. You'll have to ask Summerton.'

'We'll save it for tomorrow. I hope that you can find another brief, Mr Tillworth. My guess is that Willoughby Frankenberg will have more clients than he can handle at the moment. Perhaps the duty solicitor will be available.'

Trussell, took out his phone, snapped a couple of pictures for the record and then told the uniformed officer to handcuff him. 'Don't look too pleased, Mr Tillworth. You're under arrest as well,' he told the unfortunate estate agent, as he cautioned him. Trussell turned to the uniformed constable. 'Take Mr Tillworth to the Woodchester A & E now and get him some medical attention. When the doctors have finished with him and say that he's fit to leave, take him to Woodchester Police Station and lock him up. I'll talk to him later.'

'Well, Jackie, I think that's mission accomplished. We can leave the rest to DCI Simpson and his team. It's their problem now. Sorting out the factory. Looking for drugs. More than enough to keep them occupied.'

'Shall we get back to Woodchester now, then?'

'We ought to. We'll need to supervise the processing of the prisoners. The Custody Sergeant will be complaining about the number of customers we've sent him. I expect it's probably getting a bit overcrowded.'

66

Day 42.
Monday 1ˢᵗ April. 9.30 am.
CID Office, Woodchester Police Station.

'Have we organised a brief for Arthur Tillworth yet, Jackie?'

'Should be arriving shortly, Jim. Duty solicitor. Name of Michael Dexter. Not met him yet.' Jackie Joynton picked up the phone to speak to the duty sergeant on the front desk. 'Alan says that he's just arrived, Jim.'

'OK. Get Custody to bring Tillworth up to the interview room. We'll introduce him to his solicitor and give them ten minutes to get acquainted. Then we'll have to make a start. Have you seen Tillworth since he returned from A & E? I assume that they've passed him fit for questioning.'

Jackie Joynton shrugged her shoulders. 'I wonder whether he's had time to think about things. He seemed very keen to talk. To get himself some sort of deal in exchange for information.'

'We'll see,' said Trussell. 'I've thought he might have a lot of the answers since the beginning.'

They walked down the stairs to the main entrance, to see a man standing in the lobby, carrying an executive case. He was of average height, dark brown hair and smartly dressed in a dark grey suit with a red striped tie. Trussell thought that he was probably in his mid-thirties. Shuffling his feet. Clearing his throat. *Looks a bit new to all of this* thought Trussell.

'Can I help you?'

'Er, yes please,' the man began nervously, ' I'm here to represent a Mr Tillworth. I'm Michael Dexter, duty solicitor. I'm looking for DI Trussell.'

'You found him,' said Trussell, showing the identity card hanging round his neck. 'Come this way,' opening the door to the interview rooms. The door to Room 1 was open, and Trussell ushered him inside.

'If you'd like to take a seat, we've arranged for Mr Tillworth to be brought up from the cells. We'll make the introductions and then you can have ten minutes with your client. He seems quite anxious to speak to us.'

'He looks a bit knocked about,' said Jackie Joynton, 'not by us, I'll add. One or other of his former colleagues was responsible, but I've no doubt he'll tell you more. We had him checked at A & E before we brought him here yesterday.'

Arthur Tillworth arrived with a uniformed officer holding him by one arm. His face had been cleaned up at the hospital but several bruises had appeared. He was sporting several stitches and a couple of plasters. He still looked worried and uncomfortable in his surroundings. He had lost that brazen self-confidence that he had shown when they first visited his agency.

'Right, Mr Tillworth,' said Trussell, 'this is your solicitor, Michael Dexter. You can have a few minutes with him in here, then we'll make a start.'

He and Jackie Joynton waited outside the interview room while this discussion took place.

'He seemed very keen to do some sort of trade yesterday when we found him in Brandford, Jim. I wonder how he feels about it today now he's had a chance to think about things?'

'His brief looks a bit nervous. Perhaps it's all a bit new to him.'

Trussell looked at his watch.

'Let's find out. He's had his ten minutes.'

Trussell tapped on the door and opened it. They walked in and took their seats opposite Tillworth and his solicitor. Jackie Joynton slipped a fresh disc into the recorder and looked in Trussell's direction. He nodded, so she started the recorder and asked everyone to identify themselves.

'What do you need to question my client about?' began Dexter, somewhat nervously. 'I understand that he has not been charged with any offence as yet.'

'Correct,' said Trussell. 'He did express a wish to cooperate with our enquiries when we arrested him at the factory in Brandford, so let me start with what we know about your client already. That might persuade him to tell us what we want to know. He expressed a willingness to do so.'

'Go on, Detective Inspector.'

'Mr Tillworth was responsible for running Summerton's property empire in Brandford when the opportunity arose to buy Mr Trott's estate agency. Mr Tillworth already possessed the necessary experience to run such a business and it would provide other opportunities to handle money and future property transactions for his boss.'

'That's no evidence of a crime being committed, Detective Inspector.'

'It's what came afterwards, with the purchase of properties in Brandford and raising large mortgages against them in fictitious names, to defraud the Society. Then there were the murders of the surveyor and the solicitor to ensure that the perpetrators would escape justice.'

'So, what is it you want from my client? You've apparently already made arrests.'

'When did he first suggest to Summerton that it would be possible to defraud the High Weald?'

Dexter looked to Tillworth who shook his head.

'My client refutes that suggestion.'

'Let him answer for himself,' said Trussell.

'It was Stevie Winterden who came up with the idea,' said Tillworth. 'It was her plan. She works at the Building Society and understands the mortgage market. She had the access to the manager to influence him to agree to the mortgages. She's got some sort of hold over him. Not sure what. I just identified the properties and set up the first contacts.'

'Tell us about Stevie Winterden's role.'

'She's Jack Summerton's daughter although she's done her best to distance herself publicly from her Brandford roots. That's why she changed her name. It was all part of the long-term planning. She's as ruthless as her father. She has both brains and physical strength. Summerton has been preparing her to take over the organisation. The others are all frightened of her.'

'Is Summerton funding her lifestyle?'

'Yes. He owns the flats where she lives for free at Breckenridge. I can tell you that the rents there are astronomic. It's a smart place to live. Organised her car too. Top of the range SUV. Range Rover. He pays the lease. Funds her sports activities and her membership at the Country Club. His little girl wants for nothing.'

'What about the surveyor, Edmund Royston?'

'Stevie knew that he was vulnerable. His business was failing and he'd started drinking. He was very weak. It was easy to persuade him that there was easy money to be made. All he had to do was to overvalue the properties when he surveyed them and then leave the rest to Stevie. She was able to influence Barnaby Scoular to agree the mortgages.

Unfortunately, Royston got cold feet and had second thoughts after the event.'

'So, who set him up, then? Arranged for him to visit the Oatleys' house?' asked Trussell.

'That was Stevie. She phoned him from my office so that the call couldn't be traced at the High Weald. It was easy for her to arrange the time and place to deal with him. He was used to getting instructions from my office for surveys.'

'What about the solicitor, Marcus Culverton ?'

'Culverton was easier to get on board. He had taken over Fotherby and Co. when the original owner retired, but hadn't done proper due diligence. The firm was in a desperate state financially with outdated practices and a dwindling client base.'

'Who suggested it to him?'

'Stevie did. They had a hold over him. He was already addicted to the drugs supplied by Summerton's organisation. Culverton saw the mortgage fraud as a means of escaping his financial problems and disappearing when he was paid. Like Royston, when he became a problem, then he had to be eliminated. Stevie dealt with that problem.'

'Tell me about Jason Tubbitt. '

'They will all deny it, but he is the son of Brian Kirby and Shirley Tompkins. They had an affair twenty-odd years ago and Jason came along. Brian has been a bad influence on him – the kid never stood a chance with his background. Shirley invented the father's name as Tubbitt to disguise his parentage, on instruction from Kirby and Summerton. She had a job as a front, running Summerton's factory so that he could keep an eye on her. They control her by fear and threats.'

'What about Tubbitt's relationship with his mother?'

'She disowned him after he threatened her and got violent. The police were involved. Summerton persuaded her to drop the charges against him. Still had to speak to him, as he was part of the firm – sort of trainee enforcer. Summerton found him useful. He was well rewarded for that which allowed him to indulge his passion in expensive motorcycles.'

'Did Stevie acknowledge him as a half-brother?'

'No. She wanted nothing to do with him. Knowing her as I do, I wouldn't have put money on his future. He wouldn't have had one as soon as she took over. You probably noticed that Summerton is a very sick man these days. Terminal illness.'

'Let's talk about Eddie Sprawson's role in the matter.'

'He'd known Summerton from the old days. Jack was his snout all those years ago. Eddie tipped them off that the police were taking an increasingly close interest in the estate agency. He convinced Summerton that I was getting nervous about the attention and persuaded them that I wanted a bigger piece of the action. Not true of course, but he used me as an excuse to get more for himself. That's when Summerton decided that something would have to be done about him.

'So, he was summoned to Brandford. Sprawson thought that he was about to be rewarded for keeping them updated on the progress of the police investigation, but it was just so that Jack could tell him the facts of life. Sprawson wanted revenge for that and tried to contact the Eastern Europeans who are trying to take over the town. Brian Kirby reported that to Summerton and he told him to deal with the situation. The rest you know.'

'What about the mortgage fraud? Where did the money go?'

'You'll have to ask Summerton. Maybe Stevie knows. It would have come back at some stage and been reinvested in more property. That's what I did for Jack. In the end he was more prepared to believe Sprawson and that's why I was dragged out of the shop and brought here to talk things over. You can see the result of that,' he said, indicating the state of his face.

'Thank you, Mr Tillworth,' said Trussell, gesturing to Joynton to terminate the interview. She switched off the recorder.

'I'll now discuss the matter with the CPS and see what they want to do about Mr Tillworth,' said Trussell to Michael Dexter. 'In the meantime, he'll be returned to the cells until we get a decision.'

'What about bail?' asked Dexter.

'Not in his interest, I fear,' said Trussell. 'Can't have him running around loose, for his own safety.'

Jackie Joynton stood up and indicated that Tillworth should follow the uniformed officer who had been silently watching the proceedings.

'Take him back to the custody suite, please.'

67

Day 43.
Tuesday 2nd April. Pm.
CID Office, Woodchester Police Station.

'Do you think that you could pop round to the High Weald branch, Jackie?' Trussell asked.

'Certainly. What do you want me to do?'

'I'd like you to talk to Susie Albright and show her Brian's picture. Check whether he was the man she saw talking to Barnaby Scoular early one morning in the office.'

'OK. That shouldn't take too long. Anything else?'

'I suggest that you give John Hansworth a ring first, just to make sure Susie's available. Use discretion, of course. You might also ask him if there have been any developments. Has he noticed anything unusual? What are the staff discussing? Any gossip about Barney Scoular or the mortgage problems?'

Jackie picked up the phone, tapped in the High Weald number and asked to speak to John Hansworth. A few words and she finished the call.

'OK, Jim. All fixed. I'll pop round there now.' She grabbed her coat and left the office.

Spring was in the air now and the weather had improved. It was noticeably warmer. The High Street was busy with people rushing about in all directions, many of them either on their phones or just texting. There was the usual background hum of passing traffic.

Ten minutes later, she arrived outside the High Weald branch. As she opened the door, she saw John Hansworth talking to a customer. He noticed her and indicated one of the two empty glass offices on the right of the shop before finishing his conversation. A moment later, he joined her. They shook hands.

'I understand that you want to speak to Susie Albright?' he asked.

Jackie Joynton nodded.

'She's in her office at the back. Would you like to come through? We can talk in my office.'

Jackie followed him out of the glass office and through the door at the back adjoining the two tills. Maureen Scoular paused for a moment while dealing with a customer to give Jackie a brief smile of acknowledgement, and then resumed her conversation.

'Come in here and take a seat,' said Hansworth, leading the way into the manager's office and indicating one of the two guest chairs. 'I'll get Susie.'

Joynton glanced around her. It was a windowless office filled with a desk, three chairs and a couple of tall wood-grained filing cabinets. The impressive antique style desk was covered in neat piles of files, and one lay open on the desk with an A4 pad on which Hansworth had started making notes. There was a sense of orderly chaos about the place. He had to manage the branch and, at the same time, see what he could contribute towards helping to solve the mortgage problems.

A couple of minutes later, he reappeared, followed by Susie Albright, carrying a number of files. She looked very apprehensive. Wondering why the police should want to speak to her now. Her conscience was clear. *What could it be?*

'Sorry about the delay,' said Hansworth. 'Susie was hiding in the filing room,' he said, smiling. He pointed to the other guest chair. 'Sit down, Susie. Don't look so worried.'

Jackie looked at her. She noticed that there was a diamond ring on the third finger of her left hand. This gave credence to James Howditch's statement when she had interviewed him with Trussell at the police station on the Nineteenth of February. 'Nothing to be concerned about, Miss Albright,' said Jackie, pointing to the ring. 'I see congratulations are in order.'

'Thank you.'

'We just wondered whether you might be able to assist us.'

'How?'

'When we last met, you mentioned that you had seen a mysterious visitor sitting in Barnaby Scoular's office early one morning when you first arrived. Then you said that he had disappeared.'

'Yes.'

'Do you recognise this man?' asked Jackie, handing her Brian Kirby's picture.

She studied it carefully. Thought for a moment. 'I don't want to get anyone into trouble,' she said.

'Don't worry about that,' said Jackie. 'Have you seen him before?'

'Yes. Definitely. That was the man I saw speaking to Mr Scoular that morning.'

'Thank you, Miss Albright,' said Jackie. 'That's all I need from you.'

'That's OK, Susie,' said Hansworth. 'That's all that the Detective Sergeant wants. Just don't mention this to anyone else.'

She got up from the chair, still looking rather worried, and walked out of the office to head to the public area, holding the files she had been carrying when she walked into Hansworth's office.

'Now,' said Hansworth, 'is there anything else you need, Detective Sergeant?'

'Has there been any further discussion here about Mr Scoular's disappearance, the mortgages or the unfortunate deaths of the surveyor and the solicitor?' asked Jackie. 'Comments or speculation?'

'No, but there's something you and Detective Inspector Trussell need to know.'

'Oh?'

'Through that doorway,' he said, pointing to the back of the office beyond his office and the staff area, 'there are two more rooms. One is our filing room, and the other was mysteriously locked and no one seemed to have a key.'

'What about Stevie Winterden?' asked Jackie. I understood she has the keys to the branch.'

'She claims that she only had keys to the front door, the staff room and the archives. Apparently not to that room or to the back door, which she says were never used. She is adamant that she was never given copies of those keys. In fact, she tells me that she has never seen either door open, not even when old Mr Thompson was the manager.'

'Really? Do you believe her?'

'I have no reason to doubt her at the moment. After consultation with the CEO, Mr Hartman, I brought a locksmith in after hours when everyone had left for the day. He opened the doors without any difficulty, and has now provided me with keys for both that room and the rear entrance. He also made some recommendations about future security in that area, which we shall be implementing.'

'Interesting, Mr Hansworth. I'm sure that you're going to tell me why you think that DI Trussell and I would need to know.'

'Certainly,' said Hansworth, rising from his chair and producing two keys on a ring from his pocket. 'Come with me and see for yourself.'

Jackie followed Hansworth out of his office and through the door at the end behind the staff area. He opened it and went immediately to the door on the left, inserted one of the keys, twisted it and the door swung open.

'This is what you need to see,' he said to Joynton, as he reached inside and turned on the light.

Joynton looked into the room, amazed at what she saw, as she recalled some of the previous evidence they'd taken from witnesses.

'Have you touched any of this stuff, Mr Hansworth?' she asked.

'Absolutely not,' he replied. 'I took one look and decided to stay outside. I did touch the light switch, of course.

'Then, please ensure that no one else comes in here,' she added.

'I wonder what these things are doing here?' asked Hansworth. 'They've obviously been used recently, otherwise you'd expect them to be covered in dust.'

'We'll need the forensic people to look at this and record everything,' she said. 'I think that we'll have to arrange for them to come in here either via the back door, or after close of business to avoid any public scrutiny. Someone in the branch must know about this stuff. I don't want to alert them.'

She looked at the contents of the room; a dark-framed mountain bike, a dark blue anorak hanging on a hook, a pair of blue jeans and a pair of trainers and a rucksack on a shelf. Trussell would need to know about this as soon as possible.

'Can you lock the room again, please Mr Hansworth? she asked. 'Make sure that no one goes near it. Someone must have a key. Obviously, Barnaby Scoular must have had one, but I believe that the contents of that room have possibly been used to commit at least two crimes that certainly postdate his disappearance. I'm talking about the deaths of Royston and Culverton.'

He locked the room and led the way back to his office.

'I'll go back to the station now, Mr Hansworth, and discuss this with the DI. I'm sure that he will want to see this for himself. She looked at her watch.

'You'll be closing shortly, I suppose.'

'That's right. In ten minutes. I can wait behind after everyone else has gone home, if you like. I can let Detective Inspector Trussell in so that he can see for himself. That way, none of the staff will know.'

'Thank you. What time do you suggest?'

'Shall we say six o'clock. Everyone should have left by then.'

'Perfect. We'll see you then. Thank you for your assistance.'

Jackie Joynton walked out of the Society, smiling at the staff as she left. Jim Trussell would be very interested in Hansworth's discovery. This could be a real breakthrough in the case.

Ten minutes later, back in the office, Jackie Joynton shared the information about her visit to the High Weald with Trussell. He was astounded. 'So, who do we suspect, then, Jackie?' he asked facetiously.

'Well, Jim, process of elimination. I bet that it wasn't Janet MacDuff. She certainly wouldn't match the description of either of the two mysterious cyclists. I should think that Susie Albright is in the clear as well. I'm pretty sure that we can exclude James Howditch too. It obviously isn't Hansworth, so that leaves us with two suspects – Maureen and Stevie. Unless, of course, some third party, unknown, also has keys to the back door and the store room. Unlikely, but we can't rule it out.'

'Well, DNA samples from those items might help,' said Trussell. 'We'll have to arrest both the ladies to get those samples. It might be a bit early yet for that.'

'So, shall we go round to see Hansworth shortly?' asked Jackie. 'We can call the forensic team in then, if you agree.'

'Good idea. Phone Hansworth and tell him that we'll go round after six. I think that it might be a good idea for him to get his locksmith in and change the locks on the room and the rear entrance. That would certainly safeguard the evidence.'

'What about Forensics, Jim?'

'I'll take a look first. You might want to give Maurice a call and get him to stand by. If we get them down, it will need to be fairly discreet. Something like that will get all of the locals talking.

68

Day. 43.
Wednesday 3rd April. 10.30 am.
CID Office, Woodchester Police Station.

The phone rang on Trussell's desk. He picked it up. 'CID. DI Trussell speaking.' He listened intently, grabbed a sheet of paper and started noting the conversation down. 'Thank you. We'll get out there right away.'

He replaced the phone and looked across at Jackie, who had picked up on the gravity of the moment. She looked expectantly at him.

'That was uniformed, Jackie. It looks as though Barnaby Scoular might have been found.'

'Where, Jim?'

In the woods over in Ockenden. A woman walking her dog let it off the lead and she thought that it was chasing a rabbit when it ran off and then started digging. When she caught up with the dog, it had started to uncover a body buried in a shallow grave. It must have been a terrible shock for her, but she still had the presence of mind to call the police straight away and wait until someone turned up.'

'What makes you think that it's Scoular?'

'Uniformed had his description at the time he went missing, including details of the clothes he was wearing. They saw enough of the body to recognise him from those details. Obviously, we'll have to exhume him and make the usual identification to be sure. Anyway, CSI have been called, so we'd better get up there as quickly as possible.'

Trussell stood up, took his jacket from the back of his chair and, making sure that he had his car keys, headed for the door. Jackie hastily picked up her bag and followed him. Mark Green and Tim Beach just looked at one another in astonishment at this turn of events, which had effectively negated a great deal of the hard work they had put in to track down the missing person.

Trussell and Joynton got into the Skoda and he punched Ockenden into the satnav. 'About twenty-five minutes this time of day,' said Trussell.

'Thank goodness for dog walkers,' said Jackie. 'The woods at Ockenden are a bit off the beaten track. We might never have found him, otherwise.'

'We just have to hope that the arrival of the cavalry hasn't obliterated any evidence on the ground. I doubt very much whether he walked up to Ockenden and buried himself. Was he killed there or elsewhere? I know that he wasn't physically very big, but it would still take an effort to carry a body up there.'

Speculation was rife as they drove to the woods at Ockenden. When they arrived at the public car park just off the road, a uniformed officer checked their warrant cards and directed them to a space nearer to the track that led into the trees. At this time of the year, they were in full leaf, which made their journey ever upwards through the shady woods rather gloomy.

Police officers stationed along the track, there to dissuade any members of the public from encroaching on what was now a crime scene, directed them to the location. When they arrived at the taped-off area, another officer checked their ID and lifted the tape for them. The CSI leader approached them.

'Morning Maurice,' said Trussell. 'What have you found so far?'

'One white male, about five-feet-seven. He was wearing a mid-grey suit. It looks as though he's been there several weeks, I'd say. But the post-mortem will tell you more. He was buried in a very shallow grave and the body was barely covered. Whoever was responsible didn't make too much of an effort to hide it. Perhaps they were counting on the remoteness of the area to avoid discovery. Or maybe they were disturbed before they could finish the job. I'm just surprised that the local wildlife didn't get at it.'

'What about the immediate area around the site? Anything of note?'

'Well, there are some tyre tracks that stop nearby. They've been photographed already and we're trying to take casts of them. Big vehicle. SUV or four-wheel drive. Distinctive tyre pattern. One of them is damaged and it shows on the tracks. We should be able to narrow the make of vehicle down, if that's any help. If they're connected, it could mean that the perpetrator drove up here. Begs the question as to whether the victim was killed here or somewhere else.'

'Can we have a look?' asked Trussell.

'You'll both need to suit up.'

Wearing the hastily donned white plastic suits, masks and overshoes, Trussell and Joynton followed the CSI team member up the hill to where a tent had been erected. They ducked inside to look at the crime scene.

After recent events, they had both become hardened to the sort of sight which greeted them. The body had been uncovered as the soil had been stripped back. They both looked at it and were fairly satisfied that it was Barnaby Scoular. The remains resembled the photograph they had been shown and certainly fitted the description that had been circulated. It just required formal identification.

Trussell wondered whether he should ask Maureen Scoular to go through the agony of the process, or whether he should ask the brother. That would be a difficult decision.

69

Day 44.
Thursday 4th April. 6.00 pm.
The Hollows. Frattenden

It had been a bright, clear Spring day, but even that was not enough to lift Trussell's spirits as he and Jackie Joynton drove towards The Hollows, a new estate a couple of miles outside Woodchester. They were accompanied by two uniformed officers in a marked car. They arrived outside the house that had been shared by Barney and Maureen Scoular and parked their cars. A familiar silver Range Rover was parked outside. People walking past stopped to stare at this sudden police presence, aware of the fact that Barnaby Scoular had been missing for quite a while. There had certainly been enough exposure in the media and people had seen Maureen's tearful public appeal. Now something appeared to be happening. The word had quickly got around and a crowd was already gathering as the four police officers walked towards the house.

'Let's get this over with, Jackie,' said Trussell, his face betraying the disgust that he felt. There was no satisfaction for him in the final resolution of a case that had started with a Missing Person report and had left a trail of other crimes in its wake.

They walked up the garden path to the front door and rang the bell.

Maureen Scoular opened the door. She was wearing a plain dark blue dress. Her hair was just dragged back and she had no makeup. Fatigue and worry had taken its toll and her face was very pale and lined.

'Hello, Detective Inspector. Do you have any news?'

'Yes, we do. Can we come in?'

She stood aside, expectantly, and they walked into the living room which had become so familiar to them. The two uniformed officers followed them.

As Trussell had expected, Stevie was there, sitting on the settee. She was just flicking through a magazine. She looked up at them in an almost detached way.

'Stevie has been very kind, keeping me company from time to time since Barney disappeared. I've been grateful for her support.'

'We both know the reason, don't we, Stevie?' said Trussell.

'What do you mean?'

Trussell turned to Maureen.

'Mrs Scoular, I'm sorry to have to tell you that a body was found yesterday and we have already identified him as your husband, although we shall need you to do so formally.'

Maureen's hand flew to her mouth. Her look of astonishment changed to tears and then near hysteria.

Jackie stepped forward to catch her before she collapsed. She sobbed uncontrollably, the tears streaming down her cheeks. This time, the tears and reaction seemed genuine. Her guarantee of security had gone.

Stevie sat there, apparently unmoved by her friend's distress. Totally relaxed and detached.

Trussell looked at her. 'We both know about the circumstances of his death, don't we, Stevie?'

'What do you mean?' she replied, unemotional, disinterested.

'We found your car tracks up to that isolated spot in the woods where the body was discovered, Stevie. You were caught on CCTV in the Weaver Street Car Park in Woodchester High Street getting into your car with Barnaby Scoular that evening when he disappeared. You were the last person to see him alive. It's taken a while to piece all of this together, thanks to your friend, Fast Eddie, feeding us false information about the CCTV records there.'

'That doesn't make me responsible for his death,' she responded, her voice expressionless.

'Tell me it's not true, Stevie,' sobbed Maureen. 'I don't believe it. Why would you do something like that?'

Stevie stared back at her, apparently devoid of emotion. She stood up. Trussell was concerned that she might try to use violence - after all, she was highly qualified to do so as a Black Belt. Finally, she spoke. 'I did it for you, Maureen, to set you free of that awful little man. He could never appreciate you or love you the way I do. It was so that we could be together forever. I'll be the branch manager now. We'll have each other and total financial security as well.'

Maureen heard these words in total disbelief and horror.

'Whatever gave you the idea that I had any feelings for you? I thought that you were just a friend, supporting me through this terrible time. Now, I'm alone again. I needed my husband. He was my security, my future and now you've taken him away from me forever. You've no idea what it was like, being abandoned as a baby, stuck in a children's home, unwanted, abused. Barney Scoular was my ticket away from all of that and now you've killed him, you bitch! You've killed my husband!' She broke free of Jackie's supporting grasp and, screaming, arms windmilling, tried to grab Stevie.

Jackie grabbed her and held her back. 'She's not worth it, Maureen. Let the law deal with her.'

Trussell, a spectator while the scene played out, seized the initiative. He turned to Stevie. 'Stephanie Winterden, I'm arresting you on suspicion of the murder of Barnaby Scoular on or about the Eighteenth of February.' He continued to issue the caution and then nodded to the two uniformed officers. One produced a pair of handcuffs and secured her wrists.

'I have to warn you that other charges will follow. Take her to Woodchester,' he told the two officers.

They led her out of the door and down the path to their car.

There was a buzz from the crowd as they appeared. One police officer opened the rear door of their car and the other helped Stevie settle into a seat. He leaned over, fastened her seat belt and then closed the door with a bang. There were loud boos as the car was driven away.

Inside the house, Jackie still held onto Maureen, partly to restrain her and then to support her. She was still sobbing, but seemed to be mastering her emotions.

'I had no idea that she felt that way. She's never talked about anything like that. I certainly would not have returned those sorts of feelings. I thought that she was just being supportive.'

'We'll have to organise some help here, Jackie,' said Trussell. 'Can you get on to Woodchester and ask them to send a family support officer? We'll wait until someone turns up.' He turned to Maureen. 'In the meantime, is there anyone else we can contact to be with you? What about Alex Peterson?"

She shook her head, the reality of the situation only sinking in very slowly. 'I'm sure I'll be alright,' she said. 'I don't have any family, but at least I've got my friends.'

Trussell wasn't convinced.

'What will happen to Stevie?' asked Maureen.

'We'll have to leave that to the courts,' said Trussell. 'No doubt a good defence counsel might make a case for diminished responsibility or even insanity. That will be up to the jury. Either way, she'll be going away for a long, long time, I would imagine.'

He turned to Jackie Joynton. 'We'll have to arrange for Stevie's car to be taken in for forensic examination. Can you fix it, please?'

'Certainly,' she said, taking her phone from her bag.

'They'll be here within the hour, Jim,' she said. 'I've asked them to make a start as soon as the car arrives at the garage. I've told them that this one is a priority.'

'OK, there's nothing more for us to do here,' said Trussell.

Maureen Scoular had recovered her composure after the initial shock. This was now the self-possessed woman that Charles Preston had described in their first conversation.

'I'm fine now,' she said. 'You're right, Detective Inspector. I'll give Alex a call. He'll come round. There's no point in pretending any longer. I don't care what people might think. What happened to Barney was nothing to do with me. I have to think about myself and the future now.'

Satisfied that there was now no need for them to stay a moment longer, Trussell indicated to Jackie Joynton that they should leave.

70

Day 45.
Friday 5th April.
Woodchester Police Station.

Trussell and Joynton walked into the interview room. Stevie Winterden was already sitting on a chair behind the table. She gave Trussell one of her usual dirty looks. Her solicitor was sitting next to her. Willoughby Frankenberg again. Paid for by her father, no doubt. A watchful uniformed officer stood in the corner, near the door.

They took their seats on the other side of the table and Jackie Joynton put a fresh disc in the recorder. She asked everyone to identify themselves for the record before the interview proceeded.

'We'll start with the disappearance and subsequent death of Barnaby Scoular,' said Trussell.

'Insignificant little man,' muttered Stevie. 'He was pathetic. He didn't need a relationship, just another mother. I soon learned some of his grubby little secrets which would have ruined his life and career if the management had found out.

'So, you blackmailed him for power then? You needed him to rubber-stamp the mortgage applications? He had no option. Either sign or risk his secrets coming out?"

'Your words, not mine.'

'Your client has already admitted her responsibility for Mr Scoular's death in front of witnesses,' said Trussell to Willoughby Frankenberg. 'We also have forensic evidence which puts her at the scene of the crime.'

'So, what do want to ask my client, then, if you feel that you have enough evidence to charge her?'

'We want to talk about the deaths of Edmund Royston and Magnus Culverton.'

Frankenberg looked at Stevie, cautioning her to remain silent, but there was no stopping her.

'What makes you think that I was involved?'

'It really was only a matter of time before we caught up with you,' said Trussell. 'We found your mountain bike and clothes in the locked storage room at the High Weald branch. We worked out that it was yours by process of elimination. Now that you're under arrest, we'll take your DNA and that will confirm your involvement.'

'I don't know what you mean.'

'C'mon. Stevie. It's useless to deny it. We know that you were missing from the High Weald Branch just before the two men died. It was so easy for you.'

'What d'you mean?'

'You held the key to the store room and a key to the back door of the building. As the door to the office section was locked, you were able to leave and return to the building without anyone else knowing. You told the staff that you weren't to be disturbed while you searched the archives on the personal instructions of the CEO. You instructed them to contact you on your phone if they needed to talk to you.'

'Where's your proof, Detective Inspector?' asked Frankenberg.

'She had the keys in her possession when she was arrested. The staff at the branch will confirm what I've just told you.'

'Not enough, Detective Inspector, and you know it,' said Frankenberg.

'You arranged with Arthur Tillworth for Edmund Royston to carry out the survey at the Oatleys' house so that you could fake the accident. Unfortunately, Royston didn't die when you threw him over the landing as you moved the ladder. Very untidy. Very inconvenient for you that he was still conscious enough to crawl toward the front door. You have the necessary skills and strength to break his neck to kill him, and that's exactly what you did.'

'Prove it!'

'Well Stevie, Tillworth has confirmed that you both agreed that Royston should carry out the survey. He was the logical choice as he was already deeply involved in the mortgage fraud. It gave you a hold over him. He had to agree to visit the Oatleys' house. Tillworth has told us that he heard you make the call to Royston from his agency to arrange for him to carry out the survey, but claims that he didn't know that you intended to kill him, but that's another matter.'

Frankenberg intervened.

'Hearsay, Detective Inspector?'

'He will swear to it. He has confirmed that Stevie made the call to Royston from his office. He was there. He heard it. Oh, and by the way, the post-mortem confirmed the actual cause of death. Stevie was meticulous in the way she cleaned up after the crime before she left the house, but she reckoned without one thing.'

'Oh, and what was that? How can you prove that I was there?'

'The one thing you overlooked…the video doorbell. It showed you arriving and leaving the house with the timings. You were wearing the blue anorak and jeans found in the locked room at the High Weald, you know, the one that you deny having a key for. The doorbell video shows you wiping the door handle to remove any fingerprints.'

'You'll never prove it,' she said. 'Anyone could have been wearing something like that.'

'It was clever of you to copy the clothing worn by another member of your Country Club and get a similar bike. You had obviously seen him cycling to the gym and decided that would be a great way to disguise yourself. That did throw us off the scent for a while, but luckily the member concerned had a cast iron alibi. Your attempt to transfer the blame to him failed.'

'Pure conjecture, Detective Inspector.'

It was almost as if Stevie was enjoying these exchanges. *It must be her competitive side*, thought Trussell.

He continued. 'Well. There are always the wet footprints on the stair carpet from the trainers you were wearing when you went up to pull him off the ladder. The DNA will establish that they were on your feet when the prints were found on the stairs. The trainers have already been matched to the prints. Clever but not clever enough.'

She was completely unfazed by these statements. Detached.

'Then there was Magnus Culverton. I wondered why you went into the High Weald branch at 6.30 that morning. We saw you on CCTV. It was obviously to give you time to deal with Culverton and be back at the office to let the others in when they arrived at their normal times. No one could have possibly connected you with that crime. After all, you were in the Building Society, diligently working. Putting in unpaid overtime. Carrying out the instructions of Mr Hartman, the CEO, to search the archives. You gave everyone the impression that you really wanted the Branch Manager's job. You knew that there would be a vacancy as you had already killed Barnaby Scoular on the night that he disappeared. '

'Rubbish. All in your imagination, Detective Inspector.'

The same Stevie that Trussell had encountered on his first visit to the High Weald. Completely calm and in control of herself.

'So, you visited Culverton early that morning. He let you in because he already knew you. With your martial arts skills, it was not difficult to put him in a chokehold. The post mortem confirmed that as the cause of death and that he was already dead when you put him in the car. We found the marks where you'd dragged him from the house through the side door of the garage and put him in the driver's seat. They matched the abrasions on the backs of his shoes. You connected a pipe from the exhaust, started the engine and just left him there.'

'There's no way that you can prove I was anywhere near his house that day.'

'Wrong again, Stevie. There was a witness who saw you leave Culverton's house on your bike early that morning. Just before the postman arrived and heard the car engine running in the garage. That witness can identify you.'

She still maintained her composure. Remained impassive.

Frankenberg listened to these exchanges. Saying nothing.

'Let's talk about Barnaby Scoular,' said Trussell. 'It was only when he realised the enormity of what he'd been persuaded to do, that he tried to put it right. That would have implicated you in the mortgage fraud. The hold you had over him would not have been enough. His pride in his position would have overcome that, so you knew that he would have to disappear to take the blame for the crime. Taking his passport from his desk drawer was a clever way to try to convince the police that he had run off with the proceeds. You arranged to meet him after work, to accompany him to a dinner, as he thought, to rectify the problem. There was no dinner. You lured him into your car and then drove him to Ockenden, where you killed and buried him.'

'Proof, Detective Inspector?'

'We have removed your car for examination. We found tyre tracks from an SUV leading right up to that place in the woods where you buried him. The pattern is distinctive. There is also damage to one tread and this has been matched exactly to your car. I'm sure that we'll find Mr Scoular's DNA in the car when Forensics have looked at it. I understand that a spade was found in the boot and soil samples on it are being matched with the ground at Ockenden where Mr Scoular's body was found.'

'Any further questions, Detective Inspector?' asked Frankenberg.

'I don't think so,' said Trussell. 'Has your client anything to add?'

Stevie Winterden shook her head.

Trussell indicated to Jackie Joynton that the interview was over. She made the appropriate closing comment and switched the recorder off.

'Your client will now be taken downstairs and charged, Mr Frankenberg, Perhaps you would accompany her. We shall arrange for her to appear before the magistrates tomorrow and she will, of course, be remanded in custody until a trial date can be fixed.'

The uniformed officer standing by the door during the interview now stepped forward and took Stevie Winterden by the arm and led her out.

Epilogue
Day 55.
Monday 15th April. Early afternoon.
The CID Office. Woodchester Police Station.

'Well. Jackie, that just about wraps up the Scoular case, I think,' said Trussell. 'The files will be going off to the CPS and they can decide who gets charged with what. Stevie will certainly go down for the three murders and they have enough other charges and culprits to keep themselves busy for quite a while.'

'I assume that the mortgage problems will go to the Fraud Squad,' she said. 'I question whether the High Weald will ever get any of their money back. One wonders how much information they'll get out of Summerton. He's obviously a very sick man. You can't help feeling sorry for the other people in the High Weald branch who've been left to pick up the pieces.'

'Well, I wish them the best of luck,' said Trussell. 'With James Howditch now promoted to manager and running the branch, plus a couple of new staff joining the team, things should soon get back to normal in the High Street.'

'At least there have been a couple of winners in the whole sorry train of events,' said Trussell. 'Maureen Scoular will now presumably inherit the house at The Avenue and settle down with Alex Peterson. That's all out in the open now.'

'You may as well include Greeno in the list of winners as well,' said Jackie Joynton. 'Now that Sharon Webster has moved in with him at his flat, I shan't be able to pull his leg anymore. Just wish them all the best.'

'As he no longer has any daily concerns about her safety, he's been able to concentrate on our problems. While we've been tidying up the Scoular case, Greeno has made a really good job of sorting out the Supercheap pilferage issues,' said Trussell. 'I asked him to take over the investigation after Eddie's death. I've just read his final report and recommendations.'

'What was the outcome, Jim?'

'The whole thing was organised by one of the shift supervisors at the warehouse. It may just be coincidence, but he comes from Brandford.'

'Do you think that Eddie knew him?'

'It's highly likely, because he seems to have dragged the whole thing out without coming to any real conclusion about who might be responsible.

Just feeding us info to suggest that he was on top of it. It's true that their vetting system was ineffective, because a couple of people employed there had previous convictions but weren't actually involved – they were just trying to turn their lives around, Eddie used them to divert attention away from the real guilty parties.'

'Do you think it was deliberate on Eddie's part?'

'I'm certain of it now in view of the Brandford connection. My fault, I guess. I should have kept a closer eye on things but it wasn't our top priority at the time.'

'So, what's the next step there, Jim?'

'I think that we have enough evidence now to make some arrests. I'm inclined to let Greeno handle it. He's done a first-class job, picking up the investigation from Eddie and revisiting the whole thing. He's also demonstrated some leadership skills in the way he's got Sandcastle involved. He'll be the next one to think about the sergeant's exam if we're not careful!'

'Do you want me to go with him, Jim?'

'Good idea. Just be there. Let him handle it. Take some extra help with you in case.'

'OK, Jim, I'll organise it this morning.

'Now that Greeno's domestic issues have been resolved, I suppose you'll turn your attention to Sandcastle,' laughed Trussell.

She grinned in anticipation. 'I wonder what dark secrets he's hiding?'

Trussell was definitely in a more cheerful mood after all the difficulties of the previous weeks. It had taken his mind off his personal problems for a while and Jackie was pleased to see him lighten up. He could face the future, professionally, with a bit of optimism now that the worries about his team had evaporated. He had confidence in his two young Detective Constables. All he had to do now was to persuade Jackie Joynton that her future was in the CID at Woodchester and not with the Fraud Squad.

An ongoing task for another day.

Printed in Great Britain
by Amazon